CROSSING TO DANGER

As they gathered at the Platte River, young Fitzpatrick raised up in his saddle and stared back grimly at the massed Conestoga wagons.

How had he gotten into this? What unkind God had chosen him to lead this bizarre lot of people through the Western wilderness? Back there in those wagons was a gang of just-freed slaves, as volatile and dangerous as a tinderbox in a dry forest . . . A girl who'd vowed to have him even if it meant his painful death . . . A crazy old mountain doctor with a hankering for human flesh . . . And at least two powerful men who'd sworn that Barry Fitzpatrick and the wagon train would never get through.

He sniffed the wind. Suddenly there was a scent he knew very well—the smell of death. *Hostiles!*

He shrugged broad shoulders and bellowed back at the restive multitude. "Move! Move on out!"

THE
CONESTOGA
PEOPLE

Jeanne Sommers

A DELL/BRYANS BOOK

Published by
Dell Publishing Co., Inc.
1 Dag Hammarskjold Plaza
New York, New York 10017

ISBN: 0-440-01227-9

Printed in the United States of America

First printing—August 1979

Book One

THE CONESTOGA PEOPLE

1

It wasn't his clothing alone that marked Barry Fitzpatrick as an outsider in Independence. It was the way he strode along the crowded streets in them. Wide-shouldered and slim-waisted, as wiry as a sapling pine, uncaring of the unusual figure he cut in his fringed buckskins, moccasins and beaver cap, he seemed to dwarf many of the plain-garbed emigrants in town—but as much as by the fluidity of his motion as anything else. He was clearly a man of the wilderness, something the emigrants were yet to be, and he wore his wilderness garb as casually as they did their skins.

Fitzpatrick was just slightly older than the mud-streeted hamlet of Independence. He'd been born in a Missouri town himself, Columbia, though he hardly remembered his childhood there, having left home and his father's stockyards at the impressionable age of seventeen. Mostly, he'd lived in dugout hovels, trapper's cabins and Indian tepees extending from the Missouri River to California and from Kansas to Montana. The education that mattered to him had been derived from fur trappers and hunters. Ordinary men to him, but legends in their time to others: Jim Bridger, Rocky Mountain Jim Smith, Henri "Frenchman" Maquette, Pie-eyed Pete Landusky, and his uncle, the famous Tom "Broken Hand" Fitzpatrick. In his mid-twenties, he was a man of their world now.

What the emigrants didn't know was that the bustle of Independence tied his stomach into knots of uncertainty.

"Look out, you blitherin' idiot!" he swore.

A whip cracked through the thin April air; a wagon behind a team of sweat-lathered dray horses sank into the street's thawing brown mud and rolled out with a sucking sound. As it did, it kicked mud spray onto Barry's trouser legs, and Barry's black Irish temper soared. On the long trek from Wyoming he had kept this set of buckskins carefully rolled so that he would be clean and presentable on this very special day.

A merchant unloading a cart near Barry had also been sprayed with mud by the wagon.

"Damn Mormon . . ." the merchant scowled, as though it explained everything. For ten years the robust, overcrowded hamlet had been a way-station for those who sought to follow the Church of Latter Day Saints to the promised land. Because Independence had been the Mormons' headquarters prior to 1833, many who came after still acted as though they owned the town.

"Near makes a man wonder what God's up to," the merchant said, wiping his face with a kerchief. "Had one tell me last month that I was an agent of the devil 'cause I sell tobaccy in my store. Me, a deacon of the Baptist church for the past ten years. Told my old woman that very day that there'd be no more trade from the Mormons. So now what do they do? That's what they do!"

Five or six grimy emigrants stood a hundred feet away, shouting and waving tinware and cloth they wished to exchange for flour, ammunition and tools. It was an amazing sight to Barry Fitzhugh Fitzpatrick. The trading of furs for goods was a quiet, subtle exchange done by hand signals, with hardly a word spoken. The noise of this banter grated on his ears.

But everything about Independence was beginning to grate on his nerves and senses. As he stood there, brassy music blasted from a nearby tavern as the door opened and a drunken Indian stumbled out. The Indian was wearing velvet knee britches and a bowler hat with an eagle feather stuck in it. Barry was angered by the impression the Indian was giving white onlookers. He knew Indians in the plains and mountains. He knew Gros Ventres, Cheyennes, Crows, Blackfeet, Shoshones and Utes. He respected these Indians. He knew they'd be embarrassed by this one, dishonoring them by such a public display.

His anger then turned on a trio of French-Canadian trappers, their leather-fringed costumes smoke-stained, with pelts thrown over their shoulders that showed signs of improper curing and shedding. They were out to make a fast dollar. It bothered Barry that they were giving all trappers a bad name.

A cart swung by. Four women in gaudy silk dresses, wearing flowered bonnets, waved their hands and called out. Looking up, Barry realized that they were hailing him. He averted his face and flushed crimson.

The merchant was amused. "Lord-a-mercy, listen to them chippies howl at you, boy. Reckon they ain't seen a man of your cut for a spell. Mormons ain't much for payin' for a woman when they can have as many wives as they hanker after. Damn fools, I say. I've a hard enough time listenin' to the harpin' of one woman, let alone several. But don't get me wrong. I've no use for this cut of woman, either."

Barry swallowed. "Do you mean those women are . . . ?"

"Nothing else but," the merchant laughed. "They ride out from Kansas City a couple times a week. Oh, they know better than to try anything here, but they have a way of lettin' a man know where to find them if he wants to ride five miles west for the evening."

To Barry's further embarrassment the women had the cart driver stop in the middle of the street so that they could blatantly stare at him. He was unused to such attention. The women were unused to such a male specimen. Barry was a shade less than six feet tall in his moccasins, but his wiry frame made him look taller. His face, beneath his straight black hair, was lined and craggy, his cheekbones high, his mouth thin lipped, and his eyes as deep black as a well-bottom. His nose had been broken, more than once, by both man and animal. His chin was jutting and square. It was an attractive, even handsome face, with a quality of sensuality Barry hardly knew he possessed, so seldom did he think about it in the mountains.

Still red-faced, he said, "I wish they'd move on. I have business to attend at the Fremont house. Could you direct me?"

Instantly, the merchant turned cool. "I can, though I don't mind sayin' I've little use for the man and his explorin' ways. He's going to open this country up so wide it'll start being just like the damn east. You'll find the house a block over, sitting on the corner. Best warn you though, he ain't one for seein' people without an appointment. Thinks his shit don't smell."

Barry nodded. He was curious enough to ask for the merchant's further opinions about John C. Fremont, but before he could, the man hoisted a flour sack onto his shoulder and strode, mumbling, back inside his store.

Jessie Benton Fremont had been lucky to find a large, stately brick house for rent in Independence. It had none of the comfort of her childhood home in St. Louis or the luxury of her parents' brownstone in Washington City, but it kept her close to her husband of two years and that was all that mattered to her.

On that day nothing had gone properly. John had left early to discuss with someone his next exploration of the western frontier. The fire had refused to start throughout the day. Two scowling gentlemen awaited John in the cold parlor, and the servant girl her father, Senator Thomas Benton, had given her as a belated wedding present claimed that her womanly curse had started that day. Standing in the center of the hall, ready to weep, Jessie heard a heavy knock, and waited for the sullen Kitty to answer it.

Her intuition told her at once who the caller must be. She sailed forward as soon as she spotted him in the doorway.

"Thank you, Kitty," she said sweetly. "I'll handle it. You must be Barry Fitzpatrick. Welcome and come in. I'm Jessie Fremont."

Barry hesitantly doffed his beaver cap and shyly entered. Coming from the sunlight into the dim hall put the woman and everything else into shadowy focus for him.

"Thank ye, ma'am," he said. "I'm here to see Major Fremont."

"I expect him shortly. Won't you come into the sitting room to wait? It gets the westerly sun and soon should be rid of the chill. I must apologize for our inability to ignite the fireplace properly, Mr. Fitzpatrick. I've never been capable of it and my maid seems equally inexperienced."

Barry noticed she was wearing a heavy shawl. He followed wordlessly, finding the ill-lit room warm enough for himself in buckskins but perhaps indeed too chilly for her. As was his manner, when he saw a chore that needed doing, he took over at once. He dispatched Kitty for dry firewood and plunged his hands into the grate to re-ignite the charred tinder fragments and make it work. It was not until the fire was blazing and the de-shawled Jessie Fremont had returned with a bowl of water and towel for him that he had a good look at her. She was a young girl.

He saw that she was lovely. Once before, Barry

Fitzpatrick had known a young girl perhaps as lovely, but that was years before when he was a callow teenager and the girl, Maria DeVises, had all but broken his heart. A quick pang at the sight of Jessie Benton brought Maria to his mind again, just for an instant. He looked and saw she was of a different order of loveliness. Her blond hair was of a shade so light as to be almost silver. Her lips were not the shell-pink usually found in pale blondes but deep rose, and her eyes were sea-green, soft and velvety. She was slender rather than thin, high of bosom, soft-curving, and she swept along as though entering a Washington ballroom. Maria DeVises wouldn't have been at home in a ballroom, only in the mountains.

But then, Barry didn't know Jessie yet.

Jessie Benton Fremont didn't know the meaning of the word fear. Her father, Thomas Hart Benton, had been the senior United States Senator for the State of Missouri for the past twenty-three years. She had grown up surrounded by such men as John Quincy Adams, Andrew Jackson, Martin Van Buren and William Henry Harrison—all presidents. She could have had her pick of a couple dozen young swains, but to the chagrin of her parents was adamant in her choice of a man eleven years her senior. And she would stick with the controversial Major Fremont come hell or high water.

"Now, that is what I call a real fire, Mr. Fitzpatrick. I do believe fire-laying is an art and you have the knack for it."

Barry, embarrassed, said, "I'm sure your father could have done just as well."

Jessie cast him a sidelong glance.

"Hardly, sir," she said. "His tongue is capable of creating more sparks than he was ever able to produce with a tinder-box." She stretched her hands to the fire and then turned back. "Oh, that feels so good. I must confess, Mr. Fitzpatrick, that I am not a winter person. I should have been born a bear so that I could hibernate and emerge only when it was glorious spring."

"It's more spring here than where I came from, ma'am. I've seen it snow in the mountains as late as mid-July."

"Then you must enjoy your life, Mr. Fitzpatrick, or you would get away from such conditions. Have you family?"

"Mainly myself."

Jessie was studying Barry, her eyes soft and innocent.

Too innocent, Barry realized suddenly. This one knows men, he thought. With an Indian squaw there did not need to be study or prolonged flirtation. If she liked you it was a simple matter to spend the night in her tepee, leaving when you were sated, or staying to sate yourself again. This one would want more out of him than he had ever given a woman before. But she intrigued him. He had never slept with a white woman.

"I suppose it is best you have no family," she said. "I consider myself a strong woman, but I don't know if I would be strong enough to endure the hardships of a western trek. There are enough privations right here in Independence. But, I suppose if a woman loves her man deeply enough she will follow him anywhere."

Barry looked at her suspiciously. He had heard of women coming to the middle-frontier because the male-female ratio was ten to one—and a hundred to one farther west. He wasn't quite sure of what young Jessie had in mind.

"I ain't been around women much, ma'am," he allowed, "but I reckon you're right."

"Ah, here's Kitty," she beamed. "I took the liberty to have her fix you a light repast, Mr. Fitzpatrick. It is small reward indeed for the fire. What would you like?"

"Well, ma'am . . ." Barry hesitated. Despite himself, he was stirred up by Jessie's flirtatiousness. If he allowed himself to speak the truth of his feelings, he would have told her directly what he wanted, namely herself. Instead, he chose to say, "Anything, ma'am, anything at all. Tea and sandwiches will do just fine."

The front door opened and closed while Barry was gingerly picking at his unaccustomed lunch and Jessie was, most charmingly, continuing to flirt. She had just referred to some trappers' tales she had heard to the effect that young Indian girls make savagely passionate lovers. She wanted to know if Barry believed this too.

Barry's eyebrows lifted when he heard the door close. "What I believe, ma'am," he said tonelessly, "is that we both done just been caught in amorous dalliance."

Jessie burst out laughing.

A tall, rangy man with a coal-black beard and mustache entered the sitting room doorway. His black hair cascaded down to his shoulders. He heard Jessie's laugh and took in the scene with small, fiery eyes all but lost in his plump face. "What ails you, woman," he boomed. "Are you daft?"

"No, John," Jessie smiled. "This gentleman just said something terribly amusing, that's all. John, this is the man you've been waiting for, Barry Fitzpatrick. Mr. Fitzpatrick, may I present my husband, Major John C. Fremont."

Barry stood to greet the major, studying him.

"About time," Fremont snapped. "I was beginning to fear I would have to leave before your arrival. It is good to meet you, sir. However, I had anticipated a much older person."

Barry's sentiments were the same. He had envisioned Fremont to be a man in his mid-fifties. This darkly handsome man of thirty seemed far too young to have accomplished so much in life.

"Age doesn't count in the west, sir," Barry said coolly. "I've been training under Jim Bridger for the past year. Now, if you would like to hear his plans . . ."

He had, he saw at once, struck the right note. John Fremont hated to waste a single moment of his life with unnecessary detail. He worshipped industry and ambition and men of action. In spite of his insane jealousy over his young wife, it was she who had helped make him such an outstanding success. Jessie had actively engaged in the furtherance of his enterprises from the time of their marriage and was a remarkable sounding board for his sometimes impetuous nature.

Fremont's eyes moved quickly, taking in Barry's muscular build. My God! The man could pull a wagon west all on his own!

"Yes, John," Jessie whispered sweetly, "he's a real mountain man."

"Come into my study," Fremont said incisively.

"I want to see if you think my explorations can be put to their truest test."

But Jessie put out a hand and stopped him.

"There is no fire in the parlor, John. Mr. Fitzpatrick was kind enough to lay this one for us but you have two other guests waiting there. A Colonel Herbert and a Mr. Corinthwyeth."

"What good luck!" Fremont enthused. "I was unaware of their arrival. They will have two of the three segments of your wagon train, Fitzpatrick. I'll go greet them and bring them back here. I think Kitty should prepare three more places for dinner, my dear. This is marvelous, just marvelous!"

The sudden change in Fremont startled Barry. Seeing the expression of wonder on his face after the major had left, Jessie said:

"My husband lives to see his dreams fullfilled."

Seeing that Barry still did not understand, she added quickly: "He was like a small boy last year when he found the South Pass through the Wind River chain of the Rocky Mountains. Now he needs to know if it will bring about a faster and safer route for the emigrant trains. That's why he was so thrilled to learn that Jim Bridger would help on the project. His is not an official government operation. You do know that?"

Barry nodded noncommittally. He was aware mostly of Bridger's prophecy that the days of the wilderness were numbered and the days of the settlers were at hand. Barry was still unsure if he wanted to be a part of that change. He loved the unsettled west and didn't want it to become like Independence, now that he had seen Independence.

"John will make you famous," Jessie said
smugly. "Some day you will be known as the man
who took through the first great wagon train."

I rather doubt that, Barry was thinking. He was
still smarting over the way he had allowed this
woman to soften him up with her smooth and
flirtatious talk.

Jessie, intuiting his thought, lowered her voice
to a tense conspiratorial whisper.

"Before John returns I deeply wish to apologize. Flirting with you was very unkind of me,
and that is not my nature. It is a deep compliment
to a woman to be wanted by another man and at
your expense I was relishing the compliment you
were paying me with your eyes. Can you please
forgive me? I would much prefer it if we could be
Barry and Jessie to each other."

Barry felt his blood race anew. Oddly, her
apology stimulated him. Before, when he thought
she was seeking him, his interest had been only
lukewarm. Now that he'd seen she was not available, his desire returned. He supposed he was still
angry at her. He wanted to accept her apology
with a hard kiss. He wanted to crush her in his
arms, feel her exciting lips upon his, the softness
of her breasts pressing close against his chest.
Deep in her eyes he saw that she was totally reading his thoughts. It seemed to him she was thinking that it might not be too bad an idea to give the
mountain man exactly what he wished.

But both of their thoughts were washed away
by the jolly re-entry of John Fremont. He had in
tow two men of such dour expression that Fremont seemed like a jubilant law officer who had

just captured a couple of desperate criminals.

As Fremont enthusiastically gave a sketchy background on each man, Barry had a chance to weigh and study each, in the same manner he would have on meeting an Indian or trapper for the first time. A man's past history meant little to him. It was a man's eye and bodily reaction while he was being talked about that could unearth his whole personality.

One man called himself Colonel Thomas Cuthbertson Herbert, but Barry's animal instinct told him that the title was self-imposed. The man was fat, nothing against him, but he sweated profusely as he leaned forward nervously in his seat, patting daintily at his balding dome with a soiled silk handkerchief. Although Barry judged Herbert to be in his mid-fifties, his hair and mustache were jet black, quite obviously dyed to make a youthful impression. He cupped his mouth with his hand quite a bit when he spoke, as if he didn't want his lips seen when he told lies. All in all, Barry saw him as something of a confidence man without much confidence. Colonel Herbert was from Alabama. His suit jacket front seemed to contain a record of what he'd eaten since he'd left home.

Bradford Cornithwyeth was the colonel's opposite. A small man with paper-thin skin and a delicate bone structure, his hands fluttered like birds unable to find a safe landing spot. His clothing was homespun and puritan in simplicity. He had a thin, eager face. Although a man of few words, he seemed to weigh each of them carefully so as not to err or be misunderstood.

Colonel Herbert and Bradford Cornithwyeth shared one thing in common: an instant and total mistrust of Barry's youth.

"I was under the impression," Cornithwyeth said slowly, "that we would be gaining the services of Mr. Bridger."

"Fitzpatrick?" Fremont said, prodding Barry for the answer.

The matter was one Barry had wished to discuss first with Major Fremont, but he had no recourse but to answer. He directed his comments to Cornithwyeth, who had asked for them.

"You shall, sir. Eight hundred miles down the trail you'll be thankful that he stayed to greet you and not lead you."

"At journey's end?" Colonel Herbert snorted disdainfully. "What help shall that be to us?"

"Hardly journey's end," Fremont laughed. "Hardly even halfway. You face two thousand miles of prairie, plains and mountains, gentlemen."

The colonel fixed beady, doubtful eyes on Barry.

"What has Bridger in mind, Fitzpatrick?" Fremont said.

"Not in mind, major. It's already fact. He's selected a spot with an abundance of water, grass and game. A blacksmith shop is already built and the corral stocked with horses and cattle. It will be a welcome way-station come the end of summer."

"But, my boy," Cornithwyeth mused suspiciously, "surely you have erred. My company, The New England Emigrant Resettlement Association, figures the trip will take no more than thirty-five to forty days from Lancaster, Pennsylvania. The emigrants should reach Bridger long before summer's end."

"Perhaps," Fremont said quickly, "I myself am prepared to answer you, Mr. Cornithwyeth. If I am not mistaken you informed me that your sixty wagons would all be of the Conestoga class. You are dealing with a piece of equipment that requires six horses each. You are also dealing with a part of the country which would amaze young Fitzpatrick's eyes if he went back east and saw it. Roads, sir. Your train will be progressing on routes that have become well travelled. You have pockets of civilization to see you many miles along the way.

"Beyond a point, however, there are no roads and the only civilization are nations of Indians who are going to be hostile at your intrusion. You are not going to be able to travel in a straight line. Water supply will determine your course and your speed. Because of the size of the train Bridger wishes put together, you will be lucky to make eight to ten miles per day."

Cornithwyeth felt as though he had just been lectured by Fremont and it rankled him.

"I stand corrected, major," he said dryly. "You have no doubt made a fairer assessment than I. However, my associates and I, well aware that we were embarking on a risky business, have demanded that each group in our party equip themselves with a new wagon, and we have given grave consideration to every other aspect of this journey. . . . Are you, Fitzpatrick, sure that you are capable of taking the train on through?"

"No," Barry said, "I'm not sure." It was the

truth, but Barry also knew that he had to take command of the discussion at that very moment or lose it. "But I am very sure of the man who has trained me for the job. He's drummed into my head certain rules and conditions that we'll travel by and that will be our law."

"Eh?" Colonel Herbert said, tugging at his lips with his fingers. "I'll wish to hear each and every rule before I consent. My forty wagons are all what you might call 'family,' gentlemen. They will be looking to me for authority and not to a stranger."

Barry rose and walked to the fireplace, carefully turning the log as though he were the host in the house. When he turned his face was firmly set. He was used to dealing with strong-willed mountain men. He felt he had a fair measure now on these two men.

"We'll not have time to remain strangers for long," he said evenly. "Nor will I have time to wet nurse each and every wagon. You each will be left in charge of your individual segment of the train, just as will the third man and his party."

"Third!" Cornithwyeth exploded. "I was not informed of this! It will surely slow us even more, Major Fremont."

"Fremont has nothing to do with it," Barry declared. "You each sought his advice and he gave it as an individual. Others have approached him and others will surely approach me before we leave. Any group that meets my conditions will be considered, and that includes present company."

An uncomfortable silence filled the room. To break the spell Jessie Fremont rose and quietly announced that she would go and look in on the dinner preparations. Only Barry seemed to have been aware that she had been in the room at all. As she turned their eyes met and he was buoyed by the respect for him he saw mirrored in them.

"It is my understanding," Barry went on, "that Major Fremont is due to leave on his next expedition shortly. His intention, gentlemen, is to further survey the South Pass and area beyond. He will no longer be of use to you locally. The spring runoff will be at its peak by the end of May. By then I will expect us to be formed together on the south bank of the Kansas River and ready to cross the prairie."

John Fremont's estimate of Barry Fitzpatrick had grown rapidly. The young man was as gritty and cocksure as Jim Bridger, but he also had a sensitivity and intelligence that the older mountain man didn't ordinarily show. In Fitzpatrick's speech there was a trace of the political acumen of Fremont's father-in-law. The army engineer was secretly enjoying seeing the arrogant southern gentleman and the pious New Englander caught up in a match that they did not quite know how to contend with.

"Perhaps," Fremont suggested almost devilishly, "it is not too soon for you to suggest to these gentlemen what you will expect from them prior to that departure date, Barry."

It was the first time Fremont had addressed Barry informally. He was quick to pick up the acknowledgment and felt grateful for the silence.

"Thank you, major," he said in agreement. "I do think it is time. In general, here is Jim Bridger's scheme. We'll be a wagon train carrying a great number of women and children. I'll want recorded a list of doctors, preachers, even those who might have abilities to teach school to the youngsters. It's a long boring trip and a little teaching can help take their minds off of it each day. It may sound personal and embarrassing for you to ask but I've got to know when each woman had her last child and if there is a possibility of her having one on the trip. One birth could stall the train for hours or for days.

"Now, we don't leave until each man can show that his wagon's in prime condition, with spare yokes, tires, axles and extra shoes for all of his stock. As I said, you'll not be finding another blacksmith till we hit the Sweetwater. Which brings me to the next list I require on each wagon. No man will be allowed to start without farm tools, as well as weapons, ammunition and at least one hundred pounds of flour for each month between here and the west coast. Then, we need to know what every wagon is carrying. Bridger says most folk tend to bring everything with them except their relations left in the graveyards. It only means trouble later on, so you'll have to tell your people no heavy loads from the start."

Barry stood for a moment, wracking his brain to see if he had covered every point that Bridger had insisted upon. It was the longest speech he'd made since he'd come back from the mountains.

Bradford Cornithwyeth had listened carefully and intently. He did not want to play the hypocrite and goad the young man into showing he was incapable of the burdensome task, but in his mind there were some glaring omissions in the rules.

He cleared his throat as though to speak for an equal length of time as Barry. "Adequate measures so far," he admitted. "But, and I feel it is necessary for me to say this, the New England Emigrant Resettlement Association is going to vast lengths to assure ourselves that our families will be bound first and foremost by the Ten Commandments. We will be sixty God-fearing families, to be sure. Reports have filtered back to us of the fornication that has been a part of other trains. We shall not allow it! What say you, Colonel Herbert?"

Herbert licked his lips nervously.

"Ah, as I said, sir, mine is already a family unit, so to speak. I anticipate no problems with my people as long as I am left *fully* in charge of them. Besides, you'll not be finding a more Christian woman than my wife, gentlemen. Miss Mary Sue Herbert will be the real voice to keep our people in line. You can count on that. Ain't a one of them that don't love her and her genteel ways."

2

Huntsville, Alabama

Dahlia Dee Herbert sat alone, lonely. Her breakfast cooled without being touched. A month before she had been totally oblivious to the steady decay and deterioration of the plantation house; today she saw it in stark reality, because suddenly the house was gone, no longer theirs. Now, she thought, she would never be able to hold her head up in respectable society. She suddenly had a premonition that sometime, in the very near future perhaps, something even more terrible was about to befall her family. As she thought the word family, something strange happened to Dahlia Dee. She understood how little a family they really were.

She had been twelve, her brother Harmon fourteen, when their mother had died and they had been spirited away, the day after the funeral, from their Georgia home. She had hated Alabama from the first, loathed the new plantation and detested her new step-mother. In the next four years she developed an outer shell. She overlooked all that was past and allowed herself to concentrate only on the present gowns and county balls she could attend. Her four-year hibernation had been knocked into a cocked hat when her father had announced that another move was of dire necessity and that he was leaving to plan for it. He had fallen at that moment, in her eyes, to the same loathsome level as his second wife.

The squeak of carriage wheels on the hard gravel brought her to her senses. She shook her head in dismay. Her stepmother was home, but she was not alone. Beside Mary Sue Herbert in the carriage sat Harmon. Behind them, nestling a new-born baby protectively to her bosom, sat a colored wet-nurse.

She bumped into them in the front hall. They paid scant attention to her or each other.

She said uncertainly, "Good morning?"

Harmon's eyes were stone gray and dark and they burned at Dahlia Dee with a restless, resentful fire. She had to catch her breath. This eighteen-year-old young man was her brother, yet she'd never seen him like this before. The grim, taciturn man-boy spoke to no one. He entered the dining room and sat and ate silently, his eyes on his plate. When he had finished, he mopped his plate with a whole biscuit and stuffed it into his mouth.

Mary Sue had taken a single cup of coffee and

stood drinking it at the bay window. The plantation was coming to life, but for the first time in
her life Mary Sue really didn't care. At forty she
felt terribly tired and very old. Four years before
she had been an attractive childless widow.
Landed and monied, she was wooed by every
available man along the Alabama River. Her
marriage to Thomas Herbert had provided the
people of Mobile Bay with months of gossip and
four years of consternation. He was a penniless
Georgia planter with no stock, slaves or apparent
ambition. Adopting the title of 'Colonel' he spent
the widow's money lavishly and foolishly. At first
Mary Sue didn't mind. She didn't love Tom Herbert, but she loved what he had been able to give
her—his children.

She was just as much responsible for the spoil-
ing of DeeDee and Harm as the colonel. It
brought back her own youth to dress and pamper
and turn Dahlia Dee into a stunning belle. It still
gave her a touch of pride to view the uncommonly
beautiful girl with the rich raven hair set against
alabaster skin and the high proud bosom and carriage. Much too late she found she could not buy
the girl's affection and now they were silent, battling enemies.

Henry Harmon Herbert had kept his stepmother at arm's length from the first day he arrived at the plantation. Even at fourteen, he had
sensed that Mary Sue might make demands on
him that would be more than motherly. It was a
situation he was incapable of discussing with his
father and so the matter was left to ferment for
four years.

Now he had become the man, physically, that Mary Sue knew he would become, but hardly the man, mentally, she had desired. Tall and muscular and as blonde as his sister was dark, he had gray eyes that seemed to probe and pierce and make provocative suggestions without a word spoken. Outwardly, he was a head-turning giant who made the county belles and colored girls dream dreams that were forbidden. Inwardly, he was as vacant and void of thought or ambition as the sands of the Gobi desert.

Mary Sue cleared her throat, then said a little stiffly, "The girl died givin' birth."

Harmon pushed his chair back, crossed to the door and turned. "Sure you didn't help push her in that direction?" The curtness of his tone had a way of making everything he said sound like a fact.

Mary Sue ignored him. "Go get that bastard, Pomeroy, then you bring your goddam nigger-sleepin' self back here."

Harmon shrugged and left, as though he were not a part of the storm that was about to break.

DeeDee looked at her with large solemn eyes. After a second, she said, "There's the baby to consider."

Mary Sue said abruptly. "Just another mouth to feed, as far as I'm concerned. The girl couldn't even be sure if the father was Pomeroy or Harmon. Damn men, anyway."

DeeDee crossed the room and unexpectedly took Mary Sue's hand. "There's nothing we can do about that now, mother. But we do need Harm and Pomeroy now. Mr. Larkin was here again last night. He's set on collecting the debt by the end of the week. We must stick together until we hear from father."

Mary Sue frowned and looked out through the window to where the canvas-covered body of the baby's black mother was a frightening sight for the other slaves. None dared approach the wagon, but stood, in an ever-increasing circle, to stare and jabber.

Aaron Pomeroy did not need to be summoned. He came bounding out of the crowd like a wild, charging bull.

"Leave us alone," Mary Sue commanded.

They glowered at each other across centuries of suspicion: Mary Sue sure, capable and white, with the hard, uninhibited eye of the master. Her people had been on this Alabama land for over a hundred years. She had grown up with every slave on the plantation and could call each and everyone of them by name. They had been her 'family' until the arrival of Colonel Herbert. It had been her new husband's suggestion to send to Georgia for Pomeroy and make him overseer.

The rangy, beefy-faced man was totally unacceptable to Mary Sue from the start. His black ancestry set him apart from the white world, and his white ancestry made him instantly suspect among the slaves. He wanted the best of each world and was denied both to the point that at twenty-seven he had become hard, cruel and calculating. No one ever knew where they stood with Aaron Pomeroy, because he wasn't quite sure where he stood with himself.

"The girl claims that you might have been the child's father."

"Could be," he drawled, indifferently.

"You listen to me, Pomeroy. I sure as damn hell expect a straight answer or the black part of your hide will feel the rawhide."

The tall man had to turn away to hide his mirth. He knew the dainty, small woman to have a loud bark, but a heart that was far too compassionate. She was the only person he had ever been able to summon up an ounce of respect for, and a great deal of that had to do with his long secret desire for her. He had never looked upon her as a woman thirteen years his senior. Her body was still as subtle and well-cared-for as Dahlia Dee's. He would overlook the streaks of gray in her mousy brown hair and the wrinkles beginning to appear at the corners of her eyes and across her forehead. It was the soft round curve of her firm breasts and the seductive way her pelvis moved when walking that always held his attention. He just couldn't ever picture her lying beneath the fat, officious, pig-like colonel.

"Ain't much to answer, ma'am. You know the colonel wanted me to help improve the breeding stock."

Mary Sue glowered. "And I recall forbidding such a practice. Are you the one who put the idea into Harmon's head?"

"No, ma'am," he laughed. "Ain't no one has to put bed-wenching ideas into his head."

"It would seem to me," she said sternly, "that you would be the first to be against such a practice. Have you seen the child? It will be mulatto, for sure."

"And thus a better price. It's something Larkin's overlooked, Miss Mary Sue. He's only counting heads, not quality. It may be a harsh question, but what are you going to be able to take with you?"

The question hit Mary Sue like a lightning clap. She ambled back to the window like a mammoth moth lured to the light of truth. She had never given the future any thought until three months before. Only then had Tom Herbert confessed to her his gambling debts to Simon Larkin. It had nearly torn her heart out to send some of her best slaves to auction in New Orleans. Then had come the startling news that Colonel Herbert had taken the money and gone north to Missouri.

At first she could not believe the message she had received from him. She did not believe the south to be old and used up. To start up anew in the west was an alien and frightening thought. Her French ancestry rose to the surface and she set her mind to giving up a husband before she would the land and her slaves.

Then Simon Larkin, with his pock-faced giggling wife, came to view the plantation and stun her with the actual truth. Colonel Herbert's gambling debt was five times the amount he had admitted to her. Even if he had come back from New Orleans with the slave profits it would have been too little.

"How did he ever figure," she said aloud, "that we would be able to get to Missouri with forty wagons and the people to man them? I've just been fooling myself, Pomeroy. Everything you see will become Larkin's. It's hopeless."

"May I ask you something?"

"I can hardly stop you."

"All right. You got any money hidden away at all?"

"Yes. Some that my grandmother left me when she died last year. But hardly enough to solve my problem with Larkin, Pomeroy."

"Let Larkin solve his own cheating problem. He ain't been too quick to get the sheriff to help him gain his winnings, now has he?" Pomeroy watched her with his dark, hunter's eyes; watched for a movement, or a gesture, some head-nodding assent. In vain. More than anything he wanted to put her into his debt. "Colonel Herbert ain't been the first fool to be suckered into Larkin's trap. He may be the biggest, but not the first."

Mary Sue said nothing.

"Now, it seems to me, the colonel wanted you to do something a bit shady to begin with. He knew the debt, but still told you to bring forty wagons and your people north. I'll grant you, he knows little about the plantation, and our rolling stock is right old and in need of repair."

"I don't see your point," Mary Sue said coldly.

"Because you've never had to cheat and steal and run for your life before, ma'am. How can you blame the colonel for trying to lam out? What else was there? But he's giving you a chance to keep from holding the whole bag. Do you see that?"

Mary Sue did not reply.

"I suggest you let me know how much money is available, so we can look at the facts more clearly."

"I . . ." Mary Sue grasped for the right words. She had been more than honest with Tom Herbert about her wealth and he had squandered it on his children and gambling. Did she dare expose the last capital she might ever possess to another man? ". . . I . . . expect it's only a few thousand."

For a long time Pomeroy searched her face for something he could not find.

"Is it enough to gamble on your future?"

"Future?" Mary Sue repeated softly. "That's a funny word. My husband didn't consider my future while he was losing my money. His children have never considered my future at any time. Now, you speak of *my* future. Doesn't it secure theirs as well? If I was any other type of woman I would just take my grandmother's money and run like hell."

"But you are not any other type of woman," Pomeroy said with sudden fierceness. "To hell with your stupid bastard of a husband, and your stepdaughter who is too damn afraid to learn what a prick is for and a stepson who knows too damn well what his prick is molded to fit into. When I speak of your future, I'm speaking of your real family, the blacks. They hate my goddam guts, but if you told them to walk through fire they'd all start takin' off their shoes and boots. They'll follow you and strip this plantation to the bone if you just give the word."

Mary Sue, her face immobile, her body rigid, blinked once and gave Pomeroy a quiet solemn reply. "What is the word and how can we do it?"

His smile was very unpleasant, its amusement malicious. But it was not directed at Mary Sue. He was taking a first step in a daring gamble to gain revenge on Simon Larkin, Tom Herbert and his son. If he won he would claim Mary Sue as the prize.

"Simple," he said quietly. "You still own the cotton warehouse in Mobile. We'll start sending a few wagons down each day as is normal. Larkin will think you're trying to sell everything in sight and that's all that concerns him. He's only interested in money. Believe me, I've owed him before. He'd only sell this land and the slaves the day after you left, anyway. But we won't be sending down cotton. The wagons will be loaded with the people and goods. Your job will be to take your money and make passage arrangements for us."

"Passage?"

"Right now those wagons will be doing good to get to Mobile. But given time, while they are being shipped to New Orleans and then upriver to St. Louis, Aaron Pomeroy will bank his life on the fact that they will be ready to get you to Independence and beyond."

"And how far behind us will be Larkin and the sheriff?"

The rangy man shrugged. "Maybe he'll be here before we ever pull it off, but I'd love to see his face if we do pull it off."

Mary Sue laughed. It was the first time she had laughed in weeks and it brought dimples to her cheeks and a glint to her eyes. "Yes," she mused, "that would be a sight to see. You had best go put the plan into operation before I regain my senses and change my mind. I have never done anything illegal in my life, you know."

She was so absorbed in making mental plans that she was startled when Harmon repeated impatiently: "You ordered me to come back, remember?"

She walked to him, rigid and straight, her face a mask of glacial calm. Yet, as he looked at her in silence, without emotion, he saw a strength and determination in her that had never been there before.

"I do not wish to discuss the girl or her child with you ever again, Harmon. We, all of us, are going to be leaving this place. Pomeroy will need your help to keep Larkin from learning of it."

"Isn't that illegal?" he pointed out in a hard thin voice.

"Illegal, illegal, illegal," she cried. "Damn all of you saints around me! Illegal for your father to gamble with my money and land! Illegal for you to screw every black girl you can get into! It's also illegal to transport slaves to where we are going. Think on that! And while you are at it think on how these slaves have fed and clothed you for these years. You've been a leech, Harmon. Judgment day for you is near at hand. I'm giving you another chance to prove that you are more of a man than just what dangles between your legs. If you don't want the chance, you can leave."

He didn't answer. Their eyes clashed. He didn't have his father there to back him up and he was suddenly afraid. He was only a little boy masquerading in a man's body and he did not have the will to stand up to her. He hung his head, nodded and left.

The tears welled into Mary Sue's eyes and she cursed herself. She loved him so very much and could do nothing about it.

3

PINETOP, TENNESSEE

Howard Tedder seated himself at the table and looked into his wife's face with a smile:

"Lydia, a king could ask for no more. Good food. A good wife and children. That's blessin' enough, I'd be sayin'."

He saw them as he wished to see them and not what they had become. Lydia was still his bride and not a woman who had been slowly wasted away by the strenuous backwoods life and the lung-filling consumption that she kept as a secret from all. Howard's "baby child" was as red-headed and freckle-faced as her mother had been, but was hardly a child any longer. Maybelle Tedder, at fourteen, resented her freckles, resented the pain in her growing breasts, resented the fact that most mountain girls her age were already

with husband and child and she was already
nearly an old maid. She wanted a man of her own
more than anything else on earth, but there was
not a man within fifty miles that she thought
worthy of herself.

Howard, in his earthy way, had prayed hard
for his first-born to be a man-child. He was doubly
blessed and forever after looked upon Theodis
and Nazareth as 'little angels'. After sixteen years
they were still russet-haired, brown-eyed imps
right out of the bowels of hell. If there was mis-
chief afoot, what one didn't think of the other was
most likely to dream up.

The supper over, Howard smoked his pipe before the cabin fire of blazing logs while his wife
cleared the wooden dishes. Maybelle, who had a
knack for disappearing when chores were at
hand, had climbed into the loft and sat day-
dreaming. The twins had been dispatched on an
errand that had amazed and confounded them;
and Lydia and Howard were left alone. He
watched her get the paper, goose-quill pen and
ink as a prisoner sees the scaffold building for his
execution.

"Now we're all ready," she said cheerfully.

Howard laid his pipe down with a helpless
look. A brief respite flashed through his mind.
Maybe he could sidestep this chore before she
pinned him down.

"Lord, Lydia, I forgot my gun. I must grease
her right away," he said.

He rose with a quick decisive movement and
took his rifle from the rack. She knew it was use-
useless to protest and let him have his way.

Over every inch of its heavy barrel and polished

walnut stock he rubbed a piece of greased linen with loving care, drew back the flintlock and greased carefully every nook and turn of its mechanism, lifted the gun finally to his shoulder and drew an imaginary bead on the head of a turkey gobbler two hundred yards away. A glowing coal of hickory wood in the fire served for his game.

He lowered the gun and held it before him with pride:

"Lydia, she's the prettiest piece o'iron that wuz ever made inta a weapon. She'll be servin' us well agin varmints and Injuns when we get out west."

"Perhaps," his wife said with a shake of her graying red head, "if we ever get out of here."

"We'll be gettin' within a week and that's a fact."

"Without some record doin'?"

"I reckon not," Howard laughed. "We got to work hard at it."

"Then it's time to get to it." She gently took the rifle from his hands, placed it on the buck horns and took her seat at the table.

The man looked ruefully at the stool he was to sit on. He really didn't know if he could face leaving Tennessee. He suddenly straightened his massive frame, lifted his hand above his head and cocked his eye inquiringly:

"May I git er drink er water fust?"

Lydia laughed in spite of herself, and nodded assent. Howard seized the water bucket and started for the door.

"Where are you going?" she cried in dismay.

"I'll jest run down to the spring fer a fresh bucket—"

Before she could protest he was gone.

He managed to stay nearly a half hour. Lydia put the dishes away and sat waiting with her pensive eyes gazing at the leaping flames. She really didn't want to leave her home either, but knew it was the only answer for Howard and the children. Their land was too rocky and the winter too severe. In spite of a constant stream of new people into the valley there seemed to be less and less work for Howard's carpenter skills. In the west, they'd kept telling each other, there would be many opportunities for her and the boys. She knew she might never see the west, but her children and grandchildren would. If, that is, she took charge of the leaving.

She heard him stop and answer the call of an owl from the woods. A whip-poor-will was softly singing from the bushes nearby. He stopped to call out to that bird also, and then found an excuse to linger ten minutes more fooling with his hunting dogs.

The laggard came at last and dropped on his stool by her side. He sat for five minutes staring helplessly at the paper she had set before her.

"Don't know my letters that good, woman," he protested.

"Better than any in the valley, Howard Tedder," she scolded. "If'n it weren't for you knowin' we'd not be affordin' the move. We gotta set down each family agoin' and what they are a payin' or it'll be squabbles all the way."

"All right, woman, I'll be at it," he protested, and bent his huge shoulders low over his task. Big beads of perspiration stood on his forehead as he recorded each family name, the name and ages of each of their children, the number of their

wagons and livestock, the charge for guiding them
to Missouri and what would be due for the guide
on west. It took over an hour before he reached
the twentieth name.

"Can't finish till the boys bring me Ned Conroy's information."

"I think I hear them now."

But it was only Theodis who came in the door,
hesitated and tried to quickly back out. He was
startled to see his parents still awake and a candle
lit on the table.

"Where ya goin', boy," his father demanded,
"and where be yore brother?"

The young giant reentered, his head hanging
and mumbled:

"He's sittin' a spell, paw."

Except for their general build, hair and skin
coloring, the twins were quite opposites. There
was a timid shyness in Theodis' makeup, whereby
his brother was aggressive, brash and foolhardy.
When Theodis acted as he was acting now, Howard Tedder would feel the hair rise on the nap of
his neck and automatically know that Nazareth
was up to no good.

"He'll not be sittin' fur long if'n I have to whale
him. Nazareth!" he bellowed. "Git yore ass in
here!"

There was a long pause, then Nazareth appeared in the doorway. He came into the room
slowly, head down, feet dragging in the dust of
the dirt floor. Instantly Lydia was on her feet and
made a lunge in his direction. Howard's big hand
flicked out, snapping her to a halt. "Leave 'im
be!"

"But I can see he's hurt."

Lydia shook the restraining hand off, angrily, but waited while Nazareth came forward. His shirt was torn, his hair full of dust, and his nose was still dripping blood.

Howard looked from one to the other for an explanation. Theodis, whose face was as small and pretty as his mother's, hung his head even farther. Nazareth raised his square jaw almost proudly and gave his father a wink with the eye that was swelling visibly. Howard could have been looking into a mirror image of his own face at age sixteen.

"The Conroys ain't got no right to call you a cheat, paw," he declared, as though it answered everything.

"How'd it happen?"

Nazareth swallowed painfully. "We did as we wuz told, paw. Got the number of wagons and stock and told 'im the charge. Then you wuz called a cheat."

"By Ned Conroy?"

"No. By Neville and Billy Joe. They said their ole man didn't need to pay you no money and they'd make it on their own."

"And so the two of you had to fight the two of them?"

Nazareth grinned and then winced at the cut in the corner of his mouth. "No, paw, not Theodis. He jest likes to watch me fight more'n one at a time."

Howard looked down ruefully at the paper where the Conroy name had been laboriously printed. He had very little use for the drunken Ned Conroy and his always-ready-to-fight parcel of boys, but the man's five wagons meant very needed dollars to the Tedders' purse.

He snorted. "Git you both up to bed. I'll be handling Ned myself on the morrow."

Theodis started to open his mouth and was given a dangerous warning glance from his brother. They quickly scampered up the loft ladder, the one feeling a foreboding sense of guilt and the other a sense of satisfaction that he had escaped, for the moment, a worse beating from his father than he had experienced from Neville and Billy Joe Conroy.

Lydia paused until the boys were out of earshot and whispered:

"O Howard, we can't lose Ned and his money. It would mean one wagon less for us. I'll not be leaving as much behind as I was forced to do when we came from Virginny."

He patted her hand gently but said nothing. Defeat was an animal he had lived with for all of his thirty-six years. This time he thought he was going to thwart it. But he could feel it in the dark, shadowy corners of the room waiting arrogantly to jump out and claw at his back and bring him back down into the mud and mire of forever being forced into remaining poor. It made him so tired and heartsick that moments after they were abed their pallet he was sound asleep dreaming of the life that might never be his.

Through the still April's night his wife lay with wide staring eyes. Over and over again she weighed how the wagons could be packed if they were forced to leave one behind.

*   *   *

Lydia rose quietly and went the rounds of her daily work, while Howard scurried off to see Ned Conroy and the children were given chores in the barn and smokehouse. She moved in a trance-like silence. When her husband did not return all morning her heart grew heavier.

A savory dish of stewed squirrel and corn dumplings served for lunch. The twins' faces were one glorious smear of joy and grease at its finish and for once they were not reprimanded for their animal-like table manners. Nor was Maybelle scolded into helping clear the table and the three children looked at each other in puzzling wonderment.

Leaving the dishes lay Lydia took the bucket from its shelf and walked leisurely to the spring, whose limpid waters gushed from a rock at the foot of the hill. Before filling the bucket she listened again for Howard's horse, and could hear nothing. A death-like stillness brooded over the woods and fields.

The afternoon dragged wearily. She tried to read the one book she possessed, the Bible. The pages seemed to fade and the eyes refused to see.

"O Howard, Howard, why don't you come home!" she cried at last. "We'll go without some of the damn furniture and supplies!"

There was a slight noise down the road. The chickens cackled with louder call. Five minutes passed and then it was apparent that it was more than a single horse. She paused a moment, listened, and then lifted her small, slim form and advanced to the door.

Never in her life had she seen such a rig. Two soldier-like figures sat atop its high perch, driving a matched set of horses with quiet dignity and ease. The landau carriage was topless and its two occupants shielded themselves from the April sun with parasols, and Lydia was unable to see them until they made the turning and headed directly to the cabin.

She knew they had to be lost, because even wagons had a difficult time making it from the road up the double ruts to the Tedder farm. Most didn't try.

Lydia's children came scampering from the barn and stopped in awed bewilderment.

"Did ya ever see the likes, ma?"

"Never. It's like something a princess would ride in, I reckon."

Her voice was low and steady and her knees were without tremor as she walked off the porch. Judging the turning area in the yard the driver halted the carriage and motioned for the coachman to jump down and make their business known. He scrambled out of the rig and came toward Lydia.

"Awfurnoon, mum," he intoned, with a smart one-finger salute to the brim of his high hat. "We'd be seeking the Tedder farm."

Nazareth nearly doubled over in mirth at the man's heavy British accent. A scowl from his mother kept him from making it vocal.

"I am Mrs. Tedder. How might we help you?"

"Mi'lady seeks your husband, mum."

"He's not ta home. Perhaps I could help."

The man nodded and went back to the carriage. They could not hear his whispers, but the parasols came down at once. Maybelle let out an anguished gasp and the twins stood pop-eyed.

A regally beautiful woman sat ramrod straight listening to the coachman. Her hat, almost as wide as the parasol, was a billowing mass of brightly colored ostrich plumes. There was about her face a chiseled elegance, as if she had been captured in stone by a Parisian sculptor. As many hues as were in the plumes were recaptured in the high-necked traveling outfit that seemed to rainbow over her bosom. The nod of her head was almost imperceptible to any but the coachman.

But it was her traveling companion who held the interest of the twins and Maybelle. She was a young girl about Nazareth's and Theo's age. In spite of the dusty road conditions she was attired completely in white linen and lace. Dozens of tightly twisted chestnut curls cascaded over each shoulder and with near seductive devilment she viewed the muscular farm boys from between half-lowered eyelashes. Her facial features made it immediately apparent that she was the daughter of the haughty woman, but hers was still the glowing cream-smooth beauty of youth.

With a flick of his head the coachman motioned Lydia forward. The shy Theodis clung close to her side and his voice was husky as he spoke:

"Ain't you afraid, ma?"

The calm answer rang forever through his memory:

"I don't know what there is to fear, Theo. It's not the first time your mother's talked with a proper lady."

There was something totally different about

Lydia Tedder as she stepped forward. The hunch disappeared from her back and her normally tired gait was springy and youthful. She gave no thought to the fact that her apron was splattered with squirrel grease and a brush had not touched her hair that day. She was twelve again and the woman was no more imperial in bearing than had been her maternal grandmother upon their first meeting. Theodis viewed it all with a new reverence and awe. He respected his father, tolerated his sister, cowered under Nazareth's superiority of having been born five minutes earlier, but saved every scrap of his earthly love in his shy soul for his mother.

"Mum," the coachman said, with a tinge of pomposity, "may I present the Lady Pamela Buttle-Jones. Mi'lady, Mrs. Tedder."

Lady Pamela acknowledged the introduction with a crisp jerk of her head. "How soon do you expect your husband, Mrs. Tedder?"

Lydia was amazed that the woman sounded almost as insufferable as her grandmother. "I haven't the slightest," she said, with a slight smile. "He departed on business early this morning."

Lady Pamela pondered the information at such length that Lydia was forced to go on:

"If'n I can't be of service to you, perhaps you'd care to get outta our unseasonal hot sun. Our cabin ain't much, but of a summer's eve we mostly take a spell under those spreadin' oaks. Spring has a pure pleasurable water, if'n you've a mind."

"Oh, Mama!" Selena Buttle-Jones chirped. "Do, please, say yes. I'm as parched dry as my corset stays."

The look she received from her mother was

scathing, but her words had spurred Nazareth into instant action. He raced to the cabin for a bucket and ladle and was back to the spring before the two women had been helped from the carriage by the coachman. Aping his brother, but more to please his mother, Theodis ran to the oak trees and began to comically dust the birch-twig benches with sweeping motions of his felt hat.

Before anyone could be offered the bench seats the air was filled with flying hoof beats and a stormy-faced Howard Tedder came riding hard into the yard. He reined the beast abruptly at the oak trees, scowled so threateningly at Theodis that the boy blanched, then as he drew closer, blinked in surprise at the unexpected guests and their fancy trappings. He sat on his plow horse and gaped at them.

Lady Pamela was a woman of quick convictions. One look at the rugged Howard Tedder so expertly handling the bulky plow horse, as though it were an Arabian stallion on a fox hunt in Devonshire, told her that her backward trek from Memphis had not been in vain. He was the type of man she would have selected to be the gamekeeper for her hunting lodge in Scotland or the general manager of her tenant farms in Lancaster. He was virile and strong. He also, from the awed look on his face, seemed highly susceptible to however she might choose to manipulate him.

"Ahaa!" she cooed, sweeping forward as he alit, "Mr. Tedder, I assume. You are more than I anticipated and far above the reports given. Forgive me if that sounds rude, but this past week I have been in a state the like of which you would not believe. I am Lady Pamela Buttle-Jones and this is my daughter Selena. We are but three months out of Liverpool and find ourselves at the hands of nothing but thieves and gypsies. Pray, be an honest gentleman amongst this apparent country of heathens."

Howard Tedder blinked at the imperious yet pleading lady before him. Selena Buttle-Jones arched her eyes and eyebrows skyward. Rarely had she heard her melodramatic mother simper so sickeningly. As a rule, she would not lower herself to talk with such riff-raff. But, then, they were no longer in England where the family name would have brought quick results.

Howard doffed his cap and said with concern:

"Ma'am, ya'all sound troubled."

Lady Pamela lowered herself to the bench and used the parasol handle to poise and rest her hands upon. Over her face came a look of pain and sorrow.

"Sir," she said, smiling sadly, "you make the word trouble sound simple in comparison to our present plight. Our trip has been extremely difficult from the first and now we have been cheated and deserted. Can you be of assistance to us?"

He looked down into her somber face with a smile.

"Perhaps," was his gentle answer, "but I'll need to know the problem fust."

"Of course," she said. "But I hardly see the necessity of discussing such matters in front of the children. Perhaps your daughter and sons would be kind enough to entertain Selena while we talk."

Howard nodded his head in assent and gave an unspoken command to his children. Then he held Nazareth in a flinty glare.

"Don't be gettin' beyond earshot, boy. I wuz the whole day fixin' broken axles fur Ned Conroy and wish words with you and your brother about it."

The boys slunk away, knowing they'd be visiting the woodshed before sundown. To get revenge over the fight they'd lost to the Conroy boys, they had taken the wheel pins out of three of the Conroy wagons. At the time it had seemed an amusing, devilish thing to do. They had pictured in their minds the amazement that would come over the faces of the Conroys when they started to drive their wagons and saw the wheels go rolling off on their own as the heavy beds went crashing to the earth. Now it did not seem so amusing. Nazareth was busily determining how he could lie them out of the trouble.

Maybelle shouted for joy and took Selena's hand as if they were already fast friends. Selena started to pull away and then thought better of it. The house seemed a marvelous structure to her. It was the first home she had ever seen built of logs and to see its interior she would momentarily have to befriend and let Maybelle guide her.

Howard, not accustomed to discussing things with a woman other than his wife, was thankful that Lydia had made no move to leave him alone with the lady.

Lady Pamela wasted no time launching into her story. She and her daughter, she said, had landed in New York City because a distant relation of her husband's there possessed papers she would need to secure a western land grant that had been held by her husband's family for years. Besides the coachman she had two maids who were overseeing her possessions in an inn in Memphis.

Accustomed to traveling in England, she had not taken into consideration the enormous size of the United States and its territories. She had left the preparations for travel to her husband's relative. Besides her own personal carriage he had arranged for two additional wagons, teamsters to drive them and a guide. She was charged five hundred dollars in American gold coin for their services.

"And once we arrived at the Mississippi," she went on evenly, "they flatly refused to go on to the Rockies unless I paid them triple again. In my country, sir, a bargain struck is a bargain kept. I, naturally, refused. The next morning we awoke to find our personal possessions piled in a heap in the inn courtyard. Those were not rented wagons, sir, but purchased outright. They blatantly stole them. That is where I stand, Mr. Tedder, although I have purchased new wagons."

"Then you'll be needin' drivers?"

"No. Within the week I'll have drivers arriving by steamboat from New Orleans. They are some of my husband's people and should have arrived from England by now. I can see that is the passage I should have taken as well."

A worriment nagging at Tedder's mind was suddenly relieved.

"I see," he almost sighed. "Then your husband will be meetin' you in Memphis."

"Hardly," she said, pathetically. "I'm a widow

for the past six months. When I say my husband's
people, I speak of tenant farmers who saw this
journey as a new start."

Howard started worrying again. She would be
a husbandless traveler, even though she did have
the two coachmen. He had already turned down
one widow because he didn't want the responsibility of a helpless woman on his hands. His voice
was hesitant when he spoke:

"I can see your problem, but . . ."

"But you are about to tell me what every man
in Memphis has been telling me, that a widow
with a teenage daughter puts a burden on the
rest of the train. I am a strong and capable
woman, sir, and have the money and supplies to
be self-sufficient. I am only asking you to name
a price for me to join your train and then the
train from Independence."

Howard pulled at his chin whiskers and pondered. He didn't need to look at his wife to know
that she was staring holes into him. The Conroys
would not be going with him. The boys' prank
had helped lose him the five Conroy wagons for
sure and nearly a day's labor in rebuilding three
broken axles. Still, this woman had only the carriage and two wagons. He did not see how he
could charge her enough to take an extra wagon
of his own. It was a decision he felt duty-bound
to share with his wife.

"What think ye, Lydia?"

"We can't leave her stranded, Howard!" was
Lydia's hearty answer. Lydia had already figured
out how this woman could pay her for her own
extra wagon. "If'n it's fair to her, say ten dollar
a wagon and carriage to Independence and twen-

ty-five per afterwards, as we'll all be payin' beyond there."

Howard paused before answering. He saw the
woman's lips suddenly close and he saw a shadow
pass over her creamy, sensitive face. He swallowed nervously.

"Hit may sound a heap, ma'am," he apologized,
"after you wuz tooken so, but I promise ter look
out fer you as well."

Lady Pamela rose slowly and with emphasis.
Lydia could feel the refusal coming and her
heart sank.

"It is not the price," she said, frowning. "It is
reasonably low and I thank you for it. It was your
kind promise that suddenly worried me. I cannot
go on with such a bargain without being candid
with you. When my husband died I began to have
trouble with his family. They were never in favor
of our marriage and have never recognized my
daughter as an heir. They wished us to end up
with nothing. In my eyes I left England with
nothing more than I thought was my due for
eighteen years of marriage. All I claim now is
the land in Mexican Colorado. A family friend,
Lord Dunraven, who has a similar claim, will up-
hold my right to the land. I tell you this not to
frighten you but just to inform you that the
Buttle-Jones family are very jealous of their possessions and may seek to redress what they consider their wrongs."

Howard frowned. "Can't see why they'd git all
heated up over a couple of wagons of people 'n
goods, which sounds like all you took."

Lady Pamela laughed in mockery, not directed
at Howard.

"Sir, with what they think of as their money, I paid passage for seventeen tenant farm families and all of their goods. That depleted the Buttle-Jones farms in England. Warranted, or no, Lord Buttle-Jones has placed criminal desertion charges against each and every one of us. It is a fact unknown to the tenant farmers and I would wish to keep it that way. They elected to leave their farms and take a chance on this new land with me out of respect for my late husband. I have been as honest with you as I dare be, but I will fully understand if you have to decline my nineteen wagons and carriage in your train."

"Nineteen!" Howard gasped.

"Naturally," Lady Pamela said, as if he should have realized that all along. "That is the number I have purchased in Memphis awaiting the arrival of the steamboat. I have almost eighty people in my charge."

Howard shook his shaggy head. For the moment he was not thinking of the windfall of money that these people would represent. He was wondering how many horrible hours it would take him to list eighty names and the requisite information about them in his records.

"That's a goodly number—reckon we can handle—"

He paused again and a dreamy look overspread his rugged face. Memphis meant hardware stores loaded to the rafters with all manner of carpenter tools he had dreamed a lifetime about but could never afford. So as not to be tempted, he had planned on rafting the wagons across the Mississippi north of Memphis and heading northwest across the Ozark Plateau. Now the woman was giving him reason for going into Memphis and fulfilling his dream.

"Are we near a bargain?" he asked in an awed whisper.

"Done!" Lady Pamela laughed.

"Except for one thing," Lydia Tedder said darkly, and looked up to see a sight that made her nearly blanch. Howard's face had turned as fierce as it had been when he came riding in from the Conroy farm and the English woman's glare was suddenly cold and friendless. Lydia went on, determined. "We'll be needin', ma'am, a listin' of everyone of yore people and children by age. Also what goods and supplies each wagon will be carryin' west."

"Is that all?" Lady Pamela said with a long sigh. "It's a simple matter. I have all of that information from their ship's passage."

Now Howard Tedder was able to bask his wife in a loving smile. He could almost hear Major John C. Fremont repeat the words he had spoken on that spot six months before:

"You are the man to bring the folk from Tennessee, Tedder, because you've got a woman with more grit and brains than the men you'll be leading. If you've got no trust in God, put it all in Lydia Tedder. She talks to Him like they were personal friends."

4

Slowly but surely the indomitable will within Barry Fitzpatrick conquered his fears of his mission. He went about the preparations for the wagon journey doggedly. There were maps to draw from Fremont's original ones, long meetings to hold with Herbert and Cornithwyeth and quiet evenings to pick the major's mind. Barry had been backward about the Fremonts' invitation to stay at their house, but both John and Jessie would have it no other way. Then, almost too quickly, Fremont was off on another effort to gain political support for his explorations.

Temptation arose in Barry. It was hard to resist. It rained on Saturday and he stayed at home with Jessie. They cracked walnuts and hickory nuts before the fire while the rain pattered noisily on the board roof. Barry had a definite suggestion for Sunday that would break the monotony of "city" life.

"Let's me an' you go into the country tomorrow?" he ventured for a starter.

"I've got meeting."

He made a wry face. "I went with you and John last time and the preaching near put me to sleep. I guess I'll pass it up."

Jessie smiled indulgently. He seemed so young —although five years her senior—far too young yet to know the meaning of true religion. She was a Baptist, and the first principle of her religion was personal faith and direct relations of the individual soul with God. She knew it would not harm her soul to miss a Sunday meeting.

"All right," she said graciously. "If the weather's fair, we'll go to the country."

He reveled in the thought that night. He saw himself the hero of stirring scenes in her eyes. He had a religion too. It was the spirit of freedom born of the mountains and woods. He had never shared his inner feelings with a woman before, not about that. It was time he took the privilege.

It turned out to be a glorious sunny day. The wagon had no sooner stopped than Barry's moccasins came off and he was flying with swift bare feet along the path that led to a side creek of the Missouri. It was the hottest day of the spring, with a close air and broiling sun to be remembered longer than the hottest day of August.

They walked for a mile up the creek without pause, made impressions in the sand on the banks of the creek and shouted their simple joy of being alive. They explored the deep cane brakes and stalked imaginary buffalos and bears without number, encountering nothing bigger than a grey fox and a couple of muskrats.

"Let's cross over!" Barry cried. "Look at that shallow pool. Perfect for swimming. Here's a log!"

Jessie looked dubious, measured it with her eye and shook her head.

"No. It's too little. It'll wobble. Besides I have no swimming costume with me."

"Who needs a costume?"

Jessie laughed. "As a married woman, I do."

Barry blinked. Since a boy he had often swum with naked Indian girls without arousal or giving it a sexual meaning. It suited him now to think Jessie would be no different.

Before she could make further objection, Barry quickly stood on the swaying log and agilely hopped across, grasping a tree limb on the other side for support.

"Come on!" he shouted. "See how easy it is!"

Jessie looked doubtfully at the log and wished she had gone to meeting. It wasn't that she was afraid now, because she had seen Barry do it, it had more to do with propriety. But, in youth, Jessie could not resist the adventurous dare. She took a deep breath, lifted her skirt and stepped out.

Halfway across the log a movement on the bank diverted her attention. Without an ounce of embarrassment Barry, nude, strode into the water and yelped at its coldness. Jessie gasped. She was a bride of two years and as yet had not even seen John totally nude. Even conjuring up an image of John in her mind's eye suggested there would be no comparison between the two men. All she could think at the moment was, my God, he is huge—*everywhere!*

"Watch your step!" Barry yelled.

Jessie looked too late. She lost her balance and toppled head downward into the deep still water.

Her mouth flew open at the first touch of the chilly stream; she gasped for breath, and weighed down by her skirts, began taking the few mad strokes she needed to get to the other side. But the water was ice-cold as it soaked through her petticoats. She could not breathe and, in terrror, felt herself going under despite her efforts.

Her hand touched Barry's thigh as she sank. Instinctively, she encircled it, then felt strong sure arms lift her by the waist to the surface. She clung to him, oddly warmed by his nudity. She lay motionless as he lifted her easily in his arms, walked up the river bank, and deposited her gently on a grassy knoll.

For nearly a half hour Barry let Jessie lie and rest without speaking. Then, as common as commenting on the weather, he suggested she should get out of her wet things and let them dry in the sun. She amazed herself by rising and instantly complying, carefully placing her clothes on a mulberry bush and feeling the sun touch every portion of her body.

She was instantly aware that Barry was looking at her no differently from when she was fully clothed and she soon found she could look upon his nudity in the same manner. She felt as she imagined Eve had felt with Adam before sin had narrowed their focal range.

They swam back across the creek and found a beautiful spot with an immense sand bar and wide shallow safe waters. They rolled in the sunny sand and laughed. From the wagon Barry brought down their lunch and they shared it with a family of squirrels. Then they ran naked through the woods to a branch that flowed into the creek, followed it to the source and drank at the spring.

Through the long afternoon they lived in a fairy world of freedom, of dreams and make-believe. They talked of how great the west could become and what they each wished for it.

The sun was sinking toward the western hills when Barry went back to retrieve their clothing. To Jessie, her clothing loomed as symbols of her restricted world. She went behind a bush to dress and felt stupidly embarrassed, as if dressing were a prudish act.

They didn't speak until they were back to the wagon. As he started to help her up her foot caught on the step and threw her back. His arms encircled her a s she started to fall and it brought their faces close together.

It was so easy for Barry to place his lips upon hers, a custom the Indian women did not like. It was like tasting spring honey right out of an old tree. Jessie was warm and soft and fresh-smelling, nothing at all like the squaws. Never had he desired a woman more.

"No, Barry," she whispered and gently pushed him back. "It's been a wondrous day and our eternal secret forever. Please take me home now."

"All right, Jessie, it's all right."

She had expected an instant argument. When

Barry, kissing her once more, tenderly, and saying no more, got into the wagon and started the horses up she felt the guilty party.

After a long silence she ventured:

"Are you angry at me?"

"How can I be?" he laughed. "For most of the day you've been an Indian squaw. They don't do it at the swimming hole or when they're naked, you know. And if you try to kiss in the white man's fashion they kick and scream. So I'm a little ahead."

Jessie blushed scarlet. She was not used to such frank sexual talk. Then she saw the humor in his statement.

"That's the first time," she laughed, "that a kiss didn't suggest something further." She grew sober and thoughtful. Then she said quietly, "This day has meant more than mere kisses to me, Barry. If there is such a thing as mental sexual satisfaction, then I think we have experienced it. Does that make sense?"

He nodded. "I think so," he said. "Maybe it's in the soul more'n in the head, but it's there somewheres mysterious."

He felt sated. Yes, he still wanted Jessie physically, but the desire was easy to put off until an imaginary tomorrow. She could never be his, of that he was fully aware, for she loved John Fremont and he loved . . . well, the mountains. But she had given him something unique, a blend, like, of the world he knew and the world she knew. She'd given him that feeling, at any rate, and he felt the larger man for it. He knew he'd be hard put to find another woman like her.

They reached the house just as Bradford Cornithwyeth came storming up to the door. Barry hurried to put the horse and wagon away to see what was troubling Mr. Cornithwyeth this time.

"May I ask where you've been, Mr. Fitz-patrick?"

Barry took no offense at the effrontery, for he felt by now that he understood the man.

"In the woods," he said, shrugging. "They're awfully pretty now with the dogwood all in bloom."

"Really," Cornithwyeth snapped, "and on the Sabbath. My, oh, my!"

What he wasn't saying, Barry fully guessed, was, "On the Sabbath, in the woods, with a married woman!"

"And what brings you out on a Sabbath eve, Mr. Cornithwyeth?" Barry asked quietly.

"A dispatch this morning from my good woman in Pennsylvania. We have not as yet heard from the Geddy party. We might be forced to leave without them."

"What seems to be the problem with the Geddys?"

"Really," he huffed, "how am I to know way out here? I'm sure it must have something to do with Mr. Geddy's indentured servant."

"What in God's name is that?"

As if realizing he had said too much, Cornithwyeth replied hastily, "Merely a legal term, my boy. They are people who must work out their passage to America with labor, that is all."

But the way he'd said "indentured servant," with a slight smirk, made it sound more than that to Barry. "Now, look here, sir. The first rule set down by Jim Bridger is that he won't guide any man trying to bring slaves to the west. It's not just that it's against the Missouri Compromise law. Jim saw enough of slavery when he was in the south."

Cornithwyeth went immediately on the defensive. "Then you are a blind fool, sir. What's good for the goose is good for the gander, as I say."

"What goose and what gander?"

"Really, sir, don't be blind. Colonel Herbert is quite the big mouth about exactly who he is bringing west."

Barry looked at him stonily. He was not about to start fighting a fire until he saw the flames.

"Tell you what," he said shortly, "you worry about getting your Geddy party in order and I'll worry about what Colonel Herbert shows up with. Goodnight, sir."

5

WESTMEATH, IRELAND

The day before they had hanged a farmer in
Westmeath as a warning. The hanging did not
serve as a good deterrent, for the farmer's crime
was committed daily all over the island. He had
stolen two loaves of bread cooling on a window-
sill to feed his starving children. He swung from
the gallows longer than his trial had taken. They
left him overnight so that every farmer would
have to view him on their way to market at dawn.

In his heart, Garth Fergus did not want to look
upon the man's face, but as he came abreast the
gallows on his horse he stopped to say a kind
word, as the Irish say, and his heart chilled. The
young man had been a good father, a good husband, a good farmer and Garth's neighbor.

Garth was a big golden man and this was a

sunny April dawn. Yet he shivered. He said in Gaelic, "Go with God!"

The English soldier guarding the gallows frowned at the ancient tongue and motioned Garth on. "Unless you want to join him, bloke, move along."

Now Garth trembled with rage. "That's the English answer," he continued, but in Gaelic. "Kill off the whole nation of us."

"Garth!" Donald Geddy hissed, moving in alongside the huge farmer and his horse. "Don't be a fool. Some of these monkey guards know enough of our tongue to get you into the same noose!"

"I'd love to put young Queen Vicky in that noose," Garth seethed.

He turned toward the market square. Geddy danced his short legs along to keep up with his long stride. "Don't you think the queen worries as much as we over the famines and crop failures?" he said.

Garth didn't think so. "Do you worry, Donald Geddy?"

The little man flushed. "The man they hanged was, after all, my tenant. Who will I get to till his two acres? Are you capable of adding it to your three?"

Garth stood silent. The thought had not entered his head.

"Your debts may be less than others," Geddy went on, "but they are still debts."

Garth said nothing, only glowered.

"Still, you are smarter than most. Did you again plant only one acre in potatoes?"

"You know that as well as I," Garth said

softly, looking into Geddy's round, troubled face. "Don't credit me for having to act like a poor man. When we lost two crops in a row, the land was forced to lay idle.. Who has had money for but a single acre since then?"

"Many," Geddy answered sourly.

Garth laughed, a dry and brittle sound. "And got further into your debt because the yield was so small. How many went to debtors' prison last year from hereabouts? How many of their families starved because of it, Geddy? How many have had to sell themselves into slavery to start anew in America?"

Geddy was delighted that Garth had brought up the magic word. He knew he had to skate very carefully around the subject that had been on his mind since he'd heard of the hanging. It wasn't by accident that he had run into the farmer that morning.

"Aha," he brightened, "that reminds me of news. I had a post from my brother in America yesterday and he speaks very highly of Bertha's work."

Garth frowned. "That's kind of him. You might inform the good doctor to take a switch to the lass. Her mother worries and we've had but two letters in the three years she's been gone."

Geddy nodded and let the subject pass for the moment.

Garth found an empty stall and hesitated before taking the covered baskets down from his horse. He knew the kind of bartering that was about to transpire, because he had been through it many times. Finally, he sighed and began to set out his wares.

Geddy's eyes glowed as the freshly washed vegetables were quickly set out in small rows.

"Lovely," he exclaimed. "Mrs. Geddy will know at once that I stopped by your stall first."

And Mrs. Fergus would know as well, Garth thought sourly. He would be coming home with less cash than anticipated and it would cause a real to-do. It was hard to make the landowner see that these early spring vegetables were the result of his wife's labor in their home-fashioned greenhouse. There was no greenhouse like it in the county and hence no other early spring vegetables such as Martha Fergus raised.

"There," Geddy said when he had selected the finest of the scallions, radishes and tiny new carrots, "give me a price and I'll take it off your tally."

Garth darkly mumbled a price far lower than that the cooks of the rich landowners would willingly pay and Geddy methodically recorded it in a little black book.

"My, my," the merchant exclaimed, although he reviewed the account pages daily, "I was unaware how well you've reduced your debt. A good crop this year and your slate will be clean. Perhaps then we can talk about the two acres next to yours."

Garth would have loved to talk about them at the very moment, had he the money. The land had hardly been used in the past four years and there would still be time to get in an acre of flax and an acre of potatoes.

Again Geddy let the subject drop. "Oh, by the by, you may be of service to me. It seems that my nephew will soon be setting up his own medical practice, in the western part of America. He will take your Bertha along as a nursing aide. My brother will then be looking for another maid. Do you know of such a lass?"

Garth shook his head and stilled the retort in his throat. He hated the entire indentured servant system, even though it had kept him in farming and his family alive for the past six hard years. But there was still another pain eating away at his heart. After the heavy crop failures he had come to learn that the absent Dr. Mark Geddy, and not his brother Donald, was the true owner of a great portion of the tenant farms around Westmeath. Dr. Geddy had been sympathetic, but, like most others, Garth had fallen two years behind in his rent and had no money for seed crop.

Reluctantly, he had allowed his fifteen-year-old son, William, to go to America under a seven-year indenture to the doctor. William had hated the city life from the very beginning and loathed his work in the doctor's South Boston clinic. He wrote his parents pathetic letters about how he was looked down upon more by the Bostonians than he ever had been by the English at home. Then the letters stopped coming.

William Fergus, like so many other indentured servants, had vanished. Under the law, the Ferguses were forced to send thirteen-year-old Bertha to Boston to serve the five years remaining on her brother's contract and an additional two years to pay for her passage. Much to Martha's sadness, her errant son had never been heard from and Donald Geddy was always very careful not to raise the subject with Garth Fergus.

Geddy turned as if to leave and then turned

back. "He is only looking for a four-year person. One year to cover the cost of passage and three years clear. I'm sure he could afford the whole amount in advance, if a person was really interested in putting more acreage to the plow."

Garth blinked. "What are you suggesting?"

Geddy's eyes became cold and business-like. "The lass, Pearl."

Garth nearly choked. "She's but a child of twelve."

Geddy looked amazed. "Such a big girl for her age. I took her to be nearer fifteen. My, just a year younger than when Bertha went across and so much older-looking. Well, good day to you, Garth Fergus. Lovely vegetables, lovely vegetables!"

The farmer did not see the merchant's moon face break into a beaming smile as he turned away. Geddy was quite pleased with his morning's work. He had planted a seed that he knew would not die in the mind of Garth Fergus. The man was a born farmer, had the soil under his nails from birth. His only secure future was to obtain more land to cultivate. Nor did he wish Garth to know that his brother had purposely requested him to approach the family for the services of Pearl.

As Garth anticipated, Martha Fergus was furious at his selling the vegetables to Geddy.

"It may reduce the debt," she scolded, "but it keeps me from doing with the money as I see fit. Bah, you men are all alike."

Garth loved his wife, but hard times had taught him to close his ears to her constant harping. Twenty-three years of married farm life had altered her from a generous, beautiful lass to a dry and brittle and bitter woman who looked ten years older than her forty-three years. Garth, who was the same age, was just the opposite. His tanned face was smooth and boyish, his eyes as flashing blue as the morning sky. Even during the darkest days he had always had a word of cheer for his children and neighbors. He was loved by all, and that was another sour note in his wife's mind. She was highly jealous of her husband.

Garth drew off his cotton shirt and splashed his face and muscular chest from the basin water. He knew what was going to be said before it was said.

"And don't be splashing water on my bread," Martha grumbled. "I've just set it to rise."

Garth smiled politely. "And a lovely batch it looks to be, lass."

He was drying himself when Pearl walked in with his evening mug of grog. She was wearing a smock that made it apparent that Donald Geddy had been quite correct. She was nearly as tall as her mother and already possessed more bosom.

"Time for a new dress for you, stringbean," he said.

Garth had wanted to hear her normal childish giggle, but he had to think back to the last time he had heard the sound. With Geddy's words uppermost in his mind, Garth now took stock of his daughter, seeing her not as a loving, protective father but as any male stranger she might meet in America might. It was a difficult thing for him to do. He thought her breasts lovely, not perched like pears as one might expect in a girl her age but soft, full and giving, low with rich nipples. She carried herself with a calm pride and dignity. She was exactly as her mother had named her, a pearl. Unlike her horsy sister Bertha, not cute and cuddly like her baby sister, Meg, hers would be a beauty that would drive lads wild with desire. He was almost sorry that he was her father. He still had an eye for a well-turned ankle.

Suddenly, Garth was happy that his last three children had been girls. His son, weak and secretive from childhood, had been a great disappointment to him. A girl with proper looks and good training stood a chance of marrying up out of her station. A man was stuck with the lot he was born into.

Garth raised his mug.

"You will marry well," he predicted. "Probably to a very rich American."

"Oh, papa," she laughed, "we don't get very many rich Americans coming to Westmeath."

"Is that a fact?" he kidded. "But one finds many of them in America itself."

Even as he said it a great grief gripped his heart. He had been able to stand the departure of William and Bertha without too much sorrow. Without Pearl to make him smile, to fetch his evening grog, life might get exceedingly dreary.

"What's all this talk about America?" Martha demanded.

"Nothing," Garth waved airily. "Except that Geddy heard from his brother yesterday. Seems Bertha is doing quite well and will be taken west by young Dr. Thomas Geddy as his nurse."

"Nurse indeed," Martha scoffed. "Seems to me she fainted every time we had to wring a chicken's neck for the pot."

Pearl cried, "Oh, mama, that's different. I have to look away too, especially when papa lets the poor creature run headless about the yard flapping its wings."

"But you seem to eat your share, young lady— when we're lucky enough to have one for the table."

Pearl sulked as her mother turned away to punch down her bread loaves. Of late she had been unable to say or do anything that seemed to please her mother. Without meaning to, she was growing to hate her.

"Well," Garth said slowly, not knowing how best to attack the subject, "there's a possibility, Martha, that you could have chickens again this summer."

"And the kingdom of God could come in the same time."

"I'm quite serious," he said quietly. "Geddy has made me an offer on the two acres next door."

He could sense, rather than see, his wife's back grow rigid. "And the offer?"

"Nothing specific, as yet," Garth said. "Depends on finding someone to replace Bertha when she goes with young Dr. Tom."

Martha spun and shook her floured hands at her husband. "Nothing specific? Then why all the blarney talk to Pearl Mae about America? Girl, leave the room! I'd have words with your father!"

The girl did as instructed without a glance at either of them, but once she had closed the scullery door she pressed her ear close to learn what this fight would be about. Garth Fergus knew that it was best to remain silent and let his wife have her way.

"Haven't we already sold two of our children into slavery? Have you so soon forgotten what it did to our son?"

"I have no son," he retorted.

"Well, I had," she screamed, "until you sold him."

"And what did he do to us in return, Martha? He would be home, and Bertha would be home, if he had an ounce of pride in his body. He deserted us! What manner of a son is that? And here you have me discussing a subject I forbade in this house."

Martha Fergus sat down weakly and folded her hands in her lap. She had never been a good fighter. She was too easily moved to tears. Will had been her pride and joy and a piece of her had died when he left for America. She felt like the rest of her died when they learned he had run away.

"Each night," she said softly, "I pray that Bertha will write that she's found our Will. Is it so large a country, husband?"

"It is, my girl. They say that all of Ireland would fit quite snugly into their New England states."

"But Will hated it so. Why does he stay?"

"He has no other choice," Garth said firmly. "It would mean jail if he returned here. Besides, he may look at it quite differently now that he is free."

"Free?" Her belligerence returned quickly. "How can you say such a thing?"

"When we were so frightened over what Dr. Geddy might do to us, I did some careful asking about. Of the thousands of indentured ones who run away very few are caught and returned. They go to an area where they can be free and start a new life."

She sobbed. "Then Bertha will never find him."

"I doubt it, Martha. I seriously doubt it."

"Do you really hate him so, Garth?"

"Can one ever?" he sighed. "I even had doubts about myself when things were at their darkest and I saw men three times Will's age desert their wives and children. Perhaps what I did was even more cowardly, sending my children instead."

They sat for many minutes in total silence.

"When must she go?" Martha finally said.

The question so unsettled Garth Fergus that he sat benumbed. It was as though the decision had been made without his choosing it. Martha quickly rose from the table and went to gaze out the kitchen window. She didn't want to think about the hanged farmer she had often seen plowing the acres in her view.

"Make it quick, Garth," she whispered. "Make it happen before summer comes. The gardens and the chickens will keep my mind busy and pre-occupied. The gloomy winter days give a person too much time to brood."

In Martha Fergus' mind the matter was thus resolved. Oddly, it even gave her a twinge of delight to know that for a while she would not have to compete with her daughter for her husband's attention. She still had little Meg, who reminded her so much of her firstborn. She would hold onto her and put it all in God's hands.

Garth rose, took a fresh shirt from the hook and left. He knew that if he didn't go and talk with Donald Geddy that very moment he might never bring himself to do it. The two acres seemed suddenly very small in comparison to losing Pearl.

Pearl Mae wasn't thinking about her father. She was already dreaming of new dresses and slippers and ribbons for her hair. She was going to get away from poverty and worry and doubt and marry a rich American.

Pearl's new dress was of highly starched black cotton with a dicky collar and apron of spotless white. Her hair was adorned, from morning to night, with netting and a white doily. The new shoes she'd received were a pair of button boots that pinched at her toes and made her calves constantly itch.

Her last joyous moment had been her father's goodbye in Dublin. Seventeen days later, devastated by motion sickness, she had been removed from the packet by stretcher. She had spent her first few days in America in Dr. Geddy's clinic. The doctor was so concerned over her dehydrated condition that he ordered Bertha Fergus to stay with her and force liquids into her system.

"Bother!" Bertha scolded. "You're making matters worse for me, rather than better."

Pearl, so long had she not seen Bertha, had barely recognized her. She saw a tall, gangling woman dressed in pure white. Growth had to a certain extent filled out her sister's long face and made it more of a piece with her large bosom. At sixteen, Bertha's mature figure and stance made her appear formidable, far more than she had ever been. Even the older nurses in the clinic were quick to sidestep any altercation with Dr. Geddy's "pet lass." Bertha had made the best of her situation and thought her sister Pearl should do the same.

"How is the patient today?" Dr. Tom asked.

"Wearing me out, doctor. Come on, Pearlie Mae, open your eyes. I want you to meet Dr. Thomas Geddy."

Pearl opened her eyes and was greeted by a winning, boyish smile. The smile made her eyes dance as she smiled back.

"Well," the young doctor laughed, "maybe all your sister needed was my bedside manner."

Bertha felt a twinge of jealousy. She had been all but forgotten in her father's eyes after Pearl had been born. She was not about to let Pearl get an upper hand with the handsome and shy young man.

"She should have been at her duties days ago," Bertha snapped. "You didn't see me taking this long to get over the crossing."

Dr. Geddy laughed and took Pearl's wrist to find the pulse. Tremors of utter delight shot through her body at his very touch.

"People react differently, Bertha, even when they are related. Humm! Still a little rapid and erratic. I would say a day or two more."

"That's good for her, but I'm exhausted."

"I can well understand," he said, with genuine sympathy. "No need for you to stay another night in the clinic. Is my father still here?"

"Just preparing to leave, doctor."

"Then ride home with him. Please let my mother know that I am staying here for the night."

Bertha Fergus almost declined. She remembered Pearl as a ten-year-old child. Now she could see that she was maturing into a beautiful creature who would put her into the shade. But Bertha calmed her reservations for the moment. She had been planning her moves almost from the first day she stepped into the Geddy house on Beacon Hill and she would not let a snip of a sister get in her way.

All of Thomas Geddy's handsomeness he had obtained from his mother's side of the family. He also had from her his aloofness. His father was short, rotund and, with a flushed and freckled face with a large nose, not especially good-looking. But Mark Geddy was attractive in his own way. He had learned early in life that if he behaved in a cheerful manner people soon forgot his looks. So he grinned and laughed a lot and people called him a remarkable doctor. That he must have been, for his clinic was constantly filled with poor patients who always seemed to pay him before they did their butcher and grocer.

He had been in America for half of his fifty years and in each of those years he had been able to send money home to Ireland to purchase land. No one, not even his wife, knew what his true worth was in land and in the money his brother squeezed out of the tenant farmers. He was compassionate toward his Irish-American patients who were sick, but cared not a hoot for his Irish tenant farmers who were starving.

The Fergus family appealed to him, however. He had been overjoyed to attain the indenture on William Fergus. Here was a lad, he had thought, whom he could bend to his will and train into hardy manhood—not like his own son, whom he saw as weak and simpering as his mother, the woman he now regretted marrying.

Dr. Mark had been severely disappointed when Will vanished from sight. He needed a replacement, yes, but in addition he felt the Fergus family should suffer for the boy's failing him. He had decided to take Garth's daughter from him.

In Bertha, despite her equine features, Dr. Geddy began to see and appreciate a deep natural intelligence. It had taken him nearly three months to get the thirteen-year-old virgin into his chamber while his wife was away. Even as he seduced her he was still cursing Garth Fergus for having sent him such a worthless son.

He had not intended to touch Bertha again, but during the weeks that followed, he came to her room more and more often and as time passed she grew more and more bold with him.

For after that first time it was the humiliated Bertha who was planning revenge. She would let the ugly little man use and misuse her body until she was ready to turn it against him. She would stoke his lust with her own considerable sexual powers. Then she would blackmail her way into a marriage with his son.

When Bertha had first presented her marital intention, Dr. Geddy had welcomed it, chortling inwardly. He would have some secret knowledge, some secret power over that son of his, whom he kept regarding as spineless and weak nevertheless. Tom couldn't even get aroused by a naked woman patient, something he had little trouble doing. Certainly Bertha, whose aggressive sexual behavior he knew well, would either destroy the young fool or give him the chance to prove himself a man. Which Dr. Geddy, in circular fashion, kept thinking that his son wasn't.

But what amused him most of all was the thought of the proposed marriage's effect on his wife. Mildred Geddy had been scouring the Boston social registry for a wife for her son almost from the day of his birth. She had gained in social standing by marrying the affluent Dr. Mark Geddy. He resented her rise. He dreaded that she would leave him for someone handsome and above him in station, not Irish perhaps, and he loathed himself for that dread. The way to get even with Mildred for tormenting him was to see her beloved son married to Bertha. The prospect excited him and made him laugh.

So Dr. Geddy did not react to Bertha's blackmail threat with anger, as she halfway expected. He merely told her the marriage would have to be "arranged." Meanwhile, he could continue to take his pleasure from her and from the Fergus family.

On the coach ride back from the clinic with Bertha that night, he closed the hatch so the driver could not look down upon them and lowered the shades to dim the rumble of the omnibuses. He patted Bertha's knee knowingly.

"And how is your sister?"

Bertha pulled angrily away. "That's not what's on your mind. And the answer is no. I'm tired tonight."

He smiled. "Mrs. Geddy is going to the opera."

"Mrs. Geddy is always going somewhere."

He sighed. "Then you know my condition very well."

"And what of my condition?"

He chuckled. "A very good point, my dear. Do you like to travel?"

Bertha turned, suddenly wary. "What is that to mean? I am to travel soon, a short distance with Tom, whenever and wherever he chooses to go."

Geddy shook his head and patted his pudgy hands together. "No. I must inform you otherwise. A certain document came into my hands recently, mainly because it was only addressed to Dr. Geddy. It made me view Thomas in quite a different light. I see that he may be developing a will of his own. When he first raised the issue of establishing his own practice in the west, his mother and I naturally assumed that he mean no farther west than, say, Albany, New York. This letter was from The New England Emigrant Resettlement Association. Impressive sounding, though their paper is quite cheap and the address questionable, but all of that is beside the point. It seems that Thomas, quite on his own, has made a down payment on something called a Conestoga wagon and desires passage with this group out of Lancaster, Pennsylvania."

"Oh?" Bertha said. "What is a Conestoga wagon?"

Dr. Geddy ignored the question. "And, of course," he went on smoothly, "I assume he will wish to take along a reliable nurse, just as he had intended to take to Albany. He's really not a very good doctor, you know."

"Go on," Bertha said narrowly. "Get to the point."

"My dear," he smirked, "we do know too much about each other to be coy, don't we? For reasons of my own I have kept the document from my son. It seems that the association will allow none except married couples to join their train to Missouri. Now, neither of us can force him to marry you, can we? But what will be his reaction when he arrives in Lancaster and learns of this rule? Some of the persuasion rests with you, of course, but you have my blessing. By the by, the opera starts at eight."

Bertha turned and gave him a winning smile. "You may come to my room at eight-thirty."

Dr. Mark Geddy sat back and sighed. His plan was working admirably well. He would get rid of Bertha who was becoming bothersome and at the same time gain a bit of revenge against his son and wife. The delightful salaciousness of Bertha would be gone, to be sure, but he would still have the enticing Pearl Fergus in his home. There was no doubt in his mind that he could win her to his bed as easily as he had her sister.

Thomas Geddy had all but forgotten his anger at not having heard from The New England Emigrant Resettlement Association. Under the thumbs of his father and mother, the young man's enthusiasm waxed and waned.

"I assume this post is for you," Mildred Geddy announced one morning, coming swiftly onto the sun-drenched veranda.

Thomas was quite used to his mother assuming things. He saw that she had assumed the right to open his mail. He took the letter hurriedly and scanned it. He was thankful that it was only an acknowledgment of his deposit with Bradford

Cornithwyeth and did not mention what the money was for.

"Well?" Mildred demanded.

Thomas had given his parents only a general idea of his plans. The letter would help him keep it vague.

He said hesitantly, "I put a deposit with this group to find me space, that's all."

"All? Tommy, you are making a complete fool of yourself. Emigrant Resettlement Association, indeed. You know as well as I that you have no intention of leaving Boston. It isn't you. It's high time we forgot this foolishness and center our thoughts on marriage for you. The right girl is not going to let you cart her off to the backwoods someplace. She'll want to stay right here, in Boston."

Mildred Geddy had always believed it was her strength of character that had preserved her family. She was a big-boned, no-nonsense woman. To her way of thinking her husband and son were weaklings whom she had to guard and guide by her greater force of virtue and intelligence.

Therefore, she was astonished and angered by the amused smile with which Thomas turned to her. He had never really opposed her before, but now his dark gray eyes held hers without flinching.

"Mother," he said gently, "I am not ready for the marriage altar. I'm not even sure that I am ready for a medical practice, here or anywhere else. I have been thinking about myself . . . and things. Please don't treat me as you do father. Don't push me in the direction that suits you best."

Mildred regarded her son with icy contempt. Only the appearance of Pearl Fergus kept her from storming at his insolence.

"Excuse, mum. Mrs. Wurth's arrived for tea and is in the sun parlor."

Mrs. Geddy frightened Pearl. The woman had a way of never answering servants or dismissing them. Pearl stood with downcast eyes and waited.

"That would be Denise Wurth's mother, Thomas," she said coldly, ignoring Pearl. "I have it on good authority that you made a favorable impression on Denise at the Cabots' spring ball. I fully intend to pursue the topic of Denise's availability."

"You are a tyrant, mama," said Thomas, without malice. "I don't want to hurt you, but you are not going to impose a marriage on me that I do not desire. Denise is a brainless ninny."

Mildred's haughty face was a study. Pearl was incredulous and unsure how to back away from such a personal family discussion. She stared at Thomas as his handsome face darkened.

His mother marched to the door and then turned to give her son a parting shot. It made Pearl cringe.

"Of course you are young, Tommy. You are hardly mature. Yet. I still have hopes that you will eventually become more of a man than your father. At the present time, however, you are a feckless imbecile and shall do exactly as I say as long as you care to stay under my roof."

Mildred sailed away.

Thomas' eyes burned. He drew in his mouth until it was a white-lipped slit. His eyes did not leave his mother's retreating back.

Pearl reluctantly cleared her throat. "Might I be excused, sir?"

Thomas turned heavily to the girl and blinked. "How boorish of us, Pearl. We seem to treat servants as inanimate objects. Shadow creatures who cannot think or feel or understand. Because she would never do it, I shall apologize for both mother and myself."

"It's quite all right, sir." But still she had not been dismissed, and that had been the first lesson the housekeeper had drilled into her head, to wait until she had been.

"Do you know what slavery is, Pearl?"

She shook her head. "Only the little I read in school, sir. We don't have slavery in Ireland."

"You are a slave, in a way. So am I. We are both owned by my parents and expected to do their every little command without a whimper or a bellow. Do you believe that parents still have the right to arrange marriages for their children?"

Pearl was puzzled. The second lesson the housekeeper insisted upon was that no servant was permitted to involve herself in a personal conversation with the master or his son. Mrs. Geddy didn't count because she never talked to the servants in the first place.

"I've got me work to do, sir," she demurred, although she loved being around the young man. He was warm and comfortable to be with, somewhat like her father. But whereas her father was big and golden, Thomas was dark and willowy. His slender hands were always moving as he talked and seemed to be an extension of his soft voice. And when he spoke his dark gray eyes looked at her direct without flinching.

Thomas smiled. "You see, you are a slave. The master's son should be able to say, 'Forget your work and stay and talk with me.' But you are afraid of the overseer."

Pearl frowned. "Overseer?"

Thomas laughed. "Mrs. Harding, the housekeeper."

The mention of the name was enough to strike fear into Pearl's heart. "I really must go, sir."

"Wait! You haven't answered my question."

"And what question did you pose to her, Master Thomas?"

The toneless bark of Mrs. Harding from the doorway made Pearl start and turn. Thomas was momentarily perplexed. The housekeeper was obviously put out with Pearl. It was not his business to interfere with the running of the house; indeed, he was intimidated by the sharp-tongued Mrs. Harding, who was close with his mother. But Pearl's consternation touched him deeply, overcoming both his fears and his scruples. He did something alien to his nature. He told an outright lie:

"The question, Mrs. Harding, was if she was scheduled to run errands today. I have need for some new cravat silk."

Pearl swallowed nervously; she could hardly believe the young master was lying on her behalf. But she remained afraid of Mrs. Harding. She dared not look at either of them.

"Silk, is it," Mrs. Harding said, with a sour smile. "I don't recall a servant having to purchase such for you before."

Summoning more of his courage for the lie, Thomas said, "Mainly because I have not been

home much these past months. I would go myself,
but mother might call me in for tea with Mrs.
Wurth."

Mrs. Harding pursed her thin, dry lips. If Mrs.
Geddy might do that, she felt it best not to make
it impossible for her. "Very well. I have no
errands for Pearl, but you may send her along on
your own authority. Mind you, you'd best have
the money, for I'll not have such coming out of
my household account."

Thomas capped the lie by pulling money from
his change purse and giving Pearl precise directions as to the color he desired and on how to get
to the shop most likely to carry the article.

Pearl took it as a form of dismissal. She nearly
ran from the house.

The day was very hot for late April, the glitter-
ing air swirling with dust and chaff. Pearl didn't
care. She felt as if her life had been saved and,
aside from removing her maid's cap so that her
long hair might flow loose, sped through the
streets heedless of the swelter. She was alone, free
temporarily from her near-constant fear of Mrs.
Harding and Mrs. Geddy, and from the nightly
demands of her sister Bertha that she do her
chores better. Bertha was not in her mind now,
nor was Dr. Mark Geddy, whose strange eyes
upon her usually turned her spine cold.

The shop in question had every shade of blue
but the required one. Pearl was not displeased.
The longer she stayed away from the house, the
better she felt. The other shops she looked into
were lively and amusing, full of many wonder-
ments, the smell of cloth and leather, trinkets and
laces. Gay carriages rolled by on the cobbled

streets with gay people in them. Pearl's spirits
rose. Boston was certainly no Westmeath with its
tiny, dusty, old-world shops. She had all but
forgotten the cravat in her excitement of exploring
this strange new world, when she heard a mascu-
line voice exclaiming at her elbow: "Now will you
answer my question?"

It was Thomas Geddy. Pearl turned and saw
his amused, smiling face.

Flushing deeply, and hastily putting her maid's
cap back on, she stammered, "I haven't found
your cravat as yet, sir."

"I thought not," he said drily, holding a package out to her. "I bought the last one they had
yesterday. Luckily, Mrs. Harding didn't know
that."

"But . . . but . . ."

"It was a ruse to get us both out of the house.
Really, you must have flown from shop to shop
on wings. I've had a deuce of a time catching up.
Are you hungry?"

Pearl hesitated. "I'd best get back," she murmured, almost inaudibly. The fact was she was
starved and didn't want her adventure to end so
quickly.

"Will you please quit avoiding my direct questions, young lady? And take off that silly puff of
lace. You are far too pretty to be taken for a
childish maid," Thomas said, with an affectionate,
warm smile.

Pearl was silent. Her heart beat rapidly. She
had not thought her adventure in freedom would
include Thomas Geddy himself, and that it now
seemed it would thrilled her. She let him take her

arm and steer her through the crowded streets, feeling almost as if she were floating.

Lest he be seen with Pearl and have word of it get back to his mother, Thomas took her away from the shopping district and down to the water-front. Just before they entered a small restaurant there, they saw, on the quay, long lines of black men and women being boarded onto a ship. Pearl stared at the blacks, remembering her and Thomas's conversation about slavery.

"Do you know I've never seen an African before?" she said wonderingly.

"Poor creatures. They wish they were African. By their age I'd say that most had been born right here in America."

"Where are they taking them?"

"Back," Thomas said dully. "To their masters. They have been caught trying to escape. By our damnable laws they are pieces of property that must be returned to their rightful owners. We will have war over this question of slavery."

"Is it this way all over America?"

"To deny it would be hypocrisy, Pearl. The northern states that rail against black slavery per-petuate as inhumane a kind. You've seen some of the men and women in my father's clinic. Sup-posedly they are free men, but they carry a chain of indenture around their ankles that binds them as tightly as these blacks are bound. Not everyone is as compassionate with their indentured servants as my father. I've listened to some of those men while treating them, and their tales are heart-breaking. Yes, they get free passage from Europe and are given jobs, perhaps in the shoe factories, along with housing and food. But the housing is owned by the factory and the workers must buy their food on a charge account at the company store. Each month they end up owing the company more than they make in wages and this debt is added on to their indenture time. When they can stand it no longer they run away, which gives the company the right to force their families to send others in their places. That's what happened to your family, isn't it?"

Pearl nodded. It was the first time her brother Will had been mentioned to her by anyone since she'd arrived in America. She was curious to see if Thomas had information about him. She held her question, however, until they were seated in the restaurant. And then the question escaped her because of her wonderment.

The small establishment had neat white tables, plated silver, dark-panelled walls, a crimson carpet and black-frocked waiters. Pearl had never eaten in a restaurant before. She gazed about her, enthralled by its discreet and dim charm.

Studying Pearl's young and innocent face, Thomas felt tenderly protective towards her, as if she were the little sister he'd always wanted but had never had. He liked feeling needed; it was not a feeling either his father or mother gave him. He reached across the table and took one of Pearl's hands, so white and thin and firm.

"I'm sorry if I stepped on a tender spot by mentioning Will."

She was aware for a moment only that Thomas was holding her hand and that her heart was fluttering. He was kind, intelligent, handsome; she was falling in love with him. She stammered as she struggled with her emotions: "I'm glad you did. Do you remember him? I was only five years old when he left home."

He smiled. "Will and I were both fifteen when he came, so that makes me ten years your senior. Now I really must look upon you as a little sister."

Pearl's color increased with sudden distress. She did not want to be just a little sister to him. She wanted to be that but more, much more. But she said nothing.

"I suppose my father saw Will as a good companion for me. Mama thought differently. She saw him as a crude ruffian who would lead me astray." He laughed. "For once mama was right without really knowing it. I was a spoiled little mama's boy who knew nothing. Will knew everything about all the wrong things. I know my father loved him more than he did me." Thomas frowned. "At first I think Will returned that love, for Papa showed him a world that he had never seen in Ireland. Then they had a falling out. I really shouldn't be telling you about this, but perhaps it will help you see why he went away. We were always getting into trouble when papa wasn't around, but it was only Will who would be punished. Mrs. Harding hated him—that's possibly why she gives you and Bertha so rough a time. I really don't know what precipitated Will's leaving. I was away at school when he left and no one's ever thought to discuss it with me."

"Do you think he's still in the city?"

"Good heavens, I hope he's smarter than that. If caught he'd be in a worse pickle than those poor blacks."

"Even though we are serving his time?"

Thomas shrugged. "They'd still consider him a fugitive and make him stand trial."

"Oh, but your father wouldn't let that happen, would he?"

Thomas frowned, fearing he might have carried the story too far. He had been naive before going away to school. Only in later years did he come to see that his father held Will beholden to him for his efforts in educating him. Even closer to the truth, his father felt towards Will as many a white southerner felt towards an escaped slave. There was in his father a lust of some kind—to browbeat Will, to take revenge on him, he knew not what else. Except that he did know. He hadn't caught them at it, but he knew his father had had as insatiable a sex lust for Will as he had for young women. And he knew that it would not be a hand that Mark Geddy would raise to help Will Fergus, but a thumb to squash him.

"Ah, food!" Thomas exclaimed, glad at the reprieve from answering the embarrassing question.

The waiter brought them a steaming plate of oysters, clams, scallops and fish cakes, fresh bread, a spring salad and coffee. They ate as if it were the last food they would see in their lives.

"Now, let's get back to my original question," said Thomas, leaning his elbows on the table and scrutinizing her fondly. "Do parents have the right to impose marriage partners on their children?"

"It seems the custom, as far as I know, sir."

He slapped her hand playfully. "Stop calling me sir. My father calls me Thomas and my mother calls me Tommy. I'd like you to call me Tom."

"Then I shall," she giggled.

"Then do it!"

She giggled again. "Tom."

"That is much better." He drew his fob from his pocket and studied his watch. "But better for us if we don't prolong this outing any further."

There was a sudden quenching of the light in her face. The adventure was ending. "I know," she said softly. "I've already broken most of Mrs. Harding's rules. We shouldn't even be talking, let alone eating together in a rich place like this."

"This is hardly what I would call rich."

She lifted her eyes now, and they were full of anguished tears. He took her hand again.

"Would you really like to see an expensive restaurant, dear Pearl?" he asked.

"Yes!" she cried.

He smiled. "Then we shall. I shall not ask you to break Mrs. Harding's rules. She can be cruel, I know. But your next afternoon off leave the house alone. I'll find you as I did today."

He had the hackney-cab let her down a block from the house, and there he took her hand.

"What a wonderful afternoon," he said gently. "We shall have many, many more." He brushed her hand with his lips.

His choice of the waterfront restaurant had not been discreet. The Brewster cook, walking in the district on her afternoon off, recognized Thomas Geddy, if not the girl. She did, however, recognize a maid's uniform when she saw one. Because the Brewsters did not recognize the Geddys socially, she was not on speaking terms with the Geddy cook and could only pass her information along to the Cabot cook as she passed their mansion.

The Cabot cook was aware that the Lodge cook was a sister-in-law to the Geddy cook. And so the story traveled.

Mrs. Harding was flushed with heat and annoyance when Pearl returned. She had been forced to clear away the tea cart from the sun parlor and answer to Mrs. Geddy for Pearl's absence. Mrs. Geddy had been furious that Mrs. Harding had let Pearl go on such a frivolous errand. The two women, warriors in their own rights, hardly ever confronted each other, and Mrs. Harding did not mention Thomas's part in the errand. It was Pearl alone she was blaming for blemishing her relationship with Mrs. Geddy.

"Oh, there you are, you loitering little minx!" cried Mrs. Harding, advancing menacingly upon Pearl. "Where have you been?"

Pearl timidly held out the package. "I had to go to many shops, mum, and I don't rightly know this strange city."

"Likely story," she harrumphed. "You Ferguses can always find a way to get out of work. Bloody waste to let your sister lollygag her time away down in that clinic, says I."

Pearl blanched but held her tongue.

Maude Harding loathed the Irish just a mite more than she feared rats and mice. She herself was English. She explained away her position in the Geddy household by reminding herself that Mark Geddy was already a professional man when he migrated and that Mildred Geddy came from good "second generation American stock."

With a vengeance she tore the paper parcel, then stared at the length of silk. "Why, this is madness! He just bought a silk of this blue. I saw it in his room this morning. And I think this is the same shop paper I saw it in!" She glared at Pearl, furiously, as though about to strike her. "Where on earth have you been, girl? I'll not countenance any lies, mind you!"

Pearl began to shake with mortal fear. Just then the bell-pull from the kitchen began to peal insistently.

"What is that fool cook up to?" Mrs. Harding cried. "Has the whole house gone mad?" She turned on Pearl with a glare. "I'll settle with you shortly, young woman. Go to your room and change into your evening uniform. And make sure that it is fresh and clean. The Wurths are coming back to dinner with their daughter. I don't want that Wurth woman, of all people, to think we scrape the bottom of the barrel for maids."

The Geddy cook, Lottie Henderson, was a born gossip and a natural elaborator. It was in the latter capacities that she had rung for Mrs. Harding. She was not aware that she was speaking of Pearl when she related the story of Master Thomas and a local serving girl, but by the time she had filled Mrs. Harding's ear with the tale, the hand kiss of Thomas's that had been reported to her had become a passionate embrace.

"Not another word, Mrs. Henderson," the housekeeper warned. "I'll handle the matter from here."

Lottie smiled, curtsied and looked up at the big kitchen clock. It registered five minutes to five. Normally, Mrs. Harding would be taking her afternoon nap at this time. Now she saw her charging angrily towards Pearl's room. Lottie sighed. At the stroke of five she fully expected to see Mrs. Geddy sneak down the back stairwell to check if the dinner preparations were more to her liking than they were to the housekeeper. For years Lottie had gone along with the conspiracy, dreaming of the day she could advance from cook to head housekeeper. She had come to America ten years before to serve out the time left open by her own vanishing husband. When his time had been compensated for, she had remained and made herself an indispensable part of the household. She had a rapport with Mrs. Geddy that Mrs. Harding did not share. Now she smelled a rat and would turn it to her own advantage.

"Trollop!" the housekeeper screamed, as she barged into Pearl's room, catching her only in her chemise. "I'll have the truth!"

"I don't know what you mean," Pearl quavered.

The housekeeper snatched at the heap of Pearl's discarded uniform and shook it. Totally forgotten by Pearl, the money that Thomas had given her for the cravat jingled out upon the wood floor.

Maude Harding said narrowly, "I suppose you know nothing about that money, as well?"

Pearl could only look down on the coins in dumb confusion.

"Bloody little whore!" the woman cried. "I should have known that you would be as evil as your brother and sister. I'll fix you proper for what you've done!"

Before Pearl could cry out, Mrs. Harding hit her sharply across the face. Stunned, she stood motionless, blinding tears coming to her eyes. Mrs. Harding hit her again, equally as hard. Pearl sobbed. She tried to dart away, but the woman, though heavy set, was quick and strong. Her hands grasped at Pearl's chemise and ripped it from her back. Then, as Pearl cowered and begged for understanding, she began to pummel her sadistically with a stick she carried. Pearl began screaming hysterically as her back, thighs and stomach reddened from the repeated blows.

"Very effective," Mildred Geddy murmured. She'd quietly entered the room and was watching, the door closed gently behind her. "But hardly informative, my dear Maude."

Mrs. Harding stopped beating Pearl and re-garded Mrs. Geddy coldly, her stick poised in mid-air. Mrs. Geddy never called a servant by her first name unless she was going to make a sharp and telling comment. Pearl, bent double in pain, looked at Mrs. Geddy with astonished grati-tude; despite the mistress's menacing tone, she saw her as coming to save her from further physi-cal torment.

"Clever of you not to bruise her face with that stick," Mrs. Geddy said, her eyes as cold as the housekeeper's. "Either of the two doctors in the house would want to know how it was done."

"Bitch!" the housekeeper whispered.

Mildred Geddy laughed. "I'm not sure if you mean me or the girl, Maude. Possibly, you're cursing Lottie Henderson." This time her laugh was low and cutting. "Naturally, Lottie read your intentions and told me. I'm grateful to her. Any reprisal against her she will report to me at once. Do I make myself quite clear?"

They glared at each other until the house-keeper lowered her eyes and nodded.

"Now," Mildred Geddy said in a conversational tone, "we come to a sensible question. Have you thought to examine her as yet? If not, do so at once."

Maude Harding didn't need further instruction. She shoved Pearl down onto her cot-bed and tore away her pantaloons. Pearl was too frightened to resist the raising of her legs and the intimate exploring of her private parts.

Maude shrugged. "She's virginal."

Mildred Geddy sighed. Pearl was aware of a horribly long silence. "Make sure that she is not," Mrs. Geddy then said quietly.

Mrs. Harding was appalled. "How?"

Mildred smiled. "Did I have to give you precise instructions, you who dealt with her brother? Be quick about it. The Wurths are due for dinner within the hour. I'll expect the house in order by that time."

She did not leave the chamber, but stood waiting for her command to be carried out.

Maude Harding was momentarily unsure of herself. With Will Fergus it had been different. She had detested the boy from the first for the influence he wielded over little Thomas, exposing the lad to sexual practices she thought disgusting. The Fergus boy had been an abomination. When a young maid had become pregnant she had not believed the girl's story that Dr. Geddy had forced

Will to have intercourse with her while he watched. The story was an incredible lie that the loathsome Fergus boy had no doubt planted in the girl's head. She had lashed Will Fergus with a whip, slashing its tip into his scrotum until it was raw and bleeding. Then she had broken his manhood with the whip handle so that he would never be able to use it again on a woman.

Now she pondered Pearl, a female rather than a bestial Fergus male. But Pearl was evil too— just as her brother had, she threatened to steal Thomas away from them all.

Without another thought she inserted the stick in Pearl's vagina and pushed. Pearl screamed. The thrust was so sudden, so painful, she did not realize at first that it was her own scream; the sound seemed to come from the walls of the chamber. Then her vision blurred. As long as she was to live, she would never forget the two women's faces seen through her haze of tears: Mrs. Harding's maddened gleam of pleasure, Mrs. Geddy's smug, complacent smile.

She heard them talk, as if in a dream:

"I hardly think it is necessary for me to tell you this, Maude," Mildred said sweetly, "but your troubles will only begin if one word of this reaches the ears of my husband or son."

"I understand . . . madam."

As the woman left, Maude Harding tried to reassert her lost authority. "Be dressed and in the kitchen within the half hour," she ordered Pearl. But the tone of her voice had grown dull and lifeless, drained by her exertions in beating and deflowering the girl, drained still more by her sense of having bowed so quickly to Mildred Geddy's demands. She knew she had in some way lost a measure of control over the household.

In the kitchen Lottie Henderson had heard the scream. She had calmly poured herself a cup of coffee and sat down to drink it. She had waited a long time to get even with the arrogant Mrs. Harding. She could wait a mite longer for her own promotion. This was America, she told herself, the land of opportunity. She had long since learned that opportunity here came only to those who fought for it, as viciously as need be. America was a cruel and heartless land. Only those of strong stomach could arise from its melting pot.

6

After their dinner guests had gone, Mildred Geddy and her husband looked at each other in a long and peculiar silence. Mildred's eyes glinted angrily as she waited for Mark to make a comment. Mark, knowing one was expected of him, smiled faintly and smoked one of his strong cheroots.

It was Mildred who was forced to speak first.

"Well?" she goaded him, a nerve in her cheek twitching with impatience.

Mark, pleased with his cunning, laughed mirthlessly. "Well?" he echoed. "You will of course agree that it would be a mismatch from the start."

Mildred refused to agree. She frowned, tapped her fingers on the arm rest, and pretended to give the matter great thought. "Why do you say that?"

His smile became broader. "Perhaps you were

not as uncomfortable as the rest of the party. Wurth may be a fox in the munitions industry, but the pulse in his temple gave him away. He didn't like being here one damn bit."

"I blame Leah for that," Mildred snapped. "I don't think the man knew that the discussion might tinge on marriage."

Mark refrained from commenting that Mildred had kept him in the dark as to her discussion plans as well.

"It must be a sore point with Wurth," he laughed. "He must fear that he will be stuck with the silly little ninny for the rest of her life. My god, she is ugly!"

"Don't be cruel, Mark. Denise is a very nice child. I'm sure that Aaron Wurth wants only the best for her."

This caused him to roar with laughter. "But we don't, my dear."

"How can you say such a thing?"

There were times that Mark Geddy felt sorry for his wife.

"Mildred," he said wearily, "although the man tries to hide the fact, everyone is aware that he comes from Jewish stock. He's looking for a marriage which will hide the fact even further. I don't see why we should become part of the trap."

Mildred bit her lip. "Now look at who is being prejudiced!" she stormed. But when her husband did not comment further, she breathed a sigh of relief. She was forced to acknowledge inwardly that the dinner party had been a disaster from beginning to end. The Wurths were vastly monied and undeniably ungraced. Aaron Wurth had eyed everything, including Thomas, as though putting a price tag upon it. The man and Mark Geddy had nothing in common and all but said so openly. Leah Wurth had not acted as sure of her purpose as she had at tea time, leading Mildred to fear that she had already heard the rumor about Thomas and the maid. But Mildren's greatest disappointment centered around Denise Wurth. The girl all but avoided Thomas, as though he were not worthy of her. All in all, the dinner had been a mistake. Mildred would not let such a mistake happen again.

She rose and was preparing to say her good night when the door bell-pull interrupted her. No servant went to answer it, which infuriated her, but before she could comment Mark calmly marched from the room to answer it himself. After a moment, Mildred's curiosity made her follow him into the foyer. She got only a fleeting glimpse of a policeman before the door was closed and her husband sharply spun about.

"Bertha's sent word that there's a bad fire on the southside," he said grimly. "I'll hitch up the surrey. Tell Thomas I'll need him at the clinic."

Mildred started to protest. Before going to bed, she had planned to talk to Thomas about Pearl Fergus and related matters of importance. She decided her chat could be postponed, in view of this little emergency, whatever it was. She went to Thomas's room and relayed her husband's message.

"And Tommy," she added, "though my day is quite complicated tomorrow, I wish for you to free yourself from the clinic the day after so that we can have a long talk."

"Not if it is going to center around Denise

Wurth," Thomas said as he quickly began putting on his coat.

"I don't see—"

"Exactly," he interrupted. "You don't see."

Mildred's anger flared. "She's no less desirable than our scullery maid!"

Thomas blushed scarlet at the reference to Pearl. He stood still, with his coat half on.

"You're guilt is apparent," his mother said coldly. "I will not be humiliated in this fashion, do you hear? We can cancel our little talk, for I can say what I wish to say right now. When you return from the clinic tonight I will expect you to pack and prepare to leave in the morning for at least a two-week stay with my Cousin Minerva in New York. When you return you will marry whomever I say."

Dr. Geddy's urgent call from downstairs kept Thomas from having to confront his mother's demands then and there. He had no intention of going to New York. He had no intention of marrying Denise Wurth. For the moment did not look upon his afternoon with Pearl as anything he could not explain simply and innocently.

But Pearl was now uppermost in Mildred Geddy's mind. A week at the most, she thought, is all I need to make the girl so wretched that Mark will have no choice but to send her back to Ireland or face open rebellion in his home. And two weeks, she determined, gave her ample time to cower Leah Wurth into making wedding arrangements. Mildred Geddy again felt the mistress of her world.

*   *   *

It was not stoic resolve which had enabled Pearl to do her evening's work. Her body and brain were so benumbed with pain that she moved mechanically, almost mindless. She was sick with fear as well as pain. Lest she be beaten again for it, she had determined not to say a single word of her mistreatment to her sister, unless the bleeding did not stop and she was forced to.

The fire-victim patients had kept Bertha and the two doctors at the clinic until near midnight. Bone-tired, Bertha almost forewent her nightly custom of looking in on her little sister. But a ray of light beneath Pearl's door stopped her short.

"What!" Bertha exclaimed, her large eyes widening. "You're still up and dressed!"

"Can't sleep."

"You won't be fit for anything tomorrow," Bertha remarked crossly. "Now get that uniform off and get into bed."

Pearl started to rise from the rocking chair and felt a pang of nausea. Now Bertha saw her feverish face and dull sunken eyes. She came further into the room the better to scrutinize her sister.

"What's the matter with you?" she demanded. "You look ill."

Pearl pressed the back of her cold hand against her burning cheek. "I'm just not too well this evening," she admitted.

Bertha scowled. "I hope you're not sickening with something. You've hardly started work, as it is."

"I'm not sickening," answered Pearl staunchly. She drew a deep breath. Her chest and back hurt her. Then she felt the blood begin to flow again. She prayed that Bertha would leave her so that she could sit quite still and perhaps stop it. But it was too late. Bertha knitted her thick brows together and stared at the dark stream running down Pearl's thigh. She misunderstood what she saw.

"Good God," she said irritably. "It's that, is it? Child, didn't mama tell you about the curse? God, you seem almost too young. Don't you know how to care for it?"

"It's not that," Pearl said, beginning to sob quietly despite herself.

Bertha stared at her uncomprehendingly, and then Pearl's tears came in a rush. She had held them in so long that it was hard to stem their flow. As she told of the beating and what had prompted it, Bertha got her onto the bed and did a cursory examination. She knew at once that it was a situation she could not handle on her own. Her only concern was which doctor to consult. Because of Thomas's involvement, she decided to wake him. She did so, quietly, and brought him to Pearl's room.

Pearl faintly heard Thomas's questions, which she duly answered. He examined her carefully, tenderly. Mostly, she felt the comforting pressure of his hands. She fixed her gaze on his concerned slate-gray eyes as he cleansed her wounds and applied ointments, gently rubbing them into her skin.

A bitter hatred swelled in Thomas's heart as he prepared to sew up the jagged wound in her vagina. Almost thankfully, Pearl fainted from the initial pain. He proceeded with the operation, finished it with frowning concentration, applied a dressing, then motioned Bertha out of the room with him.

"Look in on her from time to time. In the meantime get packed up," he said tensely.

Bertha gaped at him. "Why must I be sent back, just because she is my sister."

"You're not being sent back."

"Well, I'm not leaving as Will did," she objected self-righteously. "My family has had enough trouble already."

"Not as much as mine are going to have," snapped Thomas. "I saw that father's study lamp was still on as I came here. I want this settled tonight."

"And your mother?" asked Bertha bluntly.

His gray eyes turned icy. "I never want to see the woman again as long as I live."

Bertha scoffed. "That's easy to say. Your mother has a way of not seeing her difficult."

Thomas shook his head grimly. It was as if Fate were forcing him to a decision he could not make on his own. "The three of us are going west," he said.

"Impossible."

Thomas ignored her. "I never really had reason to go before. Now, I can't stay and I can't leave Pearl behind. She's come to be like a little sister to me." He frowned. "Somehow I'll have to resolve your indentured status with papa so that your parents won't suffer for your leaving."

"It's all so sudden." Her heart beginning to soar, Bertha nevertheless watched him narrowly, testing his determination.

Thomas straightened and drew in a deep

breath. "Is it, really? My medical supplies and equipment have been crated and stored at the clinic for six months. There's a great deal of coward in me, Bertha. You're going to have to be my backbone and strength. I won't be able to make it without you."

Bertha had waited three years to hear those words. Her heart burst into inexplicable poundings. To her mind he had all but proposed marriage. Now she would follow him anywhere. She didn't even mind dragging Pearl along, now that he had made it plain that he regarded her only as a little sister. She knew that she didn't love Thomas Geddy. She considered him even weaker than he considered himself. She could live without love. She wanted a financially secure future.

Dr. Mark Geddy had never seen his son so upset. It amused him.

"I have been lying to you and to myself," Thomas admitted. "It was not Albany but further west I had in mind. Mother forced my hand tonight. I won't go to Cousin Minerva's for two weeks and I damn sure am not going to marry Denise Wurth. I am going to go ahead and set up my own practice in the west."

Dr. Geddy applauded his son's decision. But he frowned when he heard that Pearl was going.

"That's absurd, Thomas. Why would you have need to take both of the Fergus girls?"

Thomas had not wanted to tell his father the full truth about Pearl. He wanted to protect him from the knowledge of his mother's heinous behavior. But he felt he had to explain and could do so without bringing his mother into it—only, if need be, Mrs. Harding. "I'm taking Pearl to save her life," he said.

Mark sighed. "Your mother always did love to keep gossip from me, but not Lottie Henderson. I was informed of the beating incident while I was selecting a wine before dinner."

Thomas's anger flared. "And you did nothing. That's inexcusable in a doctor."

"What has doctoring to do with prattling cooks and vindictive housekeepers? If the story of ah, your affection for Pearl is true, which I doubt, it gave me hope for you. I was beginning to wonder if you had any interest in girls."

"Not as much as you, perhaps," Thomas said, brutally. "Only enough to know that even a servant girl is a human being."

"But to be handled in a discreet manner, my boy. You don't go about practically seducing them in broad daylight."

"What in the hell are you talking about?" Thomas cried. "Pearl is a child! I did nothing more than take her to lunch and kiss her hand goodbye. The punishment hardly befits the crime."

One thing that annoyed Dr. Geddy about his son was his insufferable way of talking about a subject without coming to its core.

"Thomas," he said sternly, "you know very well that I do not involve myself with your mother's running of the house. She has very strict rules about a servant's proper position."

"A rule you don't seem to mind breaking," Thomas shot back.

Dr. Geddy sighed. "I'll overlook that outburst, young man."

"I don't think you can." The perceptions Thomas had had about his father, perceptions which he had tried to repress, burst forth from him in his anger. "You must think me a fool and a blind idiot. You gave permission for Bertha to go with me only when you knew Pearl was on her way from Ireland. Bertha was a virgin when she came from Ireland. She no longer is. We both know how careful mother is in disallowing the servant girls to have men friends. A certain conclusion is unescapable."

Dr. Geddy's cheeks reddened. He fought to control his voice. "I will give you a chance to stop right there, Thomas."

Thomas had never stood up to his father before. His knees grew weak and cold sweat broke out under his shirt collar. "You can't stop me now," he said, thankful that his voice did not break. "The New England Emigrant Resettlement Association requires personal health information, and to comply I had to give Bertha an examination. As we are the only two doctors who have ever attended her, one or the other of us has performed an abortion on her in the past year."

The look that passed between father and son was a thin rapier of total contempt. But the father would not be stampeded.

"A necessary step at the time," he said coolly.

"Naturally," Thomas sneered. "You feared mother would detect the source of the pregnancy."

"I do not wish to discuss the matter any further and hardly see the link between that incident and Pearl. Your mother will punish her for a few days and then forget the whole matter. Your sudden departure may even make her forget the punishment altogether."

"Bastard!" Thomas screamed. "I've just finished taking twenty-two stitches in the girl where Maude Harding, *at mother's command,* used a stick to take away her virginity, to say nothing of the beating her poor little body also took. And don't tell me that this is the first time you've heard of such beatings taking place in this house."

Mark Geddy had listened with profound attention to the horrifying description of what had happened to Pearl. A sickness grew in his heart. Still, he did not want to release his hold on the girl before he had even gained it.

"Oh, Thomas," he said wearily, "these are poor peasant girls who sometimes carry a story a little too far. I grant you that Mrs. Harding is sometimes a bit too harsh and if it will ease your mind I shall see to her dismissal. But how can you believe that your mother would stand by and allow such a thing to happen?"

Thomas banged the study table with his clenched fist.

"This is as good a time as ever to speak the truth, all of it. You wanted Will Fergus and I to be good friends. Didn't it ever dawn on you that friends talk? God, I learned right away how you showed Will and Molly Snyder to do it with each other. It took me nearly three months to get up the courage to try it also because I was jealous that you hadn't told me yourself. Wouldn't you know that Mrs. Harding would catch us just as Will was starting to show me what to do to Molly? Odd that I wasn't punished, papa. But with my own ears I heard mama tell Mrs. Harding to

punish Will and Molly. I also heard mama tell
Mrs. Harding that Molly was pregnant and the
matter would have to be discussed with you. What
happened to Molly, papa? What happened to
Will Fergus? I was sent away to school the next
day and all I've ever been told is that Will vanished. I'd like to know the real reason why he
left."

Mark tried to bluster, sheepishly. "Come now,
what else am I and your mother to be accused
of that has happened around here?"

"It amazes me," Thomas said, heavily, "that
you and mother ever were in bed long enough
for me to be conceived. Now I see clearly what
part of each of you I gained from that single
union: your hatred of her and her hatred of sex.
What a legacy."

All through him Mark felt the pounding of
giant pulses, gathering and rushing to an excruci-
ating crescendo of defeat. Could no one understand his loneliness, his desires, his needs, his
simple need for love? He was no more than a
tool, such as one he would use in his operating
room.

He felt it had always been thus. He was the
tool his family had used to educate and send as
a doctor to America. He was the tool to supply
the money back to Ireland to make their lives
financially secure in a troubled country.

He was even the tool his family had used to
broker him an American-Irish wife to bolster
their foundations. He felt he was more a slave
than any indentured servant he had ever brought
across the ocean. And what had been his pleasures
in life? He knew that he was a short and unat-

tractive little man, even in his prime. Thomas
never knew how near the truth he had come about
his birth. Mark Geddy could count on his hands
the number of times he had been allowed into
his wife's bed in their twenty-four years of marriage. But being Irish Catholic they had accepted
their lot and not once thought of divorce.

Thomas's birth had given him a fleeting moment of pure joy, and then Mildred had skillfully
alienated the boy from the father. Will Fergus
had been a gross mistake on his part, but he had
coveted the love of a son and this had made him
too openly truthful with the youth. He could not
remember his own father, but could readily recall
his older brother teaching him about girls in the
same manner he had taught Will. Where had it
all gone wrong? Was it really revenge or love he
sought from Bertha Fergus? Was it sexual or
paternal love he sought from Pearl Fergus?

He ended his unhappy thoughts on a note of
pride. His weakling son had at last come to face
up to him like a man. Unless he wanted to lose
the only shred of love left open to him, he would
have to handle things very carefully.

"For what it is worth," he said slowly, "I shall
answer your questions, although you may hate
me forever. Unlike Bertha, Molly was sent back
to Ireland and arrangements were made for her
to marry a tenant farmer who would see after her
and the child when it was born. As for Will, it is
not a pretty story. Please don't force me to go
into details. He was put to Mrs. Harding's whip
and I had to take him to the clinic to treat him.
The next morning he was gone from his hospital
bed. Wounds such as his would have required

medical attention for at least six weeks, and were of such rare circumstance that any doctor would have gossiped about treating him. I made inquiries as far north as Bangor, Maine, and as far south as the Carolinas. Nothing. Without medical attention there was no way he could have survived. Here, and I must say this candidly, I was caught up in the same cowardly legacy I gave you as a father—I could not stand up to your mother and Mrs. Harding. Like a spoiled child I went into a shell to lick my wounds. I began to blame Will for deserting me, rather than blame the people responsible for the tragedy. Yes, it is best that you take both of the girls away. Leave the problem of your mother with me."

Thomas had listened to his father with slowly dawning, then compassionate comprehension. When he'd finished, he shook his head, then offered a solution.

"It may not be that much of a problem, if she thinks I've done as she commanded. If she thinks I've gone to Cousin Minerva's. . . ."

Dr. Geddy laughed harshly. Yet, as he spoke it was with appalling slow sadness.

"Your mother will not give you up without a fight, once the truth is known. But we will do it in this manner. At breakfast, after you've said your goodbye, I'll suggest we dine out tomorrow evening and that she give the servants the day off. That should give you ample time to make the ten-thirty train. Before I retire I'll draw up the necessary papers turning the girl's indenturedness over to your keeping. I'll also see to it that you have necessary capital to carry you through."

The hatred for his father had disappeared from

Thomas's face. Now it was full of his self-loath-ing.

"I suddenly know what a blackmailer must feel like. He has won a certain battle, but lost much in the taking."

"You should not feel that way. I'm thankful that one member of this family has an ounce of decency left in him. I don't know why I always fail people, but I do."

Thomas wanted to leave the room before he became unmanly and burst into tears. He started to walk swiftly from the room but at the door turned back.

"That's wrong, papa. I can see now that we have all failed you. I've never said this before, but I do love you."

It was Mark Geddy who was left to cry lonely tears.

7

The manner in which Arabelle Cornithwyeth
handled the affairs of the New England Emigrant
Resettlement Association were as blowsy and
opulent and warm as herself. Some of the male
emigrants thought her intrusive, but Arabelle
loved her work. Perfectly at her ease, she would
put her rosy plump face deep into their wagons,
sniff loudly, and with quite unrefined delight, tell
them what could be taken along and what must
be discarded. Through her personal effort she
had already surpassed her husband's goal of a
sixty-wagon train.

In her morning "uniform" of sprigged muslin,
her hoops swaying vigorously, the tall, stout Arabelle had become a familiar sight on the streets
of Lancaster. Her daughter, Anne, a brown spare
little sparrow of a girl at twenty, would follow

her mother about on her wagon-train business, listening to the bustling Arabelle speak, endlessly it seemed, about food supplies, the deportment of children, the livestock and the wagons, the rules the emigrants would have to live by. Anne listened with an attentive, knowing smile. As warm and loving as her mother appeared to others, she could be quite another person when the two were alone.

"There is something about that man that strikes me wrong," Arabelle sniffed, as she swooped away after speaking to one emigrant farmer.

"He seems quite civil and refined," Anne remarked mildly.

"My point, daughter. He seems too civilized and too refined to be a simple farmer, as he claims. True, he has farming equipment, but that could have been newly purchased. And I'm not sure he's a widower, as he claims."

"What do you think he is, then?" Anne said impatiently. "If he is a widower, a pretty man like that won't stay single for long."

Arabelle paused on the board sidewalk, and turned quickly to her daughter. Her face grew stern. "Put thoughts of him from your head, Anne. He is far too old for you. Besides, how would an ugly little thing like you ever hope to capture him?"

"I don't regard myself as being ugly," said Anne, flushing in her indignation.

"Well, you are, dear, and let's not banter words about it. What is our next stop?"

Anne was not really offended. She had spent twenty years being told that she was plain and simple and ugly. She had come to the point where insults from her mother were almost tests of her courage, and she could pass every one with high marks.

"The hotel," she answered. "The Geddy party came in by train last night."

"I do not recall they were to be a party," said Arabelle with fresh indignation. "I was under the impression it was to be just a Doctor Thomas Geddy. When will these people learn that this is a very complicated matter getting them organized and that they can't add on people at whim. Well, we'll settle this quickly."

The hotel proprietor had warned Thomas about Mrs. Cornithwyeth, but Thomas still felt as if he were being advanced upon by a ship in full sail. He rose and crossed the lobby to greet her.

"Well, land sakes," Arabelle gushed, "you hardly look old enough to be a doctor."

Thomas smiled. He summoned his strength to begin living the lie that he and his father had concocted. "I am not a doctor," he said smoothly. "The original arrangements were made by my father, but he is unable to travel at this time. I trust that will not pose a problem."

"Hardly." Arabelle laughed warmly. She had instantly decided to make as few problems as possible for this young man. "It is in my nature to handle problems easily, Mr. Geddy. My daughter, Anne, sir."

"Miss Cornithwyeth, my pleasure."

"Anne is my brains," Arabelle rushed on. "But as I recall your father made a deposit on a single wagon."

"That's correct," Thomas agreed, "but I shall have need of a second wagon, if such is available."

Arabelle's eyebrows arched. "I'm sure it can be arranged. Might I inquire as to the size of your party now?"

Thomas hesitated. Only at the last moment had his father given him the Association document that outlined the marriage demand. It had nearly made him go sour on the whole scheme. Then he'd decided that he was brainy enough to side-step the issue.

"There will be three of us," he said simply.

"Three," Arabelle echoed, as though it were only a grain of the information she sought. "I shall require a listing of each by name, gender, age and marital status. If the third member happens to be the driver for the second wagon, then it's only fair to warn you in advance that we will not condone taking along single people."

"Driver?" Thomas said, as if perplexed. "How foolish of me not to think of that."

Arabelle cringed inwardly. She thought she had already run across every conceivable form of ignorance and unpreparedness. Now she had another monumental challenge to face. She indicated that Thomas was to be seated, then launched into the long list of the Association's requirements for each wagon and each family. The young man, it turned out, was totally uninformed; indeed, his naivety left Arabelle stunned. Fortunately, she was able to give him many warm and friendly pieces of advice.

"I have never," she stormed at Anne, when they were back on the street, "run up against such an incompetent man in my life. I strongly doubt we will see the Geddy party with us, my dear."

"Don't you think he will take your advice?"

"Hardly," she said. "The man has a sister-in-law who is not married. She must be, to make the trip. A rule is a rule and I'll not bend it for him."

"Do you think that he himself is married?"

Arabelle scoffed. "Foolish girl, why do you think I insisted upon seeing a marriage license. They'll have to show it to me. Strange people. Strange people, indeed. Can you imagine arriving with nothing but crates of medical supplies when the doctor will not be coming until he is well enough to travel? If he is anything like his scatter-brained son, I'd never want him laying a hand on me. Oh, fuddle! I left my parasol. Run back and get it and then meet me at the mercantile store."

The parasol was exactly where Arabelle had left it, but Thomas Geddy was gone. Anne was rather disappointed. She had instantly liked the shy young man. But, then, Anne instantly liked every man she saw, in spite of age, size or degree of handsomeness. She wanted a man of her own. She even resented the fact that, as Arabelle's daughter, she was exempt from the strict marriage rule.

Just as she was turning to leave the lobby she saw Thomas Geddy coming back down the stairs with a woman. She hung back to see what type of woman had captured him in marriage. At first, because of a floppy, brimmed hat, she could not see the woman too clearly, other than that she was as tall as the young man and of a bosom size that left Anne astounded. They came right by her, but were so engrossed in heated debate that they paid her no mind.

"Of course you would say marriage is a simple matter for us," Thomas growled, "but that is hardly the answer for Pearl."

"You act like I'm the one forcing you into it," Bertha retorted. "As far as I am concerned it can be a ceremonial thing for the trip only. But that seems the least of our problems, what with all the other demands you say they are making. We can never accomplish all of that in four days time."

So they were not married! At least, not yet.

Anne smiled to herself as they passed out of earshot. She debated on running to her mother with this tasty bit of gossip. Then she recalled Bertha's face to her mind. She had never before seen a woman who more resembled a horse. It almost made her giggle. Then she felt a tinge of compassion for Thomas Geddy having to marry her, even if it was just for the trip.

She started toward the mercantile store and then stopped short, an idea occurring to her. In a way, she thought, Thomas Geddy would be a somewhat single man on the trip. That would give her plenty of time to show him exactly what a talented, sweet and caring woman she could be. Suddenly, she knew that Thomas Geddy was the man for her and she would have to secretly work to gain him. But first she had to make sure that he was included in the wagon train.

Setting immediately to work, she sought out the farmer her mother had distrusted.

"Ah, Mr. Hartwicke," she simpered. "I was just this very moment thinking of your problem and how the Cornithwyeth family could aid you."

Lester Hartwicke politely doffed his hat and

smiled. It took him a moment to recall who she was, because she was not standing in her mother's formidable shadow.

"I'm obliged, Miss Cornithwyeth."

He granted her now a warm and friendly smile. It gave her a chance to measure him against Thomas Geddy. They were equally tall and equally handsome, she noted. But there was an underlying smoothness about Lester Hartwicke that belied his homespun attire. He had almost a military stance and tilt to his square-jawed head. His eyes didn't merely look, they pierced one. But this, she concluded, was perhaps due to the extreme pale yellowness of his hair, brows and lashes, so that the powder blueness of his eyes was doubly pronounced and made him appear cold and calculating.

"It would seem, sir, that another party has an opposite problem from your very own. The Geddys are travelling with an unwed sister-in-law. I wouldn't want my mother to know that the suggestion came from me, but you might consider approaching Mr. Geddy concerning a marriage of convenience, so to speak. You will find them staying at the hotel."

"It's something I'll ponder upon, Miss Cornithwyeth," Lester Hartwicke said coolly and walked away.

Anne felt deflated, as though she had handled the situation quite incorrectly. Now she would be unable to tell her mother anything and she did love to gossip.

Lester Hartwicke did not want to give her the satisfaction of knowing that the idea might have some merit. He was the type of man who never let anyone know what was on his mind. But he had too much at stake to miss this wagon train. Because of his past it would be far too dangerous for him to attempt the trip on his own. He needed the anonymity of the wagon train and a wife would make him fade even farther into the picture.

That evening, taking his supper in the hotel dining room, he nearly balked at Anne's suggestion. It was obvious to him that Geddy's wife was not only a very unattractive woman but unmistakably Irish. His English hackles were raised and he felt he was degrading himself by even approaching their table and introducing himself.

"It would seem," he said, after being invited to join them, "that I, as a widower, am being denied passage because of no wife. It's rather a disgrace to suggest that an Englishman cannot control his lust, but the woman seems most set in her rules."

Thomas agreed and Bertha remained silent. The man reminded her of every Englishman she had ever met—pompous, puffed up and pitiable. Her opinion of him was not changed when he immediately came forth with Anne Cornithwyeth's suggestion. Pearl? He wanted to marry *Pearl?* Thomas was aghast and looked to Bertha for an answer.

In spite of her instant dislike of the man, Bertha was not about to let Thomas out of her clutches. A 'ceremonial' wedding for Pearl would ease Thomas's mind about their own. She rose very slowly and each man expected a cutting refusal.

"Thank you for your interest, Mr. Hartwicke,"

she said sweetly. "It is, however, a matter I must discuss with my sister. Perhaps you might care to join us for dinner tomorrow evening for her answer."

Each man was equally surprised. Hartwicke because she had handled the matter with class and diplomacy; and Thomas because she was even considering it at all.

Bertha didn't discuss the matter with Pearl. She flat-out told her what was expected of her and made it ring with authority by coupling Thomas's name in the discussion. Pearl was still so sick and feverish that she agreed without knowing what she was agreeing to. Early the next morning Bertha took command of Thomas's affairs.

"What is she up to? What is she up to?" Arabelle demanded the moment her daughter returned from her snooping mission.

"Plenty," Anne snickered. "First thing, that old Bertha marched herself over to Hiram Hanson and bartered for his wagon and household goods. He'll take his sick wife back to Bedford. Says that's as far west as he ever intends to go again."

"She's got grit," Arabelle admitted, "but that's only one problem solved."

"More'n that," Anne corrected. "You'd best put the Corey brothers and their wives back on the list. They only got one wagon, so she hired one of the brothers to drive their second one. They got the money to pay you now, mama."

Arabelle grinned broadly. "You see, Anne dear, it's just as I've always said. A man ain't worth anything more than the woman doing his thinking for him. I'm beginning to like this spunky gal and I ain't even met her yet."

"You'll be meetin' her and hearin' about her, I expect. She gave ole man Robinson a real to-do at the mercantile store. Told him he was chargin' a dollar more a barrel for flour than she could get in Philadelphia. He told her to go on back and get it and she told him right out she would go on the next train and bring back flour for any of the women who wanted it. Robinson's flour is now a dollar less a barrel."

"Lands, I never thought of that ruse against that skinflint." Arabelle chuckled. Then she quickly sobered. "Still, the most important rule your father set down is still lacking. I'll not bend, Anne."

"You won't have to, mama. With the money she saved on the flour she bought a right pretty dress and two lengths of bridal veil."

"God be praised!" Arabella shouted. "Kneel child, so we can pray. You see how His wonders do work?"

Anne knelt and averted her face. She prayed that her mother would not ask until too late who had been helping Him to work his wonders.

Lester Hartwicke was not allowed to see Pearl until they were standing before a justice of the peace and strict ground rules had been established by Bertha.

The wedding was scheduled for the day before departure. Arabelle, who was most anxious to see the mysterious Pearl, made sure that she was in attendance as an uninvited guest. Anne attended so that she could gaze upon Thomas Geddy. They almost went unnoticed in the crowd of eighteen couples taking mass vows so that they too could make the trip.

Arabelle smiled wickedly. "Your father would be amazed to see how many liars he recruited. Look, even the Parnells are taking vows, and they've four children already. And the old saw does come true, Anne dear. Just look at Bertha Fergus. She is as radiant as a bride would be and not the least bit horsy. But surely—"

A loud hiss stilled Arabelle, but could not divert her eyes from the couple who came to take their place beside Bertha and Thomas. Her fleshy mouth gaped, but not over the sight of Lester Hartwicke as the selected husband. She could hardly believe that the two women were sisters. Pearl, in a new dress of pink cotton, made the simple garment appear as if it had come out of a fashionable New York shop. Pink ribbons held the white lace to her head and were in vivid contrast to her rich black hair, heavy brows and lush lashes. The fever still in her body gave her creamy complexion a rosy hue that all took as excitement of the moment. But the watery wells of her eyes belied it all.

As gorgeous and mature as she appeared, Arabelle detected her misery and the manner in which she never took her gaze from Thomas Geddy throughout the ceremony. In the back of her mind, Arabelle made a mental note to keep a sharp eye on what could become a dangerous situation. She might have been better advised to have stolen a glance at her own daughter's face. Anne had also noted Pearl's beauty and her manner of eyeing Thomas, but that did not trouble her as much as the wistful and secret glances Thomas Geddy was casting on Pearl.

"He just couldn't love her."

Almost too late she realized she had spoken her thought aloud. But at that very moment the room erupted into cheers and clapping at the ceremonies' conclusion.

Thomas Geddy, without kissing his bride, turned and came directly toward Arabelle. Arabelle kept her eyes beyond him and noted that Pearl had slyly averted her head so that Lester Hartwicke was able to give her only a peck on the cheek. She was now being quickly steered away by her sister.

"Here are the required papers, Mrs. Cornithwyeth, and the rest of our money. I trust we now have your approval to form our wagons in with the others for tomorrow's departure."

"Heartily approved," Arabelle gushed. "Here, darling, put the papers and money where they belong. I'll go and collect them from the others."

Anne did a daring thing for her, as soon as her mother was gone. "Mr. Geddy," she murmured, reaching out and laying her hand on his arm, "I trust you are not angry with me for putting Mr. Hartwicke in touch with you. I didn't want to see you missing the trip."

"I just hope he's a gentleman of his word," said Thomas coolly. "Excuse me now, we have to move from the hotel to our wagons."

Anne's sensitive nature was immediately crushed. The man had not even thanked her. The rest of the day passed like an evil dream for her, too busy, too noisy, too much time to think. It had only dawned on her as Thomas walked away that he would be sharing a wagon with Bertha as a new husband. The thought of what that meant increased in her mind to frightful proportions. She couldn't stop them from consummating the wedding, but she had to learn if that's what they would do.

With Arabelle's second stentorious snore, Anne rolled from her pallet, quickly pulled a dress over her head and jumped agilely down from the back gate of the wagon. It had been an early night for all and the campfires were reduced to glowing embers. The seventy-odd wagons would spend their last night in a helter-skelter pattern. Before dawn Hiram Cornithwyeth would take command from his sister-in-law and head them out in alphabetical order. Then they would be under his strict rules as wagon boss. But on this last evening no one was quite sure where everyone else was located.

Anne Cornithwyeth, however, had made certain of where the Geddy and Hartwicke wagons were located. Still, the camp that had been her temporary home for three months seemed strangely different. It was eerily quiet and unusually dark. She could hear her every footstep and they sounded enormously loud to her ears. She paused for a moment, listening. The night was very still. She could hear no sound from any wagon. Her heart was beating light and fast, and her mouth felt dry.

Something moved beside her feet, almost startling her into a cry, until she realized it was only a cat, on some errand as secret as her own, but apparently quite ready to welcome a partner in crime. It purred softly and began to strop itself on her ankles. When she stooped it slid away from her touch, and vanished.

It seemed she was on her own. She took a long

breath to steady her heart beats, then started darting between the wagons. She melted quickly from shadow to shadow until she was beside the Hartwicke wagon.

There she hesitated. One glance under the wagon was enough to tell her that only a single person was wrapped within the bedroll; soft breathing from within suggested the presence of Pearl Mae. Her worst fears might be nearing reality, but she could not turn back now.

She trod softly, hurrying across a clearing to the Geddy wagons, and almost immediately stepped on a loose stone that nearly brought her down. Before she had recovered, she heard other quick steps and saw the moving edge of a male shadow. She stood still, straining to see who might be lurking about. They had been warned about prowlers, but had had no trouble to date. She pressed her back against the Geddy wagon wheel and felt a calm assurance that if she had need to call out Thomas would come quickly to her side.

Clearly, ten yards away, she heard a deep cough, then the scrape of a match. The man had stopped at the corner of the second Geddy wagon, and was leisurely lighting a pipe.

The flaring match seemed unnaturally bright. For a moment it kept Anne from recognizing his face.

"Sheriff Bealle," she gasped.

His head jerked round, and the match dropped into the dust and fizzled out. Anne moved towards him, her fear replaced by wonderment. "Why are you here, sir?"

"Why, Miss Cornithwyeth! I might be asking you the same."

She laughed. "I've still a million things to do before we leave. And you?"

"Ah, yes, just a little courtesy check for the Boston police." He sounded unworried to the point of indifference. He leaned a shoulder back against the Geddy wagon, gesturing with his pungent pipe at the other wagons. "It's like a maze I remember as a boy in England. Hard to find what you are really looking for."

"Exactly what is it you are looking for?"

"Might be just some needles in a haystack. Some lady in Boston wants the wagon train held up until she can get a private investigator down here. A Mildred Geddy, by name."

Anne stiffened, head cocked. She said quickly, "Whatever would be her reason?"

"Mainly, two runaway indentured servants. The message didn't give more than that they were females aged twelve and sixteen. Judge Farris told me he married a Geddy man today. Thought I'd talk with him and see if there was a connection. Didn't know everyone would be to bed so early."

"They won't be," she whispered softly, "if you don't lower your voice. I don't see how there could be a connection, but we can go back to my wagon to look at the records, if you like. We had a doctor of that name scheduled but he took sick and his son came in his place. He was the one married today to his fiancee. When you see her you will know that she is not a girl of either of those ages."

Sheriff Bealle had not liked the sound of the message from the first. He did not like other lawmen, especially private detectives, coming into his territory, and he had been pleased not to have any trouble out of this group of people whatsoever.

Besides, his brother-in-law owned the wagon factory, was making a tidy profit from this group and saw great hope for the future. Trouble with the first wagon train would mean trouble with every one that followed.

"I figured about as much," he said slowly. "Your maw is a stickler for keepin' out the riff-raff. I ain't about to hold up your departure, but I'll have to tell the man something to report back to Mrs. Geddy. Think you could help by pointing the man out to me in the morning?"

Anne had a sudden burst of inspiration. "It will be no problem, sheriff, although we will be quite busy. But my Uncle Hiram does plan on making them move out in alphabetical order. Just wait for the Gees to form. You'll hear it called out. G-e-t-t-y."

Bealle frowned. "That's the spelling?"

Anne smiled. "I should know, sheriff, I keep all of the records."

Bealle sighed. "That about does it. The Boston woman is G-e-d-d-y. I think I've disturbed you enough. Goodnight and good trip."

Anne stood, watching him weave his way out of the wagon skelter. She was not aware that the scudding clouds had vanished and the area was basked in silvery moonlight until she looked up and saw the ashen face of Thomas Geddy peering down at her through the wagon flaps.

"I'm eternally grateful for your lie," he said, "but I assure you I've done nothing illegal. This is not the time for it, but I feel I owe you a full explanation."

She acknowledged that promise with a winning smile. Then something made the hair rise up the back of her neck. She turned to see Bertha scowling at her from the second wagon. Words did not have to be exchanged for each to know that they had become combatants over the same man. Bertha's leer suggested that she already held the upper hand by being Thomas' wife. Anne leered right back, buoyed by the thought that they were in separate wagons on their wedding night.

Anne, when she returned to her own wagon, took no care in not disturbing her mother. She lit a lamp and took out the Geddy papers that she had failed to read after they had been given to her.

"Fool," she chuckled, at seeing how utterly honest Thomas Geddy had been. The Fergus girls had not only been listed by their proper age, which stunned Anne, but he had listed their status as indentured servants. She touched a corner of the paper to the lamp and watched it curl brown and then burst into flame.

She would hold the secret in her heart until she was ready to use it to gain Thomas away from his 'servant girl.'

Book Two

THE GATHERING

8

"Niggaahs! Niggaahs am a comin' up de trek!"

Missouri was a slave state, but around Independence blacks were mainly household servants of long standing. The "farm folk" along the banks of the Missouri and Mississippi Rivers were far to the east and of little concern. For most this was the largest gathering of blacks they had ever seen and their parade through town was greeted by a sullen silence.

Barry Fitzpatrick stood on the porch of the Fremont house. He was livid with rage. He could understand now why Colonel Herbert's records were a mishmash of confusing information. Only in the first passing wagon had he spied any white occupants. Then, with each wagon passing, his heart had sunk deeper. Never had he seen such

139

ill-cared-for people or equipment. He was utterly amazed that the forty-odd wagons had stayed together for the trip from St. Louis. Most hobbled along on wobbly-bent wheels, their wood siding all but weathered away. Each was so overloaded with goods, people and chicken coops that he expected the crack of axles at any moment. There wasn't a horse or donkey whose ribs were not easy to count from thirty paces and they looked far healthier than the dour-faced slaves.

It was such a disheartening scene that Barry almost missed the wizened little old man uncaringly tugging a pack mule behind him in the wagon's dust. But the squat little man squinted at the porch, broke into a toothless grin, dropped the burro's reins and came flying across the small yard with his fists a-shaking.

"Son of a hoot-toddling ole wallar," he cackled, "if'n it ain't ole 'Five Fingah Lad' 'imself."

Barry balked, blinked and roared with delight. "Jehosephat," he cried, "the devil's done opened the graves and let his demons loose."

The old man eyed him with mischievous devilment. "That ole varmint ain't got his hooks into Doctor Merriweather Freitag in sixty and three years, boy, 'n I'm still runnin' faster'n any jack rabbit."

Barry clasped the scrawny man to his chest with an instant admixture of regret and elation. The man reeked of rancid body odor and wood smoke, a smell Independence had divorced Barry from but which now made him aware of his homesickness for the west and his mountain man life.

"Hot dang, you're a great ugly sight to me. Where'n'the'ell you pop up from?"

Doc Freitag threw a thumb over his shoulder at the wagon train parade.

"Tagged wid 'em outta Saint Louie. Odd lot, but docile folk."

Barry laughed. "What was an ole coot like you doin' back there?"

Jessie Fremont, who had been waiting with Barry for the Herbert train arrival, took a step back when it was apparent introductions were not in order. She was somewhat amazed in the change in Barry. It was as though the weird little man in buckskins had cast a magic spell and even Barry's speech and language seemed to alter.

"Makin' a damn fool mistake." Freitag chuckled until spittle formed at the corner of his mouth. "Went back east ta my beginin' and my sorrows. Foolishness! Damn ole man foolishness. Thirty-odd years east of the Miss and thirty-odd west of the Miss gave me a hankerin' ta see which was fur me. I'm goin' west ag'in, boy. An' lest you'd lak folks ta know why ole Doc calls yah 'Five Fingah Lad' thought ya'd find a place among yah fur an ole broken down medicine man."

Barry blushed, and tried to hide it from Jessie. "Always find a place for you, old man. By the way, let me present Mrs. John C. Fremont."

A remarkable transformation overcame Merriweather Freitag. He snapped to a West Point attention and bowed. "Honored, ma'am," he grinned. "Was beginnin' ta think the lad had lost all the good bringin' up his uncle pounded into his thick skull. Well, 'scuse me. If'n this be your train, bar-boy, you'll have need of a sawbones. Seen Injuns bettah cared for by witch doctors. Ma'am."

"What an unusual man," Jessie exclaimed, when he scurried back to his mule.

"You don't know the half of it." Barry grinned. "Some idiot set a bear trap wrong and I had to stumble into it a couple years ago. He set and re-broke my fingers and set them again until they would heal right."

"That's genius. What in the world is he doing in the west?"

"Thank the Lord he is. I don't care to retell his story without his permission."

Jessie Fremont could easily accept that. The same thing was true of her father and many of his political friends in Washington. You met a man and then learned to accept or reject him on the merits you found in him. At the moment she didn't care to have the smelly man inside of her house.

Her mind might have altered if she could have read Barry's at that moment.

Merriweather Freitag was a legend in his own time. Born at the close of the American Revolution to a three-generation family of doctors he was sent to Europe for his education and was already practicing medicine by the time he was nineteen. Reaching his mid-twenties he was performing surgery unheard of for that era. He came home to America not only as an honored doctor of note, but also as a gifted violinist, artist and man of letters. Philadelphia matrons tended to overlook his squat ugliness. He was a most sought-after bachelor for many social seasons, a frequent house guest at Mount Vernon and Monticello due to his wit, his language ability and a depthless knowledge of world history and politics.

Then, at age thirty-two, with America at war

again, he was instantly commissioned as a surgeon-general and personally chosen to serve under General Andrew Jackson. After the Creek nation was defeated at Horseshoe Bend a trace of scandal began to erupt around him. Other doctors began to complain that he was doing too much unnecessary surgery on the wounded. There was even a rumor that the dead were being buried without their livers and that said livers were finding their way onto the officers' mess tables. Only Freitag's reputation and friendship with Jackson averted an investigation.

But after the Battle of New Orleans in 1815 the allegations began to spring up again. This time his enemies claimed that Merriweather Freitag and his accomplices were growing rich by butchering the dead and selling portions of the bodies wholesale to a butcher shop in New Orleans. Because of inefficient record-keeping, over fifty bodies could not be accounted for and Jackson was forced to ask Freitag to relinquish his post until a full investigation could be completed. It was not enough for those who sought to ruin him and they demanded his immediate arrest.

Without Jackson's knowledge he was sipirited away, manacled and sent north to St. Louis by steamboat. British agents had sabotaged the boat and it blew up fifty miles south of Cairo, Illinois. Two days later Dr. Freitag was found on the western bank by a hunting party of Ozark Indians. He was taken into the mountains and cared for until his recovery. Learning that all but ten people had perished in the accident, he decided to let his own death stand as fact.

He cast aside all of his past and became a wayward doctor to the hunters, trappers, mountain men, Indians and an occasional pioneer family. In twenty-eight years he had become as rough as the land he traversed. Only three men knew his real background, Barry having gained his information from his uncle.

In spite of the fact that Cornithwyeth claimed to have a doctor coming from the east, Barry felt relieved to know that he would have Doc Freitag along.

His relief was short-lived. No sooner had Doc Freitag disappeared into the dust than a rider came out of it. It was apparent that Major Hudson Warren was coming to see him.

"Mr. Fitzpatrick!" Warren greeted him, sliding easily from his saddle. "Glad that I caught you! Mornin' Mrs. Fremont!"

"Major," Jessie said coolly, for she disliked and mistrusted the man. "I'll leave you gentlemen alone."

Barry looked at the army commander keenly. Warren was seldom so effusive. In this, as in all other matters of dealing with the government, it paid to know your man.

"Well," Barry drawled, "glad to see you so cheerful. Makes a body think you've been transferred back east."

"Nothing that good," Warren laughed.

He's nervous, Barry thought, damned nervous . . . I wonder what the hell he's up to.

Hudson Warren was a West Point graduate book man. It was uncommon for so young a man to have such high rank in peace time, but Warren made sure that the proper authorities always knew the right things that he did.

Warren leaned forward confidentially.

"Ever hear of the slavery movement laws?"

"No. Never did. What are they?"

"A simple protective matter to keep new areas from becoming slave areas. Seems to be all blacks that just drove through town. Lucky I was down from Kansas City to see it. If you move them across the Missouri, I'll just have to bring them back with federal troops."

"That's great," Barry said, his voice heavy with sarcasm. "You've just been dying to stop me in any way that you could, haven't you?"

"Now, wait a minute!" Warren said. "I'm trying to avert trouble before it starts."

"Which," Barry said, "is another way of saying you'll try to avert trouble in my other trains as well."

"Agreed. But that is my job—and I intend to do it. Look, Mr. Fitzpatrick, this is government business. This is a little place, no more than a hamlet. If you put together the size train you intend, the news will spread fast. The army doesn't have the manpower to guard every damn fool who wants to go west. Washington would rather see fewer pioneers out there until we can get a fort system established. We're having enough trouble with the Indians as it is."

Barry frowned thoughtfully.

"Why," he said quietly, "I thought the army was just itchin' for a fight with the Indians."

Warren smiled.

"You know that isn't official. A good skirmish now and then does keep the cavalry on their toes. But we are getting away from the point in question."

"The blacks," Barry mused. "I know it's illegal and I'm against it. But what's to stop Herbert and his men from taking them on their own and not paying my price?"

"I doubt they would want a confrontation with the army, Fitzpatrick. If they fight, they will be breaking an even more enforceable law. They are only three white men and two women. It's illegal to arm a slave, for any purpose. They will be a millstone around your neck even if you do find a way to include them in your train."

Barry studied Warren in silence.

"I'll let Herbert know tomorrow," he said.

"Tomorrow may be too late. Either you tell him unofficially, or I'll do it officially."

"I'll tell him," Barry said, and walked off the porch without a goodbye.

The rest of the day Barry was very busy. He went from person to person and asked questions. It checked: every word that Warren had told him was true. The army had every right in the world to keep slaves from crossing the river. The loss of that many wagons was going to put him into a financial bind. He had already used a goodly portion of Colonel Herbert's down payment to purchase a chuck wagon, team, extra saddle horses and supplies. He would not be able to repay the man until he had collected from Cornithwyeth and also had the Tedder payment.

He went to the Herbert campsite at last, his head aching. The condition of the wagons and people was almost unbelievable. It was obvious that the Herberts had been foolish in attempting to bring along so many slaves. They were all dressed for the south, and the Missouri nights were still cold in May. The children looked frightened and unsure of what was happening to them. It also seemed to Barry that the rations had been skimped upon in their month of travel. Other than the slave issue newly raised by Warren, he saw a thousand other reasons why he could refuse to take the Herbert party along.

He was saved from the tangle of his thoughts by the approach of Colonel Herbert. With him was a woman, a slim creature who had been decidedly pretty in her youth. But it was not the woman who caught Barry's attention. It was the girl whom she held by the hand. He took her to be less than sixteen years old. Her delicate beauty was magnetic. Her bearing was womanly, yet there was in it that same curious grace that attracted Barry to Jessie Fremont. Women like this girl made him uneasy; they made him feel like a wagon mule next to an Indian pinto pony. Then Barry's discomfort increased with Harmon Herbert's running to catch up with the group. This young man was commanding, a prince born to plantation life. His eyes measured Barry with a look that had already found, Barry knew instinctively, few men his equal and none his better.

"This," Colonel Herbert said with simple pride, "is my Miss Mary Sue, my daughter Dahlia Dee, who we'all call DeeDee, and my son Harmon."

"Howdy!" Barry rumbled. "I'm pleased, ma'am. I've heard the colonel talk about you three for a month. It's a little late to invite you to Mrs. Fremont's for supper, but Harvey's can always set a few extra places."

"Is that anything like Antoine's, papa?" DeeDee demanded suddenly.

Colonel Herbert threw back his bulbous head and laughed aloud.

"No, my sweet," he chuckled. "Harvey's is the boarding house where I've been staying. It's just very plain northern fare. Did you eat at Antoine's when you were in New Orleans?"

"Hardly," DeeDee said gravely, with a scathing look at her stepmother. "We hardly had that much money."

"Dahlia Dee!" Mary Sue said.

"Papa said I was always to tell the truth," she smirked.

"That's right," Colonel Herbert agreed, "always tell the truth, sweetness. Harm, ya'all tell Pomeroy ta pass out the rations to the niggers and then you catch up with us, hear?"

Barry used the first part of the meal to study the family and determine how best to break several pieces of bad news to them. The meal was served family style and he could not help but notice an oddity in the hands that passed him bowls and platters. Three appeared as though they had never done a day's work in their lives, but Mary Sue's were rough and reddened from hard toil.

It was left to Harmon to relate the various events that had transpired since they left the plantation. Colonel Herbert, who had been only half-listening to his son, looked at his wife tenderly as he spoke to Barry.

"Folks didn't cotton to me marryin' up with Miss Mary Sue," he said. "They all said it were her comedown, the Dubois plantation bein' one of the richest in the south. But things seemed to sour. She all worked like bloody hell to save that place, she did." His glance fell on his wife. "We all will have a plantation in the west as big as the whole state of Alabama—or my name ain't Thomas Cuthbertson Herbert."

"Hush, Tom!" Mary Sue warned, good naturedly. "Mr. Fitzpatrick is not interested in our failures or day dreams. He appears to be a man with troubles of his own without taking on ours."

"Your troubles and mine are about the same, ma'am," Barry said quickly while an opening presented itself. "I can't help but notice the condition of your wagons and people. It's going to take a heap of work and money to right all the wrongs before I can agree to take you."

"What? What?" Colonel Herbert blustered. "Hell of a time to be tellin' a man a thing like that!"

Mary Sue stretched out her hand across the table to soothe her husband. "He only speaks the truth, Tom. Aaron Pomeroy and I discussed it at length on the trip. You see, Mr. Fitzpatrick, we were unable to get some of our wagons repaired on the journey as anticipated. Thankfully they lasted this far, so we can now make the necessary repairs. My husband has the needed funds for the repairs and supplies. How long do we have?"

"Perhaps too long," Barry said gruffly. "The government says you can't take that many slaves —any number of slaves—across the Missouri. I've checked everything possible and have no answer for you."

"Damn them!" Herbert growled. "They can't do that! I own those slaves legal and will do as I damn well please with them."

"The army will only force you to bring them back."

"Shee-it!" Harmon sneered. "We all will whip their asses. Got ourselves some damn fine huntin' niggers in our group."

"That will get you into even more hot water," Barry warned. "It's illegal to arm slaves."

"I don't give a damn about legalities," Colonel Herbert stormed. "I can't go back 'n so I'm goin' forward—with or without you!"

Mary Sue stared at her husband with a strange expression on her face. If he had divined her feelings, he would have been roaring with rage. For the expression in her eyes was total pity.

"Is there a lawyer in this town, sir?" she demanded.

"There are a couple," Barry said. Then, gently, he said, "But, ma'am, I talked with them both."

"I don't want to sound rude," Mary Sue said sweetly, "but you talked with them with limited information. As a slave-owner I have far different questions to pose."

When her husband started to balk she waved him to silence, rose, graciously thanked Barry for the meal, and went to arrange accommodations with Mrs. Harvey for herself and children.

Barry bade the remaining trio a calm goodnight and gazed quietly after the swaying bustle of DeeDee. He tried to picture her swimming naked with him and couldn't quite bring the thought into focus.

Colonel Herbert was relieved when Barry declined his offer to join him and his son in a pint at the tavern and jerked the boy soundly away when Harmon tried to persuade Barry.

"What'n the hell's yore problem?" Harmon scowled.

"Shut up! We got ourselves more trouble than this damn nigger business, boy!"

"I only thought—" he began, but his father interrupted harshly. "It would be the first time," Colonel Herbert growled. "Now, tell me how much money Mary Sue brought with her."

Harmon shrugged indifferently. "All she had, I reckon. Most went for boat passage up the river."

"Damn the woman," Herbert said flatly. "I only wanted her to bring along the best breeding stock. The old ones and children will only be a drain on our supplies. You and Pomeroy best see to sellin' off a batch tomorrow."

Harmon thought earnestly. His knowledge of the slave operation was exceedingly vague.

"Might be hard," he said at last. "Ain't seen hardly a plantation in this state."

"Gotta be done!"

"Y'all been gamblin' again?" Harmon demanded.

Herbert's brows knitted with his frowning. He made a helpless little gesture with his hands.

"What else's a man to do in this godforsaken place?"

"How much?" Harmon demanded impatiently.

"I'm owin', boy. Promised the man I'd get the money from Mary Sue when she arrived. We just gotta unload some of the blacks tomorrow. But don't be lettin' Mary Sue know what we are up to."

The next morning, Mary Sue dressed very carefully in her best gown and poke bonnet. With very little difficulty she found the office of Ralph Morrison, Attorney.

Wonderingly, the old man led the fashionable woman into his book-filled office and sank behind a paper-laden desk. There was no mistaking who she was; everyone in town had become aware of her the afternoon before. He feared he would be giving her the same free advice he had given Barry Fitzpatrick. A New Englander by birth, he had no sympathy for the slave system whatsoever.

"Your government," Mary Sue began flatly, "says I can't take my servants to the west, is that correct?"

"Not exactly," Morrison said. "Slaves and indentured servants are the case in point, ma'am."

Mary Sue's face brightened.

"But what if the servants are free people, sir?"

Morrison's thin face split into an enormous grin.

"Interesting point," he chuckled. "Can't see how the army could raise a fuss, in that case."

"They are like family, sir," Mary Sue said sadly. "I would wish everything to be quite legal and air-tight."

"Think deeply," he said gruffly. "You can't free them just to get around the law and then renege on it when you are in lawless country."

Mary Sue had been pondering that thought all night long. Try as she would, she could not shake the feeling that this was her only course of action. What good would it be to start anew unless she had the people to help her build? She could not take them along as slaves, but she never once questioned that they would not blindly follow her as free servants. They were children, no matter what their ages. And never once did it cross her mind to discuss the matter with Colonel Herbert. He was perhaps her biggest child of all. Making one of her characteristically swift decisions, she took a sheaf of papers from her purse and offered them to Morrison.

"These are the bills of sale on each slave that I own, Mr. Morrison."

"But, ma'am—" the lawyer started to protest. He got no further.

"I anticipate your comment and can save your breath. I am Colonel Herbert's second wife. Nothing of mine, including the slaves, was ever put into his name. Can you handle this matter for me?"

A few minutes later Mary Sue signed away her fortune in human flesh and was given a receipt for the bills of sale.

"Now," the lawyer said, "it is binding from this moment, although it will take my clerk a few days to draw up manumission papers for each person."

"And the government can't stop me now?" she demanded.

Morrison frowned.

"I think not," he said finally. "Although it has never been tried before. You also have to keep in mind that once you give them their manumission papers they are free to leave you and do as they wish."

"Rot," Mary Sue said. "They will still look to me for food and clothing and transportation. Nothing will really be that different." Then she rose and left the office, holding the receipt tenderly in her work-roughened hands. She was not about to let a stupid law stop her.

Colonel Herbert nearly stopped her by committing murder. If Aaron Pomeroy had been a minute later in arriving at the Herbert wagon he would have found the woman strangled to death. He had little trouble pulling the mountain of flesh away from her small body and tossing the man out into the dust. He would have jumped down and soundly thrashed the man, but with amazing agility Colonel Herbert scampered to an upright position and began running for town.

"Wha'da hell?" Harmon cried, coming on the run.

Mary Sue coughed and rubbed her throat. "It's all right, Harmon. I took your father by surprise. The only way we were going to be able to take the slaves was to free them. I did it this morning first thing."

Harmon and Aaron Pomeroy stared at each other in stunned disbelief. They had been since sun-up culling out the slaves they might be able to sell. Pomeroy had been furious upon hearing from Harmon that the Colonel had gambled away the money Mary Sue had been counting on. Now his fury was near to murderous rage. He didn't want to be the one to tell Mary Sue that her impulsive act could be their death knell.

"Harm," Mary Sue said, "give your father a chance to cool down and then you and Aaron go to him. In time he will see that I am right, but my fear at this moment is the money he has left from the New Orleans sale. I'll feel safer if it is in my keeping."

Both men knew that it was going to be a fool's errand, but Pomeroy was relishing an inner glow.

The woman had called him by his first name and with a note of respect in her voice. Now, more than ever, she was going to need a strong man around her and he was determined to be that man.

"Shit!" Harm spat, after his stepmother left them. "With no bill o' sale we can't sell a single damn nigger. The ole man ain't even got the fifty he owes the card shark at the tavern, let alone the money she's expectin' us to talk him outta. Wha'da we gonna do?"

Aaron Pomeroy put up with Harmon Herbert because he could feel superior around his simple-mindedness. He had heard from a Georgia trader that the Arabs bought white folk as slaves. He would have loved to sell the whole Herbert family, except for Mary Sue.

"First," he answered slowly, "we're gonna nose around and see if anyone wants to buy some black meat on the quiet, if you know what I mean."

"Not the wenches!" Harmon insisted. "We ain't about to sell a single wench."

"Don't fret yourself, boy," Aaron said. "You don't even know if they'll let you cut them now that they are gonna be free and I won't be able to bull-whip them into your bed. 'Sides, it's time fur you to start learnin' what a white one feels like. I wonder if yore ole man has learned if there is a whorehouse in this town."

They learned that there wasn't even before they went to Colonel Herbert's room at Harvey's boarding house. He wouldn't have been able to answer them even if he had known. He had tried to drown his rage from the whiskey jug and had passed out, face down, on the bed. Pomeroy would have loved to have held his massive skull deep into the pillow until he stopped moving forever.

Harmon slumped into a chair, the picture of dejection. Pomeroy, knowing Herbert to be a bland-faced liar, silently began to search the room for hidden money. He had never before seen five thousand dollars all together at one time and it boggled his mind that Herbert could have gambled such a sum away. He was being extremely quiet and cautious, because the walls were paper-thin and he could hear every movement that the person in the adjacent room was making. The noise began to intrigue him and he pressed his ear flat against the wall. When there was a knock at the next room's door, he motioned Harmon to total silence. It took the occupant so long to answer the door that a second rap came. Pomeroy smiled to himself at the sounds he detected.

That morning Barry had realized he had erred and that he had slightly more than a hundred dollars left. He had no intention of touching this last reserve, no matter how much Herbert might cry for his money back. Now, standing in Cornithwyeth's room, his face mottled with rage, he swore that he was being hoodwinked.

"Yesterday," he roared, "you told me your train was still a good fourteen days out of Liberty! And now I learn from an army scout that it's no more than three! But that's not what gets me, Cornithwyeth. You never once mentioned that you'd hired an Injun scout. Now I can see why you've been stalling me on a down payment. Why, you dirty, bloodsucking little leech, I've got a good mind to . . ."

Cornithwyeth's face was ashen with fear. He spread his hands wide.

"Mr. Fitzpatrick! Mr. Fitzpatrick!" he implored, "Control yourself! I told you the truth about their arrival as I knew it. I have nothing to gain by tricking you. My wife must have hired the scout for some reason or other."

Barry's big hands came down slowly to his sides. What Cornithwyeth was saying could be the truth. Why then was he being stalled on the money?

Cornithwyeth saw his advantage and pressed it.

"Mr. Fitzpatrick, it is true I have been reluctant to advance money until I could see the condition of the other trains. But for a very sound business reason, I can assure you. Our people will have nearly all new equipment and will not wish to dawdle along with the likes of what came into town yesterday. That was a disgrace. I feel justified, but am thankful that Major Warren is going to disallow them to go further. We can now discuss your fee."

Barry's face cleared, but a nagging doubt clung like a burr in his mind.

"Suppose," he said, "that losing the Herbert party forces the fee to go up. My expenses will stay the same, either way."

Cornithwyeth objected. "There has to be a limit, sir. The fee was high enough in the beginning. My people would have difficulty in meeting a new demand. I'm not sure who established your fee, Fitzpatrick, but they must not have been aware that twenty-five dollars is a man's entire wages for a month in the east."

Cornithwyeth hoped he had been convincing.

What he had not told Barry was that he was already charging each wagon eight times over what Barry was charging him and wanted to keep all the tidy profit for himself. He did not wish to pay for the loss of the Herbert wagons from these profits, any more than he wished to pay the Harvey's for board. Miserly in nature, he preferred eating at a local tavern, where a lunch was available for the price of a beer.

A suspicion that Cornithwyeth might be a swindler gnawed at Barry. Still, he could not afford to lose a hundred wagons before ever leaving Missouri.

"Price stands," he conceded. "When can I get some money?"

Cornithwyeth sighed. "Then that settles Herbert's hash."

"Not really. I understand from Lawyer Morrison that he is drawing up manumission papers for all the slaves."

Cornithwyeth looked at him in amazement.

"But you just said . . ." he spluttered.

"I said suppose. I've no idea what the colonel is up to. He may have the money. Even if he does, I don't think he has a chance in hell of ever getting those wagons ready to my satisfaction. But that doesn't concern you, Mr. Cornithwyeth. My demands for each wagon train party have been the same. You're overdue."

Cornithwyeth was flustered. "Naturally, but you must realize I do not keep such sums on my person. You may accompany me to the bank, but keep in mind that I do not intend to pay any more than ten percent of the total until I see the total rolling stock from the east."

Barry was agreeable. The advance would give him more than enough to resist Herbert's demands when they were made, and he suspected that they would be before the day was out. Faced with the loss of his slaves, he fully expected Herbert to turn tail and run.

Aaron Pomeroy waited until no further sound in the next room or hallway indicated that Cornithwyeth had gone. He tried to keep his excitement masked as he turned back to Harmon.

"Boy," he drawled, pulling every coin he possessed from his trouser pocket, "git yourself as quick as you can down to that mercantile store. We got ourselves a heapin' need for as many harness rings and washers you can buy for this amount. Hush! Don't go askin' foolish questions that'd get yah in trouble later. Move!"

Pomeroy took time to see how deep was Herbert's drunken stupor and to watch through the window Harmon's race down the street. Then he went into the hall. At Cornithwyeth's room, he slipped his Bowie knife between the door and jamb; three deft strokes brought the lock bolt back and gave him entry. He closed the door softly and quickly familiarized himself with the room. Then he closed his eyes and tried to recreate the sounds he had heard through the wall. He had listened well. He was able to walk directly to the place where Bradford Cornithwyeth had hidden the gold coins he had heard him desperately scrape off the table at Barry's knock.

Aaron found four leather pouches of money, a mind-numbing store of twenty, fifty and hundred dollar pieces that Cornithwyeth had not trusted to a bank. To Aaron, who had never stolen more than a turkey before, taking it all was fraught with danger. He was aware of the figure Colonel Herbert should have had, could not calculate what he must have paid Fitzpatrick, and finally took a handful from each pouch and stuffed them into his pockets.

He was weak from mental exhaustion by the time Harmon came back to Colonel Herbert's room. Harmon's eyes widened at the heaps of gold coins he saw deposited on the bureau top.

"Gimme," Aaron demanded and began to fill his pockets with equal handful amounts of washers to compensate for the stolen gold. "Count it! I ain't got much time!"

Never again did Aaron Pomeroy want his heart to beat that fast. Back in Cornithwyeth's room, it seemed to take an eternity to put the washers in the bottom of the pouches and cover them with gold coins. For a moment his mind blanked out and he grew frantic trying to remember where the pouches had been hidden. He recalled the spot at the moment of his greatest fear, when he heard footsteps approaching in the hallway outside. Fortunately, the footsteps passed. Relieved of his agony, he replaced the pouches and hurried back to Colonel Herbert's room.

Harmon was counting the stolen money.

"How much?" Aaron demanded.

Harmon gulped. "Jeeesus! Thirty-three hundred dollars!"

Pomeroy scowled. "Goddamn me fur bein' a stupid sonofabitch! My fault, fur not bein' able to count! Ah gotta go back, Harm!"

"Where—" Harm gasped. "Where'd it come from?"

"I—I don't want you knowin', boy," Aaron faltered. "Is there enough there for your maw ta do good with?"

"Should be," Harm panted.

"We can't let her know where it came from."

"What—what of the ole man?" Harm demanded.

"Oh, corn hole the bastard!" Aaron groaned. "Think, damnit, think!"

"Aaron," Harmon whispered. "I'm scared. All I can think is—"

"Yes?" Pomeroy urged gently.

"We can't let either one know the real truth," Harmon said miserably.

Pomeroy nodded. "Agreed. But how do we explain the money?"

"We'll make her believe that this was all the money we found after he paid Fitzpatrick and gambled some away. That'll sound honest to her and still make her mad as hell at him fur a few days. We tell him this is all the money she has left from Alabamy and she's ready to skin him for losin' the rest. He'll keep his distance."

"And can you keep your silence?" Pomeroy whispered.

They stared at each other like statues, their eyes cold, a long forgotten challenge between them rekindled.

"You figure that out for yourself," Harmon said mockingly.

It was quiet in the room after Pomeroy had silently re-pocketed the money and left. So still that Harmon could hear the drunken note of his father's breathing. Never before had he felt hatred as strong as he felt for the man who had just left and the one still with him. He somehow knew, in that strange moment, that a time would come when events would force him to kill one or the other of them, or perhaps both. He never once considered that they might have the opportunity to kill him first.

Jessie Fremont's admiration for Mary Sue Herbert's decision to free her slaves was instantaneous.

"Oh, Barry," she cried, "use a bit of common sense. You're obviously not aware of slave prices. Do you have the foggiest idea of what she has signed away with a single stroke of a pen?"

"I'm not sure I really want to know."

Jessie's Benton temper flared. "Well," she snapped, "I'm going to tell you whether you care to listen or not. I am not for the slave system, but I'm well aware of what a person in her circumstances has invested and can't really afford to lose. Had she wished she could have sold each and everyone of those individual black souls for three, five, even a thousand dollars. Think on that sum times the amount of slaves she has out in those wagons. A fortune greater than you or I could ever imagine. And yet, this evening she came to you with the remainder of your payment, asked for a little help and you sat there mute and silent. I thought I was beginning to know you, but I guess I was grossly mistaken. You're beginning to sound like my father to me, able to speak out of both sides of your mouth at the same time."

"They'll never be ready," Barry said sourly.

Jessie hesitated a moment, then slowly put out

her hand. "I would rather see people of her courageous spirit inhabit the new west than people like Cornithwyeth. Mark my words, you'll have more trouble with that man and his people than you will with a woman like Mrs. Herbert. Help her, Barry, please."

Barry wouldn't have minded helping Mary Sue Herbert as a person. It was the overall situation he regarded as hopeless. And events that might did little more than re-enforce his feelings of despair. Bradford Cornithwyeth made sure that the central topic of conversation in the tavern was the freeing of the Herbert slaves. Those who owned slaves looked upon the act as mad and feared the knowledge getting to their own slaves' ears. Cornithwyeth stayed in the tavern throughout the afternoon and evening, amazing the proprietor by buying mugs of beer for those who would sit and listen to his strident voice.

"I've been poor too long, my friends," he said. "I'm sorry for those poor black devils, but they'll cause more trouble free than slave. I think it's a ruse on Herbert's part. He's setting them free and will take only the best. The rest you are going to get stuck with right here and they'll demand to work for a wage. I say they should be chased back east before that happens."

By ten o'clock enough beer had flowed and enough words had been spoken to bring forth action. Twenty men were willing to follow Cornithwyeth, armed with rifles, clubs and revolvers.

Cornithwyeth marched his drunken crew out to the Herberts' campsite, ignoring the rain that had been falling for hours.

"We want you to move out," he called out to

the blacks there. "Don't want a one of you left by morning."

The blacks huddled together under their wagons. The wind whipped the rain down in gusts, leaving them few places for protection. Miss Mary Sue was not there to tell them what to do and so they wisely did nothing. One man left his shelter and sped to Aaron Pomeroy's wagon. Aaron was already awake and going to rouse Harmon. He set the man back to tell the slaves to come out and stand together. He did not tell them to arm themselves, but survival instincts made them pick up stones and pieces of wood.

"Look who's behind it," Aaron growled, when he had Harmon out of the wagon.

"Because of . . . ?"

"Shut up! Let him do the talking."

As Cornithwyeth's vigilantes moved forward, the slaves began to gather. Cornithwyeth could see that his group was outnumbered, but had no suspicion that the slaves were armed. He wanted only to scare and scatter them.

Suddenly, as they approached, a slave threw a rock. It struck a farmer on the head, felling him. Immediately the air was filled with flying objects.

"Don't shoot!" Cornithwyeth roared at his men. He might as well have addressed the wind. Revolver fire cracked in the rain, then riflets. Blacks fell sprawling in the mud, amidst the angered screams and shouts of their fellows. As the fallen slaves bled and moaned, the rest charged Cornithwyeth's men en masse.

Aaron and Harmon swore and started running toward the fray, in the vain hope of saving the Herbert chattels from further damage. Before they could reach it, the issue was decided. In their maddened surge, the blacks wrested the whites' arms from them. Though a few whites were able to fire again, shooting down other blacks, they too were quickly overwhelmed. Weaponless, they ran off zigzagging through the rain while the slaves knelt and fired ineptly with the captured guns. Not a shot hit its fleeing target.

Aaron saw Cornithwyeth fleeing with the others. He raced after him, gaining steadily. He'd almost caught up with him when Cornithwyeth's body seemed to leap into the air, spin like a puppet on a string and come crashing down into a mudhole. Aaron turned and saw Harmon with a rifle at his shoulder. He'd grabbed it from a slave and was still aiming it. For a moment Aaron was sure he was to be Harmon's next target. But then Harmon lowered the rifle, a peculiar grin crossing his face.

They woke Barry a little after eleven. The town was crying for revenge. The Herbert slaves were being blamed for the incident and there was a demand for lynchings, even though Bradford Cornithwyeth was the only white who had suffered a serious wound.

Twenty-seven slaves had been massacred. The Herbert family alone was seeing to the needs of the survivors.

Throughout the night Barry's concern centered on Cornithwyeth. The man had to live, he felt, to avoid the lynchings and further disasters. Aaron Pomeroy had carried him into town and left him with Dr. Fowles. The young doctor expressed little hope for Cornithwyeth's survival; the bullet, he pointed out, was lodged against the man's spine. Barry offered the services of Doc Freitag, whose aid Fowles at first rejected. Near dawn the old sawbones removed the bullet. But even he gave the man little hope.

In the iron grate at the Fremont house, the fire burned feebly, and the room was cold. Barry stood by the window looking out into the leaden dawn through the thick swirl of rain. The wagon-train enterprise seemed doomed. Dreams were ending—Fremont's, Jim Bridger's, and Barry's too. He had never felt more discouraged.

He was aware, after a time, that someone was knocking at his door. He roused himself and went to open it. Major Warren stood before him in the rain.

"Come in," Barry growled.

"Thank you," Warren said. He strode into the room and stood there looking at Barry.

"I came to tell you that you have won," he said. "We cannot tolerate a second incident like last night's. Tomorrow army rafts will be available for you to get your people across the river. I want you to know I do not approve of you moving blacks west. I simply do not want to be forced to order my troops to fire on whites to save them."

Barry did not answer.

Warren continued. "I've heard that Cornith-wyeth stirred up the insurrection. I cannot accept such action, either. I will keep troops in town until you have your train moving."

"Thank you," Barry mumbled.

"I feel sorry for you," Major Warren said. "You mean well, but last night is only a taste of

what lies ahead. If the rest of Cornithwyeth's
people are like him, you have your work in store
for you."

He left. The fire leaped and flared as the door
opened and closed behind him.

Alone, Barry sat and stretched out before the
fire. He had difficulty assimilating the turn of
events. He had thought he wouldn't be able to
move on. Now it appeared he was being *shoved*
on—by the army.

When Jessie Fremont awoke and joined him
for breakfast, he didn't discuss his plans for the
day with her. But he already had them firmly in
mind.

9

When Barry rode past Harvey's boarding house, Colonel Herbert came out and waved him to a stop.

"I am not about to cross the river," Herbert said. "Do what you wish with the niggers, but I want my money back."

"Too late," Barry said gruffly. "Your wife has already offered me the second half of the payment."

"She hasn't the right to do that," Herbert said savagely. "I wish nothing more than to leave the damn savages here and take my family back south!"

"That might be dangerous," Barry said. "The people are in an ugly mood."

"I'll chance it," Herbert answered. He turned back into the boarding house.

Barry spent the next hour helping the blacks bury their dead. They were sullen, he noted, but quiet, as if resigned to their losses and resigned too to being helplessly far from any place they could call home. He had a sinking feeling that the Herberts might already have abandoned their former slaves. Not even the overseer was to be found.

Presuming on an authority he did not actually possess, Barry ordered the black men to prepare the teams and wagons for the trip to the river. He was met with slow, sullen stares of resistance, until finally Mary Sue, her children and overseer did arrive.

Barry noticed a change in Mary Sue. She had donned a gray cotton work dress as though she were back on the plantation and she sat her horse confidently. She asked the slaves to gather around and then jumped to the tail gate of a wagon to face them.

"My people," she said, "what happened here last night will cause me sorrow all my life. I didn't want anyone hurt. I wanted only to give you freedom so that we would be able to cross the river. Ask Fitzpatrick here!"

Barry nodded.

"But now," Mary Sue went on quietly, "they want us to leave here. I've been all morning trying to decide what to do. The lawyer says I can't give you orders. You are free. You can do as you please."

"Miz MarSue," an old black man broke in, "wat am ya'all gonna do?"

"Me?" Mary Sue said, a note of anger creeping

into her voice. "Well, I sure can't go back to Alabama, Amos. That land is lost to us. And they'd figure a way of making you a slave again if you return."

The slaves looked puzzled, but, to Barry's great relief, much less hostile.

It was the old man who answered his own question.

"We'd best go wid ya'all, Miz MarSue. Ya'all gonna have need ob us."

"Exactly! I'm happy you see it that way. Separated we will all be lost. Together, we can be just like we were on the plantation. That's the way we should have been on the whole trip, but change frightened me as much as it has you. Let's stop being afraid!"

She had them now. These were basic facts and they knew it. Mary Sue had been the only constant in the slaves' misery-laden lives and they were not about to desert her.

Barry was impressed with the miracle she had worked with words, but still doubted that the Herberts would be ready to leave on time. The Cornithwyeth party was expected in three days, and he calculated that the Tedder party would arrive before then, both groups pushing him to form up and depart within a week. There was no way, as he saw it, that the Herbert train could be ready in less than a month.

He had not counted upon Mary Sue's determination. Throughout the day Barry stayed on the eastern bank, supervising the loading of the wagons onto the rafts and keeping a constant flow moving across the river. He was not used to working with blacks, but because he seemed to be in special favor with Mary Sue, they jumped as his commands faster than had Aaron Pomeroy been in there cracking his whip.

In the afternoon, when he rode across with the last rafted wagon, he was witness to an astonishing sight. The canvas tops had been removed from each wagon and tents had been made of them. A dozen wagons were on their sides. Their wheels and axles had been removed and repair work had begun. Mary Sue came to greet him, her eyes bright with happy tears.

"Aren't they magnificent, Mr. Fitzpatrick?" she cried. "We had all but forgotten that a plantation is a town unto itself. My family had lived on that land for nearly . . ." She laughed. "Bringing up the past is rather foolish of me, isn't it? We are in the present. When we departed I told them to bring what they thought necessary." She laughed again. "They did! But what was necessary to them! The blacksmith brought his anvil, the carpenters their tools and I could rattle on and on."

"You love them, don't you?" Barry smiled.

Mary Sue started, looked around, then turned back with her cheeks a deep scarlet.

"Why yes," she said, embarrassed. "I never had to think of it in that way, Mr. Fitzpatrick, but yes, I do love them."

Seeing Mary Sue Herbert's spirit helped to renew Barry's vitality in the project. Daily he would see to it that barges and rafts would be available to ferry across the supplies she would order and pay for in advance. No longer did the blacks seem sullen and starved to him. Wagon after wagon was repaired by them and put in prime condition. The goods that had been brought from Alabama were carefully gone over, considered, and the worthless turned into campfire material. Because the smokehouse meats were already turning rancid, steers were purchased, slaughtered and cured to make jerky. The field hands, without other skills, foraged the countryside for spring greens. No portion of an animal or vegetable root was cast aside. Barry's stomach at first rebelled at the gelatin substance made from cows' innards and giblets, until he found that 'head cheese' was as tasty as jerky and far easier to eat.

In those days Barry came to look upon the Herbert slaves as he did some likeable Indian tribes he knew. They were industrious, wasted nothing and were committed only to the day that they could see dawning around them. Yesterday was a myth left to old men to muse about; tomorrow was a vague promise that might never come.

With each passing day he began to create excuses to stay with them on their side of the river.

"What's in those?" he asked, pointing to several large wicker baskets stacked to the side.

Before the black woman he had asked could answer, Harmon Herbert answered for her.

Harmon had first been assigned to follow Barry so as to learn what he might know or suspect about the Cornithwyeth robbery, which still had not been reported. But Barry had soon puzzled Harmon. Here was a man as arrogant as his father but without apparent malice. He was forceful, like Aaron Pomeroy, but he was neither sadistic nor cruel. Harmon had never met a man like Barry.

To him, Barry was a paradox. He couldn't stay away from the man. He wanted to taunt and test him to see what made him tick.

"Corn," he smirked, "what in hell do you think?"

Barry said nothing for a long moment. He had a sense of what Harmon was about. More than that, he had observed Harmon's vicious treatment of the blacks. Until he took full command of the train he couldn't order him to stop these practices. He turned to Harmon finally and said quietly, "I think taking corn might be a waste of space."

When Harmon started to protest, Barry motioned him away from the black woman's ears.

"You don't need to tell anyone I said this," he whispered, "but that corn on the husk is taking up twenty times the space in the baskets that ground meal would. You might make such a suggestion."

Harmon eyed him suspiciously and then grinned. "Might do that." Then he thought he should do a favor in kind. "Ya'all stayin' the night?"

"Might."

"Then I'm aimin' to fix y'all up with a real hot black pussy. What a hell of a child we could get out of a stud like you."

Barry only nodded; he was a bit too stunned to speak.

Aaron Pomeroy, nearby, did not need to hear what the two men were talking about. He sensed it, and it infuriated him. More and more he had seen Mary Sue turn to Fitzpatrick for advice. Now Harmon was playing up to him. Aaron was jealous and unsure of how to handle the feeling. He prayed for Barry to make the kind of mistake that would give him an excuse to kill him.

For several days it had been unseasonably hot. The rise in the river from spring run-off went unnoticed. Late in the day Barry decided that the easiest way to avoid Harmon's invitation was to go back and spend the night in Independence. But before he could even leave camp the deluge came. All the horizon-to-horizon clouds seemed to break open at once. Within minutes the Missouri began to leave its banks and snake over the land. Its backwaters rushed up the Kansas River, only to be met by greater amounts of water surging down.

In a matter of minutes the campsite turned into a lake. Tents were evacuated. One after another wagons were rolled to higher ground. As the sky continued to darken, some of the superstitious blacks began to moan and chant.

Then a scream pierced the eerie atmosphere. It was Mary Sue, off some distance from Barry, and she was wailing, "DeeDee! It's DeeDee! She's asleep in that wagon! In the river! Oh, God!"

Barry looked up. One of the wagons that hadn't been moved in time was now fifty yards offshore, caught in a raging torrent that was swirling it like a top.

Swearing, Barry leaped to his feet, kicked off his moccasins, ran to the river's edge and dove. He came up spluttering, feeling the icy water seep through his buckskins, sensing the tug of the current as it spun him in circles and then dragged him under. He fought to the surface, gasping for breath. Battling the current just to stay afloat, he

searched for the wagon and found it. Then, putting his head down, he set out towards it with
strong, powerful overhand strokes. Lifting his
head to breathe he saw a fallen small tree come
sailing by him from the rear. He grasped at its
branches and was towed along for a few yards,
giving his lungs a chance to refill. An elongated
lightning flash gave him an instant image of the
wagon, now closer, being sucked beneath the
surface of the flood, then rising like a brig on an
ocean swell. He let go of the branch and started
swimming again.

Then a miracle happened. As Barry's lungs
came near to bursting again from his efforts, the
wagon swirled by the current, made a complete
turnabout in the middle of the river and started
heading back towards him and the shore. At first
Barry thought his benumbed brain was playing an
ironic trick on him. Then, when he realized what
was happening, he struck out even more power-
fully, with renewed hope.

When he was within a few yards of the now-
bobbing wagon, he saw DeeDee Herbert crawl
out of it to the driver's seat. He tried to shout to
her, letting her know he was there, but his voice
was lost in the rush of wind and water.

Thinking herself alone, DeeDee pulled herself
upright, holding on desperately to the first arched
rung of the canopy frame. She could not swim.
But the wagon was going under, she felt, and she
prayed that somehow she would get to shore on
her own and with God's help. She inched to the
edge of the wagon and began to let herself down
into the water. It was like trying to hold her feet

on a moving platform. By the time she was in as
far as her waist her body was streaming away
from the wagon like a limp rag. Terrified, grabbing at the wagon tongue, she tried to haul herself back to the wagon, then realized how weak
she was. Her muscles trembled with the impossible effort. She couldn't hold on. She let go.

She was below the surface and choking to
death when Barry's hand closed around her arm.
She fought him, sensing only another alien force
trying to drown her. Barry thrashed with her. She
got her head above water momentarily and
screamed in panic. Her eyes were glazed with
horror, as if she were looking into an abyss rather
than into the face of another human being. Hold-
her arm only, Barry kicked himself upwards as
far as he could. With one arm free of the current,
he slapped her with all his might, full in the face.
Her eyes looked shocked. They they focused; she
saw him. "Go limp!" Barry shouted. "Limp!" She
did what she could to comply. Barry spun her
around on her back. He cupped her chin and
pulled her along, inch by inch, wave by wave,
towards shore.

But the rescue had taken its toll on DeeDee.
By the time Barry had reached a muddy bottom
he could stand on, she was half-insane with fear
again. She struggled to get free. He did not let
her go, for he felt the water was still too deep
for her. She turned and bit hard on his forearm.

"DeeDee, you damn fool!" But he'd released
her and she was gone, flailing ahead until she
could stand, then racing up the bank and disappearing into a grove of trees.

Cursing, Barry strode through the water and followed her. He was tired, drained emotionally as well, but felt a need to make sure the girl was all right. Ahead of him through the trees, he caught a brief glimpse of her. He began to run, splashing through the underbrush in pursuit. He ran some fifty yards calling her name, then stopped. DeeDee hadn't answered and was nowhere to be seen.

Barry walked unsteadily to a log and sat down. Where was he? Looking back through the trees at the shoreline, he gathered that the current had swept them about two miles downriver from the campsite. He would have to walk back, but he was dog-tired now. He lowered his head into his arms, closed his eyes and sat that way for a long time. Only when he heard the snap of a twig did he become somewhat alert again. He lifted his head, his fatigued eyes bare slits, and saw DeeDee peering at him from behind a tree. Her face was caked with drying mud. Her eyes were not the haughty and seductive eyes of Dahlia Dee Herbert. They were the eyes of a frightened animal.

Barry said softly, "I'm sorry that I scared you, Miss Herbert. It was the only way I knew to help you. I'm Barry Fitzpatrick."

DeeDee let out a sobbing cry. Barry jumped up as she ran forward, catching her in his outstretched arms. She didn't speak a word of her gratitude, if gratitude was what she felt. More than gratitude; it was perhaps a passion for life born of her close touch with death. Almost in desperation, DeeDee wrapped her arms about his neck and pulled his head down so she could hungrily kiss his eyes, his cheeks, his mouth. Once, after that first dinner in Independence, DeeDee had determined this man to be hers. Now he was more than an object of desire; he was her savior. She didn't care that the two of them were muddied and wet; she wanted him to be her very first man and at that very moment.

Sex with DeeDee was the furthest thing from Barry's mind, but, sensing her feelings, he gave what he could of himself. He felt sorry for what she'd been through and he felt tenderly towards her—towards her youth and her present emotional state. He kissed her, brushing his lips against her forehead. She relaxed in his arms, with a secret smile. Speaking soothingly, he smoothed back her hair and cleaned her face with his handkerchief. DeeDee closed her eyes in anticipation of his next kiss. After a moment, she felt herself being lifted into his arms. He's taking me to a dry, safe place, she thought drowsily. She moved so that her head lay against his wide shoulder. She could feel his breath upon her neck. She wanted to taste his lips again. She was sure she would, soon.

"We have to get you back to camp now, Dee-Dee," Barry said gently. "They'll be worried about you."

Disappointment began to gnaw at DeeDee.

He started off through the woods, carrying her. She lay in his arms, her feelings becoming so entangled that she could not sort them out. He had saved her from drowning, yes. But couldn't he see how empty she had become, how drained of life by her fears? She needed him to lay her on the ground, cover her body with his, pump and thrust excitement and life into her again. He wasn't doing it. Why not? Wasn't she beautiful? Everyone said she was. A sense of deprivation, then of resentment, grew in her. She raged at Barry. She would have him. Nothing could stop her.

Barry strode on wearily, unaware of the seething emotions of the girl who lay in his arms. He had it in mind that the campsite lay a bit to the east rather than due north and he slanted off in what he hoped was the right direction. He could not encourage DeeDee to walk, except for short spells; she complained of a cramp in her leg, though to him she appeared more paralyzed by dread than anything else. One way or the other, he had to carry her most of the way and it took him well over two hours to reach the camps.

Mary Sue, who had seen Barry reach DeeDee in the river but had lost sight of them afterwards, had lit beacon fires, hoping against hope that her stepdaughter had not drowned and would have these means of finding her. When she saw DeeDee and Barry come from the woods, she let out a gasp of joy and ran to meet them, followed by Harmon and Aaron Pomeroy.

DeeDee, seeing her, struggled free from Barry and fell into her arms, sobbing and wailing.

"Hush, child," Mary Sue soothed, hugging her tight. "It's over now. Oh, thanks be to Mr. Fitzpatrick for saving you!"

DeeDee said something that astonished Barry.

"Ain't all he done to me," she bawled.

He stood there disbelievingly. There was a moment of stunned silence as Harmon and Pomeroy stared at him. There was no mistaking DeeDee's implication.

"I—I—" Barry stammered.

"Wha'd yah do to her?" Pomeroy demanded. Contemptuously ignoring DeeDee, his hatred for Barry glowed in his eyes.

"Pomeroy!" Mary Sue snapped. "I will handle this! Take some men and see if you can rescue the wagon."

"But he did kiss me and do it, mama!" DeeDee wailed.

Mary Sue had to step between Pomeroy and Barry. With the same look she warned Barry to silence and told Pomeroy to do as he was told. She felt her nerves could not tolerate more turmoil and she was suddenly very suspicious of the accusation. Any time Dahlia Dee started calling her mama her guard automatically came up.

"Harmon," she said quietly, "take your sister and find her some dry clothing. I'll speak with her later. Mr. Fitzpatrick, an army messenger arrived about an hour ago. Two of your trains have arrived in Kansas City. You'll find the messenger in the camp waiting for you. Pomeroy, move! Amos, let's see to getting some breakfast started around here."

Barry watched them all go, his gaze on DeeDee the longest. Then, shaking his head in continued puzzlement, he walked with Mary Sue towards the waiting messenger.

Off by themselves, Harmon and DeeDee discussed her experience, but in a truer light.

"Did he? Did he really?" Harmon whispered, chuckling.

"Don't be an ass!" DeeDee snapped. "It's because he didn't. But who's to know?"

"Know," he bellowed. "Mary Sue'll know when she takes a look up you 'n see's ya'all ain't been touched yet."

DeeDee stopped and stared at him wide-eyed. "She'll do that? If you're funning me, Harmon Herbert, I'll whop you one."

"Hell, ya'all sure are dumb if'n yah don't know lookin' at your hole's the first thing she's gonna do."

She pursed her lips. "Then you gotta help me."

"How?"

"You gotta poke me with your thing to make it look like he poked me with his."

He stared at her. "You're sick, DeeDee. Even a dumbass nigger knows betta than to poke his own sista."

DeeDee's eyes narrowed. "Then I'll just go get me a big black stud to do it to me."

"Over my dead body," he snarled. "Let me catch ya'all with a nigger stud and I'll kill yah."

"Why," she insinuated, "is it any different than you bedding a nigger wench?"

Harmon shook his head. "You are sick and stupid, gal. It ain't the same thing at all. Ever'-body know that. Now, ya'all better start thinkin' up a new story to be tellin' Mary Sue, cause I ain't helpin' yah no way. And yah better figure on Fitzpatrick givin' yah a wide berth from now on."

"Why?" she asked innocently.

"Dahlia Dee, ya'all are sick, stupid and *blind!* You don't even know when you embarrass a person. He wouldn't poke yah now if'n yah was the last pussy left on earth."

DeeDee went into an even deeper sulk than she'd been in before. She still didn't feel defeated, only cheated.

10

Swearing under his breath, Barry met with the army messenger. He still felt ashamed of himself for letting DeeDee put him in the position she had. She had a good deal of the spoiled brat in her and he should have known better. He was thankful for Mary Sue's wisdom in the matter.

The messenger told him that two of Barry's trains had crossed to Kansas City from a point on the Kansas River a few miles to the north. Major Warren wanted Barry to get there fast. They could wait until dawn, the messenger said, to allow some time for the weather to clear up and for Barry to rest. But he had two horses ready and they'd have to ride at daybreak.

"What's Warren's all-fired hurry?" Barry demanded.

"Search me, sir. They ferried one of your trains

across all of yesterday and were planning to start on the second this morning. I figure they've done it by now since there was no flooding up there. Major just said get you there fast."

Much good it'll do me to worry, Barry thought grimly. But it puzzled him why the trains would cross at Kansas City rather than come to Independence.

Next morning, after crossing the river and galloping up a rise, the messenger pointed down to a valley. "There's the encampment of the first train."

The sight pushed the Herbert incident from Barry's mind. This is how he'd hoped an incoming wagon train would look. He counted over forty white-topped schooners neatly circled, with campfires ablaze. Outriders lazily watched the cattle and horses graze on the lush grass. The ring of a hammer on wheel-metal mingled with the cries of children at play. Barry and the messenger had been spotted and were conveyed down by a rider from the encampment.

"Who is the captain of the train?"

Howard Tedder's rangy face broke into a broad grin. "Meself. I'm Tedder from Tennessee. You Fitzpatrick?"

"Sure am. Glad to see you, Mr. Tedder. Your party's a mite larger than first reported."

"Middling," Tedder grinned, "just middling." Then he sobered. "Hope that ain't no problem."

"No problem," Barry laughed. "Looks like a handsome group."

Tedder beamed. He had amazed even himself with the ease of the journey and everyone's acceptance of his leadership. "Come along and I'll introduce you and show you the rigs."

"How about the major?" the messenger insisted. "Is he here?"

"Oh," Howard chuckled, "near plumb furgot, what with all the orders he flies off with. He's up at the ferry crossing and wants ta know when Fitzpatrick git here, all right."

The major's absence suited Barry. He first wanted to see and assess the encampment for himself. He was grateful when the first person he met promptly stuck a tin cup of steaming coffee in his hand.

"Thank you kindly, ma'am."

Lydia Tedder's instincts told her she could have as much faith in Barry as she had in her husband.

"Would you care to sup with us tonight, Mr. Fitzpatrick?"

"Pleasure, ma'am, if you call me Barry."

"All right," she said, "and I am Lydia." Then she smiled lovingly at her husband. "But some folk just don't cotton to their first name."

Howard groused. "Tedder's good enough, Barry."

Tedder was good enough for Barry, too. They went from wagon to wagon for introductions and an inspection. The man had backwoods common sense that appealed to the young mountain man.

"Now I've never heard tell of that," Barry exclaimed, watching Nazareth Tedder go from wheel to wheel with a nasty looking bucket and a cloth-wrapped stick. "What's he smearing on there?"

"Bear grease," Tedder proudly instructed. "Don't let a wagon roll each day until each hub gets a splash of the goo. Hav'ta find something else when we run out."

Barry was delighted to see that Tedder had undercoated the wagons with pine pitch so that in fording rivers the wagon beds would be watertight and thus be in less danger of rotting.

"Now," Tedder said, a little grimly, "before we come to this next group I'd best say a piece. The woman is a lady. Real English toff type. Ain't givin' me any trouble, herself, but her people are a mite strange. Tenant farmers, she calls 'em, but ain't a one of them my boys didn't have to teach, up to harnassin' their team 'n wagon. Cold types that don't mix much. But I ain't much of a mixer meself. Oh, by the by, Lady Pamela's got herself a young'un. Pretty mite, but scared ta death of her maw or sumptin' or t'other."

After the introductions to the nineteen English farm families Barry felt he might have initial trouble in distinguishing one from the other. The men were all in their early to mid thirties, polite and yet cool. They were almost Quakerish in their simple garb. Their women seemed dour and went unintroduced. Whereas the children from the rest of the families were off yelling and laughing in play, the English children sat docile and vacant-eyed.

Lady Pamela Buttle-Jones, however, was definitely not cut from the same mold. Barry's first surprise came in viewing the landau carriage and the two men laboriously polishing and waxing its already brilliant siding.

"They always dress in red?" he asked.

"Nope," Tedder chuckled. "They got black, blue and pea-green uniforms as well, 'pending upon what the lady wears. Driver's kind of closed-mouth old weasel named Hufford. Lad's his son, Donald. Ain't a bad chap."

Donald was slim and blond, with hair not two shades darker than his father's pure white. He straightened up as they approached, with a motion like a startled faun. Then he stood very still studying Barry through golden lashes that seemed too long for a man's. Barry had an impression of effeminacy which did not sit well with him, given the arduous journey they were to make.

"Sorry to trouble you, sir," young Hufford said to Tedder. "But that blacksmith bloke in Memphis was a bloody fool. I'll be a while reshoeing the carriage horses. Get to it as soon as I can."

Barry, revising his impression, grinned. The young man's hands, he saw now, were strong and calloused. As long as he worked as eagerly as he obviously was working now, it didn't much matter what he looked like.

Tedder nodded. "Donald, this here's our guide. Barry Fitzpatrick. Would yah mind tellin' the lady he's here?"

Donald wiped his hands, shook hands with Barry and left with the message.

"Told the lady, Barry, that it was damn foolish to take this fancy rig, but comfort am comfort, I guess," Tedder said, shugging. "It's what she wanted."

Barry squatted down on a knee and examined the landau's undercarriage.

"Mighty low," he mused. "We won't be having roads from here on. How's her springs?"

Old Hufford glared as though he had been personally insulted. "Finest!" he snapped.

Barry laughed. "I can sure see that, sir. Right handsome way they've put those lengths of metal together. But my fear is that the wheels are too low and too narrow. Had any trouble with them?"

Hufford nodded. Apparently he didn't want to clarify the trouble, but his son, returning, did.

"Milady will be with you shortly," Donald said. "And yes, we have had some trouble with bottoming out."

"Mmm." Barry mused. "Troubles only starting then. Hit a couple of bad ruts and you'll not only break some wheels but tear those springs right out."

"Can hardly leave it behind," Hufford objected.

"I'm not suggestin' that, either."

"What is it you are suggesting, sir?" a woman's voice said.

The soft-spoken question turned Barry about. He was looking at Lady Pamela Buttle-Jones. The woman, alerted by Donald, had put on a dress of blue velvet that marvelously matched the blue of her eyes. She was strikingly lovely, Barry saw, by no means old—she was possibly still in her thirties —but richly mature-looking. Her cheeks were flushed and rosy, her eyes danced with adventure. Her lips were full and coral pink. When she smiled, as she did now, those lips appeared even warmer, more inviting.

"You certainly fit the part of a guide, Mr. Fitzpatrick, but are you an expert wagoner to boot?"

Barry flushed. She wasn't so much jeering at him as holding him in suspension with her voice, her smile, her look of cool interest in what he had to say. But it was her extreme beauty that was holding him, too. Unlike Jessie Fremont, hers was a cultured beauty, the kind he had never seen before.

"Ma'am," he said slowly, gazing at her. "It's just common sense. Be lots better for the wagons if you fitted them with new hubs to take regular wagon wheels."

"Really," Lady Buttle-Jones exclaimed. She looked at her coachman for confirmation. Old Hufford shrugged noncommittally.

"Fact is, we were advised against doing that in Memphis, milady," Tedder said. "Man said it wouldn't work."

"In my opinion," Donald Hufford said, "the man was too lazy to tackle the job."

"Well," Lady Pamela crooned, "now we have still another opinion. Mr. Fitzpatrick?"

Barry was being faced with his first command decision. "The carriage won't make it this way," he said shortly.

Lady Pamela's smile was suddenly acidly cold. "Which leaves us exactly nowhere."

Tedder grimaced as he saw the lady's change of expression. The guide was getting the same treatment he had undergone for weeks. She was sweetness and light when she wanted something and sour apples when she couldn't have her way. He was thankful that she was now Barry's responsibility.

"No," Barry drawled, "not exactly nowhere, ma'am. If your men could take the rig five miles

south to the Herbert camp, we've a fine blacksmith with that train. Shouldn't take him more'n
a day to fix it up. It'll ride comfortable enough
when he gets through."

"Excellent!" Lady Pamela smiled. "Hufford,
see to it!" Without further comment she started
to turn away. Immediately, she turned back. "I
dine with my daughter at seven, Mr. Fitzpatrick.
Please join us."

Barry gulped. He was now sorry that he had
been so quick to accept Lydia Tedder's invitation.

"Sorry," he stammered, "but I'm expected else-
where."

Lady Pamela nodded, as though he had just
closed the door to any further invitations. She
coolly walked away.

As far as Howard Tedder was concerned,
Barry had shown himself to be a good measure
of a man. He was proud to see that the guide
had not been cowered into changing his mind.
Old Hufford, too, was impressed; though he had
not liked Americans since he had faced them as
a British soldier in 1812, he had to admire common sense and decisiveness in any man.

"I say," Donald Hufford laughed, "you're all
right, Mr. Fitzpatrick. I thought the job could
be done, just couldn't get 'em to believe me."

"Boy," his father said impatiently, "don't prat-
tle. What's to be done, sir?"

Barry found out quickly that Hufford, once he
stopped kowtowing to Lady Pamela, had a razor
sharp mind. He listened attentively to Barry,
added some excellent suggestions of his own and
prepared to depart with the rig at once. Barry
stored away his impressions of the man's abilities

and intelligence. It occurred to him that the old
man might be a good mind to have on the camp
council he intended to form.

Barry regretted not having had the opportunity
to meet Lady Pamela's daughter. He wondered
if she was anything like her mother. He was planning to ask Tedder about her, but when he got
back to the Tedder wagons, he found an im-
patient Major Warren waiting for him. He
thought the major was waiting to take him to his
other arriving wagon train and had no reason to
believe otherwise when the army man merely
barked at him, "Come along, will you!"

They rode for nearly a mile in total silence.
Warren was noticeably angry. His mouth kept
twitching, a gesture Barry put down as having
nothing to do with him since the man's mind
seemed a thousand miles away.

Finally, near the top of a rise, Warren reined
to a stop. "Fitzpatrick!" he snarled. "I'm a damn
good soldier, but sometimes I have to blindly
follow idiot orders from Washington."

Barry sighed. "Don't tell me your troubles,
Warren. Just get me to my other wagon train."

"They'll get into Liberty tomorrow."

"What? I thought they were here already!
Damn it, what train *are* you taking me to?"

"Just hear me out!" Warren looked at Barry,
his eyes tired and grave. "It's this: I've been
ordered to put another train in with yours. I'll
get back to them in a moment. There's something
else. We have had a very good army scout with
some of your other people since they left Ohio.
Ransam Beaver Pond, by name. He's a Sioux
half-breed. He's going with you as your outrider,

whether you like it or not, because we have information that the whole Sioux nation might be gathering to stop you. The Sioux trust him and he might be able to save a few of your damn scalps. But that's not the main reason he will be joining you. Come to the crest of the hill and I'll show you what that is."

Barry blinked when he reached the hilltop and looked down. Then he burst out laughing.

"What in the hell is that—a circus?"

Major Warren snapped, "That's a caravan. At least, Count Justinian Khominy likes to call it that. He also likes to be called Count Just, though you'll find very little that's just about the man. He is the nephew of the late Tsar Alexander of Russia and until a few weeks ago was the Russian ambassador in Washington. He is a very rude young man with rather weird ideas and tastes. Because of several tactless things he did in Washington the Tsar was forced to call him home. He refused to depart on an American vessel and wouldn't wait for one to come from Russia. Hence, he is here."

"What in the hell do you mean? How did he get here and where the hell do you expect me to take him?"

Warren laughed. "I wish you could take him to hell, Fitzpatrick. In actual fact, he disappeared from Washington with most of the Russian embassy staff. He was finally traced to a Russian colony in Ohio, where he put this caravan together. Now he wants to get to the Russian colony at Fort Ross, which is in northern California. He can't be turned back. He's royal family, despite his antics, and it could cause an international incident if we tried. We can't let him be killed by Indians, either. Same reason. It's ticklish. You are the answer."

"Me!" Barry groaned.

"I once said I felt sorry for you," Warren went on, sincerely. "Now it goes double. We will do everything we can to have you ready to roll by tomorrow."

"Impossible! What about the Liberty train?"

"Aha, the point to return to. Beaver Pond will take them directly northwest to the Platte. It will save time and you will join up in a couple of weeks."

Barry growled, "That's the Cornithwyeth train, the New England group. What about Cornithwyeth himself? He's laid up bad and may not live."

"Yes," Warren said simply, "a point to be considered. If he is well enough to move, move him. If not, leave the bastard behind. Now come and meet Count Just."

Shaking his head, Barry rode down into the Russian encampment. He felt like an alien in his own country. Everywhere he looked he saw bear-skin-hatted Cossack guards, their tunics banded with rows of rifle shells. The wagons were drosh-kies, drawn by three horses, their sides wooden-framed like houses on wheels. Each side-panel was decorated with bright flowers and designs. The tents were sewn-together strips of material in rainbow hues. But the heavy-busted women with their coarse-braided hair made Barry gape the longest. Their colorful skirts stopped halfway between the knee and ankle. He had not seen that many ankles and thighs since visiting his last Indian village.

He exploded, "Christ almighty, what will the other woman say?"

"About what the Washington women have been saying. That he has a harem and doesn't mind advertising the fact. In here."

Before they could enter the tent an uproar from inside burst upon their ears.

"You fool!" Count Justinian was screeching. "You utter incompetent *kulak!*"

A manservant came scurrying out, moments before a flying *samovar* and china cups and saucers.

"You're on your own," Warren chuckled.

"I'd rather face a rattlesnake," Barry groaned.

He stepped onto the handsomest carpet that had ever been beneath his boot and gazed for a minute about the interior of the tent. Doc Freitag had once told him about the fancy whorehouses in New Orleans and he felt this was the nearest thing he would ever see to compare them with. Golden lamps hung from golden chains. Even the chairs were gilded. A canopied four-poster bed took up most of the area.

"Stop! Who are you?"

Barry had to look about to see where the voice was coming from. He couldn't find it.

"Fitzpatrick," he said. "The wagon train guide. Major Warren brought me."

There was a crash as a three-panelled screen was knocked over. Then Barry saw Count Just. He sat in a portable wooden bathtub lathering himself as though he were still alone. His beard and mustache were closely trimmed, which seemed to enhance the needle sharpness of his nose. He peered at Barry out of small, suspicious eyes.

The count grunted. "You seem young to be a guide."

"And you seem young to be an ambassador."

Justinian tilted back his head and roared. "Da! That is good! At least you speak more truth than the *kulaks* in Washington. Bring yourself the seat."

"What's a *kulak?*"

Justinian winked. "Best you not be one. They're neither serf nor noble. Most are whore-born paper pushers in government offices. But, to business. When do we leave?"

"Tomorrow."

"Why the delay?" Justinian groaned. "It seems the *kulaks* rule my life."

"I don't see that," Barry said. "We'll be leaving three days before I thought possible. You won't lose much time."

"Oh, won't I, though! Since leaving Washington they have tried to stall me everywhere. Why can't we leave today?"

"Because I already have other people committed for this journey."

"Others!" Justinian shrieked. "You are not taking me and mine alone?"

"No. Up to near two hundred wagons and over a thousand folk."

The rest of Barry's words were lost in the clatter of the count's jumping from the tub and rushing to the tent flap.

"Warren!" he called, his voice shrill. "Major

Warren! Come here, you creature out of a slut!"

Major Warren smiled quietly and approached the Russian. Justinian was trembling all over as though he had the ague.

"Come in, come in!" the count scowled, holding back the flap. Warren entered.

"You said I would be guided to California," Justinian said. "Why this big train? It will take forever. I wish another guide."

Slowly Warren shook his head, the hint of a smile playing about his face.

"There is none other available, Your Grace. If it is a question of the price being too high. . . ."

Justinian's voice again rose to a frenzied shriek.

"Price!" he cried. "I will pay nothing!"

"All right," Warren grinned. "Thanks for coming over, Fitzpatrick. I'll just have to get new instructions from Washington and they'll have to get them from St. Petersburg."

"No, Major Warren! Get out of here! Fitzpatrick is the guide for me. I will keep him."

The count paced the Persian carpet until Major Warren had left, unembarrassed by his total nudity.

"Fitzpatrick," he decided, "I'll give you twice what you are getting to take me on alone. This is fair, is it not?"

Barry shook his head. "You'll pay me twenty-five dollars per wagon same as the rest," he said quietly.

"That's fifty thousand rubles!" Justinian moaned. "You robber! You thief!"

Barry rose and started to leave.

Count Justinian flopped down on his bed and

pouted. Finally, a glint of amusement appeared in his shrewd young eyes.

"All right," he said. "I now know your price for taking me with the train. What is it alone?"

"I can't do that."

"Come, come. Every man has a price. Is it women? I can offer you some of the finest from all of Mother Russia."

Barry shook his head.

"Aha," Justinian said slyly. "I forget that you are a mountain man and they sometimes have different tastes." He rose and posed in a sensuous manner. "You must admit that I have a most handsome male body. If that is your desire, it is yours for the entire journey."

Barry again shook his head. "No offense, sir, but I wouldn't know what to do with another male. The price and conditions are as stated."

The Russian shrugged and drew a leather pouch from beneath his satin pillow. He weighed it in his hand and tossed it to Barry.

"That is Russian gold, but gold is gold, is it not? I like you, Fitzpatrick, because you are not afraid of me. My cousin is afraid of me and that is why he wants me home. Poor little Nicholas is Tsar and shudders to think of skeletons in the family closet. I somehow doubt you have any skeletons to hide. I like that. Nor do you seem to be a man who can be bribed. So I say this to you in all honesty, get me to California with honest haste and you will never regret having befriended Count Justinian Khominy."

Barry nodded, "Now you have a deal, sir." He tested the weight of the gold in his hand and knew it had to be triple the amount agreed upon. "How would you like me to address you—Count, Your Grace, Mr. Khominy, what?"

Count Justinian rolled about on the bed in delighted laughter. "Oh my," he chuckled, "the list could be endless. I think I have been called everything and accused of everything. My mother was the Grand Duchess Maximova-Manilov. She detested my father, who affected the foppish mannerisms of the court and insisted that I be named Justinian. Hideous name. You know, I am twenty-five and have not talked this honestly with another person since my mother died. She called me Max. Would you honor me by doing the same?"

11

Back at the Tedder camp, Barry said little about the Russians other than they were coming along. Howard's group would see them soon enough, for themselves. He was glad he was back. He enjoyed the Tedders' homespun hospitality and warmth. The twins reminded him of bear cubs at play and Maybelle reminded him of a coy otter wanting to be noticed but slyly scurrying away when she was. In a way the youngsters made him homesick for the mountains.

He sat with Howard and Lydia a spell, chatting and winding down from his ruckus with the count. Then one of the Buttle-Jones farmers came to call him away.

Lady Pamela's landau looked like a brig that would never come down out of dry dock, so high did it sit off the ground on its Conestoga wheels.

But the wheels would do the trick and Hufford was plainly elated.

"Nary a bump or jar, sir," the old man said softly, as if it were his and Barry's secret alone. "And Mrs. Herbert had one of her men build me these fine little steps for Her Ladyship to climb the new height. I'd have been lost not driving me rig, sir."

Donald Hufford motioned Barry over to him. His face was grave.

"Really, sir," he said, "you might have warned us of the situation. They were all black, sir. Really, quite black. I was most embarrassed."

Barry studied the blonde young man's earnest expression. Sometimes he wasn't sure he'd ever get the hang of people. Here was a chap he'd thought he could count on for sense, a non-flustering sort who'd do his work and mind his business. Now this.

"That's odd, Hufford," he said coolly, "I wonder how embarrassed *they* were."

"Sir? I must have misunderstood you."

"I don't think you did. The work they did on your carriage proves these people are not stupid. I'm sure that some of them have it well in mind that it was you British who captured them and sold them in slavery. Goodnight, Mr. Hufford."

The young man blushed scarlet. "Sir," he stammered, "I meant no offense, I assure you. You've made me feel like a cur. I—I—"

"Forget it. Nothing's changed. You're a good man," Barry said simply and walked away. He didn't know if Donald's attitude towards the blacks spelled more trouble for him, or if it was just a passing remark meant to gain his attention.

Even that possibility bothered him, given his initial reading of Donald's effeminacy. Jesus, what did they all want from him? He was beginning to wonder if he could cope with the many, varied people he was responsible for bringing together.

Passing a wagon, going back to his horse, he heard a girl's giggle and then some sort of throaty demand from a boy. He reached the tail-gate just in time to be knocked to the ground by someone escaping from the wagon. He grabbed hold of the figure and twisted it about until he was looking into the frightened eyes of Theodis Tedder.

"Hey," Barry said, hardly amused. His stern tone so further frightened the youth that he clawed his way free and scampered away.

Curious, Barry rose, dusted himself off and flapped back the tarp on the wagon. Inside, frantically pulling up his pants, was Nazareth Tedder. The girl with him was patting her skirt, calmly, as though it had never been raised.

Barry needed no introductions to the girl. She was a perfect copy of Lady Pamela, her mother, though on a daintier scale. Barry almost whistled. He couldn't really blame the Tedder boys for what they'd been up to.

Barry scratched his head. He didn't know quite what to say. "Miss Buttle-Jones," he said then, "your carriage has been repaired. You might care to inspect it."

Selena Buttle-Jones eyed him as though she had every intention of suggesting he would make a better wagon mate than either of the Tedder boys. Barry didn't move a muscle. Her look turned cold. She smirked as she jumped from the wagon and brushed past him.

That left Barry alone with Nazareth.

"Some looker," Barry said indifferently.

"My folks ain't gotta know, do they?"

"Know what?" Barry asked innocently.

"Gee," Nazareth gushed, "weren't nothing horrible. Ole Theo's never been . . . never done . . . he just ain't, you know. He's sweet on Miss Prissy Pants and I thought I'd . . . augh . . . well, he didn't wantta."

Barry didn't smile, recalling that Nazareth seemed quite ready to take over for his shy brother.

"Sure," he drawled. "Well, wish your folks a goodnight for me, and tell them that I went back to the Herbert camp. Dawn is going to come right soon for all of us." He took a few steps away and then turned back. "Oh, Nazareth, you forgot about three buttons on your fly. A man checks thinks like that."

The boy blushed as deep as the red in his hair, but his eyes did not flinch from Barry's. He had been caught dead-to-right in a punishable offense and was being treated as an mature equal. He now felt honor bound to the man.

Barry felt less honor bound than he did binded by circumstances. Although he got some rest riding his horse slowly back down to the Herbert camp on the Missouri, there was no let-up once he got there.

"Fitzpatrick!" Colonel Herbert roared, as soon as he spotted him. "Off your horse!"

Barry didn't budge. The return of the colonel, and the lurking presence of Pomeroy, told him that accusations were to begin anew.

"By what authority," Herbert screamed, "have

you been given the right to command work out of *my* people? Now that I am back I forbid such practices. My people will be kept separate!"

"That suits me," Barry said, his voice heavy with sarcasm. "Move 'em out when you wish, colonel. Give the Indians something to keep their minds off the rest of us."

"Now, wait a minute!" Herbert roared. "You can't strand us this way. You've already been paid."

"Exactly," Barry said quietly. "And I'll stay in command, unless you have a better reason for replacing me."

Colonel Herbert squinted furiously. He had no reason other than having been made to look foolish in the man's eyes. Barry tried to read the overseer's face, but Pomeroy averted his head. Colonel Herbert had been told nothing of DeeDee's accusation because Mary Sue had ordered it kept silent.

"I see," Barry mused, when no answer was forthcoming. He turned to Pomeroy wearily. "Look, there's a valley three miles up the river where we will be forming. If you break camp at four you'll be there by dawn. I'll meet you there later because I have to bring across the chuck wagon, horses and drovers. Oh, we'll have to use one of your wagons temporarily for Doc Freitag and his patient, Mr. Cornithwyeth."

He left them with Herbert blinking in confusion and Pomeroy's face a study in rage. He thought they were upset only because he had given them orders and brooked no opposition to them.

But fording the river back to Independence,

Barry suddenly threw back his head and laughed aloud. The irony had just struck him that they had reacted most violently to his mentioning Cornithwyeth's name. The Herbert people and Cornithwyeth would be stuck with each other for a couple of weeks. Neither group would like that one bit.

For reasons of his own, Hudson Warren had lied to Barry. The New England Emigrant Resettlement train had come nowhere near Liberty. Over the strong objections of Arabelle Cornithwyeth they had been diverted to Fort Leavenworth, twenty miles northwest of Independence.

Arabelle couldn't understand the army order. The train had been outfitted so carefully that very little restocking was required at the fort. She was eager to be on her way to join her husband and the main train. A part-Indian army scout joined them at Leavenworth, but he was close-mouthed; she was not able to get much information out of him.

When Major Warren arrived at the fort that evening he first paid his respects to Arabelle. Adeptly, he never once touched up on the subject of her husband's condition. She was soothed into believing that the change in route was at the suggestion of Bradford Cornithwyeth and Barry Fitzpatrick. Graciously, the army would leave the scout to guide them to the meeting on the Platte River. He asked for the scout, and, learning his whereabouts, went to the fort commander's office to meet him.

When Warren entered, Captain Willingham stood up and faced him soberly.

"Major," he growled, "damn his Indian's hide to hell. He won't tell me anything."

"No," Warren said. "Why should he? It's his orders. We would like the use of your office now, captain."

"Very good, sir." Willingham saluted stiffly and left, his ears burning with resentment.

"You come highly recommended, Beaver Pond."

The man turned away from the window and Warren stared. He was nearly six and a half feet tall but seemed much taller because of the three feathers sticking out of his battered old cavalry hat. His glossy black hair was plaited into twin braids that hung down onto his chest. He wore only a leather vest, buckskin trousers and moccasins. His bare arms were like corded ropes of steel. He made the major feel puny.

But it was more than his stature that kept Warren staring. Except for his hair and coppery skin tone, he hardly seemed of Indian origin.

"Your stare does not embarrass me, Major Warren," Beaver Pond said arrogantly. "You do not have to remain curious about my handsomeness. I have learned to live with the mark my Swedish mother gave me. The Kaws felt that I should have had their flat, wide nose. The Arapahoes were most disturbed that my eyes were blue and not black like their own."

"Kaws? Arapahoes?"

Beaver Pond explained.

"Sooner or later you would have been forced

to ask, so I tell freely. My grandfather was a trapper. My mother, as a girl of twelve, wandered away from his camp and was found by the Kaws. The Kaws did not know of white women. Because she was blonde, they thought her a goddess and smuggled her back from the mountains to their winter camp on the plains. The Arapahoes learned of her and wanted the goddess for their own. When he knew his tribe was to be attacked, the Kaw chief let the young braves come one at a time to have my mother for good luck. They were defeated nevertheless. Once she was captured the Arapahoe braves also used her for good luck. I'm told that twenty of their braves were with her on that first night. That she did not die proved to them she was a goddess and she was no longer touched. But the Kaws wanted her back and warred for her. I do not know if my father was Kaw or Arapahoe, but I do know that when I was born, each tribe claimed me for its own. The Kaws, if they could have had the child-god, would have let the Arapahoes keep my mother. When they could not win me in battle, they bartered for me. But my mother would not let me go for any amount of ransom. The goddess had spoken sternly. I was given the name Ransom Beaver Pond. My mother and I lived one season with the Kaws, the next with the Arapahoes, so as to bring peace to the tribes. I learned the tongues of both people, and later the tongues of many tribes in the Sioux nation. To them all I am Beaver Pond. It is only among my mother's white people that I am Ransom."

"I see." Major Warren had listened carefully,

impressed by the man's princely mien, but some- what at a loss to judge where his alliances might be. The major hesitated, then nodded. "Ransom it is, then. Do you understand the mission?"

Ransom Beaver Pond nodded curtly. "Yes, major. The Russian is not to reach Fort Ross until the Siberian ports have already frozen shut."

"Yes," Warren sighed, "just as simple as that. I do not intend to ask any questions about how you will bring it about."

"I shall see what I can do."

The scout's face thereafter remained impassive. He was familiar with the white man's lies and be- trayals in the service of a selfish end. To appease Russia and gain a secret treaty the Americans thought nothing of putting a thousand innocent lives in peril. He had nothing further to say to Major Warren. His own plans remained locked in his mind. He had been waiting thirty long years for an opportunity such as this.

Hudson Warren rode back to Kansas City that night already imagining his promotion to colonel. He chuckled over the spider's web he had woven around Count Justinian. The Tsar did not want the trouble-making count to return to Russia but was not anxious for his death, either. Wash- ington was concerned about the Mexican govern- ment which might precipitate a war now that American emigrants were moving into Mexican California. Washington would enjoy seeing Rus- sia sever diplomatic relations with Mexico. By delaying the count's return, they would be in a position to bargain for this. Major Warren was not overly concerned about whether the bargaining would succeed or not. It might actually stir up a war with Mexico. If so, he would be ready to fight. He saw himself as a general in that war.

Barry Fitzpatrick's emigrants, who might suffer from the delay of the train, were not the major's concern at all.

At that very moment another man, this one in the Cornithwyeth camp at Fort Leavenworth, was thrashing about with his private concerns.

Lester Hartwicke laid on the straw pallet in his wagon and fumed. The delay and change in route were thwarting his plans. Up ahead, out of his reach, was Lady Pamela Buttle-Jones. It was not chance that had put Hartwicke on this particular wagon journey. He was on a secret, revengeful mission and he was ambitious to complete it quickly. A few weeks delay could mean his ruination, for who knew what protective alliances Lady Pamela might be forming? He could not afford to let her slip from his grasp. He could almost taste her pain at his hands.

Then, too, there was sex.

For the first week out of Lancaster, Hartwicke had paid little attention to Pearl Fergus, the little girl he had married as a means to an end and who now lay on a pallet beside him. But Hartwicke was highly sexed; he'd hardly been without some form of sexual contact in twenty years. Even if there had been an older woman on the train available to him, Arabelle's hawk-like patroling would have smelled her out.

In the second week he had used the cold night air as an excuse to sleep within the wagon, rather than on the ground as he had at first. He had assured Pearl that she was quite safe with him. But the desire inside him now was elemental and brutal, and it mingled with the rage he felt toward Lady Pamela for escaping him so far. Gradually, he substituted Pearl in his mind for the English woman.

One night, before Pearl could cry out, her mouth had been clamped shut by his palm and his weight was atop her. As she stared up at him, wide-eyed and terrified, he had raped her, again and again. He hurt Pearl, badly. Her stitches from Thomas Geddy's operation were still not completely healed and she began to bleed profusely. Hartwicke relished the bleeding as a sign of her virginity.

She did not scream or later report him for the simple reason that he threatened to kill her before any investigation into the whys and wherefores of his husbandly rights could commence. There was something in his cold eyes that told her he would do it, no matter the risk to himself. In that, she was right. Hartwicke was already dead inside, dead in his heart; it did not matter to him that his body might stop existing, as long as while he could still move it he could have his way.

Pearl began to hate the setting sun and the nightly blood-letting until she screamed out the real reason for her bleeding. Hartwicke then backed off from sexual contact, with a vague fear of contamination. He began experimenting with all of the mental and physical tortures he wished to use on Lady Pamela.

One day, when he thought they were nearing

their rightful destination, Hartwicke went and spoke to Thomas Geddy.

"A couple days more and we can end this farce, Geddy," he said. "Once we join the main train to hell with that harridan and her rules. You can have your little sister-in-law back with no questions asked."

Arabelle's announcement that they would not be joining the train as planned but would be delayed at Fort Leavenworth for a few more weeks sent Pearl into near shock. She didn't think she could survive another night with Lester Hartwicke.

As for Hartwicke, rage at the delay almost consumed him. That night, as Major Warren rode away from the fort and she lay sleeping near him, he rose from his pallet and raped her again. Then again and again.

For a while, he was satisfied.

Book Three

THE JOURNEY

12

Jessie Fremont would have it no other way than to come across the river and see the beginning of her husband's fondest dream.

Astride her horse on a high mound, with the feeling of old America thousands of miles to her back and new America literally forming at her feet, she could not keep the tears from her eyes nor the shout from her throat:

"God bless these hearty souls!"

From three directions they came as the first pencil light of dawn announced to the coyotes that their wailing serenade would soon be pushed westward, as well. The dawn clamor came up:

"Move 'em up! Head 'em out!"

Jessie thought: Goodbye mountain men! Goodbye trappers! On this day in May of 1841 the ordinary people were moving. This would go down in history as the day that the west was really won!

Breakfast for all had been a sullen meal in pre-dawn darkness. Those who refused to rise and missed it snuggled close to their fanciful dreams. One man saw his destiny as the Tsar of all the Russias. And here was a woman who saw herself carving a piece of the British Empire out of a Colorado dust bowl. These two slept late in their wagons. Perhaps only the blacks who first kicked the horses onto the trail had little hope. It would have been just too fanciful for them to imagine that in little more than two decades, a President of the United States would set them free.

"It's a glorious morning and a wondrous sight," Jessie enthused, as Barry rode back to join her. "Look at that! They are still forming and the first are already to the horizon line. What ever will it look like when you join the northern train with it?"

"An armada!" Barry exalted. "Last night I had my doubts, but this morning I feel like Lord Nelson with a fleet at his command."

Jessie Fremont leaned over from her saddle and gave him a quick but expressive kiss on the mouth.

"Good luck, my young admiral. I love you! I love my husband! If that sounds confused, it's because I am a woman. Come back to me so that we may go swimming again!"

She had planned her farewell so that he would not be able to answer. She turned the horse and sped away, tears streaming down her cheeks. She had been raised not to be unfaithful, and she loved her husband deeply, but she vowed vengeance on any woman who did not treat Barry as the gentleman he had been with her.

To her kiss and quick departure Barry reacted in his own manner. To him, the kiss was almost a cleansing agent, a finale to his eastern adventure. It gave him a chance to turn his eyes westward to the barbaric, the abounding, the beautiful. He was going home!

Then, gazing from the valley to the wagons fading on the distant horizon, he chided himself.

"I'm a damn fool," he muttered. "These idiots will ruin the place!"

His words rose to haunt him as the sun rose higher in the sky. The people lacked experience in unblazed trail travel, the animals were unruly without well defined roads or wagon ruts to follow. The train formation, clumsily trying to conform to a single column, soon lost order. The women began to complain about choking on the dust of the wagons in front of them, so the men began to veer off to travel on their own. Children ran off to explore the wonderous new world and frantic mothers would force their wagons to a halt until the children caught up. The men were unaccustomed to watching the ground ahead for ruts and rocks hidden by the tall prairie grass. The first half of the day brought five broken wheels, a splintered axle and a wagon that became high-centered on a small knoll, its wheels spinning foolishly inches off the ground. Each accident brought all of the wagons to a halt to help out.

Barry was getting no time to blaze a trail. He galloped back and forth, exhorting, adjuring and trying to restore some order. But he was dealing with independent men. They saw no rhyme or reason in his demands. The landscape seemed so wholly free of danger that even experienced men like Howard Tedder let down their guard and ambled along as though it were a pleasure jaunt. Barry was well worn when at mid-afternoon he halted the lead wagons, five miles out from their starting point.

"Now what is the delay?" demanded Count Justinian, riding up from his own wagons, far at the rear, and accosting Barry. "We can go five miles further, maybe ten, if we stop this infernal stopping."

"This is it for today," rejoined Barry. "We'll be getting nowhere if we don't get this train shook down and some order established."

"Which is exactly what you are being paid for," commented another voice. Colonel Herbert eyed the count as though he had found an ally. "But this whole day you have done nothing but see to broken wheels. Why can't they be left behind to make their repairs and then catch up?"

"Right now it doesn't matter," Barry replied. "We are in more or less friendly Indian country. Out yonder it's different and anyone left behind is as good as dead. I don't want anyone getting the habit."

"A brash answer, as usual," scoffed Herbert.

Other men were now arriving, wondering the same question as had the count and colonel.

"Camp tonight where you stand," Barry told them. "I'm going to set up right over there. Right after supper I want to see every man to give rolling orders for tomorrow."

His straight gaze kept them from further comment. Herbert turned and rode back with Count

Justinian. When they parted the count went to pay his respects to Lady Pamela, covertly instigated and encouraged by Colonel Herbert. Avoiding Howard Tedder, the colonel aired his complaints against Barry to anyone who would listen. He was determined to get cliques and factions started.

After Barry had given his orders to the hired chuck-wagon cook-driver and the six drovers, he rode back to the Herbert train to find Bradford Cornithwyeth. The man was ashen gray and not taking the journey well at all.

"How is he?" Barry asked, climbing into the wagon.

"Middlin'," Doc Freitag frowned. "Hossback ride ovah here opened the wound. Ah had him flat all day ta stop the bleeding."

Barry sat crossed-leg near his head. "Mr. Cornithwyeth, I was able to get the things out of your room at the boarding house. I've got it all stowed away in the chuck wagon."

Cornithwyeth was feverish and his mind unable to concentrate. He nodded and whispered: "My wife?"

"The army is seeing that her train is being taken to the Platte. We'll join them there."

He nodded again. "She's been kind."

Barry frowned.

"He's talkin' bout Miz Herbert," Doc Freitag interpreted. "Made him feel right ta home."

That's one small blessing, Barry thought. He started to say something about his main reason for coming and saw that the man had drifted off to sleep. Well, he decided, no one but the man himself knew he'd had four heavy bags of gold in his room. Barry didn't like the responsibility of keeping them hidden in the chuck wagon, but he had no other choice until the man was well enough to handle his own affairs.

He nearly crashed into Aaron Pomeroy jumping down out of the wagon. The Herbert's overseer was standing at the tailgate.

"Sorry," Pomeroy apologized, "I was wondering if you meant fur me ta be at the meetin' too?"

Barry wondered why Pomeroy was being so servile. "I want every man there."

Pomeroy made a wry face. "Blacks, too?"

"Every man!"

Pomeroy shrugged and walked away. Whether the blacks came to meeting was the least of his worries. He had learned exactly what he had come to overhear. The old man's money had no doubt been taken from his room but it was reasonable to assume that Barry Fitzpatrick was unaware that any of it was missing. He wanted to keep it that way until he could figure out how to keep Cornithwyeth from learning of his loss also.

The hundred-odd campfires of the scattered train stretched out over a mile of grove and glade at the end of the first undisciplined day. By ones and twos the men came to sit and stand around Barry's campfire. It was soon obvious that two groups had absented themselves purposely. Barry crawled up onto the chuck-wagon seat so that he could be seen and heard.

"Gentlemen, if you can't hear me come closer. But first, we seem to have some stragglers from the Herbert and Russian wagons."

"Hardly," Colonel Herbert said gruffly. "I will

handle any instructions that need to be given to my people."

"They are not your people," Barry said. "No more than the Cossacks are the count's. This is the first time that we have all been together. Now, I'm not one for long speeches, but damn it, we're not going to get mixed up tomorrow like we were today. When I say every man, I mean every man."

Silence for a time greeted his demand. The Tennessee pioneers, Tedder's men, looked uncomfortably one to the other. It was one of the English farmers, whose ear Herbert had caught, who rose at length.

"We have been wondering, sir," he said, "if your guide duties include the bully-boy tactics you have been employing today. We departed England to get away from kingly rule."

There were murmurs of agreement.

"Damn it," Barry shot back, "we won't get anywhere without some organization!"

"Wa'll," drawled one of the Tennesee men, who had also become a Herbert partisan, "that thar's the whole pernt. Ain't agin' you bein' the guide, boy . . . but, ah think we'all need a real elected leader type."

"Very sound suggestion," Count Justinian boomed. "We are very fortunate, although I only met the man two or three hours ago, that we have a retired colonel among us. Even in Russia men with such training are asked to step forward and lead. I would strongly recommend that we elect Colonel Herbert. Will someone second that?"

Some of the bewhiskered Tennessee men stirred, but cast their eyes toward their own leader,

Howard Tedder, whose role as their spokesman was in jeopardy. To Howard's surprise, Ned Conroy had decided to join the train after all. All had been well at the start, but Conroy had begun to carp at Tedder over the repairs on his wagon axles, and some of the Tennesseans were beginning to side with him.

Howard rose, cleaning his throat. Speaking forcefully, he said, "I ain't agin electin' a leader, but we gotta know what we're electin' him fur. Ah'm one fur listenin' to what Fitzpatrick's got on his mind, first. If'n a man, no matter what his color, is gonna drive a team, tote a gun or herd the cattle, we ought to hear him too."

The approving nods of Tedder's associates disturbed Colonel Herbert. He didn't want the Tennesseans drifting away from him. He leaped to his feet, deciding to join them, but for his own purposes.

"I will go along with Mr. Tedder on that," he said grandly. He thought, if they allow the male slaves to vote, that would automatically assure him of the election. "Harmon, run and get our people back here quickly. Count, my man Pomeroy can fetch your Cossacks, if you like."

Count Justinian nodded, his face a wide grin. Oh, what fun, he thought, to see this stupid thing called democracy at work. Every man wanted his own way.

"But," the count said, "is there reason to wait for them, Mr. Fitzpatrick?"

"No," Barry said. Foreseeing another time-consuming petty squabble, he changed his tactics. "My intention in this meeting has been simply to ask you to form a train council, a leader from each of your groups, so to speak. You can go off and do that by yourselves."

Ned Conroy broke in: "Why not do it now? Then you can do yore jawin' with them."

He was hushed to silence.

"We'll need them later, not now," Barry went on. "For now, it's enough that we understand that we are going to travel in four parallel columns, separated by not too great a space, and this space is to be maintained, especially toward nightfall. Never again will we camp like this. Each night, the outer two columns will draw in together and the other two angle out, wagon lapping wagon, front and rear. That'll make an oblong corral of the wagons, into which, through the gap, the work horses and mules will be driven for the night after they are fed."

"Won't that be a danger for the young 'uns?"

"They won't be there. The tents and fires are to be outside the corral except in case of an Indian attack. Then we'll turn the corral into a fortress."

An old Tennessean scoffed: "Ain't gonna work, sonny. A saddle horse 'n harness horse'll only fight."

Barry grinned. "I haven't mentioned the transportation animals yet, but they will have to be hobbled outside each night. Each leader will have to supply eight guards each night. Each man and each boy above fourteen will be given guard duty on a schedule. The only excuse will be if he's too ill to walk."

"Hoss feathers, army stuff," Conroy sneered.

Barry ignored him. "Now, during the day, no wagon is to change its own place in the train after the start, dust or no dust!"

This brought many murmurs and inaudible complaints.

"What about breakdowns, like today?" the Count demanded. "I must get on, as quickly as possible."

"Each column will appoint men for emergency repairs, Max. They will pull the wagon out of line and try to get it fixed before the whole train passes. If not, when we camp that night, all of the emergency crews will go back to assist and tow it into the corral." Barry looked around. "Any more questions?"

A tall, good-looking young Englishman timidly rose. "Our cows, sir. You took them away. I have a small daughter who needs milk."

"Are your cows marked?"

"I have only two and they know me by sight."

The mild remark brought a laugh and eased some of the tension.

"How many men don't have their cattle branded with a mark?"

Several raised their hands.

"I've hired drovers to keep the herd as one," Barry explained. "This makes it easier for the train to move freely. In Missouri I had the blacksmith make up some extra brands. See my drovers at dawn and they'll have the fires ready to brand. They'll also tell you when your women can come to milk. Make sure they know the brand you pick out. I don't want a bunch of women squabbling over stolen milk."

"Ya'all got drovers, but can they protect the cattle from the Indians?"

"The last thing in the world the Indians will want is your cattle. They can't stand the taste of it. Buffalo is their meat, which most of you probably won't like at first. Too bad more of you don't have oxen like they have for a lot of the Cornithwyeth wagons. The Indians don't like oxen, but horses and mules are like money to them. Which reminds me, when we get onto the plains you will tether your horses and not hobble them. The grass gets scarcer and a hobbled horse can get several miles away searching for it."

"He talks a lotta sense," said a loud voice.

"A good guide, a good leader."

Herbert arose, a sneer on his face. "I think it's time we set to electing this council, as he called it, and then a leader. Not later. Now. Fitzpatrick is going to be too busy being a guide to be much else to us. Is that all right with you, Mr. Fitzpatrick?"

"Good pernt," Conroy chuckled.

"Our group's already gotta man. I say we Tennessee folk stick with Tedder."

Hearing the firm voice, seconded by most of the Tennesseans, Conroy kept quiet. Barry quickly surveyed the situation. There was no question but that Herbert and the Count would retain autocratic control over their respective groups. A reasonable choice to head the fourth column would be the wagons of Lady Pamela. The English farmers seemed hesitant to single one of their number out to command the others. Barry made a suggestion that met with their immediate approval.

"I'm sure you'll want Her Ladyship out front so she's not eating the dust of the others, so why not name Hufford, her coachman, to the council? He sits high enough in that carriage to keep a sharp eye on everything."

"Here, here." Most all the Englishmen applauded.

But when the question of choosing a leader for the council arose, the meeting disintegrated into hopeless haggling. Herbert most wanted the position, Barry saw, and he had some support from the count and the English. But he couldn't get enough backing at that point even for it to reach a vote. After an hour, it was decided to leave everything in the hands of the council without one man being higher in authority than the others.

Feeling he'd already made appreciable headway, Herbert declared: "That's it, then. A four-man council it is."

"What about Fitzpatrick?" Tedder asked. "What's his status to be?"

Herbert looked at him as though he were a fool. "He is an employee," he said tartly.

"Colonel's right," Barry said quickly, grateful that he at least had Tedder and Hufford on the council. "I got plenty of chores to keep me busy. Well, the council's formed. They're our law and order from here on and we'd best go by what they decide and say. Now, knowin' a lot of you folk retire with the chickens, and they've roosted a long time ago, I say we all call it a night."

"A moment," Colonel Herbert boomed out. "I strongly urge the council stay and have a few words with each other."

"Stay all night long, fur all I care," Ned Conroy growled, disgusted that this night made Howard Tedder a bigger man than he was before. "I'm gonna go to bed!"

The men filtered away. Most went to pass the news of the meeting to their wives and children.

* * *

Because a lamp was still aglow within Lady Pamela's wagon, old Hufford timidly knocked his briar pipe against the wagon wheel to announce his return.

"Step up in, Hufford," she called warmly, "I've been waiting for you."

Hufford had known Pamela Twedsbury since her birth, but he still stood in awe of the position she had obtained since being born to a tenant farmer on the Buttle-Jones estate. The days were long past when he could call her Pammy-lass.

In his quiet Yorkshire way he gave her an almost word-by-word replay of the meeting. Lady Pamela laughed when she learned of his election.

"They, at least, showed some good common-sense, Hufford. There's probably not a man among them with your sense and ability, I'm proud of you. But you seem troubled by it all."

"Milady," he frowned, "when you married His Lordship and took me out of the stables, I vowed undying loyalty. I've never once questioned this trip, although I'm not blind to its dangers. But I think we all might be lost if we don't follow what this man Fitzpatrick says."

"Does someone wish not to follow his suggestions?"

"That's why I came to talk it out with you, milady. This Colonel Herbert reminds me so much of Sir Malcolm that I fear the young man will never know the sharks have him until he's all eaten up."

"Well, Hufford," she said encouragingly, "we have so far out-foxed the real Sir Malcolm, so I suggest we might do the same to his pretender. I rather like this Fitzpatrick, even if he did turn down my dinner invitation. Let's put our trust in him. But that doesn't mean he needs to know our purpose for being here."

Hufford started. "Milady, my word. Not even my son knows why we have come so far from home."

Her beautiful face saddened for a moment. "So far," she said. "And yet not so far. I've longed for the days when you could still call me Pammy-lass, Hufford. Not even these vast prairies seem to take away the feeling that I am now in a Buttle-Jones prison. Will it ever end, Hufford?"

"I'm not sure, milady," he said frankly. "I've me suspicions, as I stated in England, ever since I saw how quickly some of His Lordship's men took to your side for this trip."

"But surely you've seen how unfounded those suspicions were."

"Possibly," Hufford admitted. "Yet I cannot rid myself of the feeling that you are being followed. The spy—" He shrugged. "The spy could be in this camp. He can be in another. We do not know."

"Seventeen of these so-called farmers were soldiers under my husband," Lady Pamela said firmly. "You know that. And you know they would protect me from anyone who wishes me harm." She thought for a moment, then smiled. "Perhaps I have eighteen champions."

"Milady?"

"Fitzpatrick," she said, as though he should have understood. "Between the two of us we shall see that he remains the only voice of command on this journey. In return, he will be our protector. Is there something I can do to help bring that about?" Then she giggled, and it made her look like the devil-may-care child she had been. "I am asking as the somewhat maligned niece of your late wife, Uncle Hufford, not as the regal cold beauty the Buttle-Joneses thought they created for their lackluster son."

"Pammy-lass," he grinned, "you can use all those high-flown words you learned from Lady Agatha on the Russian count. If you can side him with me and that chap from Tennessee, the votes are ours."

"Done," Lady Pamela said. She touched her cheekbones with a haughty gesture, then lifted a finger perkily. "I shall tame the Russian bear anon."

"I've got the strangest feelin'," Howard Tedder whispered, lying next to his Lydia in one of their wagons.

"Put it from your mind," she chuckled. "I'm not about to start another child goin' cross-country like this."

"Oh, woman!" he roared, "ain't that. It's that damn council. I ain't a smart man, but something stinks 'bout the way they're tryin' to push Fitzpatrick out of the way."

"Well, man," she sighed, "if you smell a stink then you ain't dumb, jest too lazy to sniff out the source."

He was quiet for a long time. "Night, Lyd."

"Night, husband."

Lydia Tedder lay perfectly still so that the con-

sumptive cough in her chest would be still and
not disturb her husband. She was proud of him
getting named to the train council. She saw no
reason why he should not have been. In her eyes
there was no other like him on earth. Her only
friend on the train was Miriam Conroy, even
though their husbands did seem to be at swords-
point. In the morning she vowed to put her ailment aside and get out to meet some of the
women from the trains other than her own. She
had faith in her husband, but a lot of faith in
herself, as well.

Mary Sue Herbert lay alone and lonely. The
colonel had not shared her bed since the first year
of their marriage. No one had reported back to
her on the men's meeting and she resented the
fact. It hurt her that Tom Herbert had taken back
over as though he had always been there. It had
been the same in Alabama. It would be the same
no matter where they were. He was a man and
she was a woman and he always came back as
king and master even if he was a slovenly bum.

But of one thing she was deeply thankful: no
one had dared mention DeeDee's accusations
against the young mountain man. Her husband
would never have thought to check the girl out
carefully, as she had done. The girl's membranes
had been bruised, she had noted, but hardly more
than an hour before Mary Sue had examined her.
She felt sorry for the girl for wanting a man so
badly she would resort to such tactics, but she
knew she had to be severe. But what punishment
did one give out in the middle of a wilderness?

13

With the council unable to make a single decision the train was left to run in a willy-nilly fashion for the first three or four days out. The four-column formation was abandoned the second day. The loosely knit organization rolled on in a broken-crested wave, ten, fifteen, twenty miles a day.

Even this progress was far greater than Barry had dreamed possible and so he refrained from pushing for his demands. Seeing that six drovers were far too many until the Cornithwyeth cattle were added on, Barry took two of the cowboys and began to train them as scouts. His decision was based on the simplest need for survival—water. The water barrel lashed to the side of each wagon would last the average family for days, but Barry needed to find water for the animals. Be-

tween them and the Platte were many streams and
several strong and capricious rivers. As often as
possible the rivers determined the daily encampment and not the number of miles traveled. Also
Barry and the scouts had to be constantly on the
lookout for fording places that were the least difficult and dangerous.

As with any group of people so loosely brought
together the rumor mill never stopped churning.
Ned Conroy claimed to know the ways of Indians
and because none had yet been sighted it was a
sign to him that they were gathering for a great
attack. Barry's declaration that the prairie Indians
were nomads and had long since started north for
the summer did little to scotch the rumor. He had
no answer for one story an English farmer had
heard in Kansas City, but it seemed a little far-
fetched that the Mormons who had been kicked
out of Illinois and Missouri had formed vigilante
bands to keep others from moving west.

But the rumors did take away some of the strain
of daily travel, some of the problems no one had
anticipated. By day they were assailed by green-
headed flies that left red welts on exposed skin,
and at night the mosquitoes attacked in whirring
swarms. The timber-lined valleys and open prairie
ridges were their natural spring habitat and the
train people a new invader to attack.

As the days passed the groves of walnut, oak,
hickory, elm and ash gave way to dogwood and
wild plum. No one lacked for fresh meat. Wild
game of every sort was abundant—deer and turkey and grouse, especially plover, scented the
campfire air each night.

But these niceties did not make up for trail

hardships. The most trifling matter could set off petulance, incivility, wrangling and intrigue. Men passed each other without speaking, even that early on the road. The more serious matters were taken before the council and their decision more often than not created greater problems. All of this made Barry pray for a quick union with the other train. Because of the wagons Arabelle Cornithwyeth had been able to add on during the journey from Lancaster, it was supposedly nearly equal in size to the present train. As Barry daily grew more morose and grim, he knew that he was going to have to have a strong voice in the council or they would never leave the Platte.

Noon of the tenth day brought them to the spring-swollen banks of the Platte. Barry and one of the scouts had ridden north to find a safe crossing, since where they were the river struck him as unfordable.

Late in the afternoon he finally found a crossing. It was about that time, when he was still surveying it, that the third scout, Parsons, came riding hard in search of Barry, jerking up his horse as though the action would lessen his anger.

"Boss," he panted, as though the horse had been riding him, "you'd best git back to those fool people."

"What's up?" demanded Barry.

"Gawd, boss, it's awful. That old fool colonel declared fer fordin' as soon as you turned your back. No one could stop him. He begun ta take heart when he got his first five wagons floated across. The sixth one got a little off course and the horses started to panic. The wagon flipped over and sank like a rock. It were weird. Nary a scream or cry came from the women an' chillen inside. An' not a man moved a muscle ta try 'an save those black folk. Then the ole fool Colonel ordered his seventh wagon ta start inta the river. That Hufford man tried ta stop him an' they bellowed at each other like bulls. Tedder tried to break 'em up an' then there was a shot. I think the colonel killed Hufford, boss. He fell an' I went fer my horse. Last I saw was the colonel swimmin' the river an' yellin fer his wagons ta head out fast. The train's in a panic."

It was hard for Barry to take in the scope of the disaster. He shook his head. "Parsons," he barked, "get back to what's left of those trains and head them here. Lenny, stay here and wait for them. I'm going after Herbert."

"Why'n hell would you wanta go after that bastard?"

Barry didn't take time to answer. He plunged his horse into the crossing he found. The horse sank out of sight below the rolling surface. Barry went down to his armpits, then swung off the saddle and swam on his own. The gallant horse headed for the center of the heavy current, but Barry still held his reins and turned him downstream. A hundred yards down they landed on a sandbar and scrambled up the far bank.

In a single motion Barry was back into the saddle and sat dripping. The horse, more than he, needed this moment of reassurance. Then he turned its head and heeled it into a southward gallop.

Within an hour he had spotted the wagons by their dust on the horizon. They were being driven hard and frantically fast. Herbert wagons had crossed the Platte, all right, and were fleeing west. Barry altered his course so that he could get into a position to head them off. The sun was already making long shadows upon the land and he did not like the terrain for such fast-moving wagons. It was dangerous.

Colonel Tom Herbert was not aware that the ground was getting rockier and was on a steady rise. He had done many things in his life, but he had never killed a man. But he had killed that damn coachman, he had! Frantically beating the horses to race faster, he was not aware of Mary Sue's screaming demands for him to stop. The negro driver, who had floated the wagon across the river, sat next to the colonel, clutching at anything he could find as though he feared his life would end at any moment.

Behind him, Harmon Herbert maintained the reins of the second wagon team. He felt totally inexperienced at the chore, but he had no recourse but to try and stay up with his father. Beside him, his sister DeeDee was crying. She had pleaded with her father not to send her across. But Colonel Herbert had been adamant in his belief that his family had to be the first across to ease the superstitious minds of the black slaves.

Now, Colonel Herbert was bitterly wondering if he had made the right choice in taking his family along. His wife was of little use to him and his children were next to worthless. Slaves were all that mattered. He figured he had at least thirty in the wagons behind him.

Where was his overseer? God damn it! Pomeroy had been standing close at hand when he had started to fight with Old Hufford. The colonel had heard his revolver crack, then looked down to the smoking barrel his own hand held. He could still see it dropping from his hand, hear the shout that came from his voice, feel the cold water covering his fatty flesh as he jumped and swam from the nightmare. Hell's fire, Pomeroy should either have swum along with him or seen to the crossing of the rest of his slaves. He had done neither!

The sun, as it loves to do in the prairie lands, will sink so slowly that it seems like it is stuck and will never vanish. Then, in the bat of an eye, it's gone. A sudden darkness falls that is eerily rosy. Nothing appears as it did the moment before.

The fifth wagon driver blinked a couple of times to refocus his eyes, tried staring again into the dust cloud he had been following. Frustrated because he could not see, he unconsciously jerked the reins slightly. The galloping horses responded by veering off to the right, then to the left, then to the right again. The panicking driver could not control them. The horses were trying to avoid rock formations, but could not. One split them like a knife. Wood, metal and the screaming driver smashed into the rock's granite face. In spite of the horrendous sounds of the crash, not a single wagon to the front was aware of what had happened.

Riding down the ridge, Barry saw the wagon and nearly puked. He was nearly killing himself and his horse, and for what? The Herbert train had been a thorn in his side from the very beginning. What did he owe them?

Colonel Herbert caught sight of Barry's approach. Even at a distance Barry saw the terror that took over the man's face. Herbert's mind

could only summon up the thought that Barry
was coming to arrest him for Hufford's murder.
Without even checking the course ahead, he
veered the wagon sharply, nearly toppling it as the
wheels screeched and illuminated the scene with
flying sparks.

Harmon had not been prepared for so quick a
maneuver. Barry was galloping abreast when he
started to turn his wagon to follow his father.

"Don't turn!" Barry screamed. "River cliffs
ahead!"

Barry began kicking his horse for an added
surge of speed. The animal's eyes grew wild with
fright, its breathing nearly stopped by the masses
of foaming froth that blew up from its mouth and
threatened to clog its nostrils. As he drew up to
the colonel's wagon from the rear, Barry stared
aghast at the ashen face that peered out from between the tarp flaps. Everyone had forgotten that
Cornithwyeth was a passenger in the Herbert
wagon.

"Jump!" Barry yelled, "or you'll get killed!"

Cornithwyeth looked at him frozenly. It was
plain he thought the jump would kill him as well.

With a final gallant effort the horse brought
Barry alongside the wagon team. His warning to
Colonel Herbert was met by stinging lashes of a
bull whip to ward him off. Herbert was beyond
understanding what Barry was screaming at him.
But the black man with him understood and
looked ahead.

"Miz MarSue, lookee dat!" he wailed, and
jumped free, his arms and legs windmilling.

Mary Sue climbed up into the vacated seat and
gaped. A hundred and fifty yards ahead, the

ground ended abruptly in a precipice. She tried
to cry the information into Tom Herbert's ear but
he ignored her. Desperately, she tried to wrestle
the reins from his grasp and with a shrieking curse
he swung a backhand that caught her a stinging
blow to the side of her head, spinning her away.
She reached out to save herself from falling but
found nothing but thin air and the hard ground
rushing up to greet her. She fainted before she hit
the ground and her limp body rolled along like a
wind-driven tumbleweed.

In attacking his wife, Herbert had dropped the
reins. Even as Mary Sue was falling Barry jumped
from his mount to the neck of the lead horse and
struggled to turn the team. Colonel Herbert, still
unaware of his danger, cracked the bull whip at
him in an attempt to knock him from the horse.
His buckskins afforded Barry some protection
from the stinging blows, but the whip cracks were
keeping him from gaining control of the beasts.
They surged faster ahead and would not be turned
away from their own destruction.

The wagon suddenly hit an outcropping, shearing off a wheel, the axle plowing out a three-foot
deep trough. But instead of slowing the wagon,
the loss tended to frighten the horses into dragging
it even faster.

Barry swore. He had to look to his own safety
now. He could jump now and risk smashing into
rocks. He could ride with the horses over edge and
take his chances on the water below. He chose
the latter.

Close to the instant it happened, Colonel Herbert finally saw the calamity ahead. He sat still

with an odd little grin making his clipped mustache twitch.

The four horses sailed off into nothingness, their hooves pawing as though still on solid ground. For a moment that seemed an eternity they remained poised in mid-flight, the wagon's weight holding it suspended on the cliff's edge. Then, their terrified squeals filling the air with a dreadful noise, the horses began to fall. Barry held on tightly, measuring in his mind the distance to the muddy water below and when would be the safest time to jump free.

The wagon seemed reluctant to leave the ground. It smashed down the rocky face, shearing off the wagon tongue. The horses were now free to plunge toward the water, but the wagon, now entirely wheel-less, plowed its own course as though that had been its purpose all along. And over the sound of the horses and the wagons' thunderous crashing came a noise that was eerily unbelievable—laughter. Like a child on a winter toboggan ride, Colonel Herbert was mindlessly enjoying his ride.

Ten feet above the water Barry jumped free, his powerful arms churning at the water the moment he hit to keep him away from the danger of the horses' hoofs. The current was swift and he instinctively swam against it, knowing that the entangled, overheated horses would be momentarily stunned when they hit and automatically let the current sweep them downstream.

The moment he pulled himself ashore he heard the terrified cry for help. It took him a moment to orient himself. The wagon had not turned over.

Miraculously, it had come to rest in the river fully upright. It wasn't the colonel who cried out. He still sat his seat, looking back up the trough the wagon had dug down the cliff face and giggling foolishly.

Barry ran back on the bank of the stream and reached the wagon.

"I'm trapped and drowning," Cornithwyeth wailed.

Barry cursed the man for not jumping when warned. He slid back into the frigid water and made his way to the wagon's rear. Only Cornith-wyeth's head was above the water line; the rest of his body was entangled in the wagon's debris. He wasn't trying to help himself. Damning him for a fool, Barry struggled to move the debris away from him. Every time he was able to dislodge a trunk or barrel it wanted to float or roll right back into place.

Then someone started shoving the articles forward from inside the wagon. It was Harmon Herbert. Harmon, who had stopped his own wagon, had scurried down the cliff, dreading what he might find. His father had only grinned at him and then he had heard Barry talking to Cornith-wyeth. Harmon removed the debris so Barry could grasp the small man in his arms, float him out of the wagon and carry him up to dry ground.

Now a half-dozen of the former slaves were making a rope and human ladder down to the wagon. Colonel Herbert flatly refused their help. He began scrambling up through the rocks like a mountain goat.

Barry returned to the wagon. As though it had been his main purpose in descending Harmon was removing still usable possessions and stacking them up neatly. Then he felt utterly stupid.

Timidly he put out his hand.

"Thank you, Barry," he said.

"For what?" Barry growled.

"For saving what you could. The black's got himself a broken shoulder and mama is only shook up and bruised. Paw would have killed us all, and you know that for sure."

Barry didn't answer.

"What's gonna happen to paw?" Harmon asked weakly.

Barry shrugged. He frankly didn't give a damn. "Depends," he said. "Depends on whether Hufford's dead or alive. We'll have to see."

"Is that who it was? We were already across the water. When paw came over we just followed him blindly, as usual."

He stared at Barry with dawning recognition in his eyes. "Guess that's what I've been, what I am. A blind fool."

Barry said gruffly, "No more than any of the rest of us for letting him have his own way."

"I—I guess you'll want us to leave the train," Harmon said, "after all the stupid things we done."

"I'll think on it," Barry said. "Now, you'd best get someone to help you salvage some of this stuff. I'm going to go get a fire going to warm Cornithwyeth."

When Aaron Pomeroy had fired his revolver, quickly pressing it then into Colonel Herbert's hand, he had not anticipated the bullet would hit old Hufford. He'd hoped only that the other men, judging the colonel to have gone berserk, would grab him and keep him from moving the Herbert wagons away. Pomeroy would have had to go with them. That was the last thing Pomeroy wanted. He wanted to remain close to the main party's chuck wagon, in which the Cornithwyeth gold lay hidden. It had taken him two weeks to butter his way into a talking friendship with the chuck wagon driver and Herbert's stubbornness had nearly ruined his plans.

Now that the colonel had actually left, Pomeroy was looking at the situation quite differently. Knowing the colonel, seeing his reaction to Hufford's fall, he figured he would flee and keep fleeing, just as he had in the old days when he'd welshed on gambling debts. Then he'd fled Georgia for Louisiana and other parts south. Now he expected him to head straight for California. And, mused Pomeroy, knowing the colonel, he might make it, too.

Strolling among the few slave-packed Herbert wagons that remained gave Pomeroy a sense of inherited power. He had been the one the blacks had childishly turned to after the colonel had made his escape. He was the one they would continue to turn to until the day came to take them away from the train and establish his own plantation.

The train was now encamped at the crossing where Parsons had directed them. Fitzpatrick had not returned. It was a quiet camp that night. The melee at the river had taken its toll on men's spirits and quite a few of the emigrants had gone to sleep early. Pomeroy, with a joyous song in his heart, went to a wagon in which the colonel had secreted his whisky, got a jug and casually sauntered over to the chuck wagon with it.

"Sonovagun, if'n it ain't ole Aaron!" Jeb Pierce said, his bewhiskered face lighting up at the sight of the jug.

"Howdy, Jeb," Pomeroy said, setting the jug on the ground next to the cook-driver's blanket. "Figured we might sit and talk a spell, seein' as how most ever'body else has gone to bed. Good moon for it." He looked up at the sky. "Nice out here, ain't it?"

"You betcha," Jeb said, his eyes fixed on the jug.

Cooking and drinking were Jeb Pierce's main pleasures, as far as anyone could see. Before hiring him, Barry had had to weigh his ability at the former against his propensity for the latter. He cooked up a storm of good food and he didn't hurt anybody when he drank, he finally decided. Which was true. Pomeroy had had a few nips with Jeb before. He liked to drink and tell stories about the old days, about Jim Bridger and Jed Smith and Kit Carson and other trappers and traders and guides he'd traveled with even before they got famous. The stories were interesting up to a point. Then Jeb would get sentimental. The old days were gone forever was, when he got sufficiently drunk, about the only message he could get across.

On this night, after an hour's worth of Aaron goading him to his tales and their inexorably reached conclusion, he tapped the jug and said, frowning, "Aaron, this jug's got black sand in it, like at the bottom of a river. It sucks you in, you know? The old days are sinking under me, boy. I got no place to go now, except home." He didn't say where home was. He stretched out on the blanket, drew his knees to his chest and fell asleep.

It was the sleeping, then the snoring part that Pomeroy liked best. He waited a while longer, then casually stepped into the wagon and began opening trunks and canvas bags. He was at his search for a half-hour. Finally, deep in a bag packed with clothing, his hand touched something familiar. His heart pounding, he drew out the four leather pouches. He took only as many of the gold coins that he could load his pockets with. From those pockets he took the washers he'd brought along and substituted them, weight for weight, for the gold. Then he carefully replaced the pouches in the same bag in which he'd found them and left.

Jeb Pierce was still snoring on his blanket. Aaron felt he'd have many more opportunities to get the rest of his loot.

Several miles to the south and somewhat to the west, Harmon Herbert sat staring into the dying embers of another camp fire. He too was dwelling on the gold coins he'd helped steal from Cornithwyeth's room. After the day's fiasco he had an urge to go to Barry and make a full confession of the theft. But he wasn't ready to act on his urge just yet. He felt miserable about too many other things.

There hadn't been much food in the surviving wagons, only a munching supply of dried jerky. On the other hand, no one was really hungry.

Cornithwyeth had done nothing but complain.

His father had never ceased to babble strangely. Mary Sue, though not seriously hurt in her fall, was bruised and in an uncommunicative shell. DeeDee had stubbornly refused to leave their wagon; Harmon thought she was embarrassed at having to face Barry Fitzpatrick but she wouldn't admit it. All in all, Harmon felt rotten.

"Well, my boy," Colonel Herbert said, expansively, "I think I hear your mother calling us to bed. Bank the fire good, because we don't want this fine old mansion burning down around us."

Harmon looked across the fire at Mary Sue, who raised her head, warning him to silence.

"Best you do go to bed, Harm," she said wearily.

"What about him?"

The colonel had curled up comfortably on the ground and was smiling, as if there were a thick, flouncy mattress beneath him.

"He's not with us," she said dully. "Let's just see what tomorrow brings."

Harmon had no one to talk to. He sat until he saw that Mary Sue was asleep, then went back to his wagon. DeeDee was no longer there, had apparently jumped out for one reason or another. Though he was lonely, Harmon resisted an urge to search for his sister. Probably, she'd finally gone after Barry. He hoped she'd gone to apologize for the way she'd wronged him. That's what he'd done; he'd apologized. Harmon was still hoping his own apology would pay off.

DeeDee had no intention of apologizing about anything. The way she saw it, she had been wronged, not Barry. Considering the course of the day and Barry's forced overnight stay away from the rest of the wagon train, she felt that this was her night for revenge.

Barry was fatigued, as he'd been fatigued after he'd run an Indian gauntlet once to win his freedom from a hostile tribe. He felt he could sleep for several days, right on the ground where he was. He was annoyed at the fly that kept landing on his face and escaping before he could swat at its tickling little legs.

He didn't open his eyes, because then it would see him and dart away to cunningly await another attack. He counted the seconds before each landing and posed his hand in preparation. Then he struck! But this time his hand never reached his cheek to squash the little devil. It captured instead another human hand. Then he heard giggling and opened his eyes.

"DeeDee!" he growled, and started to push her away.

DeeDee would not be denied. She dropped herself onto him, her lips slightly open.

In his fatigue, in his sudden urge to come out of it, Barry took the kiss full on the mouth, seeing if it would arouse him. It did. For a brief moment, he thought of Jessie Fremont's kiss, tried to make a comparison. Then DeeDee stuck her tongue in his mouth and ground her hips against him, and he gave himself the pure animal pleasure of the moment. His hands ran up and down her back to the curve of her buttocks. "Oh yes, oh yes," she whispered, burying her long hair in his face. "Grab my ass, grab it!" He grabbed it and pressed her close against him until her body stopped moving for a moment. Then he freed her to writhe again, bringing his hands up between them to fondle her breasts. She moaned and clawed at his belt.

She was like an Indian girl, just like an Indian girl fighting savagely and biting for blood on a teepee's pallet. Barry wrestled her around beneath him. Biting his neck she could not wait to get his pants off. She tore at the buttons and reached inside to grasp and hold, then pull out that suddenly massive, gorgeous rod she so urgently wanted.

DeeDee gasped. It was big, bigger than any boy's she'd ever held, bigger than any she'd ever imagined. It was hot and pulsing. She wanted to lick it, suck it, eat it. She wanted to swallow its juices.

She tried to move her mouth that way, but Barry held her back. He tugged at her skirt as he would at an Indian maiden's. Instantly, DeeDee pulled it up for him; she was naked beneath it. He penetrated her with his first thrust. DeeDee said, "Oh!" for she felt some pain. She put her hands against his shoulders and tried to push him away. Barry barely felt the push. She cursed him and Barry chuckled. Indian girls knew how to curse, too. She felt insulted by the laugh and lay tense and motionless. He kept thrusting. It was no different for Barry than it had been with a hundred Indian squaws. He accepted her final submission as commonplace and continued to please only himself.

Even when it was over and DeeDee had left in a silent huff, Barry was unaware of any problem. He lay back on the ground, relieved, letting the cool air and moonlight bathe his face. He'd enjoyed the sudden letting loose of his passions after days of tension. It was the trapper's way, the Indians' way, the way with which he was familiar. DeeDee hadn't objected. She'd shown some passion, too. He figured she felt about the same way he did, just wanted, like him, to be alone for a while.

DeeDee Herbert was very disappointed. She walked for a long time under the starry sky shaking with rage and frustration. She remembered feeling nothing, absolutely nothing—only his barbarian pounding within her. Maybe only toward the last had she begun to feel a slight tremor of excitement and then he had ceased to move. All that petting meant nothing. She knew there had to be more to sex than that.

Perhaps, she mused, it was like the first time she had secretly tried her father's corn liquor. It had burned like hell and tasted awful, but after a while she had grown to love the burning sensation and the warm glow it gave to her thinking. This had to be the same, she concluded. She wouldn't let Barry get away again.

She spun around and walked back to him.

"You're mine now," she enthused, "and there's no two ways about it."

Barry was surprised to see her.

"Ain't nobody's," he grumped, and rolled into a tight ball.

"We'll see about that," she chirped.

Barry grumped again and was asleep.

He awoke long before dawn, his body cold and stiff and sore from the evening before. He didn't disturb anyone, but threw the blanket and saddle onto his horse and rode for an hour to the river-fording spot where the main party was camped. The smell of Jeb Pierce's coffee was a welcome note and kept him from questioning why the old cook looked so solemn and forlorn.

Because the camp had had such a troubled night everyone seemed to be up and about and news of his arrival spread fast.

Barry was delighted to see that one of the first people to reach his campfire was old Hufford.

"I'll be damned," he said. "Thought sure I was coming back to find you dead."

"Hardly a scratch," Hufford chuckled, "although the fright nearly did me in. Wish I were younger and could take the bounder on for proper."

Barry shook his head. "I'm afraid, Hufford, it's in God's hands now."

"Dead, is 'e?"

"No. Something worse. Doc Freitag may be able to tell us for sure, but I think he's lost his mind."

Hufford pursed his lips. "Checked his knickers into the barn, has he? Can't say I'm surprised. I feel for the family."

Others were less charitable towards the Herberts. Now, when a meeting was held, children crowded in, too. They had seen a family of blacks perish at a river crossing the day before. Even this crossing loomed large to them. They wanted some assurance of safety.

"Looks full and wide to me, too," Howard Tedder said doubtfully. "All these wagons . . . Do what ye like, but I vote to take her slow an' keerful back to the east until we find somethin' narrower."

"And your people will follow you like a bunch of damn cowards!" stormed Count Justinian. "We can and must go on! Time is the question!"

There was silence. An icy voice broke it.

"Council's dissolved!" Barry declared sternly. "I am now Tsar, king, slave-owner or whatever damn name you want to give me. I'm sick up to here with each and every one of you and your petty little squabbles! We're moving across this river right here and now. That's what you paid me to decide and I've decided. If you want to go on your own you have my blessing but don't come crying to me for a refund of your money. I could walk away right now and feel we were justly even."

Ned Conroy opened his mouth to argue and Barry eyed him to silence.

"We will harness up and ride out as I dictate and camp tonight as I directed, which hasn't been done yet. Tomorrow, once passed this river, we are in the Platte Valley and the summer home of the Kaws. They, ladies and gentlemen, are Indians. Red men. *Savages!*" Then his voice dropped to a snarl. "But after two weeks with you people I've come to appreciate how civilized they are."

Ned Conroy refused to be put down. "I say we don't move 'til we bring that slave owner Herbert to trial for yesterday!"

Before he could get any support Barry shouted:

"Shut up! All of you! First, let's get one thing straight. Those blacks once belonged to Mrs. Herbert and not the Colonel. She gave them manumission. That means freedom. They're just like each and every one of the rest of us and I'll fight any bastard who says differently—especially the

ones who have seen fit to use their services and not
even give them a thank you. What happened yesterday I can't say, because I wasn't here, but you
weren't there for the end of it either. I was! The
colonel may have taken a little feeble in the head,
I don't know. I do know I'm not about to stop this
train to find out. You've got fifteen minutes to
harness up and begin to move out. Those who
don't follow my wagon across the ford are free to
go their own route."

For too long the emigrants had had four different people to rail against. Now they had only a
single authority to buck, and it drew them into a
common union against him.

"Wagon master." No one was ever to determine who was the first to use the phrase in a
coupling with Barry Fitzpatrick's name. But before the sun had even started to warm the earth
that day, and every single wagon was forded
across the river without mishap, every man,
woman and child knew that their former guide
had become the "wagon master" of their future
destiny.

14

The New England Emigrant Resettlement Association train lay banked along the Platte in utter and abject confusion. Organization there now was none. Ransom Beaver Pond was an excellent scout, but purposely had avoided taking any leadership responsibility. The trip from Lancaster had been uneventful in comparison with the two weeks of nightmare they'd had since leaving Fort Leavenworth. Not a day passed without freak accidents and hard-to-explain breakdowns in the new Conestoga wagons.

A great many of the inexplicable incidents began to be blamed on the fact that the train was "petticoat" run—by Arabelle Cornithwyeth. A hundred miles out of Fort Leavenworth three disgruntled family men made a joint decision. They took their wagons with their wives and children and headed back east.

Doom-sayers prophesied that the journey to Oregon was going to end in disaster right there on the banks of the Platte. If many more didn't turn around and go home, it was only because they wanted Bradford Cornithwyeth to reach them so that they could get at least a partial return of their money.

Arabelle would not be daunted. She walked down the wagon lines, Anne in her wake, noting the needed repairs and doing her best to get them done. Most of the men just sat and waited. Women, pale, gaunt, grim, looked at her with eyes that would have dissolved a lesser woman. Children whimpered and did not play. Even the dogs, curled nose to tail under the wagons, growled in a surly fashion.

For once, Arabelle kept her thoughts to herself and did not try to browbeat or scold or shame. She would leave all of that for her husband.

On the third day of their stay at the Platte, Arabelle awoke strangely excited. She went and sat the morning out on a grassy knoll, her eyes never leaving the southeast. Even after she spotted the slow-moving wagons kicking up columns of dust, she refrained from calling out. So disciplined were they in their four well-spaced-out lines that she thought at first they were military units on maneuvers.

But her intuition had never lied to her before, so she stood and shielded her eyes from the noon-day sun.

"Woweee!" she cried, and began to jump up

and down like a child spying its first Christmas tree. "They're a-coming! Woweee!"

The stout woman's cheer brought the emigrants out of the doldrums. They raced to high ground and began to cheer on the train themselves, as though watching a horse race. In a way it was a race, the stronger teams breaking out of the columns to gain the choicest camping sites.

At the front of the train, Barry hastened his horse to one side, needing to give orders quickly. He waved his hand for the breakaways to stop. Then he cupped his hand and shouted:

"To the right and left, columns—roll!"

It appeared to the New England people as if the drivers had been doing this wagon maneuver since leaving the Missouri. The wagons broke apart, alternating right and left, until the four columns had become two. Each of these advanced, curving out, then drawing in, until a long ellipse, closed at front and rear, was formed.

"Look, mother!" Anne Cornithwyeth pointed with pride. "There's papa on that wagon! I hope he can train our people to do that, too!"

Arabelle nodded, knowing her unexperienced husband could not possibly have worked out this maneuver. She had been watching Barry Fitzpatrick command the formation and wisely gave the credit where it was due. Even at a distance she could see that the guide of the southern train might be the kind of man who could put Ransom Beaver Pond in his place, which pleased her mightily.

Anne's gaze turned from her father to another familiar face. Her heart gave a leap, then just as suddenly chilled. She was looking at Thomas Geddy. She'd been attracted to this young man in Lancaster and maybe she still was. She felt he still owed her something for keeping his secret about the two servant girls with him. Look, the horsy one he'd married was with him on the wagon seat. That's what chilled Anne. She wasn't about to wait for him to leave that horse and turn to her. She wanted to meet new people, exciting people! Especially that young, handsome lad driving the wagon her father was in. Goodness, why did the wagon have an Alabama flag on it?

"Come on, mother!" she cried. "Let's go greet papa!"

Anne and Arabelle, needing to walk gingerly down into the valley, reached the wagon after it had stopped. Its driver, Harmon Herbert, was unharnessing the team. Anne gave him a quick, admiring glance; he was as good-looking as she'd thought he was, seeing him from the hill. But her attention was immediately drawn to her father, who looked pale, wan, quite ill.

"Bradford! What happened to you!" Arabelle stopped short, much disturbed.

Cornithwyeth looked at her coldly. As usual, she'd shown him no tenderness, not even with a hello. "I was shot," he said. "Among other things."

"Shot!" Arabelle gasped. "Who? How?"

Harmon Herbert stopped unharnessing the team. He thought it time to set one part of the record straight.

"It was me, ma'am. I can explain. I wasn't tryin' to kill him, only protect our black people after he and his ruffians killed a couple dozen of them."

Anne's heart sank. She still had not been introduced to this young southerner and now doubted that she would be.

"Should have killed them all," Cornithwyeth snapped, as Arabelle continued to gape. "Then that crazy father of yours wouldn't have had a chance to try and kill me again."

"Again?" Arabelle cried. "What is this madness? Didn't you have any law and order?"

"No," Cornithwyeth snapped. "But we will have as soon as I get back on my feet, by God! Either these black heathens are put out of the train or I'll . . ."

Barry had come riding up and Cornithwyeth cut his threat short. Sick as he was, he was not ready to take command, not yet.

Barry dismounted and doffed his cap. "Barry Fitzpatrick, ma'am. I don't need to be told that you are Mrs. Cornithwyeth and this is your daughter Anne. 'Cause you all haven't met, this is Harmon Herbert."

"I want him arrested, at once!" Arabelle flared.

Barry said slowly, "Can't do that."

Arabelle stormed. "Then I shall send back for the army, sir."

"Your privilege, ma'am," Barry said evenly. " 'Course they'll be asking your husband about the twenty-seven blacks he had killed."

"I told them not to fire," Cornithwyeth cried.

Arabelle ignored him and eyed Barry dangerously. "That is beside the point, Mr. Fitzpatrick. These savages aren't people to begin with."

Barry fought to control his anger. "Lady, you are just about as pig-headed a fool as your husband. Those blacks were people enough to feed and nurse him after what he done to some of them. Those black men had arms strong enough to lift him up a cliff after Harmon here saved his worthless life. Why don't you do me a big favor? Get him the hell out of my sight. I'll feel a lot safer going on with the blacks than I ever would with the likes of your train."

"Well! You have that a little wrong, Mr. Fitzpatrick!" Arabelle said, enraged. "From what I have just heard, I wouldn't dream of putting my people in your charge. And furthermore—"

The frantic screams of several women interrupted her. Barry looked to the south. Several Indians, perhaps thirty, had come into sight along the river bank. They were riding towards the encampment in full view and their ponies were trotting. Quivers of arrows were at their backs. Barry looked at the frightened women and scratched his head. Then he got on his horse. "Harm," he said, "get everybody inside the wagon circle and mount some guards. But tell the damn fools not to fire unless attacked."

"Where are you going?" Arabelle shrieked.

Barry said, "To palaver with the Indians. Unless you fear some of this black skin you see will rub off on your pinkness, you can invite your people into the circle for safety."

He was gone before Arabelle could form a reply. She stood there, confused. Her people had no doubt seen the Indians, but she couldn't walk back there in time to instruct them. Where was that stupid Indian scout when she needed him the most? She'd have to trust Anne.

"Child," she wailed, "run and tell the people to come here!"

Harmon had come back from the mission Barry had sent him on. People were scurrying inside the circle and guards were posted. He took a quick look at the situation and said, "You stay, Miss Anne. I can go faster!"

Anne flushed. "I'd surely appreciate it, Mr. Herbert."

Arabelle waited until Harmon was gone before she exploded. "Really, how ill-mannered can some people be. I'll not have strange young men calling you by your Christian name. A man who shot your father!"

"Mama," Anne said, some fire in her eyes. "May we get inside the circle ourselves now? Please? Papa is ill and we will have to help him."

Major Warren had described Ransom Beaver Pond quite inadequately, Barry mused, as he rode toward the column of Indians. His heart had relaxed the moment he recognized that the redmen were Kaws and that the tall scout was leading them. The heavily laden ponies told him that they were on a trading mission. He could have sat his horse and waited their advance, but continued to ride out to greet them so as to provide the fortress with a good rehearsal while they were still in relatively friendly country.

First in sign language, then in the Kaw tongue, he greeted Beaver Pond and the braves. Because respect had been shown, Ransom returned it by speaking English.

"The trains will welcome the Kaws," Barry said. "But aren't the goods they bring to trade still unskinned?"

Ransom laughed delightedly. "You have the eagle eye, my brother. Those whites I have led this far know little of hunting or fishing. They use up their supplies as though a general store will be waiting for them beyond the next bluff. I saw no reason why my Kaw brothers could not use their excellent hunting ability to bring about trade. They bring not skins but fresh game."

A good point, Barry thought, but felt he should make one of his own. "You are wise," he said, nodding, "but they will need more than fresh game to trade hereafter. I have brought people who are expert shots. Venison and wild turkey are even now being roasted on a spit."

Ransom had been noting the distant wagon circle with great interest. Barry Fitzpatrick, he was quickly coming to note, was not the total fool and inexperienced person that Major Warren had depicted. Ransom would have to be very clever slowing down this young mountain man. His first ploy, which he used with every new person met, was to launch immediately into the story of his strange birth and life. His was not a braggart's story but an interlude, a time when his mouth could be saying words so often said that his eyes would have time to study. He would learn more of the listener than the listener did of him.

There were those, like Major Warren, who listened indifferently, marking them as more interested in themselves than the other person. Or there was the shocked listener, like Arabelle Cornithwyeth, who really wasn't shocked at all and was therefore in his eyes a very insensitive person. But very seldom did he run into a person like Barry Fitzpatrick, who honestly hung onto every word he was uttering and thus revealed nothing more of himself than his warmth toward other human beings. And few, such as Barry, ever dared to question the true outcome of the story.

"That's amazing! And your mother? Is she now with the Kaws or the Arapahoe?"

Ransom laughed. The answer was only for him to know. "I think that is a story for another time, young brother. I would suggest that you prepare your people for our friendly visit."

Both trains were well prepared to have a friendly visit with each other and with the Indians. It was a time for sharing, relaxing, forgetting the past days of turmoil and strife. It was as though each and every person wished for that to be a night so full of eating, drinking, laughing, dancing and friendly gossip that he would not have to have a yesterday or a tomorrow.

For his own people, the man they called Big Rufus began to fiddle. A farmer from New England joined him with a mouth organ. Howard Tedder brought forth one of his saws and a bow to make it sing. Not to be outdone, Ned Conroy joined them with an earthen jug he could blow into to create a bass rhythm chord.

They were a widely diverse gathering, but the music brought them together to reel, to jiggle, to waltz. At first the English stayed a little aloof, although the Cossacks had to put on a foot-stamping display that made the Indian guests roar with mirth.

Because many other young couples had been caught in Arabelle's marriage demands and still weren't comfortable with their mates, the evening produced many roving eyes. The Conroy boys were dancing with anybody in sight, until their father soundly cuffed them for 'hoppin' around wid niggah trash!'

Maybelle Tedder, screwing up her courage, brazenly asked Barry to dance and was crushed to learn he had never danced a step in his life. But he grabbed the first single-looking fellow he could find and thrust Maybelle into his arms.

In doing so he almost trampled a little girl and had to quickly keep her from falling.

"I'm sorry," he apologized.

"My fault, I'm sure," she giggled. "Isn't this exciting? It's near like the farmer's fair at home."

"Is it now?" He kiddingly matched her brogue. "I've not heard that lilt for a dog's age. Who would you be, lass?"

Pearl Fergus Hartwicke knew exactly who he was. Although he was dark, and her father golden, she had taken a single look at Barry Fitzpatrick and grown terribly homesick. Now she felt suddenly awed by him.

"I'm Pearl, Master Fitzpatrick."

"Master, is it?" he roared. He somehow saw her as the child she actually was and not the woman others saw. "And where might your folks be?"

Pearl looked about confused. She had not seen Lester Hartwicke for some time. That was not unusual, but in the excitement and the crowd, she had become separated from Bertha and Tom. "They're about," she said uncertainly. "Perhaps dancing."

"Which a lovely colleen like you should be doing as well. Ah, here's a couple of likely prospects. Theodis . . . Nazareth . . . over here. Here's a little Irish lass with a lilt that will melt either of your cold hearts. She's ready for a dance."

Nazareth quickly begged off. He had a secret meeting to keep with Selena Buttle-Jones that promised more than dancing and was glad for an excuse to get rid of his twin brother. Theodis turned a glowing scarlet the moment he was left alone with the girl. For weeks he had set in his mind that Selena would be the only girl in his life, even though his brother did have more fun with her. Now, taking the Irish girl's hand to get into the Virginia Reel line, his mind boggled. Her merest touch turned his body to liquid fire. When she sashayed away from him, he momentarily could not recall her face; then, as they would be reunited, it became lovelier with each recoupling. Her natural perfume intoxicated him. He would hold her in his arms to twirl her about, and dread the moment he would have to release her to return to the women's line.

At the end of the dance he bravely begged for another and was joyous when she accepted. And Pearl kept accepting his invitations because she was having the time of her life. She had no particular interest in Theodis Tedder; she had hardly looked at him. She was just relishing this momentary escape from boredom and the cruelty of Lester Hartwicke. And when her enjoyment was at its zenith, it all seemed to melt into a rosy, warm glow and peaceful darkness. She was back in the women's line and close to fainting.

"Are you all right, child?"

The voice, so lovingly tender, and the fuzzy focus of her eyes made her think another had spoken and tenderly held her hand.

"Mums," she murmured.

"No child," the voice answered, "I am Lydia Tedder. I fear my son over-danced you."

But Pearl looked into a face that easily could have been her mother's own, it was so filled with love and compassion and concern.

"My fault, too, mum. I was having a most good time."

"Of course. You'll be fine in a moment. Are your people about?"

"Surely, mum. My sister and her husband and my . . ." Pearl could not bring herself to say it. She still could not look upon Lester Hartwicke as a husband and never could. It was a fake thing for the trip and she had spent a joyous evening not even thinking about him.

Lydia Tedder didn't press her to go on. She didn't need to be told what the look on Theodis's face meant; he had very quickly and totally committed himself to loving this very beautiful young girl. But Lydia was no fool. She had lived in the backwoods far too long not to note immediately that the girl, in spite of her young age, showed many signs of pregnancy. The girl had stopped short of mentioning a husband, but the rumor mill was already rife with the quick marriages that had been performed before the staid New England group would allow some to travel with them. Until she knew more about the girl, she would hold her knowledge back to protect her son.

Arabelle had stubbornly refused to attend the outing. She was with her husband and daughter.

She, too, was seeking knowledge of a protective sort.

"Once more, Bradford," Arabelle implored, "is there anything that Fitzpatrick has done that would make it possible for us not to have to pay his exorbitant fee and still make him lead us? It's obvious he is the only man for the job."

"Oh, mother!" Anne pleaded. "You've gone over it a hundred times. Please excuse me, for the evening."

"You're excused to go to bed," Arabelle said shortly. "I know what's in your mind and I'll not have it. Dancing is the handiwork of the devil and there are many in this camp who will hear of it from me tomorrow. Goodnight! Now, Bradford?"

Anne's feet were flying before she heard her father's answer. She feared the music would end before she reached it. She had never danced before, either, but would have gladly allowed Harmon Herbert to teach her. She would have gladly allowed him to teach her anything.

But when she came near the center of the festivities she nearly turned and fled. Harmon was dancing with the most gorgeously gowned creature Anne had ever beheld. Anne had heard the rumors about an English lady and a Russian count being on the train and took for granted that the beautiful girl had to be a member of one of those parties. Everything about her was rich and elegant and regal. She watched her in open-mouthed awe and envy.

"She is gussied up pretty, isn't she?" someone at her shoulder said drily. "But you've got no call to get upset about her."

Anne turned. "Oh," she started, "Mr. Fitzpatrick. I'm glad I saw you. I just came from my family. My father says you have some of his things to return."

"Did you come to deliver messages or dance?"

She blushed. "I don't dance."

"Nor do I," he grinned, "but I seem to be the matchmaker of the evening. He called out, still grinning, "Harmon, that's enough with your sister. Get her another partner and come on back here."

DeeDee swung away from her brother and glared. "That ape. He's not man enough to dance with me himself and now he's trying to stick you with that stringbean. God, I hate him for what he's done to this family."

"Or not done for you?" Harmon chided.

Angered at him and spiteful, DeeDee pulled away and searched for a dancing partner whom she felt sure would keep Harmon from deserting her. She found black Amos's eighteen-year-old grandson Ebner and planted herself directly in front of him. The husky youth was momentarily stunned when DeeDee put her arms about him. The dance was a lively two-step that his feet knew well, but it was decidedly awkward for him to do it with the "mass'ah's daughter."

DeeDee had judged her brother's reaction wrongly. Off to one side, he watched her for a moment and shrugged. If he had to suffer with the plain Anne Cornithwyeth, let DeeDee make a public fool of herself with a black.

Lady Pamela had viewed that particular contretemps with wry amusement and then climbed back up into her wagon. Because Selena had asked it of her, she had showed herself and watched most of the festivities. But, in actual fact, she had found the outing most vulgar and barbaric. She despaired of it. Except for Barry Fitzpatrick, she had not seen a single man she would care to touch, let alone dance with.

She had come back inside to concentrate on another problem. She did not like the attachment Selena was developing for the Tedder boy and she intended to put an end to it that very night. When she heard footsteps on the tailgate steps, she primed her comments.

"Selena, I—" She stopped short and gasped. "You!"

"Surprised, milady?" Lester Hartwicke carefully let himself into the wagon, closed the flaps and found a comfortable seat to lodge upon. "Surely, I don't take you by surprise?"

She couldn't answer. She was fighting down waves of terror.

"That amazes me," he chuckled. "For once in her life little Pamela is caught speechless."

"It's a classic tale," she murmured. "The obvious was always in plain sight."

"Not quite," he said warily. "Some things had to be carefully concealed."

"Such as your death? When the servants made me suspicious of the duke I should have realized that it was not him that they were wary of. It was you, wasn't it?"

He laughed. "Naturally. I could have linked every one of them to the assassination attempt on Queen Victoria. When that stupid pot-boy Oxford missed his target, the plan had to be quickly altered. Of course, I had the advantage. Who would suspect such a loyal subject being involved?"

She studied his face intently, as though thinking of another question. But her senses were returning and she was measuring her adversary.

"That doesn't make sense," she said. "Why pretend to be dead if you were not suspect?"

Again he laughed. "Most every plot to take over a throne involves many important people. I guess I failed to see in the planning that I was expendable. My blood line, it seems, ran a little too close to the duke's. When his henchman came to kill me, Captain Templeton saved my life and the man's mangled body was buried in my name."

"Surely the duke suspected something when his man didn't return?"

"He did and it was almost my fatal mistake," he remarked in a disappointed voice. "I popped in on the old duck and he seemed not the least bit surprised. As an uncle he never was a very loving man and thought my demands to remain dead and silent were a bit out of bounds. He quietly had me locked away in the castle. I gather you might have been brought to join me, but you tended to muddy the waters at that point."

"Muddied the waters?" she gasped. "I considered you dead!! Your family considered you dead! Demands and accusations were flying about like a swarm of locusts. Your soldiers were released from service and looked to me for their pension. You never saw fit to consult me about your business affairs and your papers were a jumbled mess of nothingness."

"You should have left matters as they were."

She clenched her teeth. He enraged her. Never had she felt hatred as she felt it at that moment, but she kept her voice soft and even.

"That, Lester, was an impossibility. Your family was out for revenge because I had had the audacity to force you into a marriage that would sully their family tree. I was accused of making you live high on the hog and squander family money. After our first two years, I never saw you long enough to have that much influence on you. When it became apparent that they were going to cut me off without a pound I went to Lord Dunraven for advice. He never was partial to the duke and suggested I take what I could and flee while I was still able. As the one land grant was in your name he said I could legally claim it."

"So I learned in New York."

"I was wondering how you traced me. Although I've suspected all along that the duke, or your father, would have someone on my tail."

"You're so damn stupid," he sneered. "Did it not occur to you that the duke might have had someone with you all along?"

"No," she snapped right back, "because those soldiers feared for their lives after what happened to you. Dead men can't tell tales." Then she gasped. "Templeton! He knew you were still alive!"

"Rubbish! It had to be one of the others that told the duke of their pending departure disguised as tenant farmers. He might have stopped them then and there, but you had already departed. He could not afford to arouse your suspicion and give you a chance to totally disappear.

Hence, he had no choice but to release me to come after you."

"Perhaps I am dense . . . but what is his purpose for all of this? They got exactly what they wanted, to be rid of me and Selena."

This time the laugh was sardonic. "I have been under the suspicion that my uncle gave you the full story when he was making his demands. Didn't you know that I was helping myself quite liberally to the family treasures? The total figure is quite a king's ransom. Now, my dear, to appease the old bastard, and give me a fresh no-questions-asked new life, please hand it over."

"My God!" she cried. "You're insane!"

He scoffed. "We really don't have to return it, Pamela, if that's your fear. As husband and wife we can live a lifetime on that gold."

"As what?" she said tartly. "You never were a husband to me. Less than a father to Selena. Once I had tears to cry over the servants snickering about Lord Lester and his latest affair. After fifteen years there are no tears left and I don't want to learn how to cry again. I buried you once and I don't want to do it a second time. As far as I am concerned you are dead!"

Lord Lester Buttle-Jones' brows came together in a scowl. "As you wish," he said absently. "But I can't take a chance of your ruining my life a second time."

"What is that supposed to mean?"

"A man doesn't like to be branded a thief, even by his own family. Now, the gold is not where I hid it in the manor house. It is far too much for a coffer chest, so I am curious as to where you could hide such a sum."

"Would you like to look through my wagon?" she asked through clenched teeth. "That is the only way I am going to be able to prove to you that I know nothing about any gold."

Lord Lester grinned impudently at her, and shook his head. "That only proves to me that it is not in this wagon. Play out your little game, Pamela, I have plenty of time. If the duke's man finds it first, he may not be as civil with you. And once the soldiers find out I am alive and here, I don't think you will be able to count on them for much loyalty. You're bound to make a mistake and I'll be waiting. Oh, I'm known as Lester Hartwicke in case you want to get in touch with me."

"Get out!" Lady Pamela said furiously. "I have no reason to get in touch with you whatsoever!"

He shrugged. "Not even for Selena's sake?"

"What of her?"

"What of her?" he repeated absently. "I would hate for an accident to befall her because you are being so stupid."

"You can't be serious. She is your daughter!"

"Does that seem fantastic to you?" Lester said gently. The tone of his voice made her blood run cold. "She means less to me than you do and you surely must know how much I care for you. Goodnight, Pamela. Pleasant dreams!"

Lady Pamela's first desperate thought after he left was to call on Hufford for immediate aid. But she had to find Selena first. Until she could figure out what to do about Lord Lester, she wasn't going to let the girl out of her sight.

"The man's insane," she said. "I wouldn't be

out in this damn wilderness if I had stolen the
gold."

"The man is insane," Tall Pine advised Beaver
Pond. "None of our people will wish to go to the
big water."

"You were wise to tell me this thing, little
brother. Go now and tell your father, our chief,
that Beaver Pond will sit with him before the
moon is halfway across the sky. I will know by
then how the man is to be answered."

With the departure of the Indians, so seemed
to depart the merriment of the evening. The emigrants had put on a brave face for the savages,
although most were not fully aware that's what
they had been about. Like dancers after a masked
ball, they returned to who they were before the
evening began.

This pleased Ransom, for he could now see
that the young mountain man's group were as
split by inner turmoil as the one he had led.
Without making it obvious he carefully studied
the Russian group and then silently slipped away
to return to the Kaw village.

For many hours he sat in solemn council with
the Kaw elders. He listened, answered quickly
when asked for facts, and respectfully waited for
these old men to listen to his youth. When everyone had their say the Kaw chief pondered it all
deeply. Though Ransom was a half-breed, He-
of-the-Buffalo respected his wisdom.

"For many moons," he said softly, "you have
been back among these people, son of the Golden
Woman. We never feared their trappers and hunt-

ers, because they were like a single storm in a drought year. Tall Pine speaks of many squaws and children. Is it their whole nation on the move?"

"No, my adopted father, these would be no more than a handful of hair out of a whole buffalo robe."

"Then we must stop them here and now!" Leaf-of-the-Aspen declared.

"I am hearing Beaver Pond," the chief growled sternly.

"I know the feeling in his heart," Ransom said quickly, for he had many missions to accomplish and wished no enemy over words. "But the many wars among our own people have reduced the Kaw lodges and braves. We have none of their firing sticks."

"You make us sound like women!" another council brave snorted.

"No Kaw is a woman!" Beaver Pond snapped. "But hear me. Trappers may have been a single storm, this group a day of rain, but there is a flood waiting to engulf us if we are not prepared."

"Are you not saying the same as I?" Leaf-of-the-Aspen insisted.

"You, who could be one of my fathers, I tell you that for the Kaw alone to strike down this group would only bring upon us the horse soldiers and their cannon. Their singing wire of words can bring many bluecoats faster than we could gain help from other nations. I am told, that to the north of this river, which has been a mother to us, stand five hundred Sioux lodges. For this year they already hang much buffalo meat, and the women are hard-pressed to dress all the hides.

Their men grow fat and lazy because they have been given no cause to war. I say let this train go and give the Sioux cause for war."

Now the chief was skeptical. "The Sioux are very slow to stir, my son. Your voice would be better heard by the Arapahoe."

"Sioux!" Ransom shouted. "They owe me! I will give them cause. I curse the Arapahoe for allowing the Sioux to steal my mother and sell her to the trappers who used her and killed her. They owe me the names of those trappers and I'll give them a thousand white scalps in exchange. If they do not want my bargain then I shall go to the Cheyenne, to the Gros Ventres, the Blackfeet, the Shoshones and even the hated Utes. I will not rest until I find her or her resting place, and it should be your vow as well!"

A slow, rhythmic beat on the ground of the tepee with the palms of their hands gave him the council's wholehearted approval.

"Have you thought it out carefully, my son?"

"I have, my adopted father, although there is risk. We must first consider this Russian man, for he has been put in my charge. He was not to arrive on the shores of the big water until the first snow had fallen. That is moons away. He has already offered Tall Pine several of the firing sticks to lead him away tonight."

The mention of the firing sticks impressed the council. They feared them, stood in awe of them, but deeply coveted them.

"But," Ransom quickly went on, "he is a man in high council in his land, but in disfavor with their chief at this time. His delay is important, but not his death."

"Why not death to him as well?" Gray Wolf asked. "Is he not also of the white skin?"

"He is," Ransom agreed. "But his nation is peopled like an ant hill. They would like nothing better than to sweep down from the land of the Aleuts and kill us faster than the bluecoats could dream possible. But I also need time to make my pact with the Sioux. As a young man, have I the permission of the council to put a plan before you?"

Greeted with thunderous approval, he grinned.

15

There were not enough curse words in the King's English to come near the number required by Barry as he stared at the empty spots in the circle. His anger was such that his calm voice seemed a far more dangerous element to deal with.

"How many?" he asked.

"Six," Howard Tedder answered, on a note of embarrassment. "His personal wagon and the supply wagons. He's left us with his women and servants."

"No Cossacks or arms?"

"Nary a one."

Figures. "Was this Nazareth's post last night?"

"Yes," Tedder blushed, "but how'd you know that?"

"Easy," Barry said so evenly it was deadly.

"He's always with that English girl. Her maw's been frantic all night looking for her. I was a damn fool not to think of this. Get her back so I don't have to ask questions."

"Already back," Tedder wheezed, in relief. "You goin' after the count?"

"No," Barry said with firm resolution.

Tedder blinked. "You went out af'ta the colonel."

"Different," Barry snorted, but didn't give his reasons, and Tedder decided not to ask after them. Barry looked around the rest of the circle and made a quick decision. "Council's lacking, Tedder. Cornithwyeth will try to take over, especially after this. If you and Hufford agree, I say we let Harmon replace his father. That's better than letting Cornithwyeth rule the roost."

But Bradford Cornithwyeth had also gotten up before breakfast that day. The deplorable condition of his wagon train staggered him and suggested nothing but delay. Knowing Fitzpatrick's penchant for running things by council-committee action, he quickly sought to form a similar structure of his own.

"Who," he demanded of Arabelle, "seem to be the most educated men among us? Men who can outthink Fitzpatrick's henchmen."

Hesitantly, since she could not abide either man, Arabelle mentioned Thomas Geddy and Lester Hartwicke. Bradford accepted her suggestions, sight unseen, and turned his attention to his possessions, which Barry had just had delivered back to him.

* * *

Lady Pamela stared at her daughter with mixed feelings of anger and relief. "My God! Where have you been?" she demanded.

"In my wagon," Selena lied, indifferently.

"No. I'll have the truth!"

Selena giggled. "Is it really that important?"

Lady Pamela sat down slowly, trying to control her temper. "Yes, Selena, it is! Your father is on the other wagon train."

Selena looked at her mother as though she had lost her mind and laughed. "You have tried many things, mother, to keep me away from boys, but this ruse is ridiculous."

"I am speaking the truth," Lady Pamela exploded.

"Sure," Selena sneered, "you are, mother, as you see the truth. Are you jealous? You were nothing more than a gardener's slut who spread her legs for an earl's son. I'm not sure what to call the boy I've spread my legs for."

The slap was so swift and so harsh that it stunned Selena. "No more," snapped Lady Pamela. "You will report to me each and every hour of the day until I say differently, unless you wish to taste the true side of his sadistic nature."

"But he's dead," Selena wailed.

"Far from it and he's claiming that we have stolen some Buttle-Jones gold. Now get to your wagon and stay there. I've a lot of thinking to do."

Ransom Beaver Pond was a puzzlement to Barry. For a man charged with the responsibility of the count's safety he seemed untroubled.

"There are greedy men in every race, Fitzpatrick. If he bribed some Kaw braves to lead him, as you suggest, we will come upon him after a few days' march."

"How do you figure that?"

Ransom grinned. "The part of me that is Kaw says it is so. A few days away from their lodges and a Kaw's feet automatically turn for home. I do not fear for the man until we get to the land of the Sioux."

It was a truth Barry could believe, but there was another point that had to be considered. He had wanted the matter settled before Cornithwyeth joined them. Now he could see the feisty little man charging toward his wagon with two men following him. He looked like a gamecock ready to fight.

"What worries me," he said quickly, "is that he took all of his men with him. I don't know if we have enough extra to drive his wagons. The sooner he's back the better for all of us."

It was just such a statement Ransom had been waiting for. "Then I go to scout him out."

Bradford Cornithwyeth, seeing the Indian riding away, forgot what was uppermost in his mind.

"Where is he going?" he demanded.

"Scouting," was all Barry cared to say at the moment.

"From now on he will take orders only from me! This is Geddy and Hartwicke. They will be my council."

Wily bastard, Barry thought. He's deadlocked the council at three and three.

"Fine," he drawled. "This is Tedder, Herbert and Hufford."

There was a general shaking of hands except

for Lester Hartwicke and Hufford. They eyed
each other cautiously, neither wishing to reveal
that they had been master and servant. Hufford
was amazed that Lord Lester was so openly dis-
playing himself. Lester thought it quite idiotic
that such an uneducated old coot was in a position
of authority. His first impulse had been to flatly
turn down Cornithwyeth's request, but then he
had seen how well it would work to his advantage.
As a leader of the train his snooping around
would go unquestioned. But the coachman might
be a fly in that ointment.

"Now's the time to get us ready for a long
march," Barry stated. "You, Cornithwyeth, seem
to need the most work. Harmon has offered the
services of their blacksmith and carpenters for
those who need them. But I don't think that it's
fair for them to work for free. Which reminds
me, we've got some finances to discuss ourselves."

"Yes, we do," Cornithwyeth said icily, pulling
a leather pouch out of his belt. "And this is all
I feel I owe you!"

He threw the bag down so hard that it hit on
the campfire rocks and split open. All that fell
out were gray metal washers and harness discs.

"Is this some kind of a joke?" Barry asked,
puzzled.

"Don't be coy," Cornithwyeth sneered. "I'm
missing seven thousand dollars in gold coin, and
you stole it!"

"What in the hell are you talking about?"

"Don't lie!" he shrieked. "You were the one
who took my possessions from the boarding house
and kept them during the trip. But when your
cook returned everything to me this morning this

is what I found instead. I want it back, you lying thief!"

For the moment Barry could only stare at him. Harmon blanched and was tempted to call Cornithwyeth the liar. He knew the exact amount he and Pomeroy had stolen, but held his silence.

"No man," Barry said through clenched teeth, "calls me a liar and thief. I know nothing about your money and am not about to accept this as the money due me."

Cornithwyeth spoke coldly, with a certain contempt that made Barry color.

"Then your services are no longer required by my Association, Fitzpatrick."

"That's enough," Harmon said hoarsely. "You're forgetting that he saved your life. If he stole your gold, why didn't he just let you drown and the theft never would have been uncovered?"

"That's how I'd look at it," Tedder soundly agreed.

"That still doesn't get my money back," Cornithwyeth insisted.

"All right!" Barry flared. "I do feel responsible because the money was in my charge. I don't know how, but I'll repay it some way or other."

"I should certainly hope so. Now, please leave us."

"I'm not the one leaving, Mr. Cornithwyeth," rejoined Barry hotly. "This is my train here and yours is over there. I'll not train up with a man who has accused me as you have done."

"The choice is not yours to make. You are only a hireling!"

"I say," old Hufford snapped indignantly, "you have no right to speak everyone's mind for them.

I think I speak for Tedder and Herbert in saying that we'll continue to cast our lot with Barry."

Unable to control himself further, Cornithwyeth wheeled and galloped his banty legs back to his own train.

"Damn," Lester whispered to Tom Geddy. "He's worse than his wife."

"I don't think we can make it under them," Tom agreed. "I'm tempted to ask for our money back and see if we can't join up here."

"Excellent thought," Lester replied. "You go beard the lioness in her den and I'll broach the subject to Fitzpatrick."

But Lord Lester's main intention was to sidle up to Hufford, which he did when he had a moment alone with him.

"It would seem that stolen gold is a popular topic these days," he murmured.

Hufford scowled. "So mi'lady informs me."

Lord Lester said narrowly, "But of course, you'd know nothing about it."

"Nothing," Hufford said and dropped the subject because Barry had come up to them.

Lord Lester was quick to make Tom Geddy's suggestion his own. Barry was a little dubious about the plan.

"I doubt the Cornithwyeths will return your money any more than I would, Hartwicke. I do have a down payment from the man on most of the wagons, although it was damn little. I suppose if a person wanted to pay me the difference direct, I wouldn't be turning them down."

Hartwicke pursed his lips. "That might be a little difficult. We all had to pay our two hundred dollars in advance."

"Damn him for calling me the thief!" Barry flared. "I'm only charging him twenty-five a wagon!"

"That's very interesting," Lester nodded thoughtfully. "If you will excuse me I'd like to discuss that point with Tom Geddy."

Barry watched him walk away.

"Tell me something, Hufford. Do all your English farmers sound as though they were born with a silver spoon in their mouth?"

The old man had to hide his mirth. "Like as not some folk like to be putting on airs in a new land."

"Funny chap," Barry mused. "Do you know that girl who fainted at the dance yesterday?"

"I recall. Pretty young Irish lass."

"She looks to be near as old as your Miss Selena, but I found out from Miss Cornithwyeth that she is only twelve. It's hard to picture her being Hartwicke's wife."

"She's his wife? Are you sure of that?"

"Yep! Many over there were forced to marry before starting out."

Hufford gulped and quickly changed the subject.

"I know it is none of my business, son, but how do you expect to repay Cornithwyeth such a sum?"

It was a problem Barry had been trying to put out of his mind ever since he'd made his boastful promise. He shook his head sadly.

"Even if I was paid up on every wagon it would only be something over five thousand. Hell, he said seven. I'm already out about a thousand for supplies and wages. Jim Bridger's gonna skin me for being such a lousy businessman."

"You couldn't forsee the theft, son. Have you any notions on it?"

Barry shook his head again. "None. I'm the only one who touched that gold until Jeb Pierce delivered it this morning. Jeb wouldn't take it. Money means only booze to him and he hasn't tied one on since we left the Missouri."

Hufford pondered a moment and then he thought he had best speak out. "That's not quite true, Barry. The night the Herberts ran away he was sharing quite a large jug with the Pomeroy person. I saw them when I had to get up in the night to relieve myself."

"That could mean something," Barry mused, recalling that Pomeroy had been outside the Herbert wagon when he had told Cornithwyeth that he had his possessions. "Why don't you keep that to yourself until I can do some checking around?"

"Gladly," the old man grinned, "and, son, I've a bit put aside for meself. It's yours for the asking."

Barry's eyes misted. "Thank you, Hufford, but I couldn't do that. It'll work out, someway or other."

When something greatly angered Lydia Tedder, she "spunked up her back," as her husband would say, and did something. With an egg basket over her arm she left her wagon and made a complete circuit of the train. Lydia was unaware that she had become a deeply loved and respected person among the other women. She never bickered or gossiped, and was the first to arrive if a woman or child was down ill. Her cooking pot always held a little extra for the emergency mouth that might need to be fed.

Because some of their husbands had been officers, while others were soldiers, there was a quiet, unspoken caste system among the English women. But each was grateful that Lydia had broken down the barrier and taught them how to cook over an open campfire.

Lydia's eyes didn't see color in people's skin and was as welcome in the wagons of the blacks as she was with her own Tennessee woman. That morning she hesitated briefly before calling on the Herbert wagons; the last thing Lydia would ever want to do was embarrass the Herberts or anyone else. But she saw a huddled group of the black women and decided she had to at least call out a cheery greeting. She was spotted and waved over to join them. Sitting in the middle of the group was one of Lydia's favorite people in the whole train.

Nearly everyone called the gray-haired, three-hundred-pound woman "Nanna." She was not really the grandmother of all the former slaves, but came close.

"Bless yah, chile," she greeted Lydia with a broad grin. Something was out of place, but Lydia could not put her finger on it at once. "Sit yahself fer a spell. We'all been hearin' bout yah special chore dis mornin' 'n are most proud ob yah."

Lydia flushed. Not from the praise but from confusion on how best to handle the situation.

"I gather," she said slowly, "that the story is travelin' faster than my legs."

Nanna laughed. It made her whole body quake. "My ole mama always did say de drums in Africa talked slower'n de wag of a woman's tongue." Then she sobered. "Near mak a body sicken to hear dat man say such a thing agin Mass'ah Barry. Hurts me, Miz Lydia, ta think ah killed one of de good layin' hens ta mak soup fer dat man when he was ailin' among us." She shook her massive, bandana-covered head. 'Ain't fittin', just ain't fittin' he can say Mass'ah Barry done stole 'is money." Then she grinned. "But 'tis right fittin' wat yah bout, you angel."

"Well," Lydia stammered. "I'm only asking . . ."

"We'all know, chile. Dat's why ah done talk ta my womens fur yah. Let's see yah basket, hear!"

Nanna uncovered the flaps of her apron and her wide lap was filled with a collection of coins and objects.

"But . . ." Lydia tried to protest.

"Ain't no buts about it, Miz Lydia. Our man's in a heap ob trouble 'n we's beholdin'. We'all ne'ber have our papers ob freedom if tweren't fer 'im."

She began to dump the contents of her apron into the egg basket and an object caught Lydia's eye that made her protest.

"Nanna," she cried. "I knew something was wrong! That's your gold front tooth."

"Sure am," she boasted. "Nanna had ta gib sumpin' 'n de good Lord'll still reck'niz me widdout it."

"And so shall I, Nanna," Lydia said, fighting down her tears. "And so shall I."

Lydia felt a little ashamed that she had never really gone too far out of her way to be real neighborly with Mary Sue Herbert. But in a certain way she found her to be far colder than Lady Pamela—and Lady Pamela she normally steered a wide course around.

"Good morning, Mrs. Tedder," Mary Sue said warmly. "Please step up and in. Harmon has told my husband and me what traspired with Mr. Cornithwyeth and it is quite unbelievable."

"Horrible," Colonel Herbert corrected. "It is horrible, Mary Sue, that a petty theft could take place on this plantation."

Lydia was quite aware of the colonel's condition and smiled politely.

"Then you may also be aware of my mission," she said hesitantly. "I'm only askin' what a body thinks they can help out with."

"What? What is this?" the colonel demanded.

"Paw," Harmon said gently, "Mrs. Tedder's been going around the wagon train trying to collect money to help Fitzpatrick pay back the loss."

There was a deadly silence while this sank into Colonel Herbert's constantly wandering brain. Harmon felt utterly guilty. His family was using that stolen money and he could ruin them if he spoke up.

"Admirable, dear lady," Herbert finally intoned. "A good cause for a fine young chap. Miss Mary Sue, our coffer, please. I think we should give a dollar a head for each and every one of our people."

"But, colonel," Lydia protested. "Nanna already has collected from each of your people. The dear soul even gave her gold front tooth because of what Mr. Fitzpatrick did to . . ."

She caught herself before going on, not wishing to bring up a subject that might make the colonel go into one of his sudden tirades. Mary Sue understood and was grateful.

"It's a handsome offer, Tom," she said gently and patted his hand. "Harmon, get the coffer box and count out the money for Mrs. Tedder." Then she pulled a gold chain from about her neck that was interlaced with a ring at its end. "Mrs. Tedder, this was my grandmother's wedding ring. She and Nanna were girls together and the day that my grandmother was given this ring, my grandfather gave Nanna her tooth. Please take this ring and let me have Nanna's tooth back. We do owe Mr. Fitzpatrick more than we can ever repay."

Lydia dug the tooth from the basket, but refused the ring.

"Not on your life," she protested, "will I be lettin' that man have either of these precious things. Ah don't mind givin' that skinflint money, but ah'm not about to give him the love that was behind it."

The dollar a head for what Colonel Herbert still considered his slaves gave a hefty feel to Lydia's basket. She had been doing so well that she never once prepared herself to meet resistance and an uncivil tongue. But she did meet resistance at the Englishmen's wagon.

"No, woman," Charles Templeton growled at his wife. "Charity begins at home. If the man's such a bloody fool to lose such a sum, it proves

he's not that worthy to lead us. My purse strings
stay pulled!"

And not as much as a single coin did Lydia get
from any of the English farmers. She noted that
the women there who had started to be friendly
had suddenly gone back into a sort of frightened
shell. She was unaware that their husbands had
also seen Lord Lester and waited in holy terror
for what obligations and demands he would once
again place upon them.

Amy Butterick wept silently after Lydia had
left. She was a bride of a year and expecting her
first child in midsummer.

"Hush!" Stephan Butterick soothed. "There's
naught to fear, lass."

Amy blinked. "I fear seeing a dead man, walking and talking. How is it possible?"

Stephan wished that he knew. He was only a
simple soldier who had followed the orders that the
officers had received from Lord Lester. He knew
nothing about an assassination attempt on the life
of the Queen and her Prince Consort. All he knew
was that he was suddenly considered a dangerous
man and Lady Pamela had given him a chance to
begin a new life with his bride. He wished he
didn't fear her so, or else he might have gone to
find out what was happening to his new little
world. He didn't have the courage either to approach Captain Templeton or Yeoman Faraday.
The six most troublesome years of his life had
been spent in the service of Lord Lester and he
had felt guilty at the feeling of gladness he had
felt upon learning of his death. In England he
would have had no qualms about escaping that

very moment. But the wilderness made him feel more a prisoner than had he been in the Tower of London.

Lydia Tedder started toward Lady Pamela's wagon, hesitated, then felt a burden lift from her shoulders as she spotted the old coachman go quickly up the wagon steps. After fifteen straight turndowns, she did not fancy facing another.

"Here you be," Howard Tedder growled. "Is a man to go lunchless these days?"

"Oh," Lydia gasped, looking up into the sky. "The time escaped me. I'm comin' now, husband."

"Lydia, Lydia," he grinned, "I'm never one for a good tease, am I? Maybelle's seein' to the vittles fer me and the boys. You go on about yore task."

"Reckon I'm most finished," she said wistfully, looking at the Buttle-Jones wagon. "Them folk ain't much interested in my project, I reckon."

Tedder grinned, with loving tenderness. "Any time you start reckonin' twice in one sentence, Lydia, you ain't finished reckonin' with things."

She didn't answer. When the thought had crossed her mind to help Barry, she had thought of Lady Pamela first. Seven thousand dollars was a huge sum in Lydia's small world, but she'd figured it might not be to Lady Pamela. She had thought the woman might give her some advice on how to collect money from the others. Then, changing her mind, she had decided to just start out on her own.

"Lydia," Tedder said tenderly, "we've come a fur piece together, gal, but today you left me and went over to stand with the angels. I ain't often

said I love you when I should have, but you've
sure honored me today. Here!"

"What's this?"

'The good Lord saw fit to give us a profit out
of Lady Bountiful there, an' you jest can't go
'round gettin' donations from everybody else and
leave out the Tedders. We're small fish, Lyd. Now
go after a catfish!'

Lydia was so choked with emotion that she
feared her consumption was going to act up and
ruin the moment. She had been so busy caring for
other people lately that she had all but put her
own condition in the back of her mind. She
fought to keep from coughing and bravely smiled.

"I think she's waiting my departure, mi'lady."

There was no response. Lady Pamela sat regarding her coachman with stony solemnity.

"It will be the best use ever for such ill-begot-
ten money. Can't you see that, lass?"

"Why haven't you told me of this before?" said
Lady Pamela, in an icy voice.

"Oh, child, would you have let old Hufford go
ahead with such a daring scheme? Can't you see
that it was for your own safety?"

"My safety," she repeated dully. "That may
have been the case yesterday. I even came near
convincing myself that Lord Lester's raving about
the gold was just a return of his former illness."

"And why not?' Hufford's voice was very quiet.
"That's when I first learned the truth about the
gold. I feared for your life from the raving mad-
man and kept me eye on him. He had more secret
niches in that manor house than a pack-rat.

Nightly, he would re-hide the gold, fearing its discovery. Some nights he'd lose track of where he'd put it and those would be the nights that he'd be at his balmy worst. Then came the border war and he was off like a shot. Soldiering being pure madness made his peculiar ways seem commonplace. When he returned, even his family thought the war had cured him of the devil in his head."

Lady Pamela scoffed. "Because they only had to see him on a rare occasion. We know that he was even meaner and more sadistic."

"Aye," he agreed, "except that never once did he look for his hidden gold. Never once in these past five years. Some forget that servants have ears, mi'lady, and one day in the carriage I heard him admit to his father that he had squandered the money stolen and was penniless. He was told to live on his soldier's pension or perish. But still he didn't touch the gold. Why is he remembering it now, unless the madness is in his brain again?"

She drew a deep, shaken breath. "That could well be, but he also convinced the duke that I must have taken the gold. He is sure that one of the soldiers is now a paid spy for the duke."

Hufford laughed. "Not a very good spy if he hasn't smelled out the gold as yet. Not even my Donald knows of it, and he's around it daily."

"The carriage!" she gasped.

He grinned, shyly. "Mostly. The newer coin I kept for emergency use and the rest I melted and poured into the doors, down the rib sides and under the floor boards. That's why I started fearing when they said we might have to leave the carriage behind. Fitzpatrick saved the carriage and the favor is due back to him."

"As you wish. After all, I suppose it is your money now."

"I am no thief!" Hufford said harshly. His face was deeply drawn. She had never seen him look so fierce. "We are family, although I tell you not to think that way. They owed you, lass. They owed you twenty times that amount. It's for your future and none other. I'll not be letting that bastard get his murky hands back upon it!"

There was a hesitant knock on the wagon steps.

"Come up."

Lydia Tedder entered shyly. She had waited a long time for the coachman to leave and finally decided that his presence might give her more courage to face Lady Pamela.

A quarter hour later she stepped back down to the ground, her legs a bit wobbly and unsteady. She clutched the egg basket tightly to her breast and stilled her heart from the secret she had just been sworn to keep. No one was to ever learn the amount Lady Pamela had donated for the nineteen English families and herself.

What had started out as a pleasant task had been turned by Lady Pamela's generosity into a great burden. The egg basket now contained nearly four thousand dollars, an amount Lydia could hardly contemplate. Her single purpose now was to rid herself of the responsibility.

She was momentarily nonplussed when Jeb Pierce told her he had not seen Barry since the morning meeting. She considered leaving the money with the cook and then thought better of it. A cry of alarm turned them both as one. Orange fingers of flame were shooting up through the canvas of one of the Herbert supply wagons. The camp became an instant surge of humanity running to drag the wagon out of the line and put out the fire.

Lydia tried to keep up with Jeb but the basket was cumbersomely heavy. She had to stop and rest a moment. Then she felt a spasm followed by a searing pain that raced through her chest like lightning. Down she crashed, gasping for air, fighting to keep the cough from starting. The pain continued to increase, and then she couldn't still the cough any longer. She gagged and spat out masses of clotted blood, but she didn't faint. She knew it was her worst attack yet and she had to still her fear and overcome it.

A surge of hope filled her on hearing footsteps running back from the fire area. She tried to cry out; the effort was too much. She was wracked by a new wave of coughing that made her spill forth a stream of fresh blood. The attack was so horrendous that she had to clench her teeth to keep her entire stomach from erupting. In the next second the last person in the world she expected to come to her aide was kneeling beside her.

How stupid of him, she thought, as he roughly tore the apron from about her middle. It's hardly the time to be wiping my face clean. But through watery eyes she saw him dump the contents of the basket into the apron and nervously knot up the corners. She tried to scream and only brought on a worse cough. This time the faint did start to come, but in her last lucid moment many things became quite clear. She had seen the man several times that morning, but never considered she was being followed. The fire had been started to draw people to it and leave her alone and vulnerable. The look on his face told her that that face was the last she would see in this life. As the blackness closed over her she made her peace with God.

16

"Lydia-girl . . . Lydia-girl . . . don't leave me alone . . " Howard Tedder's shoulders heaved with hoarse sobs that tore at every heart.

His grief was commonly shared by every man, woman and child. Even the Cornithwyeth family, with others from the estranged train, felt duty bound to walk across the field to join the silent gathering at sunset. No one spoke as the rich soil covered their lost friend and marking stones were placed; they were still stunned by disbelief and wonderment.

There were those who felt grief for the living as well as the dead; Selena for Nazareth, Pearl Fergus for her dancing partner Theodis, several of the young men for the weeping Maybelle, Lady Pamela for herself and old Hufford, both of whom blamed themselves for donating the money that had tempted a second robbery. And everybody, including Bradford Cornithwyeth, grieved for Barry Fitzpatrick.

No one had suggested it, but everyone assumed that the final solemn moment of their farewell was Barry's obligation.

He stood, feeling vastly alone. It seemed to him as if a million years had passed since Jessie Fremont had warned him that just such as this was bound to happen and prepared him by marking passages in a Bible. He tried to read the page but his eyes blurred and he couldn't dislodge the lump in his throat. The Bible should have recalled Jessie's face to him and it couldn't. For the moment he couldn't even recall Lydia Tedder's face. He raised his head and blinked, as though re-echoing an ancient cry that the task be taken away from him. One face in the crowd seemed to force itself upon his eyes and brain and demanded recognition. The eyes were clear, the brown cheeks unmarked by tear lines. On Nanna's lips was a sweet smile that suggested that she was well aware that she was only saying goodbye to Lydia for a little while.

Even as Barry opened his mouth to speak, he could not take his eyes off her radiant face.

"This Bible says that the Lord giveth, and the Lord taketh away. Today he sure took the best away from all of us. The book has a lot more words that can be said at this time. Most are right pretty words. Pretty words should be said for a pretty woman like this. I reckon I don't feel much like pretty words this evening, except for the part about not stealing and not killing. Doc Freitag says she was a mighty sick woman, but might have lived if he had gotten to her sooner. Most don't know that Doc has a bit of Bible learning in him and he says that every man and woman have their season and the good Lord declared that this was the end of Lydia Tedder's season. Lord, forgive me saying so, but I hope you're keeping the season in mind of the person responsible for this. Ma'am, I'll go to my own grave remembering what you were doing for me today, and each and everyone of these other people. If it means anything to you now, you've left a mark on each of us that no matter of soap and water will wash away. This isn't in the book, but as long as we have to leave you in Indian land, I thought it proper. *Yay-te-hay!* That can mean hello or goodbye but mainly it means 'may your face stay with me until I look upon it again.' *Yay-te-hay!*"

And that night, in the two separate encampments, divided people struggled to be reunited. Had it not been for Lydia Tedder's death the revolt against Cornithwyeth might have erupted that evening. Now, it seemed improper and the men sat around the campfires till near morning airing their grievances.

But in the encirclement early bedding down seemed the easiest way to ease aching hearts, though several beds were no more than blanket-covered lengths of firewood. Nothing moved, no sound was made, as though the camp were in a sleep of death of its own.

Several people had similar thoughts, but few had consulted each other. Harmon Herbert had no choice but to act upon his own. The germ of suspicion that had been growing in his mind since that morning had crystalized with the burning of the supply wagon and then the robbery of Lydia Tedder. He lay silent beneath his sister's wagon and waited for the shadow he knew had to pass. His wait was not long.

The figure came and removed the water barrel lid, but the sound thereafter was not that of a nightly quenching of thirst. The arm thrust into the barrel to retrieve something on its bottom sloshed the water over the rim and to the ground.

Harmon's long arm shot out and his hand clapped on an ankle, toppling the figure to the ground.

"Mighty big thirst you got, Pomeroy. I went along to keep us from ruination, but you had to steal 'n steal agin."

Aaron Pomeroy's face turned a blackish-purple hue.

"You can jest bet it ain't the last either," he whispered hoarsely. "I heared sumptin' today that'd make this seem like chicken feed."

"I don't care, you cowardly skunk! A body died 'cause of you. I'm takin' back what you got there!"

Pomeroy's hand flashed out and hit Harmon's face in a ringing blow. The boy's head jerked back, his hat fell to the ground. Then Pomeroy jerked his knees up and jackknifed them back into Harmon's groin. He rolled into a ball and nearly fainted from the pain.

Cursing his ill-fated luck, Pomeroy grabbed the dripping money pouches and started for the tethered horses. This had not been his plan, but Harmon had just reduced his chances of getting more gold out of the coachman's carriage. Muttering, cursing, Pomeroy climbed astride a saddle-less horse and headed toward the rising moon.

Harmon half crawled and half ran, no longer fearing of his own part in the original robbery. No more than three wagons along he was stopped short by a figure stepping out of the shadows.

"Barry!" he gasped.

"Hush!" Barry warned. "It's all right. He won't get far."

"No matter," Harmon moaned. "I gotta tell you or go mad. I kinda of helped him when we stole the thirty-three hundred from ole man Cornith-wyeth's room in Independence. My paw had lost all his money gamblin' and we was flat broke. Mary Sue don't know, I assure you. And I don't know nothin' 'bout the money he took from you or got from Mrs. Tedder. Oh, damn, I hurt bad!"

"Quiet!" Barry warned again. "You're not telling me much more than I've pieced together already. Jeb Pierce confessed before the funeral that Pomeroy'd been plying him with corn liquor. You just helped us smoke out where he had every-thing hidden."

"Not everything. He said he found somethin' today that would make this seem like chicken feed."

Barry started to answer and then checked him-self as another figure emerged from the shadow.

"Well done, Fitzpatrick," Lester Hartwicke en-thused. "You've caught the bloody culprit."

"No," Barry said dully. "Herbert was just at-tacked by him."

"Good show! Then you know the man that you are after?"

"Yep!" Barry said slowly, his mind quizzical. "You're out mighty late, Mr. Hartwicke."

Lord Lester laughed. It rang fake and hollow "I had hoped to befriend some of the English gentlemen in your party, but they seem to have retired. Well, good hunting."

As he turned, Lester's face broke into a knowing grin. If there was one thing he knew about his wife it was her inability to lie. She had almost convinced him that she did not have the Buttle-Jones gold. Harmon Herbert's words gave him renewed hope.

Barry turned his mind away from Hartwicke and motioned for Harmon to follow him. Beyond the chuck wagon two of the cowboys sat their horses.

"He didn't come this way, Barry."

"I know. He headed out east. Parsons and Tompkins will be circling him back shortly. You boys call it a night and let us use your horses."

Barry let the horses walk as though they were on little more than a moonlight ride. A heavy growth of trees covered the top of the first ridge and they skirted to the right of it. Barry took the lead, proceeding cautiously, and as soon as he could see over the summit halted. Harmon, following closely, saw down the slope of the ridge to the bare rolling land and the rise to the next ridge. Nothing was moving and Harmon started to comment on it.

"Sssh!" whispered Barry, holding up a warning finger. "Sound travels a long way at night."

In another moment there was movement coming off the second ridge. Barry rummaged in the breast flap of his buckskins and drew out a sulphur match. He scratched it with his thumbnail and held the flame high.

"Light travels even farther," he chuckled, "especially when you're looking for it. Figured he'd head east, so I put the cowboys out around this whole area. They'll start boxing him in shortly."

When Aaron Pomeroy'd come upon the gun-drawn cowboys, his first thought was that the robber was about to be robbed. Unarmed, he yanked the horse's head around by the tether line and raced back in the direction he'd just come. He was hard to ride without a saddle. But he was fast, and Pomeroy cared for nothing else. He listened for the pounding of pursuing hoofs in his rear. Involuntarily he glanced back. On the quarter mile or more of grass plain between him and the ridge there was not a horse, a man or anything living. He began to take heart that he could make it to the wooded ridge and hide within its protective covering.

The cowboys had been ordered not to immediately pursue, unless Pomeroy escaped them to the east. They waited until he was in the center of the plain and then spurred their horses. Once on level ground they split apart and urged the mounts into a hard gallop.

Almost too late, Pomeroy saw a rider to the north and then the south. Again he looked back and realized how swiftly the other two cowboys were closing upon him. He made directly for the densest part of the grove.

"Now, Harm," Barry shouted. "Back around to give him a welcoming party."

They were in place in plenty of time, prepared to cut him off no matter where he emerged from the trees. To the left and right of them horsemen did appear, but Barry warned Harmon back, because these were the encircling cowboys. The cowboys stopped and held their position. It was so still that they could hear Pomeroy's horse thrashing about in the undergrowth and could anticipate exactly where it would emerge.

Then Barry cursed. "Damn it all, look at that! He's turned the horse loose and gone into hiding." He drew his revolver, held it high as a signal and began moving forward. They would have to smoke Pomeroy out.

Only a few yards into the grove Barry realized what a lengthy operation it was going to be. He was amazed that Pomeroy's horse had made it through the thick entanglement at all. He and Harmon were forced to leave their horses and plow through the heavy undergrowth on foot. He could hear that the cowboys had done the same and wondered how the two easterly men were faring.

"Yoho! Barry!" A shrill shout cut through the night. "To my voice! Quick!"

"Got him!" Barry chortled.

But it was a higher power that had gotten to Aaron Pomeroy first and meted out its own form of poetic justice. All they could surmise was that Pomeroy had looked back again to check on his pursuers and the frightened horse had taken him right into the low hanging branches of a tree. His head had gone right into the Y of a stout branch, instantly breaking his neck and leaving it at an awkward half-backward angle. The look on his face suggested that he never knew what hit him.

At the first light of dawn Mary Sue ordered a grave dug, making sure that it was nowhere near that of Lydia Tedder. Unlike the evening before, there were no mourners for Aaron Pomeroy. Three strapping black youths stood by to gratefully shovel the dirt onto their former overseer. The news had been kept from Colonel Herbert, and Harmon stayed in his wagon waiting for Barry to decide his fate.

Mary Sue came to the grave site out of a sense of duty and stood alone with Barry.

"It's very sad," she said softly, "that he is leaving this life as alone as he lived it. Not being loved is a horrible thing. Perhaps the only decent thing he ever did was to steal the money so I wouldn't learn of Tom's gambling. I know it was wrong, but I hope the Lord will take his reasons into consideration."

"On that one he might," Barry said gruffly.

She sighed. "It's the living who worry me now. I've got what money is left waiting for you at the wagon."

"How much did the colonel lose gambling?" Barry asked unexpectedly.

"I assume," she said wearily, "you speak of just this last time. Taking into consideration what he had already paid out to you, it was several thousand dollars. It was hard enough getting a straight answer out of him before and now you know it is next to impossible." She paused, then quickly added: "What is going to happen to Harmon?"

He made no reply for a moment, watching the blacks finish their work and shuffle back toward the train. It had been his decision that no stones would be gathered to mark this grave.

"I'm glad the boy had the grit to tell you the truth," he said. "Now, it's something that's only known between the three of us. If we leave it that way, he'll punish himself worse than anything we could do to him."

"I'm—grateful," she said, a little unsteadily. "I'll need him now more than ever."

"You'll also need the money."

"Very true, but it's hardly mine to keep."

"Depends upon how you look at it, ma'am. Normally, the colonel only gambled with five men at the saloon in Independence, but on many occasions I saw a sixth with them. Kinda surprised me at the time, because the man was hell-bent against cards and liquor and always crying poor mouth to me. Only when Harmon told me how Pomeroy came to learn about the money did it strike me why Cornithwyeth didn't pay me in his room and hauled me off to the bank. He didn't want me to learn how big his gambling winnings were. I may be wrong, but I think he might be just as much a cheat at cards as he is in overcharging people for his services. I figure that money is just as much yours as it is his. He doesn't have to know about the theft from his room, only from my chuck wagon. You've got a lot of people to see after with what you have left."

Mary Sue gazed at Barry, astounded more by

his speech than by the emotion that prompted them.

"My dear man!" she exclaimed. And then she paused. She could not find words.

"Money! Money!" Cornithwyeth screamed at Barry. "Of course I want my money back from that thief, and it all had better be there! Because of your meddling I will need every red cent to keep me from ruination!"

"Meddling? What am I being accused of this time?" Barry laughed.

"Don't be snide," Cornithwyeth replied grimly. "There's a revolution going on out there. The tone is that I am to be tarred and feathered unless I reduce my rates and join up with your train. And you claim to know nothing about it?"

"No," Barry said bluntly, "but it sounds like the only sensible thing on their part. You might be able to manage a game of cards, but you sure as hell won't be able to manage this train."

Cornithwyeth turned scarlet. "Hush! My wife knows nothing about that, Fitzpatrick. I—I just got very lucky—for a beginner."

Barry roared with laughter. "God damn, you are a hypocrite! You can lie out of both sides of your mouth faster than most can out of the middle. I'm tempted to tell her just to see you get your due."

"That's blackmail!" he shrieked. "What do you want from me? To run the train? All right, you've got it! Name your price!"

Barry smiled. "Price is the same. Twenty-five per wagon. What you have charged these dumb bastards is between them and you. But let's settle this other matter first. You said seven thousand was stolen from you?"

"Exactly."

"Here. This is what I took off of Pomeroy's body last night."

Cornithwyeth greedily grabbed the pouch and the knotted apron and tried to push them inside of his coat.

"Wait a minute, buster," Barry growled. "I didn't open either of those and I want it counted."

"It's my money."

"Might and might not be," Barry said sternly. "The apron is what Lydia Tedder collected. The pouch don't feel like no seven thousand, so I brought the apron along too."

Cornithwyeth fumed. "I'm going to count, Fitzpatrick, and any difference is going to be your responsibility."

Barry held his silence, not wishing to expose the ace that he had up his sleeve. The leather pouch contained thirty-seven hundred dollars, just as he expected. That matched up with the thirty-three hundred that Harmon had admitted counting out. Barry steeled himself as Cornithwyeth's bony fingers worked to free the apron knots that the water barrel hiding place had shrunk. Barry had loved Lydia Tedder for her generous effort to help save him, but anticipated that she would have been able to collect only a few hundred dollars at the most. He averted his gaze from the man's rapidly counting fingers, rehearsing in his mind the blackmail tactic he might have to employ to make up the difference and keep Cornithwyeth from learning he had let Mary

Sue Herbert keep some of the money. But as the figure began to mount, he couldn't help but stare at the slowly diminishing pile of coins. When the combined total reached seven thousand he reached out and stayed Cornithwyeth's hands.

"What are you doing?"

"You got your seven thousand back and said I was responsible for the difference."

Cornithwyeth blanched. "I must have made a mistake on the amount stolen."

"The hell you did. You're counting the collected money, not your own. Pomeroy must still have another pouch hidden somewhere.'

"Then it's mine when found, remember that."

Barry looked at him as though he were a creature that had crawled from beneath a rock. "Cornithwyeth, you little bastard, you're paid in full! This money and any that is found will go back to the people who were kind enough to try and save my neck from your stupid greed. Now, start counting out eighteen hundred dollars."

"For what purpose?" he demanded.

Barry sighed, as though he had been trying to teach him the alphabet and the man was incapable of remembering what came after C. "The price on your wagons, less the ten percent already reluctantly paid."

Quite a gathering of men awaited Barry as he stepped down from the Cornithwyeth wagon. Hartwicke and Geddy stood in the forefront.

"Here," he said to Lester Hartwicke, "do me a favor and count what is in this apron. I'm tired of being accused of things. The rest of you gather round. He's paid me my charge. I'll have people here within the hour to start looking over your wagons for you. With luck I'd like to head out at dawn."

"What'd he pay you?" a New Englander called out with suspicion.

"What I always asked," Barry called back truthfully. "Twenty-five a wagon."

His words brought bitter mumbling.

"If you've got a gripe," Barry said with stern authority in his voice, "don't look to me to be your wet-nurse. What you paid him is your problem and not mine. I accept the council he named to go with the council from our train, but I'm naming myself as the head member of that group. You got that counted for me?"

"Yes," Lord Lester answered quite gleefully. "You've got three hundred and ten in gold coin American and two hundred nine in gold crowns sovereign."

"What in the hell are they?"

Lester smiled enigmatically. "British currency, old boy. But in equal weight and purchasing power to your dollar."

Barry smiled back. "Seems some of the Englishmen in my train have bigger hearts than they have smiles. Thanks for counting it for me."

"My pleasure, I assure you," Lord Lester enthused. Silently he thought what a wonderful stroke of luck that had been for him. No common soldier or officer would have possessed such coin. Only one person on the train, in his estimation would have so carelessly used them for currency. Having felt of the Buttle-Jones treasure once again with his own hands made him revise his plan for regaining every last farthing of it. Now, he was quite glad he had Pearl Fergus at his disposal. She was the very tool that he needed.

Howard Tedder's will to live was so diminished that Barry had to shame him into going and inspecting the work that would be required on the wagons.

"How soon can they be ready to roll?" Barry asked, on his return.

"Mornin'," Howard answered dully. Then he frowned, as though on a puzzling thought. "Mighty peculiar, though. Not a damn one of them repairs seem natural. Almost man-made I'd say, by a right clever man."

Barry pondered Tedder's remark as he went to make a call on Lady Pamela. He didn't know why, but there was something about the woman that always made him uncomfortably nervous in her presence. Today it was even worse. She stared at the two-hundred-odd British coins as though they were cobra snakes poised for a strike.

"You must be mistaken," she said coolly. "It is quite true that I made a donation when Mrs. Tedder dropped by, God rest her soul, but hardly as generous as the amount you possess there." Because the lie had sounded so false to her ear, she laughed. It came out such an inane sound that she now felt quite foolish. "Really, Mr. Fitzpatrick, you may check with any of my people and they will tell you what a frugal person I really am. Besides, in spite of the pomp and circumstance of a carriage and handsome wardrobe, I am probably one of your poorest pilgrims, sir."

Barry pursed his lips. "Well, it's a puzzlement, unless the money came from your English farmers."

Lady Pamela's face turned stony cold. "You bring up a very embarrassing topic, sir. Mrs. Tedder informed me that all nineteen of them turned her down without as much as a smile. Perhaps it's the climate we are born to, but the English are not known for their warmth and charm."

"I don't know," Barry smiled. "I've come to find old Hufford quite a warm and charming person. What you might call a real gentleman."

The words so pleased Pamela that it brought a natural smile to her lips. "To compliment a servant is to compliment his mistress. I thank you for both of us."

When she smiled, Barry was privileged to see again what a gorgeous creature she could be and it momentarily stunned him.

"Well," he stammered, "I've got to do something with the money."

Lady Pamela grew serious. "I was most touched by Mrs. Tedder's telling me of the generosity of the colored people on your behalf, Mr. Fitzpatrick. Of course, you could not openly give them back the money or you would be taking away what they did from their hearts. I hardly know the woman, but I could hardly help but notice Mrs. Herbert standing alone, with you, at that gravesite this morning. That took a courage that I don't think I could have mustered up. Let her do something nice for her colored people with the money, sir."

As though in a gesture of pleading she reached out and patted his hand with her own. Barry felt as though a spring robin had momentarily perched on his hand, announced the coming of summer and blessed him with good fortune. He looked up and their eyes met. Instinctively, he could feel which of her words had been true and which had been lies. Without knowing why the lies really didn't matter to him, her touch had turned him into an ancient knight and she a damsel in some sort of distress. He would not question who her tormentors might be, but would be ready to do them battle at her least bidding.

Lady Pamela drew her hand away quickly and with a muffled excuse bid him farewell. Only when she felt he was out of the wagon did she turn and watch him through the open flaps. She was glad that Barry had not detected her sudden fright at looking up and seeing Lord Lester watching them from the circled compound. As the two men met, she found herself automatically weighing them, one against the other.

Although she knew very little about the mountain man, she could not help but feel that had Barry come into her life fifteen years sooner she might have stayed as simple and loving as she once had been. But the clock, she was well aware, could not be turned back. She could not escape the fact that she was wedded to Lord Lester Buttle-Jones, even though he was parading about with an assumed name.

"Well," Lester enthused, "I see you've found the proper owner for the Queen's crowns."

"If you're talking about that British money, no," Barry declared.

"Impossible," Lester snorted. "Who else could

have such coin but a person of her station? Surely, she didn't suggest that those miserable farmers would possess such treasure."

His interest in the matter irritated Barry, without knowing why.

"Suggest!" Barry replied, on a scornful laugh. "She had it straight from Mrs. Tedder's mouth that those dour-mouthed Britishers didn't give Mrs. Tedder a penny. It was embarrassing to a nice lady like that, but what could she do? Hartwicke, I'm swearing you to your honor on this, but that widow there probably has less cash than you and I put together."

Lord Lester flustered. "Then where did those British crowns come from?"

Barry shrugged.

"Hartwicke," he said slowly then, "you're new from England, aren't you?"

"That's quite obvious," Lester said shortly.

"Well," Barry drawled, "we still got ourselves a hell of a lot of folk in the east that didn't cotton to the revolution and thought things would reverse with the war of ought twelve. They didn't. But they still got stuck with a heap of British coin in their purses. People like Cornithwyeth are trying to move west now. Hell, see this purse here. That's what the New England miser paid me off with today. Betcha it's got more British gold in it than American. That's what those folk pay off with now. How else they gonna get rid of it, lest they melt it down?"

Lord Lester's balloon had been soaring and Barry had just pricked it without realizing it.

"As poor as that, eh?"

"Who?"

Lord Lester gulped, praying the man was in total error. "Her Ladyship."

The money questions by the Englishman now made sense to Barry and he roared with disdainful laughter. "You thought she was going to be an easy mark for your glib tongue, did you? Hey, buster, she may put on airs, but when it comes to her pocketbook she's as common as you or me. If you thought of getting rich off of her, you'd do better going after Cornithwyeth's daughter. He could probably make your former king look like a pauper."

Hartwicke was left to stand and ponder the point. He had no interest in his former wife, unless she had the Buttle-Jones gold. He had no interest in Anne Cornithwyeth, unless she had an equal or greater amount of money to offer. He suddenly felt so tired and confused. What he had considered to be so close at hand had very suddenly evaporated. His unstable mind could not cope with possibilities turning into improbabilities. He had to return to his wagon and think this thing out in small pieces. He knew he couldn't be wrong about Pamela having the gold, but everything and everybody seemed to say she didn't. Again he thought of Pearl Fergus. She seemed his only hope of digging out the truth.

Harmon Herbert looked at the pile of extra money Barry had poured onto the wagon table, looked at the bewilderment on his father's face, looked at the gratitude his stepmother was heaping on Barry Fitzpatrick, heard the words that were casting him free from his own self-imposed imprisonment, and could stand no more of it.

In a flash, he was out of the wagon and running as though the devil had just come to claim his soul. His mind was a void until he came to the place where they had buried Aaron Pomeroy and he flung himself across the fresh-dug earth and beat it mightily with his fists.

"Bastard!" he cried, over and over again, until he was weak. Then he began to sob. "Why, Aaron, why? You didn't need that fuggin' extra money. We were going to make it without it, man."

Then he calmed. He sat up upon the grave and sat huddled with his knees beneath his chin. Day was drawing to a close and the campfires were being kindled below where he sat. There lay humanity of his future, but he had to sever the ties with his past.

"They tell me,' he said softly, "they said no words over you today. I'd like to. Not for what you've done lately, which I don't understand, but for the past.

"That's some word, ain't it? Past. That's final! This morning I saw you hanging from that stupid tree limb and I thought better this than from some sheriff's posse rope. I hated you at that moment. Sure. Hated you, and why not? Man, you really did a thing by robbing that woman and leaving her to die. But that's not why I came out here to talk to you. I suddenly realized I miss you.

"That'll give you a laugh, won't it? Somebody is going to miss Aaron Pomeroy, and you'll never guess why. Do you remember when you came to us, and I was a young stallion who didn't know what to do about it? My paw didn't notice, but you did. Right or wrong, you turned me in with the black wenches. I never thought about that until they buried you this morning. You were trying to teach me something and I was too wild to stop learning. Same goes when you stole the money for maw and then you kept taking for yourself. You don't know that you started teachin' again. As yore body is my witness, Aaron Pomeroy, I ain't ever going to take a thing that I ain't honestly earned ever again. And Lord, when I gotta meet this man again, wherever place it's to be, let him know my words were truthful."

17

Bradford Cornithwyeth, a sullen, discredited man, held to his wagon, his stout wife being his main source of news. For several days Barry kept as far away from the man as possible, and was thankful that he was not attending the council meetings.

The virgin timberlands, the untrod rolling hills of the prairie lands melted into a steadily rising plain. The long columns of the united train clung to the shallow-running Platte like a suckling pig to a sow. Now there was nothing but plains, vast and unchanging for miles in all directions. June was slowly melting into the airless days of full summer. Breakdowns became infrequent, but some began to chafe at a new form of delay—the frequent stops that had to be made to cool and water the animals in the blistering, never-ending heat. Even the nights were so hot and muggy that many developed the habit of sleeping on the bare ground or nearly nude within their wagons.

And once on the near woodless plains Barry gave an order that sent the women into near riot. Barry was adamant. No woman, regardless of station, was to be exempt from chores assigned to her on a given day.

"Disgusting!" DeeDee wailed, shoveling up horse droppings in a camp site they'd made one evening. "Can't see why the niggers couldn't do all of this on their own." She made a wry face. "And my hands! I can't get the stench off of them from one day to the next."

Selena laughed. "It's what it does to the taste of the food that revolts me. But, then, our food is revolting to begin with."

Her latter comment had been directed cuttingly at Agatha Crumly, a young maid her mother had assigned to stay with her constantly. Agatha was the daughter of Lady Pamela's cook.

Agatha did her best to ignore the barb. She didn't like the role of watch-dog any more than Selena liked being watched. Secretly, she had to admit that her mother's cooking was bloody awful, but she would never give the snobbish Selena the satisfaction of knowing that they agreed on something.

"Oh, look!" Selena cried, turning away from her young guardian. "Those chips look drier where Pearl is working. I'm going to gather with her."

Agatha turned as though it were a command for her to follow right along.

"You stay here, Aggie," Selena commanded. "I'm tired of you hounding me."

Agatha started to protest, then thought better of it. She could keep just as good an eye on Selena from where she was. She could go running to tell Lady Pamela if the Tedder boy came riding up on a horse. Besides, she'd rather be with DeeDee Herbert. DeeDee was a right proper lady in Aggie's opinion. Maybe she treated her black servants harshly, but she treated her just fine.

Selena walked over to Pearl.

"How're you doing, Pearl?" she enthused. "I see you've found quite a nice line of chips here."

"I have, miss," Pearl said hesitantly. "They're mostly dry and pop right off the ground."

Selena put the little wooden shovel that the men had whittled for each girl under a moon-shaped clump of chips and popped them free with no effort.

"And it doesn't smell," she giggled. "They're too old to be from this train."

"They're buffalo chips," Pearl volunteered. "The men say they've begun to spot buffalo along the trail. Mr. Fitzpatrick says these chips will burn better besides not smelling so bad."

Selena looked around cautiously and saw that Aggie was far out of earshot.

"Did you see Theodis?" she whispered.

Pearl hesitated. "For a minute. He said he'd give his brother your message."

"Oh, you're a dear, Pearl."

They worked in silence for many minutes. Each had her own secret thoughts about their frequent meetings.

Pearl, on her part, still couldn't figure out why Lester Hartwicke wished her to befriend Selena. But was happy for the friendship. Her sister had turned into a moody old grump and most everybody else in the Cornithwyeth train was less than warm. She had continued to be friendly with Theo Tedder, because she now felt sorry for him over the loss of his mother. She seemed to be the only person he would talk to now.

At first Selena had been dumbfounded when old Hufford backed up her mother's allegation that her father was married to the young girl. She had nearly balked at their demand that she befriend Pearl and gain information about Lord Lester for them. Then she saw Theo's interest in the girl and decided that she would be an excellent way for her to get messages to Nazareth.

"What do you think of him?" Selena asked, breaking the silence.

"I don't know," Pearl said slowly. "He's nice, although very shy and sad."

"No, silly," Selena laughed. "I meant your husband. He's so much older than you."

Pearl's true feelings came tumbling out. She'd wanted to speak of Lester Hartwicke for quite some time, but Selena hadn't brought up the subject until now.

"He's not my husband, Selena. Well, he is because we were preached over, but that was just so we could get in the wagon train."

"Then he hasn't been a real husband to you?"

Pearl flushed. "Selena, have you ever been with a man before?"

There can be something about a friendship, no

matter how newly formed, that commands truth and not lies.

"Pearl," she sighed, "my mother doesn't believe me, but I've never gone all the way. We've come close, and Nazareth thinks he did it, but I only held it down between my legs."

Pearl shuddered. "It's really quite horrible. I pretend to like it but I really don't. I'll be so glad when I don't have to pretend that he is my husband any more."

Selena wished she could go on pretending to herself that her animalistic father was dead. She felt sorry for Pearl having to be with him and was tempted to say so when Aggie and DeeDee came running up.

"The Indian scout's back. Let's go see what it's all about."

It had been five days since Barry had seen Ransom Beaver Pond and the report he was receiving didn't please him at all.

"How far?" he demanded.

"Ten miles—no more," Ransom answered. "No sight for women and children. You know the Sioux."

Barry mused. "What happened to his Kaw guides?"

"Left him two days ago. I told him to camp and wait for you, but he was a stubborn man. I came to see your progress and knew you'd overtake him by tomorrow."

"Did you come into camp last night?"

"For what reason?" Ransom asked blandly. "I

wished to check on him again this morning and found what I found. Like I say, best send out a burial detail before the whole train comes upon it."

"No," Barry growled. "It may spoil a few suppers tomorrow night, but even the youngest has got to learn what they might face and think I'm telling tall tales about. We're moving forward at dawn!"

Next day, towards afternoon, the emigrants came upon a sight that made even the stoutest of men turn aside and lose their stomachs. Every Russian wagon had been pillaged and burned in the surprise attack. So surprising had it must have been that many of the Cossack's weapons lay unfired. Their bodies, all without scalps, were widely scattered, with arrows protruding from them like porcupine quills.

Sick from the carnage, needing to bury its victims, the emigrants drew their wagons into a circle and camped where they were for the night. A lesson had been brought home to them, horribly. Guards didn't need to be reminded; they were at their posts long before sunset, though the scouts who rode out and back reported seeing no sign of the Sioux. One fact, a negative one, did come to light: among the mutilated, hastily buried bodies Count Justinian's was not found. Then, near sunset, Ransom came galloping back to camp. Raising fear in every heart, he motioned frantically for Barry and some scouts to follow and charged away.

The count was less than a mile away from the scene of the massacre. "Christ!" Barry said when he saw him. He was buried to his neck in an ant

hill. He was alive, but barely. His mouth had been
sewn shut with buffalo gut and his eyelids were
swollen by ant bites.

"Parsons," Barry said, gritting his teeth. "Go
back and bring Doc Freitag and a wagon."

To keep the count breathing, they first had to
clean his nostrils of the ants and then carefully
cut the threads from his lips. Digging him loose,
Barry's arms became alive with the angry, biting
ant colony; he had to stop periodically to fight the
insects off.

Doc Freitag arrived with a Herbert wagon
about a half-hour later. By then, Barry and the
count's other rescuers had him free and lying on
the ground. He could not speak and his eyes were
rolling wildly in his head. Freitag kneeled at his
side to examine him.

"Can you save him, doc?" Barry said.

"Hell, yes." Freitag spat. "His heart's good.
I've seen 'em in lots worse shape than this. Just
give me a hand, nice and easy, and we'll get him
in the wagon."

Later, back at the campsite, Freitag came over
to Barry's fire after having worked steadily on
the count for the better part of three hours.

"You ought to rest up, doc," Barry said, looking at his weary face. "You're doing the best you
can for him."

"Ain't never seen quite the likes of it, boy,"
Freitag sighed. "No Injun thought this up. Every
time they made a stitch they knotted and cut it
off."

"Nice way to kill a man."

Freitag shook his head. "Don't figger they
wanted him dead, boy. The way they did it, he

was able to stretch his lips and breathe a bit. His tongue got dry and swollen, but he wouldn't have died unless he starved to death."

"Don't sound like Sioux, at that."

Freitag scoffed. "I kind of doubt any of this mess was made by Sioux. Oh, they look like Sioux arrows all right, but I make a pretty damn good arrow myself, any tribe's."

"You thinking like I am, of the Cossack rifles they took?'

"Yep! Sioux don't go for firesticks and yet three quarters of these Russkies weapons are gone. Enough left to fool the novice, which we ain't."

Barry looked dubious. "How soon will the count be able to talk?"

"Be a spell yet."

Barry spread the word that he needed an experienced nurse for the count. He also made it plain that if the count didn't survive they wouldn't learn what they faced from the attackers. Who were Sioux, he decided to tell them for the time being.

"I forbid it!"

Bertha looked at Tom Geddy with contempt and pity. "That's the only word you seem to know anymore," she said. "You forbid me to do this, Pearl to do that. You heard as well as I what is needed. If you were any kind of a man you would reveal yourself as a doctor and help."

"No, we can't do that!"

"Can't or won't?" she sneered. "We're far beyond your mother's reach, if that girl was telling the truth."

"You heard her talking with the sheriff as well as I!"

"Not really. I have only what tale you told me the next day. I've seen no one ready to arrest us since then, but do note that her interest in you has not waned. But then, your interest in me as a wife has not increased, so I guess I should be thankful for small favors. You are not a cheat, like your father. You are just a nothing. I escaped one hell in Ireland, a second in Boston. This hell you've brought me into scares me more than all the others, but I'm not about to die like those men we saw today. I'm going to help that doctor, with or without your blessing."

"You can't," he stormed. "You are an indentured servant, unless you forget."

"I am also a wife," she said cuttingly, "but one who has never known her husband. Shall we bring both of our grievances before Arabelle Cornithwyeth? Whose crime will be the greater in her eyes? I used to detest your father, but I would exchange him for you right now without the least whimper. Crawl back beneath a rock where you belong."

Like his father before him, Tom Geddy had stopped listening to the nagging voice several sentences back. In a few moments he anticipated seeing Pearl's sweet face and that would comfort him.

"If ye want to help me right an' proper," Doc said at length, quietly, "I'll larn ye how."

The horsy-faced girl followed his directions and then improved upon them. He looked at her keenly under his bushy gray brows and shrugged. He asked for a miracle and received one. What more could he ask?

Barry had also asked for a miracle. He was unsure if it had been granted or not. By dawn no war party had been spotted and he rallied the train to form up and move out.

The wagons rolled in semi-silence. The "chip" girls were only allowed to do their gathering if accompanied by an armed rider. Around the clock the scouts rode out and back in again. There was no sign of Indians, but for a week Barry ordered a halt in their daily march in mid-afternoon. The wagons were more tightly circled now and a barricade set up at each tongue opening.

Again, odd little accidents and breakdowns began to occur. The emergency crews, under Howard Tedder's command, became expert at solving the problems quickly so that no wagon was left alone for long. Their speed, in part, came from anticipation.

"Most know what's gonna happen 'fore it happens," Tedder quietly advised Barry.

"Then it is sabotage?"

"Fear so. Lookee this rein that broke. Sure there's wear, but these tiny little knife slits sure helped it along. An' you notice most breakdowns come jest in mornin' hours after we start out."

Without mentioning their findings to the council, Tedder and Barry started their own nightly patrols. As though their minds had been read there were no mishaps for two days. Also for those two days the skies were cloudy with threatening summer storms, the air was cool, and the train made good progress because of fewer stops.

Sitting far out of the campfire glow, Howard Tedder watched two shadowy figures slither from wagon to wagon and then climb onto the Buttle-Jones carriage. Like a backwoodsman stalking a bear, Tedder silently stole to the carriage and drew his revolver.

"I'll blast ye both if'n ye don't step down peaceful."

There was a gulp and a gasp. "Hey, paw, it's us!"

Tedder cursed. "Get your asses down here."

Before they hit the ground Barry had come up and old Hufford came scrambling out from the next wagon.

"What were you doing?" Barry demanded.

"Jest joshin'," Nazareth answered sullenly.

"I'll josh you," Tedder growled, "if'n ye don't talk right fast."

"Ah, paw, we wuz jest pullin' a prank on prissy pants. We wuz gonna fill his seat wid dese red army ants."

Old Hufford agilely jumped to the driver's seat and worriedly began to inspect it.

"An' I take it we got you to thank fer a lot of other pranks?"

"Naw, paw, honest! We ain't done anything else."

"Then why this trick?" Barry asked sternly.

Nazareth fidgeted and looked to Theo for help. Theo took one look at the fierce scowl on his father's face and knew he was stuck with the explaining again.

"Well," he drawled, sheepishly, "we just wanted

ta get back at prissy pants fer what he was sayin'
bout Naz and Miss Selena, 'n fer what he said he
could do instead."

Old Hufford came down from the carriage with
a sigh. They had been caught before they had
slit into the cushions to plant the ants.

"What was it my son was saying?"

Both boys were reluctant to go any further.

"Ya'all lookin' fer a good whalin'?"

"Awright!" Nazareth exploded. "He says
he knows how to make me feel good even if
Selena—"

"Enough!" old Hufford whispered, his voice
shaking with embarrassed emotion. "I'll see to my
son's foul tongue, gentlemen."

Before Tedder could answer the air was filled
with the crack of a border rifle. Then again and
again came the thundering bark of a dragoon
revolver.

The camp was instantly awake and in confusion. All but Hufford went running in the direction of the shots and almost ran over the tall form
of young Billy Joe Conroy.

"What was it?" demanded Barry. "Injun?"

"No, a man," whispered the other. "He was
crawlin' up toward the horses. I halted him an' he
run."

"You don't know who he was?"

"Nope. Weren't one of us, though."

Nazareth scoffed. "How can yah tell, Billy
Joe?"

"Smell, wise ass!" Billy Joe sneered. "At sev-
enty yards I could tell he ain't had a bath in a
coon's age."

Before the two antagoninsts broke into a scuffle Barry took command.

"Build the fires high and every man start fanning out. I want to know what this is all about."

"No need!" a voice called out of the dark. "I'm winged."

"Come in and make yourself known."

He looked more animal than man. His hair and beard were matted, his buckskins hung in dirty tatters and his feet were wrapped in rags. He held his blood-oozing right arm up across his chest and his eyes blinked against the firelight and darted about like a trapped wolf.

"Get doc for him," Barry ordered. "And pull that box to the fire so he can sit."

"Obliged," the man muttered and weakly lowered himself. "Ain't had a horse in two days."

"An' yah was fixin' ta steal one of our'n?" Billy Joe spat, feeling the man was his captive. "Should'a killed yah 'n saved us havin' ta hang a horse thief."

"Cut it!" Barry ordered. "And get back to your guard post."

Like his father, Billy Joe had to have the last word. "I caught him an' ah say we gonna have ourselves a hangin' in the morning."

The man looked at the Tennessee farm boy as though he pitied him. "You might be doing me a favor," he said softly. "Ain't none of us going to be alive soon."

Barry looked at him, curious.

"Where are you coming from?"

"Upper Platte. Trapping. Sioux ran me out. They hung up Curly Smith and they ran me out."

He spoke each word as though it were a night-mare he was trying to forget. "They're killing and running everybody out."

Bertha came hurrying up with a basin of water and rags. "Dr. Freitag says he can't leave the count, sir. Said for me to clean the wound and then call him."

"Go ahead. Now, tell me. Have you seen the Sioux and where?"

"Seen?' the trapper said blankly. "Seen more'n I ever care to see again. They've got a village just ahead, other side of the river, that you'd never believe."

Bertha Fergus Geddy stopped in the middle of her work and stared stupidly at the man.

"Will," she gasped, "can this be you?"

He tilted back his head and gazed at the horsy woman. For a second a glint came to his eye and then quickly faded.

"No, ma'am," he said evenly and turned back to Barry. "Like I said, they're dancing to make war. Rode my horse to death getting away from them."

Frowning, Bertha finished cleaning the wound. "Bullet's still in the arm," she advised Barry. "Best he be taken to the doctor."

She turned and walked away, her Irish resolve fermenting. The man possessed her father's brogue. She hadn't seen her brother Will Fergus in many years and this man had a bushy beard, yet she was positive it was him. She didn't know why he was lying, but knew someone who could find out.

"Theo," Barry ordered, "take him over to the wagon where doc has the Russian. Nazareth, get some men and double the guard for tonight. Howard, you've been awake. You see Parsons ride in?"

"Naw, only saw Curly ride out about ten. Where's Ransom?"

Barry spat. "Haven't seen him in a couple of days. He keeps sending reports back with Parsons and Curly."

"Yeh," Tedder fumed, "an' never a damn word bout no big Injun village." He drew Barry cautiously to the side. "You know Injuns, Fitzpatrick. Are we being suckered?"

Barry frowned. "Ransom works for Major Warren, Tedder. Government isn't too happy with us pushing into Mexican territory. That bastard's just vain enough to sell us out to make himself look good."

"Humm!" Tedder mused. "Jest came to mind, what you said about Ransom. We ain't had any weird breakdowns in a couple of days, either." He stopped and pondered.

"I've got a feeling you want to say more, Tedder."

"Ain't never one to accuse wrongly, Barry, but when we fixed all them Cornithwyeth wagons everyone said their trouble didn't start until after they left Fort Leavenworth. We didn't have no such trouble, but sure as hell it's our wagons now, too."

"And every morning after Ransom hasn't been on night patrol?"

"I think we got the damn same worm crawlin' in our brains."

"Then let's keep it between us for the moment. Right now I'm banking on one thing. Ransom's not only a half-breed, but a quarter of him is

Kaw. The Sioux eat Kaw for breakfast and then spit in disgust. He'll have no voice with them."

"Still," Tedder said with resolution, "I think I'll saddle up an' ride the picket line tonight."

"Thank you," Barry said warmly. "I can't think of another man I'd trust out there more."

Doc Freitag fumed at Bertha's delay in returning. He had tended many mountain men and trappers in his day, but this man's stench nearly made him retch. It caused him to be less than gentle in probing for the imbedded bullet and the man was near a faint when two wide-eyed heads popped through the wagon flap.

The man grew rigid and moaned, "Oh no. Doc!"

Freitag thought he was the one being spoken to and was curt with his reply.

Tom Geddy bounded into the wagon, followed by Bertha. Tom Geddy had no trouble recognizing Will Fergus; he knew him instantly. He forgot that he was traveling incognito. Swearing, he drew in close to examine the wound.

"You are too close to the artery," he said to the astonished Freitag. "Bertha, more light. Cut here, into the fatty tissue, and then probe upward. He will lose less blood and it won't sever the muscle fiber. Grit your teeth, Will. It will be all right."

Freitag saw the patient relax as though a divine order had been given. In a semi-trance himself, he began to do as the young man directed. At any other time he might have baulked, but the man was using words and phrases that he had long ago forgotten and now instantly recalled. Tom Geddy's hands steadied. But Doc Freitag's instruments were old and blunted.

"Bertha," Geddy barked, as though they were back in the South Boston clinic. "Go get my bag —and hurry!"

Scalpels like Merriweather Freitag had never before seen in his life were expertly placed in his hands by Bertha. Now he did not have to saw through flesh, but made quick, deeply cut straight lines.

The pencil-line thin probes let him go gently inward until metal met metal and he was able to grasp the bullet head firmly and almost float it out.

"Bertha, sew up!" Tom Geddy commanded and quickly left the wagon.

Doc Freitag sat back stunned, watching her sew and dress the wound with quiet determination. He felt quite old and antiquated.

"Why, Will?" Bertha whispered, with a tone of hatred in her voice. "Why wouldn't you admit to me who you were?"

Will Fergus set his lips and refused to speak.

"Don't try that stunt on me, Will Fergus," she snarled. "I seen it enough times between our parents and it won't work. Isn't it bad enough that Pearl and I are both here because of your damn temper?"

"Pearl?" he gasped. "Pearl is here?"

Bertha did the sutures without answering, then turned to Freitag.

"He's finished," she said curtly, "except he needs a good bath."

"Who . . ." Doc Freitag stammered.

"No questions," Bertha said icily, "if you expect me back to help with the count. If your new patient wishes to speak, I could care less. He is dead as far as I am concerned."

It was not the patient whom Doc Freitag had wished to question her about. But he stilled his lips until he could have a chance to get Bertha in a better frame of mind.

Doc Freitag's patient was well enough by morning to sit up and eat breakfast. But it was to be Will Fergus's last meal if certain people had their way. Listening only to his son's report, Ned Conroy skipped breakfast so that he could spread the word about the horse thief and the hanging that had to take place. He took his demands to the one man he thought would aid his cause the most.

Although Bradford Cornithwyeth stood in great mistrust among his people they foolishly listened to his diatribe against horse thieves and to his advice on what must be instantly done about them. A horse was the greatest show of a man's fortune and the theft of same was more severe than the stealing of a man's wife. Because Cornithwyeth felt he finally had an issue to wrest control back away from Barry he stormed to the chuck wagon and demanded a council meeting.

"Demand," he screamed, "yes, I demand a meeting to decide the fate of this horse thief!"

"An' we're all behind you!" Conroy and the rabble rousers he had been able to muster shouted.

Few had heard Will Fergus's words about the Sioux village. Few would have believed them if they had. Barry took that into consideration, but didn't alter his words because of it.

"Get out, you goddamn stupid sonofabitch!" he swore. "Every last one of you stupid bastards! Out! Move your wagons onto the trail and do it now!"

"You are only one," Cornithwyeth stormed, "against the many."

"And he was only one," Barry shot back, "against the many. Thank God he got through to warn us in time. There are hostile Indians up ahead, you silly bastards! We move out with the guns at the ready. Those who want to stay behind can look to their own scalps!"

Within an hour Cornithwyeth was again relegated to his wagon as a dishonored leader. Silently, until Barry ordered him cut down from the tree, the train passed by the hanging body of the trapper, Curly Smith. The arrows in his chest told a vast story to Barry and Doc Freitag, but they kept their Indian knowledge to themselves. The two men knew they might never see another dawn on the plans.

And as though the Sioux felt they had not given warning enough, toward noon the train came upon the scout Parson's horse, its belly slit and the guide sewn inside to suffocate and die.

Now the words of Will Fergus took on dramatic meaning for the emigrants. Frightened out of their wits, many turned on Barry.

"Why did you let us come on?"

"We paid you to keep us out of this danger!"

"What is it? Have you lived around the savages so long that you'll take us right into their trap?"

"Where is Ransom? He could negotiate and get us out of this!"

"Fat chance! He's probably in Fitzpatrick's pay and they'll split the profits they'll get on our scalps."

The tight-knit organization of defense Barry had fought to mold began to disintegrate. Cornithwyeth was able to chip away at it with his people. Conroy secretly pulled some of the Tennessee folk away from Tedder's stern command. One look from Lord Lester Buttle-Jones and Captain Dover Templeton knew where to look for his next command. The Herbert blacks would have sided with Barry, but they were unarmed and the most frightened of all because of the stories Bradford Cornithwyeth had cunningly had spread amongst them.

"Ain't e'ber heard dat," Amos Tuttle gasped in alarm.

The New England farmer shook his head in mock sympathy. "That's what he'll do. He's been among these savages for years, my good man, and knows their tastes. They are no different than your forefathers on the dark continent. To save himself he'd just as soon see you in the Injuns' stew pots as not. He's dangerous. We need you to help us rise against him or you're tomorrow night's dinner in the Indian village."

Amos, wisely, did not himself pass on these words to the other black folk. But others Cornithwyeth told did.

When only a third of the night guard mustered, Barry was tempted to leave the train to its fate. But an inner will, or the remembered harsh voice of Jim Bridger, kept him ahorse and circling the camp throughout the night. Or was it a personal challenge he had accepted—to best Ransom at his own game?

The Sioux elders had not believed Ransom Beaver Pond when he'd told them of the might of the men who rode in the white-topped ships on the land. They had refused the gift of the Russian rifles and ammunition. They were a strong nation among the Indians because of their strength, their numbers, and their expert ability with the bow and arrow. They did not need a Kaw to tell them how to fight. They had refused as cowardly his advice that they attack at night. The night was meant for dancing and working the braves into a frenzy of total commitment. The night was meant to wear on the nerves of the enemy and let him guess as to the number of Sioux he would face at dawn.

Barry sensed the Sioux were there even before the first streaks of dawn exposed them. An hour before he had seen the shallow river water begin to darken. As it muddied to near black he could almost mentally count the number of horses that were crossing the river upstream. He sat his horse, never once looking up from the water, and waited for it to begin to clear.

Then, as though it were any other day on their trek, he rode back to the camp and ordered the night guards into the encirclement. Fires were kindled, breakfasts begun, the animals brought into the far end of the oval as though Barry were preparing to sort them out and harness them up for another day of travel.

But those whom he trusted, and who trusted in turn in Barry's leadership, drank their morning mug of coffee with their rifles across their laps.

"Paw!" Nazareth cried. "Ah can see 'em now!"

"Yep," Tedder said sourly, "an' they can see you. Jest amble to your post now."

Tedder rose and stretched, but his head slowly turned to take in the brightening western skyline. A slow grin crossed his face as he thought how accurate Barry's guess had been. There were a couple hundred Sioux waiting to attack them.

Some thought that a small number and used it as a further excuse to undermine Barry.

"My," Cornithwyeth smirked, to anyone who would listen, "is that what he kept us frightened of all night long? They would probably scatter and run if we rode out shooting."

Many began to think the same as the Sioux silently sat and didn't attack.

"Smart bastard out thar," Jeb Pierce chuckled to Barry. "Must have about popped the feathers from his bonnet seein' no guards out. Thinks he's scarin' us with his power show an' makin' us think he's standin' pat."

Barry nodded agreement. It was a masterful manuever. Rank by rank, the Indians were inching their horses forward, keeping the horizon line filled so that it appeared they were not moving at all. They wanted the first shaft of sunlight to fall fully upon them, increasing the mirage-like illusion that they were floating in place and taking

the enemy's eye off the constant movement of the
horses' hooves.

The Sioux were not used to fighting the white
man, except for small bands of trappers or mountain men. In those instances they had been able
to frighten and overpower the firesticks before
they could inflict too much damage. Again they
did not heed the advice of Ransom Beaver Pond
and prepared to do battle in their own way.

The whole plain exploded with a single shrill
cry multiplied two hundred times. It was not a
sound emitted in aggressive assault; it was a vocal
expression of the joy of killing. The line of horses
became a ripple of movement, then a surging
tidal wave that began to split and encircle the
camp.

They sped arrow after arrow against the wagons, receiving in return ball after ball of rifle and
revolver fire. Because a great many of the emigrants were unused to firing at such rapidly moving targets only a half dozen Sioux fell in the first
wave's circling. Then the war-party leader de-
ployed a second string of braves to attack. Their
success was no greater than before and he angrily
waved forward an even greater hoard of braves.

The wagons' canvas tops began to look as if
they were sprouting arrow shafts. Hundreds more
arrows had thudded into the inner circle and inflicted the only casualties for the train: four cattle, two horses and as many mules.

It was over as quickly as it began. The war-
party drew back to the horizon and sat their
horses, stunned and silent. They could not believe
that the women and children of this strange encampment had not run in panic, screaming and

scrambling for escape. Why had their braves remained hidden like cowards and not come out to fight? Messengers were raced back to the Sioux village to report this oddity to the tribal council. Other braves were waved back to the scene of the battle.

"They're comin' again!" someone shouted.

"Hold your damn fire!" Barry screamed. "They're only coming for their dead and wounded."

A heavy blue pall of gunpowder smoke hung over the train. It matched the silence as a half a hundred braves rode up slowly without a trace of fear and began to remove their dead and dying. It was an Indian rule of warfare that they automatically assumed the white men would observe and honor.

"What in the damn hell we awaitin' fer," Ned Conroy exploded. "We can git 'em like sittin' ducks on a pond." He raised his rifle to aim.

"Do that," Doc Freitag snarled, putting the barrel of his revolver right into Conroy's ear, "an' your brains are scrambled."

"Injun lover," Conroy spat, lowering his rifle.

"Hogwash," Freitag declared. "They're testin' to see if'n we're stupid enough to fire. I don't see a bow or arrow on a one of those braves." Then he cast the man with a fierce glare. "An' I don't recall your firin' that piece when it was needed."

Conroy stormed away. But his was not the only rifle that hadn't been fired that morning.

Barry was furious that some men would put their spite for him above the safety of the women and children. He glared at the council members. There was a face missing.

"Where's Hartwicke?"

"Took to his wagon ill," Tom Geddy answered him.

"Well," Barry said sourly, "don't need him anyway for what I've got to say."

Cornithwyeth cut in quickly. "We shall if our discussion comes to a vote."

"Discussion?" Barry bellowed. "Those are Indians out there, not someone dressed up for a Boston Tea Party!"

Cornithwyeth would not be riled. "And they seem to have gone away. I think it was quite wise on the part of some of us not to expend unnecessary firepower on so small a number. I suggest, gentlemen, that we harness up and get out of here as soon as possible."

"Silly ass suggestion," Doc Freitag said without malice.

"You, sir," Cornithwyeth said with malice, "are not a part of this council."

"Thank God," Freitag said. "But I aim to speak my piece anyways. That ain't someone buildin' a fire fer breakfast on the horizon. Them's signal smokes. Every brave and huntin' party for fifty mile 'round are being called home an' just for us. String this train out its full length an' you'll learn what the word massacre means."

Cornithwyeth smirked. "I'll lay any man odds that we don't see another Indian this whole day."

Barry grinned. "Why, Cornithwyeth, I didn't think you were a gambling man."

Cornithwyeth flushed scarlet, but wouldn't be baited. As was becoming his custom, he stormed away from the council meeting.

No one spoke. Then Barry did.

"Get this place cleaned up," he ordered. "They tested us to see our strength. Now they'll show us theirs."

Because the 'chip' girls would be unable to go out and collect that day, they were assigned the task of collecting up the arrows for firewood. A game was devised for the younger children. Gleefully, they raced about the encirclement searching out the spent brass shell casings as though they were Easter eggs.

The long night was going to turn into a long day and Barry was everywhere trying to keep idle minds busy and off the thought of the Sioux.

"That's a damn shame," Barry said, coming upon Hufford pulling arrows from his carriage. "Want someone to help you get them out of the old girl?"

"No!" Hufford snapped, with unusual petulance. "I'm doing nicely, thank you."

Barry looked at the carriage and scratched his head. "You know, that rig kinda worries me. Some of those damn Indians may be smart enough to figure they could jump a horse right over its middle and start swinging their tomahawks at a few heads. I think we'd be better off pulling it into the circle and closing that gap with the chuck wagon. Pierce ain't going to have time to cook today, anyway."

Old Hufford sighed with gratitude, but was reluctant to let Barry know why. The arrows had inflicted so many rips and tears in the leather seats that a close inspection might reveal what was hidden beneath them. With each arrow extracted, he had frantically filled the hole with a wad of cloth.

Harmon Herbert came along and helped them pull the carriage out of the circle. Then he was sent to help Jeb Pierce pull over the chuck wagon.

Barry stood a moment staring at the leather seats and Hufford's heart nearly failed.

"She's taking a beating from the weather, Hufford. Why don't you use one of the extra wagon tops to cover her at night?"

Their voices had been heard two wagons away. Lester Hartwicke thought it was an excellent suggestion on Barry's part. His sudden "illness" had been brought about by such a feeling of joy and elation that it had made his head swim.

During the attack he had watched Lady Pamela and Hufford to see what they would try most to protect from the Indians. When Hufford had been called away to the council meeting he had made his excuses to Tom Geddy and had quickly gone to examine the carriage. He had only a few seconds to extract some of the gold coins and now sat lovingly holding them. Come nightfall he had determined he could get more and now the canvas covering would make his chore that much easier.

Noon, and the Indians did not reappear. Cornithwyeth urged some to come back to his way of thinking. Doc Freitag and Barry were watching the many smoke signals.

"I'm afeared of sunset," said Freitag at length. "They wanted us to see 'em this morning, but they'll use the sun to blind us now."

His fear was justified. When the sun was a massive orange ball that hung forever above the horizon line, there appeared rank after rank of the Sioux, making a new dark line between earth and sky. This time they were bedecked in all the savage finery of their war dress. Ransom had finally been heard by the tribal war council. They had left their village en masse for a battle that would keep the white men from their land forever.

At first, many emigrants thought that they were no more than before, but the sun was shielding them from the horrible truth. The horizon filled and then filled again and again. This time the Indians did not have to rely upon the trickery of movement. As if someone had disturbed their ant hill, they rode forth, five hundred, seven hundred, a thousand, two thousand strong, and the ground shook under the weight of quadruple that many horses' hoofs.

They were winning the first fateful moment of the battle of nerve and Barry thought it just as well. The emigrants' frozen panic at seeing such a surging mass of hateful humanity kept the hotheads among them from firing too soon. With workman like precision, the Sioux strung out and swung wide, circling the train and riding in to arrow range. This time they did not come in wave after wave, but as a single, massive force. Despite the wide oval they were riding around, they were as disciplined as though they were one. Only when their own circle was closed did they veer to the left, discharge their arrows and quickly try to ride out of rifle range.

Two thousand arrows singing down upon the encampment sounded like a gale wind at full force. The answering fire seemed puny. No savage fell, but in the compound eight men lay dead and several women and children lay wounded from arrows piercing the canvas of the wagon tops.

The war chief's hand signal regrouped his circle and then he gave a new command—not for a renewed attack just then but for the braves to issue their piercing war cries.

The ululations rising from so many savage voices were blood-chilling. Women and children jumped from the wagon beds and ran to be with their husbands and no amount of threats on Barry's part could force them back.

He had let the Indians get in their first lick so he could time them. Now his command to fire on the second attack was almost drowned out by the screams of terrified people.

The emigrants began to suffer a terrible toll. The bow and arrow and the fear instilled in them were proving to be the superior weapon.

But some, beginning to see that Barry could not be everywhere at once, began to take command of their barricaded areas. They kicked butts and got men to kneel and fire with careful aim. Even the six-shooters, unknown to the Sioux, were effective when the painted faces rode in too close to the breastworks. After the third charge a few gaps and riderless ponies were evident in the Indians' ranks.

Three areas within the encirclement were returning little or no fire. The Herbert wagons gave the Indians a safe stretch to ride around because the colonel sat benumbed by the din, leaving only Harmon to fire the rifles as fast as the blacks could reload and hand them to him. Many of Cornithwyeth's pious followers were, as incredible as it seemed to Barry, observing the 'thou shalt not kill' commandment. He wondered if the Lord had told the same to the savages whose arrows found their way into these same New Englanders' hearts and bodies.

After the first two attacks the Indians grew more aware of the encirclement's weak spots. They concentrated their arrow power on them during the third attack to force an opening in the wagon wall so that they could enter. The English wagons were the hardest assualted, because they had not returned a single shot.

Lady Pamela had sat through each attack on the wagon floor, holding a sleeping pallet before her to ward off the arrows. So many diamond-shaped arrowheads pierced the canvas topping of her wagon that it looked like the underside of a pin cushion. The noise was such that she had paid little attention to the gunfire. She wished at that moment that she had ordered her daughter to stay in her wagon with her. Suddenly, she felt very alone and lonely. She heard the rip of the canvas and looked up to see where that arrow had pierced. With utter disbelief she stared into a face that painted red, saffron, yellow and dirty white. The Sioux had determined the weakest points of the train and were riding close enough to jump onto the wagons and make entry.

Without a moment's hesitation, Lady Pamela rose and fired the single-shot derringer point-blank. The face vanished and she did not wait to see another replace it.

Jumping down from the wagon she was shocked by the sight of the carnage across the encirclement. She called for Hufford and getting no answer screamed for Donald Hufford.

Ashen and trembling, Donald poked his head out of a blanket beneath her wagon.

"Where is your weapon?" she demanded. "Why aren't you fighting?"

"Don't know how, mi'lady," he whimpered.

"Imbecile," she snapped, looking around. "What is this? They have weapons. Why aren't they using them?"

"Waiting for orders, mum."

"From whom?"

A strong young man in another season, Donald had broken down in this one. His sobs told her all she needed to know. She had not minded Lord Lester forcing his wagon into her group, thinking it easier to watch the enemy when he was close at hand. But for him purposely to hold back nineteen well-trained soldiers from the Indian attack was utter madness.

She ran along the line of wagons, unmindful of the flying arrows. With utter contempt she glared down at the man sitting casually with his back against the wagon wheel, while his wife and two children cowered face down on the ground in terror. Without comment she snatched the rifle from his hands and felt the barrel.

"Cold," she snapped. "As probably are the other nineteen I purchased for your cohorts."

Dover Templeton looked up at her with bland coolness. "Lord Lester is back in command, mi'lady."

She expertly turned the rifle about and fired it between his legs. He was instantly on his feet, murderous rage in his face.

"You forget I was born a farmer's daughter," Lady Pamela said between clenched teeth. "Next time I'll shoot your balls off. Now, get your people on their feet and fighting the Indians, or a lot of Englishmen are going to find bullets in their backs."

Dover Templeton got up fast, muttering.

Lady Pamela raised the rifle to her shoulder, spun and caught a Sioux in mid-flight as he was attempting to jump off the top of the next wagon.

"Now!" she barked at Templeton. "On my orders!"

The jumping Indian, tomahawk in hand, had had Yeoman David Faraday as his target. Now Faraday raced toward Captain Templeton, his eyes wide.

"I'll keep your rifle," Lady Pamela was telling Templeton disparagingly as the other soldier ran up.

"What's this?" Faraday gasped.

Templeton scowled uncertainly. He had to save face. "Tell the men to protect their own."

"Mi'lady's orders?"

"Mine!" Templeton growled.

Faraday turned and hid his smile. Once again, he decided, the Duke of Chalford had been mistaken. Lord Lester had not been able to get the better of his wife; the whereabouts of the gold was still a mystery and Captain Templeton was proving to be as big an ass as always.

Being the paid spy of the duke no longer seemed important to Faraday. He had followed orders, even though his wife and children stood in danger from the savages. He might have continued to follow those orders, even though he knew full well that Lady Pamela's rifle shot had just saved his life. But it was clear to Faraday

that Lady Pamela was now in command, not
Templeton and not the duke, and he felt free of
his obligations. Not that that freedom would do
him much good. Faraday feared that the Indians
were so strong that he wouldn't live another day
in any case.

It was nearly dark when the fourth assault
came. It was fierce, and the Indians expected it
to be the last, for, though the English soldiers
and even the decimated New Englanders were
now shooting back, they had discovered the
weakest link of all. As if they'd sniffed out the
order of rot, the Sioux circled wide and came
riding at breakneck speed towards the totally unarmed blacks.

"The darkies! The darkies!" Lady Pamela
screamed as she saw the Indians, still far off,
veer in their direction. Her warning went either
unheard or not understood. Groaning inwardly,
she ran to the huddled blacks, pressed her rifle
into one man's hands and began to issue swift
orders, rousing the rest.

The first Indians attempted to jump the high
wagons, their horses getting ensnarled in the
hooped canvas coverings. Still they came, piling
on top one another, a surging mass of copper-
toned flesh that would not be denied. Within
short minutes, their kicking horses had toppled
a wagon onto its side, spilling its contents forth
into the compound.

But Lady Pamela's urgent voice and quick
commands had gotten the blacks moving, too.
Suddenly, two hundred souls bent on survival
were swinging picks, thrusting with pitch forks,
smacking down with shovel blades and clawing

out with hoes. Force met force. The Indians found their tomahawks too short to hack past the longer weapons. With cries of utter dismay they pulled back from so determined an enemy. They would tell many tales that night of an enemy whose skin was the color of a starless night.

Later, after the Sioux had withdrawn and the emigrants were quietly nursing their few wounded, Barry found time to tell Lady Pamela, "You may have saved us all this evening."

"Nonsense," Lady Pamela declared, though coloring at the compliment. "Had the darkies been armed it never would have happened in the first place."

"You might tell that to the train council," Barry suggested bitterly.

"Give me the chance before tomorrow and I shall."

Barry frowned. "Yes, they'll attack again tomorrow, I expect."

Lady Pamela looked around and her heart sickened. "Of course they will! Why not? Look at our dead! Look at their dead! I would say that we are each about equal for this day on casualties. They'll not settle for a deadlock. I say they'll be back again to finish us off."

"And I say you are quite a woman for what you did this day."

Lady Pamela colored deeply again. She hesitated. "An unlikely comment," she said then, "coming from a man who once refused my dinner invitation."

Barry shrugged, grinning. "From what I hear from old Hufford about your cook, I saved myself a bellyache."

Lady Pamela blinked, then burst into laughter. "You may well have, at that. I cooked better than Mildred Crumly does when I was ten and had no training."

Barry smiled. "Then perhaps you'd do well to start cooking again."

Pamela said coyly, "If I do, Mr. Fitzpatrick, would you consider another dinner invitation?"

"Try me."

"I shall."

It would be a dinner a long time in the coming. The Sioux, spurred on by Ransom Beaver Pond, did not wait for the morning to strike again. They attempted their first night attack. From afar, they shot flaming arrows to ignite the wagons. The emigrants had few discernible targets to fire upon in the dark and wisely saved most of their ammunition. They concentrated on putting out the fires.

At dawn, each side was allowed a respite to gather and bury its dead. The night forays continued for three days until Cornithwyeth made a sound observation, never once admitting it had originally come from his wife an hour before a meeting was held.

"I assume," he said stiffly at the meeting, "that the Indians can count as well as we can. I'm afraid that's a matter we've overlooked."

"What's yer pernt?" Ned Conroy demanded, weary and aggravated at the man's toying with them.

"Simply this," the New Englander snapped. "We show too many graves."

"So what—"

"Damn good point!" Barry injected quickly.

354   THE CONESTOGA PEOPLE

"We've had a hell of a loss and they're bound to know our true total, particularly if Ransom is there doing their thinking for them, which we ought to assume he is. Some of you may get upset by this, but tomorrow we don't bury any of our dead."

Nor did the emigrants bury their dead for several days, until the stench became unbearable. Then they cunningly put several bodies into a single grave to confuse the Indians' count.

Then the daily hostilities seemed to taper off. There were no more all-out frontal attacks because neither side was really winning anything. It was a stalemate. The minor attacks, day and night, were led mainly by hot-headed young braves who wanted to win glory in the eyes of their elders. Most never saw the light of the next day.

No one was quite sure who spoke the word first, but it became a hateful center of controversy.

"It's a siege, damn it," Ned Conroy cried. "They've got us surrounded and we'll perish when our food runs out. Fine mess Fitzpatrick's got us into!"

18

Time was on the side of the Sioux. They had
the upstream advantage to keep the waters muddied and contaminated. They had no problems
with wood or food supplies.

The emigrants' days wore on, much taken up
with duties connected with mere survival. So
wearied did the men become that many started
sleeping by day to renew their energies for the
nightly vigil. Their wives had to give up precious
pieces of furniture for the cook fires. All the emigrants began eating the horses killed during attacks, and even this meat had to be rationed. They
were four hundred miles out of Independence and
four hundred miles away from Jim Bridger. They
would need every ounce of supplies they had left
to go in either direction. Although it was never

spoken aloud, most silently thought they would never see either place.

Morale in the camp, such as it was, was lifted somewhat by three women. Mary Sue Herbert took pride in the fact that her "family" of blacks were the least troublesome group in the besieged encampment. She supervised and cared for them as she would have on her plantation. To conserve on wood her people began to cook and eat in communes. Nothing went to waste, because she was there to oversee everything done. On quiet, attack-free nights, which were becoming many, she encouraged them to sit around and sing their old plantation songs. Their rich voices gave solace to many faint hearts and, unbeknownst to them, were causing some troubled frowns on the faces of the tribal war council in the Sioux village.

If Mary Sue had a problem, it was of her own making. She was pleased with the change in Harmon, and yet not pleased. Not since the death of Pomeroy had he looked at one of the black girls in a lustful way, but Mary Sue wasn't happy now with the time he was spending with Anne Cornithwyeth. Still, she would not admit what was truly in her heart.

Lady Pamela felt her perspective on life changing. Something mysterious was happening in her heart. Her one time goal, to become Lord Dunraven's queen in the monarchy he was going to establish, she saw now as a spiteful attempt to revenge herself against the Buttle-Jones family. She did not love Lord Dunraven any more than she had loved Lester and, she realized now, she did not want the power both aspired to. Lester, as far as her heart was concerned, was dead, although old Hufford kept him alive in her thoughts because he'd reported gold missing from the carriage and Lord Lester was automatically the prime suspect.

In her waking and sleeping hours Lady Pamela could not release herself from the enthralling memory of the attack he had helped withstand. She was haunted by Barry Fitzpatrick's smile and laughter. He made her feel alive. Only in action of some kind could she be near him each day; and to that end she worked. The frills and lace came off her simplest gown. Aggie brushed her hair back and tied it in a bun at the nape of her neck. After seeing to the needs of her own people, she helped where she could with the people she had traveled from Tennessee with. They were farm folk and she had to laugh at the realization that that was all she had ever been—a farm girl at heart.

There was no petulant, self-seeking girl left in Bertha Geddy. She was the spirit that gave the wounded the will to keep living. She became as expert as Doc Freitag in removing arrowheads and sewing up the jagged wounds. Her help was so appreciated that he refrained from asking questions about her background and her husband. He knew Tom Geddy had to be a rich medical man, because Bertha kept popping up with fresh, expensive supplies every time they were needed. Doc suspected that Tom Geddy might have gone through an experience similar to his own. He knew how long it had taken for the wounds to heal in his heart before he had started practicing medicine again.

Bertha, on the other hand, felt no compassion for Tom. It was, perhaps, the one sore spot left in her heart. What love she had felt for him had withered. She didn't understand the man at all. She saw him as unfeeling and selfish for flatly refusing to use his skills. He would concern himself only with the well-being of Will and Pearl—Bertha's other two worries. Will would clam up whenever Bertha was around, making her feel the outsider. After an infection developed in his wound, he would only let Tom clean and dress it. Bertha also felt shut out from Pearl, after they learned she was pregnant. Bertha had wanted to make Lester Hartwicke stand by his wedding vow and accept responsibility. Tom Geddy would not hear of it and closed Bertha out of his discussion with Pearl.

Tom Geddy put a new dressing on the wound and looked at Will with his heart in his eyes.

"Almost as good as new."

"New, Tom," Will rumbled, the note of questioning deep in his voice. "How can I ever be new?"

"I know all about it," Tom said slowly. "Father told me everything before I left Boston."

"Not everything, Tom. Not everything. The reason he couldn't find me, was because the doctor who healed me in New York told me the truth." His voice trailed off into the smallest of whispers. "Your father made sure that I would never be a man again."

He looked up to see the color draining from

Tom's face and the pain in his eyes, as if he knew the words before they were spoken.

"You get a lot of time to think on a trip like this," Tom said, hesitantly. "At first I dropped the doctor from my name to throw my mother off the track. Then I started going over and over again in my mind what they had done to you. And something my father said kept ringing in my ears. He said that your circumstances were such that any doctor would have gossiped about your condition. That wouldn't have been the case if it was just a broken member from the whip handle. And he would not have gone to the trouble of searching for you from Maine to the Carolinas. Oh God, Will, then it dawned on me. The more I thought about what he had taken away from you the sicker I got. I vowed right then and there that I would never be a doctor again. I don't want to be anything like him."

"Don't throw your life away just because of what they did to me. It's frustrating as hell sometimes, but I go on living. Besides, you got Bertha and Pearl to think about."

"Poor little Pearl," Tom sighed. "She's too young to be carrying that baby. We were foolish to go into those fake marriages."

"Both were fake?"

"They weren't illegal, mind you. But they were just for the purpose of the trip. Surely, Will, you don't think I'd take Bertha for a bride otherwise."

"Then you haven't been a husband to her?"

"No. For the love of God, man, what do you take me for? I never want to father a child in my whole life. I would stand in mortal fear that it might turn out to be like my mother or father."

Will looked at him distastefully.

"Then I'm sorry you learned about me. I seem to stir up everybody's hatred."

"I don't hate you!" Tom said suddenly, fiercely.

"No, Tom," he said gently, "you don't hate me. You pity me now, as I once pitied your father. Hatred is just a step behind pity."

The song was sad and carried on the air like a wail. It told of the black man's desire to go back home to the land of his father. It could have been the song of any of the emigrants, after three weeks of being trapped inside the encampment. The decision had been made. The train would head back east in the morning, with prayerful hearts that the Sioux would let them leave in peace. The mood of the song was reported to the Indians' tribal council and they smiled.

DeeDee Herbert had tried every ruse in the world to get Barry alone again. He'd held her off, but that night he felt so lonely and dejected that he was glad for even her company. He had failed and knew that the last thing on her mind would be a desire to talk—about anything. He did find highly amusing the "secret" spot she claimed to have found for them.

The leather seat of the carriage was far more comfortable than the floor of a tepee, he had to admit. The tarp covering made it warm and intimate. Just enough fire light filtered through the canvas to give him a diffused look at the leering DeeDee as she daringly unbuttoned the top of her dress and fully exposed her breasts. She could see desire rise and stroked it through the buckskin. With a little giggle she guided his hand to her breast and began to arouse him. The last time had been savage and unrewarding. She was determined to have it her way this time.

She fondled him and he gasped at the pleasure of her touch. Without a qualm she dropped her head down to his lap and he tingled near to a faint at the warm contact. He was immediately appalled, delighted and bewildered. He couldn't decide whether to pull her away or leave her be.

It wasn't the only new thing DeeDee had learned well and wanted to expose him to that night. Every time Harmon had been on night guard she had stolen Ebner into her wagon. The young buck was nearly as naive as DeeDee, but at least had heard talk. Their fumbling experimentation turned into knowledgable expertise but never once did DeeDee feel she was with Ebner. He was nothing more than a stand-in for Barry in her mind. And now she had the real thing.

Suddenly, an angry voice interrupted them. "Caught you! You thief!"

The tarp had been pulled away so quickly that Barry momentarily blinked against the torch held almost in his face. He blinked again and saw the astounded face of old Hufford, showing an odd mixture of embarrassment, surprise and offended piety. But seeing the face next to the old man was like watching a candle melt from being left too near the fire. Lady Pamela had expected to catch Lord Lester stealing the gold. But as her eyes went from DeeDee's bare breasts to Barry's exposure, her expression slipped from puzzlement to hurt to utter loathing. She turned away, enough of a lady not to make a scene. But, oh, how she wanted to scream out her fury.

Instead, the air was abruptly filled DeeDee Herbert's scream. She had turned away to cover her breasts—just in time to see the savage leap from the top of the next wagon and come flying at them, his tomahawk held high to slash.

Barry didn't have time to free his revolver before the Sioux landed between them and made a double hack at DeeDee's back and buttocks. Barry grabbed for the Indian's attacking arm and tried to wrestle the weapon free. The young brave was strong and didn't fear death. He fought Barry ferociously, because he knew what they did not. He was only one of two hundred Sioux who had swum down the river and slithered their way up to the camp. Even then he knew that his brothers would be entering the camp as he had done. They knew that they would never see another dawn, but would so weaken this village that the horsemen could come riding in to avenge their honorable deaths.

"Gun!" Barry screamed at DeeDee. "Take out my gun and shoot him!"

DeeDee froze, her back wracked by pain. The loathing still not removed from her face, Lady Pamela leaped to the scuffling men, took the revolver and pressed it into the painted belly at the same time she fired.

"They're everywhere!" Barry cried. "Sound the alarm! See to her! Give me my gun! Arm yourselves!"

His voice snapped out the commands. Then

he was off and running, his gun blazing at every savage until it was spent. He threw it down next to Captain Templeton and took his. Templeton wouldn't need it. His head was split open by a tomahawk.

Yeoman Faraday grabbed Barry's revolver and tossed it to Templeton's wife, with a sharp order to reload it. As though her husband were only asleep, the woman stoically rifled his knapsack and began to reload.

The panic the Indians had hoped to bring about was thwarted by some strange, amusing and yet tragic events.

Barry, warned of his exposed condition, stopped to push himself back inside his buckskins. The man who warned him took an arrow through the heart.

Nanna, ambling down from her wagon, had a savage land squarely on her back. Toppling to the ground, the Sioux landed beneath her heavy weight and the force broke his back.

Some long-lost dream of glory sounded a trumpet call in Colonel Herbert's brain and he came charging into the compound with a jewel-encrusted sword. The sword, a keepsake, was ancient, but had been dutifully kept sharp by the Herbert blacksmith. Like an avenging angel the colonel slashed at six attacking Sioux, deftly severing arms, legs and heads until one was able to smash a tomahawk into his chest and heart. He sat back, still clutching the sword, a smile of contentment on his lips. He had at last been in battle. He had the right now to call himself a colonel.

The weakest link was not as weak as the Indians had expected, thanks to Lady Pamela's insistence that the blacks be armed. Yet, because of the short warning, the toll was great. Ebner fell and then his father.

The Tennessee men had fought Indian savages and, in feuds, each other for a hundred years. When Ned Conroy fell, and his sons got into trouble, the Tedder boys came to the aid of their youthful enemies. They were able to beat back the Sioux and drag Ned to where Bertha Geddy was nursing the wounded, but the short battle cost them the life of Billy Joe Conroy and a slash to Theo Tedder's arm that would leave it next to useless for the rest of his life.

But the real price they paid for aiding Ned Conroy would not dawn on them for some little time. Screaming for help, her cries drowned by the tumult, the freckle-faced Maybelle Tedder was seized by two Sioux who were amazed by her unusual hair and facial coloration. She was a prize not to be destroyed and they spirited her away.

Bradford Cornithwyeth was no prize. He had a poor scalp to take. Nor did he fight them back like the other white braves they had come to respect in this long battle. He was as worthless to them as the women and children, and they bashed in his hairless skull as he frantically clutched his bags of gold to his chest. And that's how his family found him, because the Sioux had not the least bit of interest in gold.

As his fat wife and skinny daughter screamed and cowered, the raiding Sioux looked on them with equal disinterest. They would leave them for the common horse soldiers who were not so snobbish about their treasures of war.

Even while fighting continued within the encampment the Sioux horse soldiers came, if more cautiously than before. They rode their circle, out of rifle range, without a sound erupting from their throats. By this time they had thought their brother braves would have opened a wedge in the wagons for them to enter. But as the gunfire grew less their hearts grew heavier and yet strangely prouder. They were the Sioux, undaunted warriors of the plains. No tribe had been their superior in 2500 years.

The young chieftain, son of the tribal chief, called a halt to the encirclement. He slipped from his pony, looking at the wagon train with a mixture of reverence and loathing and spread his hands skyward. He made sure that his words would be heard by all.

"Oh, Manitou," he chanted, "Maker of all, it is I, called Back Bull or Sitting Bull. We feel your disfavor, because you have caused all of our tepees to weep from loss. I give the blue-eyed and yellow-haired ones this victory, because they are brave. Grant me, Oh Manitou, an equal victory in my day."

Sitting Bull, as chief of the Sioux, would be granted his wish against General George C. Custer at the Battle of the Big Horn. In his old years Chief Sitting Bull would be asked to name the greatest fighter he had ever faced. He would smile narrowly, knowing they wanted him to name Custer to make headlines, but he would give an answer to confuse an historian:

"A wagon master of no name. He opened a gate. I was not able to close it again."

*   *   *

"Pull a wagon out of line," Barry ordered. "Let them come in for their dead."

"Have we won, lad?" old Hufford asked, tears welling his eyes.

Barry shook his head sadly. "No one won, my friend. It's a battle that will go on forever."

It was a sight the Indian braves would tell to their children for years to come. They took away two hundred of their own fallen, leaving an equal number of wounded and dead. It was so still that Barry could hear his own harsh breathing; not even the wounded moaned or cried out. The creak of the wagon wheels being rolled back into place dwarfed all other sounds.

Then, two screams came so close upon each other that it was an electrifying moment before Barry realized they had come from different women. He turned to see Bertha stumble out of the surgery tent, ashen and shaken. To see her thus shook Barry and he went on the run. He didn't even stop to question her, but charged right into the tent.

DeeDee Herbert lay face down on the plank table, her dress split away from neck to ankle. Doc Freitag was bent over, working on her. In the eerie candle glow Barry saw how seriously she'd been wounded by the tomahawk. The deep slice in her back and buttocks exposed raw red meat. Her face was pale and frightened. Barry could well understand why she'd screamed, but couldn't understand Bertha's cry—the nurse had seen much worse than this in the past three weeks.

Then, horribly, he saw why Bertha had
screamed.

Doc Freitag continued to bend to his work,
as unaware of Barry's presence as he had been
of the screams. Deftly, he sliced away thin strips
of DeeDee's backside flesh and put them in his
mouth.

Barry gasped, with sickening disbelief. "My
God! What in the hell are you doing?"

Doc Freitag looked up, his tired watery eyes
blinking foolishly as, close to starvation from the
siege, he joyously chewed.

"No, doc," Barry wailed. "No, not you! Oh
gawd, I'm going to be sick! Get the hell outta
here, you crazy old man!" He turned and bellowed,
"Bertha, get in here!" When he turned back Doc
Freitag was slinking out the other end of the tent.

Bertha entered hesitantly. "I—I guess I did see
what I thought I saw," she stammered.

"Forget it!" he snapped. "Is she going to be all
right?"

"We—we thought she wouldn't make it because of loss of blood. He—he sent me to get
some morphine so he could work on her back."
Nervous tension made her giggle at her own last
words.

"Damn him," Barry growled. "She looks bad.
Why did he have to pick this time for his mountain man habits to return? Can you care for her?"

Bertha shook her head. "The wounds were
deep to begin with. I—I have fifty others who
could be saved in the time . . ." She set her
square jowls and scowled. "My husband is a doctor, Mr. Fitzpatrick, but it will take a man to
wake him to that fact."

Barry didn't wait to comment. He marched across the compound, reloading his revolver as he went. Without mincing words he told Tom Geddy exactly what Doc Freitag had done to the Herbert girl and that he could just as easily kill Geddy for not helping as he wanted to kill Freitag for causing the problem. Tom's calm silence almost suggested to Barry that the man would have welcomed Barry's blowing his brains out.

"Tom," Pearl said softly, "you've got to try and help DeeDee. She's got a right to live now, just like the rest of us."

It was a child, not a man, who momentarily pulled Tom Geddy from his lethargy. He couldn't help DeeDee Herbert; she had already lost too much blood before Doc Freitag had put a scalpel to her back. But he was able to help save others. Throughout the night, patient after patient was shoved in front of him and he could not turn them away and deny them the only doctor they now had available. But for having exposed him, his heart turned colder towards Bertha, though they made an excellent working team. As the night wore on he came to realize why he both admired and loathed her. She was as hard-driving and efficient as his father, as domineering and ruthless as his mother. She would control and strangle him just as surely as Mildred Geddy had attempted to. He couldn't stand to live that way ever again. Toward dawn, when he heard that Doc Freitag had vanished with his mules, he suddenly thought of Will Fergus. Will had vanished once, and probably would again. He would secretly wait for his opportunity to do the same.

"I brought coffee," Pearl said meekly, then

gasped. "Theodis Tedder, your arm! Will he be all right, Tom?"

Tom muttered something inaudible as he cut the last stick and prepared to apply a dressing. He hadn't told a single soul how bad off he thought they really were.

"Ain't nothing, Pearl," Theo smiled shyly. "It's my feet that does the dancing."

Pearl cast the red-headed young Theodis such a warm and winning smile that Tom Geddy came fully awake. He burned with jealousy; Pearl must be his; he needed her warmth, her moral support. He needed her. Whether Bertha and Will liked it or not, he would take Pearl with him. He thought of himself as the only one capable of protecting her from the likes of Lester Hartwicke and this young punk. He was unaware that he was thinking exactly as his mother might have thought.

"Thar comin back! Thar comin back!"

The fast-approaching dust cloud on the horizon sank hearts to their lowest point of despair. They could not stand another moment of grief or nervous tension. Grown men burst into tears of frustration. An hour more and the burials would have been completed; they would have been on their way. Another fight with the Sioux just wasn't in them. They stood very still and watched as the horsemen drew nearer.

"Look!" exclaimed Barry, jumping to a wagon seat. "Look, everyone, it's Major Fremont and his army expedition! Open a path for them!"

The sight of the thirty-man column brought

heart to every man, woman and child. Now, indeed, they were safe. As the dust-covered men rode into the encampment men and women embraced, talked excitedly, wept, knelt in prayer and replaced sorrow for the joy of seeing their own kind.

John C. Fremont looked about in dismay. "Met Freitag," he said curtly. "Didn't tell me it was this bad. How many'd you lose, Fitzpatrick?"

"Near half."

Fremont frowned in puzzlement. "Why'd the old doc leave you?"

"Doesn't matter now," Barry answered sourly. "The rest of us do!"

"Right! Sergeant, take a squad of men back to that cottonwood grove and drag back some dry firewood. Barry, slaughter a couple of those cows—plenty of buffalo to replace it with up ahead. Tell the women to cook their best right away. These people need to eat. Got any music makers? Then get 'em going and play something fast and lively. Heard about your water supply so get some quinine into them—coffee, quinine, and more damn coffee. Once done, we can get these teams hooked up and move upriver. I don't care if you don't get more'n a couple miles away, but get them away from this damn place."

"They'll be glad to go," Barry said softly, "mighty glad."

Major Fremont's face was a battleground for his emotions. "A few days ago I was cursing myself for having come up with this damn fool scheme. There isn't an Indian tribe between here and the Rockies that haven't gotten wind of this battle. That you stood for so long against the

Sioux has them mystified over your power. These people paid dearly, but it's struck a fear in the Indians' hearts that will be long remembered. Now, tell me, what relationship did a Ransom Beaver Pond have with this train?"

"How did you come to hear of him?"

"One of my scouts is Sioux. He has a way of finding out things that is uncanny. Beaver Pond was the one stirring up the Sioux and telling them of your weaknesses. He had to be one of you to know about them."

Without embellishment Barry told Fremont of Ransom, Count Justinian and Major Warren.

"Warren, huh?" Fremont mused. "I'm due back in Washington before summer's end and will look into the good major."

"What of Ransom?"

Fremont laughed. "The Sioux had a problem, it seems. Since he's a half-breed they punished their half and are leaving the other half for us."

"Then he's alive?"

"Good question. Your power shamed him in their eyes. He was set free with nothing more than a loin cloth. No horse, no weapon, no moccasins. He is to be banished from every village and no one is to help him under penalty of death. It is to be as though he had never been born. I don't think he can survive."

Barry didn't think he'd be satisfied with a report of Ransom's death. He wanted to see him die as many deaths as he had caused.

The emigrants were more interested in departing than eating, but for once they silently obeyed. Then, with the wagons hitched, several truths started dawning at once.

"Aren't we heading back east? I've had enough of this Injun country."

"Ah ain't got no man fer drivin' an' my son's too young."

"Come this far, oughta go on!"

"Well," Arabelle Cornithwyeth flared, "we can drop the whole matter into the lap of the idiot who talked my poor Bradford into this in the first place. Major Fremont, you have thirty men. I shall require one of them to drive my wagon, while you escort us back to Fort Leavenworth."

Fremont scowled at her. "Lady, neither my men nor I have the time to be an escort party."

Arabelle spluttered. The angry mutterings Barry had heard so many times before rippled through the crowd. The Indians hadn't stopped them, but once more they were about to stop themselves.

He held his hand up for silence and was amazed how quickly it came.

"We have lost a lot of men, it's true. Too many, I now see, to take the wagons on. Hate to say it, but we gotta turn back. I want all the able-bodied men to pick out the best wagons. They'll only be able to haul supplies and people, so you all better start deciding what you'll have to leave behind. Sorry, but—"

"No," Lady Pamela declared hotly, pushing herself forward. "That's one answer, but not the only one. I've got an extra driver—"

"One don't help a hell of a lot," a mocking voice shouted back at her.

"Let me finish!" she demanded. "I don't remember anyone getting too upset when the count

took away all of his men and the Russian women
began driving their wagons without batting an
eye. I started out with nineteen men and two
coachmen. I've got five left. To hell with you
men! Ladies, if the Russian women can learn
to guide these wagons along, so can we."

"I can drive," Mary Sue Herbert called out,
"and there's not a darky woman here who hasn't
been behind a team at one time or other. That
will free some of the black men to help women
who can't or whose man is still mending from
his wounds."

"Hell!" Howard Tedder roared. "Ain't a Tennessee woman here who don't have to do most
the drivin' whilst her ole man sleeps!"

This brought about a hearty laugh, which the
moment needed.

"Please? Me," a timid voice pleaded. The Russian women kept so to themselves that for one
of them to speak up brought an instant hush.
"My English little. I understand. I, Ludmila Pe-
trovna. Once horse start, do good. He follow one
in front."

She got a rousing cheer for her effort to still
faint hearts.

"I'm willing to give it a try," Barry called.
"But it's got to be unanimous."

Several were still in doubt, but were too timid
to voice their opinions.

"I—I—" Arabelle stammered, "don't think I
can do it without my husband."

"Oh, mother!" Anne started to protest.

"Hush!"

"No, I will not hush! You never needed pa
before, so don't lay the blame on him. I'll learn

to drive, if need be. Mr. Fitzpatrick, the Cornithwyeth wagon goes on!"

Arabelle gaped at her daughter, burst into
tears and fled. Those who were silently mourning
could not muster sympathy for her. Those who
had been with her since departing Lancaster
knew that her grief was mainly for herself. She
had no one left to bully and boss around.

It was not as easy as the Russian woman made
it sound, but Major Fremont delayed his departure to help them get lined up and headed out.

"Thank you," Barry said, extending his hand,
"and my best to your wife."

"Thank you for remembering her," Fremont
said warmly, shaking his hand. Then he looked
far to the west, as if he could see something
Barry could not. "It's been a strange summer.
Still acting like winter in the high country and
summer's fading fast. Unless you make good time
to Sweetwater, don't try the pass till spring.
Good luck and God's speed."

19

Luck was with them, if not God's speed. The emigrants continued to lose people because of their wounds and the women had to get used to the rein sores on their hands. Their breakdowns were minor, and Barry could now look back and blame the majority of them upon Ransom and his desire to stop the train at all costs.

August was upon them as they crept into the vestibule of the mountains. The humidity of the plains seemed to disappear as the purple haze of the Rockies loomed ever closer.

No one had voted upon it, but the women took a stronger voice in the council decisions and in the chores. Mary Sue took to droving cattle to free a cowboy for scouting duty. She loved it. It made her feel useful, needed and young again.

"Oh, look, Harm!" she enthused, as he came

riding up. "I've never been what you'd call religious, but those mountains have to be where
God lives. Aren't they incredible! I feel I could
reach out and touch them."

"Barry says some of them are nearly three
miles high."

"Imagine that. It sure makes a person feel
small. I only wish . . ."

"You don't have to say it, Mary Sue. Like
everyone else, we've got to leave our dead buried out on the plains. We got ourselves and our
people to think of now."

It was the first time he had ever called her
Mary Sue. It warmed her. Since the death of his
father and sister he had become very quite manly.
He now sported a beard and it gave a firm, determined set to his jaw.

"Oh, drat," she scowled. "Here I am talking
away and not minding my chores. I've got to
go get that stray. See you at supper."

"Don't be late," he called. "The scouts shot
buffalo this morning."

As she had seen the change in him, Harmon
was becoming aware of the change in her. The
bitter, harping, nervous woman from Alabama
had vanished. The supple figure was still there,
but she was even more alert and agile. Before,
when he had caught her looking at him, he had
felt that it was lustful. Now, he saw only pride
in her eyes and it made him feel like he had
only begun to live life from the day they had
left the Platte.

The mountains, the lavish abundance of game,
the cool refreshing air made many feel that they
were beginning life again. They couldn't look

back. They were making the leap over the heights
of land between the North Platte and the Sweetwater. They were averaging a dozen miles a day,
at times spurting to fifteen or twenty miles. What
Indians they had seen gave them a respectful
salute and rode far wide of their firestick range.

Then, in the last week of August, Barry halted
the train, a lump rising in his throat. It seemed
a million lifetimes since he had left home. They
were at the entry point of Sweetwater Valley,
only a few miles from Jim Bridger's hospitality.
As if everyone sensed what he felt, the emigrants
came scrambling down off their wagons and
rushed forward.

Rising high above the surrounding plain was
a strange oblong upthrust of rock. There was
none like it around for miles. It was as if God
had purposely dropped it in this spot on the seventh day and it had been waiting patiently for
this moment ever since.

Old Nanna walked to its granite base and
looked high up at its altar-like ledge.

"Lawd, thankee! Today am sure independence
day fer dis ole darky."

She picked up a stone from the ground and
scratched an X on the rock surface. That was
her signature. It was the first of hundreds, including every prominent one ever known in the
days of the wagon trains, to be inscribed on its
surface. More than eight hundred miles out from
the Missouri, it would become known as Independence Rock.

Many would come to think its name to mean
that the emigrants had made it safely from Independence, Missouri and so honored the rock.

No one would recall it had first been uttered by a seventy-year-old black woman who had come in chains from Africa six years before the start of the American Revolution.

With a banshee wail a man in buckskins came riding out of the west, his legs straight out from the saddle, his eyes wild with excitement. His hair fell over his shoulders in long curls which had once been brown. His rounded beard and mustache were so thick they showed no opening for his constant yelping. With a flying leap he took Barry from his saddle and they rolled in the dirt, his jabbering going on without end.

"You dawg-danged hog-wallerin' lil' polecat pup of a she lion, you done did it. Gawd-a-mighty damn, you done did it. You Sioux-killin' lil' rascal. Hot damn, are we gonna have a party. Gawd love you all. Let's get a rollin'."

As quickly as he'd dismounted, he was back on his horse and riding away, tears streaming down his face.

It was the emigrants' introduction to the fabled Jim Bridger.

20

Jim Bridger hated to see them leave his settlement, but like John C. Fremont, he was also
wary of the weather. Already in the high country
the frosty nights were making the sap run in the
aspen trees and turning green mountain sides into
a floral bouquet of reds and golds. Because of his
concern he joined up with Barry to see them
across the Sandy Creek and Green River, pushing them hard to make an average twenty miles
a day. He wasn't going to feel content until he
had them up over the pass and down the other
side to the great plains valley of the Snake.

Mid-afternoon of the day they were to assault
the steepest climb through the range, Bridger
called a halt. The clouds hung so low over the
mountains that it made it look like they were
back upon the plains. But here were no vast

379

flat lands on which to circle up and the caravan camped where it halted, stretching up the foot-hills for two miles. Bridger assured the emigrants that they need have no fear of Indians. They were in the territory of the Gros Ventres, a peo-ple who may have lacked the stature and the brave trappings of the buffalo-hunting plainsmen but were as much in tune with nature as the ani-mals. For days Bridger had been searching for signs of the Gros Ventres and what he found he didn't like. The nomadic people were not to be found in any of their customary summer camp grounds. Some of the camps had been deserted for as long as two weeks. That, coupled with the sudden lack of game in the higher elevations, told him that a hard winter was at hand. He prayed that they wouldn't be stuck too many days wait-ing for the clouds to lift and the storm to pass.

"Shut that flap," Count Justinian barked, "and don't look at me once you've entered."

His luxury wagon burned and looted by the Kaws, the Russian was reduced to convalescing in one of his plainer ones. It was a great disap-pointment to Donald Hufford. Before the count's disappearance, Donald had dreamed of the chance to see the interior of the colorful tent and meet the man in person. This wagon pos-sessed nothing of glamour and the man seemed thin, bent, his cheeks hollow, his mouth still an ugly wound and great dark rings around his eyes.

"They made a mess of me," Justinian ex-plained. "Almost killed me, too. But that's not why I wanted you here. I've a job for you, young man—if you'll take it."

"Sir?"

"Although my women are quite capable, I have need for an experienced driver. All this delay has cost me dearly. Once we are through this pass, I want to press hard for Fort Ross."

"You mean leave the train again?"

"That's the only way. It will take this slow-crawling snake more than a month to reach the ocean. Four wagons, with only necessary supplies and personnel, should be able to cut that in half."

"I don't know," Donald said doubtfully. "It would mean leaving my—"

The count put out his hand.

"Leaving what? There is a reason why I picked you above all others, and I have been weighing many this past couple of weeks. You are a loner. You even seem uncomfortable in the presence of your own father. Lady Pamela treats you as if she wishes you would vanish and melt away. Shall I go on?"

Donald looked at him wonderingly and nodded.

"And there is the matter of young Selena and her boyfriend," the count cunningly continued. "There was a time, at Bridger's settlement, that I thought Nazareth might be the man for me. Not wishing to participate in the festivities, I went in search of him one night to discuss the matter. Voices from the Tedder wagon told me he was not alone, but I could not help overhearing. Interesting bit of blackmail, I thought. Miss Selena was quite willing to do whatever Naza-

reth wished of her for his promise to stay away
from you."

"Him and his dirty lies," Donald sneered.

"Really? I think otherwise or I might not have
taken an interest in you. Frankly, I hadn't even
considered you until that night. And don't start
to pout and lie to me. In my country men servants with your—shall we say, your talents are
highly favored and can become very rich men.
That is the rest of my offer. Get me to Fort Ross
and I'll take you on to St. Petersburg with me.
You will at least be with someone who appre-
ciates you."

"All right," Donald said quietly, "what do
you wish me to do?"

Justinian's smile was triumphant. "That," he
whispered, "depends upon what you wish to do
for me. Come back when the camp is asleep and
we will get better acquainted and lay our plans."

Donald nervously waited until after midnight.
Although he had daydreamed about several of
the emigrant males, he had been with no one
since leaving England. Fluffy white snow flakes
were falling when he slipped unnoticed into the
count's wagon.

It was near four o'clock when he stepped back
out, his head bursting with the dreams of glory
that had been poured into it and his body aching
from the insatiable demands it had been put
through. He stopped short and looked around.
In four hours the world had been changed. A
heavy mantle of wet snow clung to the pine
branches and wagon tops and more was falling.
He put out his hand, not quite believing that it
was actually happening. As the snowflakes melted

on contact with his feverish palm, so did his dreams begin to vanish and fade. If the snow continued to fall the wagon train would not move out the next morning, perhaps for several mornings.

On a burst of inspiration, he flung himself back into the wagon and began to whisper out his thoughts to the count. Justinian kept nodding his agreement, even as he began to dress and make some plans of his own.

Those who had started out the night on the ground had moved into the wagons. Now, with the leaden dawn bringing the cold front following the storm, they were reluctant to leave the warmth of their bedrolls. Men would dart from their wagons, push the snow away from the spot where the campfire had been the night before, curse the slow start of the fire because of the damp wood and go to huddle shivering in their wagons until the fire was roaring and in need of fresh fuel.

No one would be moving that day, so no one moved too fast to get breakfast started. It was a fairyland delight for the children, until mothers began to notice how quickly their clothing became sodden in play. Over their screams of protest they were bundled back into their bedrolls. It was hard enough to keep warm in front of the campfires, next to impossible to dry wet clothing.

Because of the strung-out condition of the train it was a while before it was noticed that four of the count's wagons were gone. The snow had covered their departing tracks completely and no one had heard a thing.

"Damn fool," Barry declared.

"Worse'n that," Bridger said sadly. "This wet stuff'll pack up undah his wheels an' leave 'im belly high. Horse'll panic an' take 'im right off inta a gorge. I'll go git our horses, son. Sun's burnin' off the humidity cloud an' we'll be able to spot his advance."

By the time Bridger returned with the horses, Barry had worked his way up to the Buttle-Jones wagons. Old Hufford stood like a stone statue peering under the tarp that covered the landau carriage.

"You'll freeze in that position, if you stand too long," Barry laughed.

Hufford wordlessly stared at him, as though he wanted to wake up and learn that it was all a dream.

"Gone," he whimpered, throwing back the tarp, "it's gone!"

The landau wasn't here. Beneath the canvas sat one of the Russian's wagons with its top removed.

"What the hell?" Barry cried. "Why would he want to steal your carriage?"

"The gold," Hufford said dully. "He's been stealing it right along, but I couldn't catch him."

Barry blinked in bewilderment. "The count?"

"Lord Lester."

"Lord *who?*"

"That will do, Hufford," Lady Pamela said sternly, stepping from her wagon wrapped in furs. One look at the Russian wagon and she paled. Then her cold reserve returned. "Send Donald for Lord Lester."

"He's not to be found, mum."

Barry looked from one to the other, totally confused. Jim Bridger cocked an eyebrow and decided he could learn more by listening than asking questions.

Lord Lester, who, as usual, was not far away, pushed forward and stared at the wagon. His face was a study in near-apoplexy.

"Where is my carriage?" he screeched. "Where is my gold?"

"Questions," Lady Pamela said, "I anticipated putting to you. What game are you playing now, Lester? Have you blackmailed Donald back onto your side, like you did when he was a child?"

"Donald!" Lester stormed. "You know my feeling toward faggots! Where is he? Where is my gold?"

"I think," Jim Bridger said quietly, barely understanding what was going on, "some answers would do us all more good than all these hog-wallowin' questions."

Lord Lester looked at him as though he were an ant that needed shooing off a picnic blanket.

"Look!" Hufford cried.

Strong winds were blowing the clouds away from the mountains. Winding their way up through the thinning timberline trees were the carriage and three wagons. For the number of hours traveled, their advantage didn't seem that great.

"He's a smart one," Bridger declared. "Switch-backin' back an' forth is the only way to make that grade. Damnation to hell, he jest might make it!"

"No!" Lester screamed. Grabbing his rifle by the barrel, he swung without warning. The butt caught Bridger on the shoulder, knocking him backwards into the snow. With a single leap Lord Lester was upon the horse he'd been holding and spurring it to a gallop. Barry raced for his horse but a growl stopped him.

"Gimme that horse," Bridger demanded, rubbing his shoulder as he rose. "Don't know what manner of critter you brought west, Fitz, but that thar bastard am mine!"

Lord Lester sensed such might occur. He veered his horse around, fired his rifle without really aiming and sped away again. Barry's horse fell even before Bridger got to it.

Cussing and fuming, Bridger went to find another mount. Now he was furious.

Barry turned an amazed face toward Lady Pamela.

"It's a long story," she said dully, wtih an indifferent shrug. "Too long to go into right now." She turned and watched the advance up the mountain as though that was all that mattered. Hufford did the same, and Barry stood feeling like an intruder in a family matter.

Wordlessly, he turned away to go help Bridger.

The rifle shot had brought many from their wagons and as rumors spread about the defection they began to gather in little knots and watch the Russian make his escape.

The horses Barry had bought in Missouri were skittish in the snow and Bridger was having nothing but trouble from the mount Jeb Pierce had quickly saddled for him. It was headstrong and wanted to follow the path Lord Lester had plowed open. Bridger thought himself smarter than the horse and didn't want to follow Lord Lester's foolish route. The Englishman was attempting to cut a diagonal path up the mountain face to intercept the small Russian caravan. Not only were there too many hazards covered by the snow, but such a track was too steep and the horse would flounder in the thinning air. Bridger tried to select a route that would still give him horsepower when he would need it most.

Dramatically, the sun shot from behind the clouds to spotlight the mountain side brilliantly. The air was so clear and crisp that the emigrants could see the movement on the mountain without difficulty. The carriage and wagons were like toys inching along a horizontal course and then switching back to rise a few feet higher on their summit-line quest.

The path left by Lord Lester's horse was like an arrow streaking to intercept one of the turnings.

Far below Jim Bridger was creating his own pattern, like a snake slithering through glass, to meet up with the caravan at its opposite turning. He now seemed more bent on warning them about Lord Lester than sating his thirst for revenge against the man.

But the people in the caravan were not blind. Both men, they figured, were out to stop them and one would come near that opportunity at the next turning. Donald Hufford checked the grade. He was almost above timberline and the summit seemed though he could reach out and touch it. Carefully, he started the four horses into a wide turning at mid-mountain, clamping down hard on the brake when the carriage swung so that it would not begin to slip and roll. When the horses felt the pull against them, he jerked the reins left and the horses strained to bring the carriage on a horizontal line again.

But the count's other wagon drivers did not have Donald's expertise. On the plains the Russian women had learned to drive without fear. Now they were petrified with fright. The horses didn't want to follow the wagon in front of them and they were not teamsters enough to "gee-whoa-haw," brake and crack the whip at the same instant. In the turning one of the wagons began to slip. In her panic the driver whipped and did not brake. The horses dug in their hooves but were unable to stem the backward movement of the wagon. Nor was the wagon behind able to steer clear of the crash into its mid-section. It came near toppling. That Russian woman was alert enough to rein her team uphill and avert a tragedy for her wagon. But the following wagon stopped short, its driven frozen with panic.

Wrapped in lap robes like his imperial uncle, Count Justinian screamed from his carriage seat at Donald. "Go lead them around, imbecile! And hand me your rifle, in case that first rider gets into range before you have them turned."

Lord Lester saw their problem and changed his own course. He felt he was within rifle range, but wanted to capture the carriage before Donald Hufford could get the wagons back on course. Then, as Bridger had feared, his horse faltered, stumbled and fell. It had broken a leg. Lord Lester was insane with rage. Donald was getting the last wagon turned about and he would never stand a chance catching them on foot. He knelt, aimed and fired at one of the carriage horses.

Even as the horse was slumping in its harness, Count Justinian was drawing a bead on Lord Lester and firing.

"My gawd, the stupid bastards!" Bridger wheezed, and spun his horse away from its course.

Below, in the foothills, the emigrants suddenly heard an odd rumbling. At first it sounded like an increasing echo of the rifle fire they had heard. They had stood spellbound by the near-fatal accident to the closer wagon, and had silently cheered its successful outcome in anticipation for the time when they would be at that same high mountain level.

But when the sound increased and they witnessed what was causing it their silent cheering turned to silent dread. No one even dared mention the word avalanche, lest the sound of his voice increase its power.

The snow, piled high on the summit, was not winter-frozen but soft. The crash of the wagon had disturbed it; the explosive rifle blasts had awakened it to life. High up, where Donald Hufford dreamed to climb to freedom and glory, it divorced itself from the rocks and no horse power could haul it back. As a single mass it began to slide and move, grinding rocks up into substance to give it weight and force. On the surface it appeared quite harmless, until it came to timberline. Then it began to chew the trees up as though they were kindling wood.

The small caravan was not even given time to cry out or know the full fear of its fate. It gulped the wagons up like a shark at feeding. They were there one moment and the next were engulfed in a swirling cloud of white.

Lord Lester had time to know his fate, but no time to avoid it. By the time the avalanche was a hundred feet from him, it towered an equal number of feet over his head. His scream was captured and locked forever within its icy confines.

From the emigrants' viewpoint it was an awesome spectacle. The entire mountain was on the move, boiling down to the gorge below. Nothing could stop it—not trees or boulders or craggy outcroppings. It was an awakened god that had little use for the puny little ants that called themselves human beings. If it could pulverize a ten-ton boulder to pea-size rock and sand within seconds, what fear did it have of skin and bones?

Barry Fitzpatrick wanted to shout out orders to harness up and turn about, but he, like six hundred other souls, was frozen with fear he had never dreamed was humanly possible. They could not run, their limbs would not move. If this was to be their death, they could not fight it.

There was no hope for those caught in the avalanche. They were buried forever under tons of snow and rock and timber. Never, as long as he lived, did Barry forget the look on Hufford's face after the roar had become only an echo in the old coachman's ears. He seemed to age thirty years before Barry's eyes.

Then, to the right of the avalanche path, they saw a single person rise and begin to stumble down the mountain. Barry felt guilty at the surge of joy he felt, while Hufford and Lady Pamela were benumbed by grief and disbelief. Barry would have known Jim Bridge's ambling gait at any distance and rushed to take him a horse.

*   *   *

"And that's the story," Lady Pamela ended sadly. "Ironic, really. The gold going back to where it came from."

Barry's Adam's apple jerked in his throat.

"Poor old Hufford," he choked. "I thought it was his son's death that did him in."

Lady Pamela fought back her tears.

"When I die, I hope it is just that way. To go to sleep and not wake up again."

"What are your plans now, Lady Pamela?" Barry asked.

She frowned.

"The first thing," she said, "is to stop being who I was. I would prefer not to be called Lady Pamela any more. Which means, I suppose, that I am automatically saying no to Lord Dunraven's offer. Now that I really am a widow, I'll use what gold Lester did steal from the carriage to make a life for Selena and myself."

"You've got time to think on that," Barry said. "Jim says there's no way we'll get these wagons through the pass till spring. It's snowed up there almost every night since we got back to the settlement."

Pamela looked at the crystal-clear water of the Sweetwater, the reds and golds and orange hues of the changing aspen. She listened to the call of a flock of geese winging south and felt the warmth of the sun on her arms and face.

"It hardly seems possible that the pass is blocked. It's just like summer here."

"We call it Indian summer."

"Is the water too cold for bathing?" Pamela said impulsively. "It's been so long . . ."

"No," Barry said, "it may not be." He cleared his throat. "Only—is it just bathing you had in mind?"

Pamela stiffened, as if she had been slapped.

No, she thought, it isn't just bathing. But she could not get the picture of Barry and DeeDee Herbert out of her mind. Oh, God, I am suddenly so alone . . . and so lonely.

She bowed her head for an instant and mastered her tears. She had been taught how to do that to be a proper lady. She had had so much practice at it. But there was still a lot of woman under the Buttle-Jones veneer.

"Barry," she said gently, "do you know a spot where I might bathe?" The hunger in her deep blue eyes was as visible as their color.

At first she thought she had misjudged him, for bathing and swimming were all that transpired. She looked at him with renewed admiration. He was more man and gentleman than she had ever encountered before.

With no regard for modesty Pamela began to put her clothes on in his presence. Why not? Hadn't she skillfully taken them off in front of his curious eyes? She was, however, amused to note by glancing at his groin that the act of donning the attire was having more effect on him than her nudity.

Pamela, now fully clothed, walked to the tall handsome man. She put her arms over his shoulders and intertwined her fingers in the scuff of his hair. His hard-lined mouth softened and met hers with brushing softness.

"You could have had anything you wanted," she cooed.

Barry looked deep into her eyes. Then he wrapped his arms forcefully around her back and waist and pressed his opened mouth to hers. The kiss was long and meaningful. Pamela felt a stirring in her stomach that had never been there before. A field of butterflies ascended to the bright blue sky. Her fingertips tingled. The blood in her veins ran torridly hot, then as chill as the icy Sweetwater. She was shaking when he pulled away.

"What I want you might not understand. I've known Indian squaws and a white girl. I've never known a woman. I swam with a woman once and felt satisfied, without doing anything. Tonight, I want to come to you, be with you, like I have never done before." He gave her a slow sensuous smile and went back to the settlement before her rattled brain could dredge up an appropriate denial for his request.

Pamela sat on the grassy bank and was once again hit by the warmth of the fall day. She took a blade of the grass and chewed on it thoughtfully. She had never before allowed love to intervene in her life. Could Barry be interested in her and not just sexually? Could she be interested in him and not just sexually? She laid back and watched the clouds play tag. A joyous, peaceful sleep overcame her before she had fully devised an answer to these questions in her mind.

21

The Sweetwater was gripped in an unbreakable ribbon of ice. The range was cloaked in a heavy mantle of white. It was an early and harsh winter, but the emigrants hardly felt its bleakness. Jim Bridger's settlement took on almost a permanent look. Trees were felled, sawed into blocks and put under the wagons. All wheels, no matter what their condition, were taken to the blacksmith shop for refurbishing. Pine boughs were interlaced to make thatched roofs for each wagon. This kept the snow from sagging down the canvas and dripping moisture; also, the boughs served as insulation and added warmth. Lean-to's were erected to serve as cook houses. Industrious souls, like the Tedders, built bough-thatched log cabins for themselves and any that wanted to pay them a wage to build the same. These permanent living quarters would later be rented out by Bridger to hunters and their Indian wives and later trains of emigrants. Many were three-sided, so the wagon could be attached as a room addition. Jim Bridger's settlement was perhaps the first trailer park in America.

And there were social activities. Christmas was coming. Women gathered for quilting bees and secret sewing sessions away from the eyes of the children. Men whittled and had secret sessions away from the eyes of their wives and children. Ned Conroy set up his Tennessee still, much to the chagrin of Arabelle Cornithwyeth.

In a teepee donated by Jim Bridger, around a Franklin stove that had been her father's, Anne Cornithwyeth set up a primary school for children between the age of six and ten. The love that she had been looking for in a man, and wasn't receiving, she gained from the children. Especially from the children out of the Herbert group.

"It's agin the law," Ned Conroy told Bridger, eyeball to eyeball. "Niggah's ain't supposed to be learned letters and figures."

"Silly-assed hog-wallerin' law, I say. This ain't the Hunited States, anyhow. This is Jim Bridger land and we go by Jim Bridger's law. That's the law says Miss Anne's gonna teach black 'uns right along with white young'uns."

Conroy's face darkened with rage. "Not my two youngest, she ain't. So stick that in yer jaw and chew on it, Jim Bridger!"

Bridger grinned so broadly that his mustache and beard actually parted.

"Speaking of laws," he chuckled. "Miss Anne's ole maw wants me to outlaw the makin' of corn whiskey. Ah'm thinkin' mighty hard on the subject."

The Conroy children attended Anne's classes without another word from Ned on the subject.

If Jim Bridger was the law in his domain, it also gave him rights and responsibilities.

"Ain't never done that before," he said of one responsibility, a little embarrassed. "I'll talk it out with Barry an' see if he knows the proper words."

A few days later, after many private rehearsals off in the woods, a very nervous Jim Bridger performed the first of many wedding ceremonies.

Men who needed a wife to help raise their motherless children sought out women in like circumstances. It was not a question of love, but of pioneer family survival. Love did have its moments, however.

Yeoman Faraday stood in the log cabin Barry had had the Tedders build for Pamela, nervously crumpling his hat in his hands. He had a favor to ask and an admission to make.

"So you see, mum," he stammered, "I was only doing as the duke ordered me. But seeing as how we aren't going back to England, I thought it best to let you know the part I was to play."

Pamela smiled to herself. The confession eased her worry on the matter, but the strings attached amused her.

"Thank you for your honesty, Faraday. But as you say, we are no longer in England and I can't help you in this matter."

His face sagged.

"But," Pamela breezed right on, "it doesn't mean that you can't handle it in the manner of our new country. Your wife is dead and you have two small children. Have you discussed the matter with Captain Templeton's widow?"

Faraday blushed. "Alicia . . . ah . . . Mrs. Templeton has been seeing to my two girls since . . . since . . ."

"Yes, I understand," Pamela said gently. Alicia Templeton had won favor in her eyes by being the first Englishwoman to step forward to learn how to drive her own wagon. Pamela had always considered her a rather pasty-faced snob while married to the captain. She could see that Faraday had come to her at Alicia's urging. "But you no longer need my approval, Faraday. The death of Lord Lester cut us away forever from Buttle-Jones rules and regulations. As an individual I can give the two of you my heartfelt blessing, but you will have to ask for her hand on your own."

He left her like a young boy who had just shot a prize marble out of the ring.

It gave Pamela a warm glow. She had never felt so happy and content in her life and it pleased her to make others feel the same. She still was unsure of her true feelings toward Barry Fitzpatrick, although she couldn't bear the moments they were separated. He was such a gentle, tender lover, but the difference in their ages troubled her. Nor had Barry ever said that he loved her, although a woman didn't need words to make a fact a fact. With the marriage fever growing stronger in the settlement, she wondered what she would answer if Barry overcame his shyness and proposed. She would have to take Selena into consideration, although her time had been so wrapped up in Barry the past few months that she saw her daughter at suppertime and that was about all. Even then, most of the time Barry was eating with them and was the focal point of her attention.

Then, a week later, a marriage took place that erased from her mind what the gossips might say about Barry being nine years her junior. The ceremony conducted by Bridger had been private and simple, but a wise old woman had seen this event coming for a long time and was prepared for the couple when they returned from Bridger's cabin.

"Ya'all gotta jump Nanna's broom," the woman cackled with glee. "Ain't fittin' fer plantation folk not ta jump de broom an' sweep away all de past ghosts. Ain't nothin' but happiness on de ober side of Nanna's broom."

Neither of them dared deny Nanna anything. Amid joyous cheers they jumped the broom and entered the log cabin that the blacks had cleaned and decorated while they had been to see Bridger.

"Somehow," Harmon said very seriously when they were alone, "there is one ghost we must speak about."

"Harm!" Mary Sue breathed in a tense whisper. "We can't! It's bad luck!"

Harmon laughed. "And you used to accuse me of becoming too much like the slaves. Why, you're just as superstitious as they are."

"Because I want the past to be exactly that."

"That's my point!" exclaimed Harmon breathlessly. "I want you to know what I've come to realize about the past. When I realized it, it gave me the courage to dare ask you to marry me. I hated you because you were married to my father. I hated you because you could never be mine. I slept with the black wenches just to see you spit and yell and damn me to hell. My father didn't do it, because he didn't care. You cared. That was love. I had to fight against it because I didn't want your love as a mother and feared what I might do to gain any other kind of love from you. I don't have to fear any longer."

"You might have to fear wagging tongues."

"No, Mary Sue," he said passionately, "the only wagging tongues I feared have already spoken. We have jumped the broom in front of our people, our family. They have blessed our marriage with their love, their cheers, their decorations. Does it matter what the other people say? No! We are a family cut off from them just as we were on the plantation. We shall survive because we are now a stronger family, a more intelligent family. They don't belong to us anymore, Mary Sue, but have you noticed something? Since you gave them their freedom we have not had a single runaway. We had had four and five young bucks a week try to get away in Alabama. They've got what they were running away to gain and now they're looking to us to tell them what to do with it."

Yes, Mary Sue mused, the man she had always wanted had grown into his shoes.

"The broom has swept clean," she said, smiling. "What now?"

Suddenly, he strode across the room and took her in his arms. "Now," he said, "is the only wedding present I'm able to afford. A trapper came through the other day and talked of a vast, fruitful valley that sounds more to our farm ways than the Oregon land. With each of our people claiming a piece, we could all grab off a chunk that would make the old plantation look mighty small.

And that's what we want, Mary Sue, land that will endure after we are gone."

"Where is this place?"

"It's to the southwest and named after the Indians who live there. Sacramento."

"I like the name," Mary Sue promptly declared. "I can hardly wait for spring."

Harmon grinned, and she knew what he could hardly wait for.

Harmon's marriage to his stepmother gave a new topic for discussion to a budding friendship between two very unlikely women.

"Tea, Arabelle?"

"Thank you, Bertha dear. You're the only civilized person left who doesn't offer one that foul-tasting coffee mixed with dry oats. Tea is so soothing. And, my dear, my nerves do need soothing. Poor little Anne hasn't dried her eyes once since hearing about that detestable Harmon Herbert."

"Oh, that's news. Did Anne have her cap set for him?"

"Really," Arabelle pouted, "I can't fault you for getting it backward, seeing how busy you were kept at the time with the wounded and dying. But, I would call it leading my Anne on, I would."

Bertha served the tea without comment. She knew what she saw in the looking glass and thought Anne should be smart enough to see the same. Other than Tom Geddy, Bertha thought Harmon Herbert to be one of the most strikingly handsome men on the train. Nor did she see anything wrong in the union. Mary Sue had always been one of her favorite people, because she was always there to add extra nursing hands when Bertha had needed them most.

"Well," she said, hoping to put an end to that subject, "we can't change it now."

Arabelle got the message and altered course. Tea was becoming a rarity and so were the women who would sit and chat with her.

"Speaking of change," she said sweetly, "how is your dear little sister?"

Bertha was sorry the talk had veered in this direction. Pearl was a real worry to her, which Tom Geddy didn't help.

"Still having a hard time of it," she sighed. "She's so small to be carrying such a large baby."

Arabelle clucked. "I rightly blame myself. I never should have forced Bradford's strict rules on one so young—*although* I was not made aware of her real age at the time, if you recall the facts correctly, Bertha dear. But my real shock, and it nearly sent me to my grave, was to learn *that* man was married to that English snob. And does she give a hoot for your poor little sister? Fiddle! Her husband was no sooner buried under the snow and she was running after that worthless buckskin-clad guide."

Again Bertha decided not to comment further. She liked and admired Barry as a person and a man. He had always made her feel needed and useful. Nor did she have any particular bone to pick with Pamela Buttle-Jones, mainly because they had never exchanged more than a half-dozen words on any subject.

"I think part of my sister's problem," Bertha

said, coming back to a neutral topic, "was my brother's decision to leave."

"Then you should have stopped him!"

Bertha laughed. "How does one stop the wild wind? I'm rather glad that Dr. Geddy loaned him the money to buy a horse and supplies from Mr. Bridger. If the trapper's life suits him, then I am glad. It made me understand him, as I didn't when he first came into our encampment."

Arabelle scoffed. "How can you say that, after what you have told me? He did you and your sister a great disservice by running away and causing your indentured status. I would hate him forever."

"Yes, I think you would," Bertha said, but without malice. "I did, until recently. He felt chained here out of family obligation to Pearl and me, just as surely as he was chained to his indentured status. I fought against his leaving, but silently. Will sensed that and took me aside one day. Have you looked at the land we are in, Arabelle? Will made me look. I was amazed. I've been looking down into wounds and sick faces for so long that I hadn't looked up. I couldn't hold him back from the promise that it holds out to every person who is daring enough to take a handhold on it. In that moment I released him from any obligation he felt he might owe me and set him free."

"But did your sister and husband do the same?"

Bertha had painted herself into a corner and had to accept the bitter gall of Arabelle's question.

"In time they might," she said simply. "More tea?"

Arabelle accepted gladly.

* * *

Jim Bridger intended it to be a communal
Christmas tree. For days he had carefully scouted
the woods for a tree large enough for the entire
gathered settlement to sit back and admire. Finally, pleased with his choice, he chopped down
a mighty blue spruce, hauled it back to the settlement, had it re-erected and then stood puzzled.
He wasn't all that familiar with Christmas cus-
toms and wasn't sure what to do next.

The Russian and English women did know,
however. Their excitement spread even to the
blacks. Men, women and children came to decorate the tree's boughs with tokens of their love for
the King of Kings. And near its base, carved and
whittled in pine by the Tedder men, grew a man-
ger scene that would one day grace the marble
mantel of the governor's palace in California.

But two faces remained absent from the tree-
decorating ceremonies. Barry kept waiting for
Pamela to appear and, when she didn't, finally decided to go to her cabin. For days he had been
wrestling with himself. He had been touched,
deeply, by a sense of love he had never known,
and it had left him baffled. He had become accustomed to Pamela's laughter, to her gentleness, to
a hundred small but important kindnesses. Outwardly he showed little sign of change, but inwardly he was coming to know himself and question what his future should be. What troubled
him was his feeling that he had nothing to offer
Pamela. She was so beautiful and educated and
refined. He was what he was, a mountain man
trapper and guide, no more. As much as he had

grown fond of Pamela, he didn't think he had the right to ask her to marry him. He mourned his decision with a sick longing that left him sleepless and exhausted.

He was doubly frustrated because of Selena's behavior. He was on shaky ground with her. Though she didn't openly question his presence during his many dinners with the family, she nevertheless made him feel an alien in the house. Every gesture he made went unnoticed or was misconstrued by Selena. When he spoke she greeted his words with stony silence. When he asked direct questions, she answered him in monosyllables.

Barry had no one to talk out such a problem with. He could almost hear Jim Bridger's hooting laughter if the subject was brought before him. Then the simple solution came to his mind with such clarity that he wanted to kick himself for not having thought of it before. He was able to talk for hours on any other subject with Pamela—why not of his love for her? It had dawned on him that he had never actually told her that he loved her. When they were in bed together it never occurred to him to express his emotions in words, and after the climax it was always a mad dash to be dressed and respectable before Selena returned.

But now, come hell or high water, he was going to have his talk with Pamela. He heard their voices before he got to the cabin. Selena's being at home almost made him turn and go away, thankful for a reprieve. But he forced his fist to knock at the door. Pamela answered at once, her face white, the cords standing out in her neck. She used her body to bar his entrance.

"Go away!" she said immediately. "I can't see you now . . . or tonight! Just go!"

The door was quickly shut. Barry stood for a moment, his mouth working.

Inside Selena looked at her mother's back. She said, hoarsely, "I hate him! I hate you!"

Barry tore himself away. It was just as he had suspected. Selena would stand in his way of marrying Pamela. He went off in search of Ned Conroy and his jug.

Pamela pulled herself away from the door and retook her seat at the table.

"You may hate me all you wish," she said brokenly, "but you have no cause to hate him."

"Don't I? He would side with you in a minute if you told him to."

"I should certainly hope so," Pamela said with gentle dignity. "But he is not going to be told. No one is to be told."

Selena looked at her mother contemptuously. Very slowly she came erect and pulled her loose-fitting dress tight over her belly.

"No one?" she laughed. "How long do you think I can keep this hidden? I figure I must be close to four months along."

"Exactly," Pamela said sternly, "which would make delivery in May. You are going to be conveniently ill most of the winter, I'm afraid."

Selena scoffed. "What will you do about him?"

"I'll send him away. Now that your foolishness has caused me to drastically alter my plans, I really don't dare see him. This train will probably leave here in April. We'll hire one of Mr. Bridger's men to take us to find Lord Dunraven's ranch."

"What about Nazareth? What are you going to tell him?"

"Nothing," she said quietly.

"Nothing!" Selena was shocked.

"Yes, nothing. He would want to marry you. I forbid that. You are destined for an important marriage, not to some hillbilly farmer."

Selena laughed derisively. "How do you intend to pawn off damaged goods like me with a brat hanging on my skirts?"

Pamela's head came up slowly, and her eyes, looking at Selena, were clear.

"I haven't given the child a thought," she said honestly. "But I shall. I shall. If we were in England it would be a simple matter."

"If we were still in England we wouldn't have the problem to begin with."

"Amen," Pamela said quietly.

They sat very quietly, each with her own thoughts. Pamela was quite proud of herself for having remained even-tempered on learning the news. She knew what she wanted and what she didn't want. She did not want Selena's young life ruined by a baby and an undesirable marriage; she herself had had fifteen years of unhappiness from such an experience. She would have to figure out what to do about the baby; she would have to figure out what to do about her love for Barry.

Selena had been amazed at her mother. She had expected a holy to-do and was thankful that it wasn't forthcoming. She didn't want her life ruined by a baby, either. She didn't want a marriage to Nazareth Tedder, at any age. But confessing that she was pregnant had had the desired effect on her mother: it was driving an unclosable wedge between her and the guide. Selena considered making a further confession, but decided against it for the moment. Her mother didn't need to know quite yet that Nazareth was fully aware of her condition. He hadn't discussed marriage and she was thankful for that.

If Nazareth Tedder was at that moment dreading the thought of marriage, was in fact fearing that his father would soon learn of Selena's pregnancy, his brother Theo was relishing the prospect of getting married himself. He missed his dead mother desperately, and felt a wife might ease the lonely pain in his heart. Having turned seventeen in November, the age at which his father had married, he felt nothing stood in his way but his shyness. It was Pearl Fergus whom Theo had it in mind to marry. Conquering his shyness, he went to make his intentions known.

The manner in which he was forbidden entrance to the Geddy cabin was so rude and heartless that Theo fled in tears. He nearly knocked over Bertha Geddy in his flight.

Coming into the cabin, Bertha took one look at Tom Geddy, his thin face gray with misery, and her heart nearly stopped.

"Don't tell me it's Pearl!" she roared. "Is she all right? Where is she?"

"She's fine," Tom said grimly. "She's not here. She felt up to going and watching them decorate the tree."

"Then what the devil is it?"

Tom snorted. "It's that young pup Theodis

Tedder. He wants to marry Pearl, now that she's a widow."

Bertha exploded, "Is that all? You nearly scared me to death, Tom Geddy. It's a grand idea. Pearl will need a man to see to her and the baby, and he's a fine young man. When will it be?"

"Never!" Tom growled. "I told him to get the hell out of here! She's only a baby."

"She has just turned thirteen and is going to have a baby herself!"

"I said no, and that is the end of it!"

Bertha's face paled.

"Oh, no, it isn't! If you don't want to make our marriage a real one, then you have no right to decide what is right and wrong for me or my sister."

Tom snapped at her, "Will gave me the right to look out for Pearl when he left."

"Will," Bertha said scornfully, "has less right than you, as far as I am concerned. If he is so worried about Pearl, why isn't he here right now? Don't try to hide behind Will, Tom Geddy. Your face says it all for you. You turned Theo down because you are in love with Pearl. You have always been in love with her. You convinced her that it was only brotherly love. Well, as long as we are married, that is the only kind of love you are going to be able to show her. I intend to discuss Theo's offer with her when she returns."

Tom rose slowly, breathing wtih difficulty.

"Say one word to her," he said quietly, "and I'll break your neck."

Bertha opened her mouth to protest, but a loud knock at the door stopped her. "Come in!" she barked.

The frightened ten-year-old boy looked at Bertha with a helpless pleading in his eyes.

"Mum," he cried, "it's me maw. Paw learn't ye saw her today and he's beat her for it. She's startin' to have the baby, but she's bad off."

"Did she send you for me?"

"No, mum," he said, hanging his head. "And my paw don't know either. He's off drinking with that Mr. Conroy."

"Run along, Timothy," she smiled sweetly. "The doctor and I will be there in a moment."

Tom Geddy was roaring with laughter even before the door was closed. "Now look who is deciding things for whom!"

Bertha eyed him coldly. "This is quite different, and you know it. Darren McCarthy believes that medicine and doctors are against God's teaching. He's forbidden me to see his wife several times, but she is in a very bad way."

"Entirely your problem," he said indifferently.

"I can't do it alone," Bertha said heavily. "We may have to terminate the birth to save the mother."

"Which runs into the face of your religious scruples, I believe."

"I lost those," Bertha snarled, "when your father aborted me. He may have done some dastardly deeds in his day, but he never ran away from a patient in need. Is it a bribe you want, Tom? All right, for Myra McCarthy's sake, I'll give you a bribe that you won't be able to turn down. Help me with Myra and I'll renounce our wedding vows. I can get Arabelle Cornithwyeth to say why they were made in the first place.

You'll be free, Tom. Free to do what you damn well please."

Tom stared at her. "Do you mean that?"

"Yes!"

"Get my bag."

Striding to the surgery wagon while Bertha went to help the McCarthy woman over to it, Tom's heart soared. He was still staggered by Bertha's offer. But he had a new lease on life. It was amazing. He would be free of Bertha, whom he had come to loathe. He would be able to guard and care for Pearl and the baby. That was all he wanted out of life. If he died at that very moment, he felt, he could not have died happier.

It was impossible to save either the mother or child, but not because Tom and Bertha didn't valiantly try. The woman's system had suffered from lack of care during her pregnancy, and her husband's ill treatment of her, through repeated beatings, had compounded her difficulties. She died on the operating table while Tom was removing her baby's small corpse.

Darren McCarthy was beyond considering the causes of the two deaths. All he saw when he stormed into the wagon was the blood and gore and a dead wife. He was drunk to begin with, and went mad from the sight. Blaming Tom and Bertha for their "butchery," he pulled borth a knife and revolver and declared himself a servant of God's justice.

In the confined wagon it was impossible to escape his unexpected attack. He fired the revolver into Tom Geddy's belly. He used the knife to repeatedly slash at Bertha's breasts. Only his son, screaming and clawing at his back, saved them both from dying before the noise brought others to capture McCarthy and cart him away to be tied up in the stable.

The horrifying incident brought the Christmas Eve tree-decorating festivities to a sudden halt. People, hearing the news, stared at each other disbelievingly. There was no way for them to encompass, to grasp the significance of or even know what their feelings were about this sudden, arbitrary, totally mad act. And yet a consequence was to be more horrifying still.

Barry was one of the many men who tried to drown their revulsion in strong whiskey. Bridger found him bleary-eyed a few hours after the disaster had occurred.

"Whar's Bertha?' Bridger demanded.

Barry fought to focus his thoughts so that he could answer. "Still in the surgery wagon," he mumbled. "Mary Sue and Arabelle are with her, but they wouldn't let me in."

"Why?"

Barry shook his head and muttered, "She's cutting off her breast."

"She's what?"

"That's what they said. Said Bertha told 'em it was the only way to stop that much bleeding. Said she wanted a hot fire and an iron. Was going to sear the wound and cover it with animal fat."

Jim Bridger swallowed and cringed.

"She ain't screamed out," he said with wonder.

"Won't," Barry said dully. "Not Bertha. Probably did the operating herself."

Bridged cringed again. "Hell of a Christmas present," he scowled. "Guess you know this means a trial tomorrow and hanging."

"And something worse."

"What?" he demanded, unable to think of anything worse.

"The McCarthy kids. Three of them. You ready to set up an orphanage? Might as well. It's all you lack in this little corner of a civilization you're trying to make. Robbers, murderers, prima donnas, momma's girls and momma's boys, cheats, liars, pimps, whores who call themselves ladies and ladies who'd be better off being whores. Ain't a person out there who doesn't think of themselves first and the other second, 'cept for maybe Howard Tedder and Bertha Geddy. You can take the rest and shove them, Bridger. After a half year with these people, I don't care if I ever see them again."

Jim Bridger sat back down after Barry stumbled from his cabin, still cussing in an angry, loose-tongued fashion. Bridger was no fool. He was able to guess, or figure out, when a waterway was likely to be getting wider, where a mountain pass would probably cut through, what sort of plant and animals were to be found where. He used his instincts now to narrow in on the prime source of Barry Fitzpatrick's rage. He felt sure Barry was seething in frustration over his love affair with Pamela Buttle-Jones. He just didn't know how to help Barry. He would have to ponder at greater length.

Bridger was saved the problem of holding a trial on Christmas day. Somehow Darren Mc-

Carthy had been able to loosen his bonds and hang himself in the stable.

And the formidable Bertha Geddy, her breast padded with bandages, eliminated any need for an orphanage. The McCarthy children, John, Greg and Tim were to become her wards. She was a woman who proved her worth again and again. In the winter months that followed, when medical assistance was required, no one hesitated to call upon her. Without benefit of formal training, other than that gained at the side of Dr. Mark and Tom Geddy, she served the emigrants' every need.

In January she delivered her sister of a seven-pound-baby boy. It was a relatively easy delivery, and a week later Pearl became the wife of Theodis Tedder.

But some of the problems Bertha faced were not so simple. She fumed over her inability to understand all of the words in Tom's packed volumes of medical books. The Latin left her puzzled and frustrated. She would slam the book shut and glare across the candle-lit table to where the docile seventeen-year-old John McCarthy sat reading his late father's Bible.

"Do you believe," she demanded harshly, "that God meant men not to know about medicine and healing?"

He looked up blinking, because his glasses were not of a strong enough magnification to continually bring the words into focus.

"I was only allowed to read the old books," John answered hesitantly. "Since my father's death I've started on these New Testaments. One of the followers of Jesus was a doctor, I am learning."

"Really?" Bertha exclaimed. "Let me see."

She pulled his Bible to her and stared in confusion. It was in Latin. Without comment she shoved the medical text she was reading across to John. "Can you tell me what these words mean?"

He translated expertly. For an hour she kept him busy flipping back and forth over pages that had left her floundering.

"Yes," she sighed. "I now understand. They cloak the mysteries of the Bible in Latin as surely as they do the marvels of medicine. Imperial men and priests do not want us common folk to know how simple some things can be. We are going to fool them, John, we surely are."

Before spring had begun thawing the ground, everyone was using an appelation for Bertha that had been coined by Jim Bridger.

"Doc Bertie," he enthused one day, "that's great. Twenty of my forty years that leg's been a troublin' me. Who but you would have thought that that lump were nothin' more than a piece of arrowhead that kept floatin' around?"

Doc Bertie married herself to John McCarthy in March of 1844. It was not a question of love, but of security for each. Bertha needed John's translation ability and John needed stability for his two younger brothers. But, timidly at first and then with growing affection, Bertha gained a sexual partner in John that was mellow and rewarding.

For three blissful weeks Bertha McCarthy wallowed in the love that had always been denied her, contented and happy. Then, in small but increasing numbers, the emigrants fell ill with burning fevers, wracking coughs and troublesome aches and pains. Everyone wanted Doc Bertie, but she stretched herself too thin and fell to the same flu bug.

In the week that she was disabled by high fever, fifty of the emigrants died, including John McCarthy. She became Doc Bertie Geddy again, and so she would remain known as, although in later years she would also marry Greg McCarthy and send Timothy McCarthy east to medical school.

She would survive wars and floods and droughts. She would see mud-hovel villages, built on the promise of gold, spring into towering cities of glass and steel. She would become so proficient in her medical practice that no one ever dared question the authenticity of the diplomas she felt useful to frame on her office wall. She would see the Conestoga wagon give way to the stagecoach—only to be supplanted by the railroads. She would be daring enough to drive one of the first horseless carriages, determined enough to make men of medicine sit up and note that women need not be restricted to nurses' work only.

Still spry and agile at ninety-seven, she made a memorable trek from Lancaster, Pennsylvania to Denver, Colorado. In a railroad train, she had accomplished in two days what it had taken months to do eighty years before in a wagon. She mentioned her journey to no one. It had, she felt, significance for her alone—a sentimental journey of sorts. But she arrived home in Denver in time to treat one of her many patients.

After he departed, she stretched out to rest. They found her the next day with a sweet smile on her face. The Denver *Post* ran a simple obituary notice: PIONEER PASSES. The story was given three paragraphs in the paper. No more, no less.

But as the spring of 1844 approached in the Jim Bridger settlement, no one was thinking about who in it might become famous or ignored by history. The emigrants were struggling for their daily lives.

"Ain't an easy subject for me, Barry," Howard Tedder said shyly. "I ain't much on words, but I know my heart an' I know what my Lydia would be demandin' right now. Would you do my talkin' fer me?"

Barry said reluctantly, "Sure thing, Tedder. But does the boy love her and want to marry her?"

They were questions Tedder had never thought to put to Nazareth. "Don't rightly matter," he said darkly. "He's got to do right by the girl and child."

Barry left silently, almost wishing he had turned down Tedder's request. He had not seen Pamela for four months. They had been long, sorrowful months. The first few times she had refused to see him, he had blamed the refusal solely on Selena. He began to hate the girl as he had never hated in his life. Then, when the rumors made it impossible for Selena's condition to be kept hidden any longer, Pamela had been cuttingly blunt.

"Don't be a blind fool," she had told Barry icily. "If I refuse to let Selena and Nazareth see each other, how can I see you?"

"That don't make sense."

"It does to me," she had insisted, and closed the door in his face again.

Slowly the realization of what her words meant dawned on him and made him burn with outrage. She had made it plain that if Nazareth wasn't good enough for Selena, then Barry wasn't good enough for her. Then, as he absorbed the insult, he had to concede he had seen their relationship no differently. But to hear it from her lips wounded him. He had wanted to run away, but there was nowhere to run to, so he had volunteered to head up a hunting party to keep the settlement supplied with fresh meat. This kept him away from the settlement for days at a time. He had kept away from her area of the settlement as much as possible and now wished he could stay away again.

When Barry reached Pamela's cabin it was nearly dark. He went in, shrugging off the notion he should knock first, and walked toward the table where Pamela sat, bent over a mug of black coffee. Her posture was an eloquent expression of her despair. Barry's heart melted at the sight of her, and he gently put an arm around her shoulders.

"Hello, Pam," he said.

Pamela looked up, startled.

"Barry!" she whispered. "Barry . . . oh, Barry!" Then she stood and fell sobbing into his arms.

"Hush," Barry murmured. "Hush, my darling, hush."

He bent down and kissed her. Pamela responded as if they had never been apart.

She drew her face away slowly, and stood looking up at him wistfully.

"You big ox," she sighed, "making me cry like that. I must be a sight."

"You look fine to me. I should have come before, when I heard you were sick."

"Then I really would have refused to see you. I have never been so sick. And all those poor souls. Funny, we rather took the deaths from the Indian attack as a part of our new life. But for so many to die from a common ailment seems a horrible waste. I thought sure I was going to die, ached and shook with such misery that I prayed to die. Poor Selena had it far worse. Bertha Geddy still has her in her cabin under constant care."

A sudden silence fell between them. Pamela had been rattling on to keep from saying the things she really wanted to say. Something's wrong, she thought. He's here for some purpose, or he wouldn't be here at all.

"Coffee?" she said. "It's a fresh pot and not a grain of oats in it."

Why did I come? Barry thought miserably. Why did Tedder have to pick on me for this chore?

"Pamela," he said hesitantly, "Howard Tedder thinks Nazareth should accept his responsibilities and obligations as a man."

Pamela stood quite still looking at Barry's bleak and forbidding face. She knew she would have to handle him in the same manner she had handled Selena.

"Please tell Mr. Tedder for me that I respect his thoughts and good intentions. But there is Selena to think of, as well. She made a gross error because of her youth and the loose morals of the young people I foolishly allowed her to associate with. She doesn't love the boy, even refuses to see the baby. You, of all people, should see that I don't want her saddled with a marriage that would be unhappy from the start."

Barry nodded. "There's the baby to think of."

Pamela said, "It's being looked after. One of the darky girls who lost her baby is wet-nursing it."

"It? Hasn't it a name?"

"No," Pamela whispered. "I've been waiting for Selena to get better and . . . it's a girl."

"A girl," Barry sad heavily. "Every damn person in the settlement knows it was a girl, Pamela. They also know that it has a crop of carrot-top hair and the face of a little angel. Like it or not, it's just not going to go away. What of the child, Pamela?"

"I don't know," she answered dully. "For a time I considered taking them to Lord Dunraven. The more I kept you away from me, the more I saw that as an excuse for me to escape and not the right answer for Selena. But now, with the talk spreading that some of the people want to go to California, I've just about decided on that course."

"For you? For Selena? For the child?"

"For me?" Pamela snorted. "I have thought only of me all of Selena's life. She is only sixteen and such a child still. It's time I started living for her for a change."

Barry stiffened. "That certainly tells me where I stand."

"Do you think that's the way I want it, Barry?" she cried. "I want you desperately, but I have a daughter to think about. Right now, if I stayed with you, she would make us learn to hate each other. Time and people change, my darling. I believe I'll love you forever, but I don't know how long it will be before I am free of Selena."

She caught him by the shoulders and leaned against him, shuddering.

"Never," Barry said darkly. "You will never be free of your dreams for her."

"Oh, take me, Barry!" Pamela whispered. "Take me to bed and hold me in your arms!"

"No," he said sternly. "You'll be my lawful wife when we share a bed again. I may be a damn fool, Pam, but you're a woman worth waiting for. Take Selena to Yerba Buena. It's a port in San Francisco Bay and is rich from the clipper ships that put in there for the fur trade. I worked for a man in Oregon a few years back. His fur company has an office in Yerba Buena. Mention the name of John Jacob Astor and his people will see to it that Selena meets only the best in that part of the world."

She pulled away from him in amazement. Every time she thought she knew exactly who he was, he startled her with another side of his character and past. If only she could make Selena see him as she saw him! But that too was her fault. She had made Selena the snob that she was and it was almost too late to change the mold. It was she who had done it. She had forced Selena into a friendship with Pearl to gain information on Lord Lester, then when the Irish girl was no longer of use to her flatly denied her the right to come in and visit with Selena. She was so accustomed to using people for her own advantage that the habit had come to be a natural part of herself. And Barry had just given her an opportunity to step right back into character.

"Oh, my darling," she enthused, "that sounds marvelous. But I can't bear the thought of being separated from you again. These four months have been hell. If you will lead us to California, you can just introduce me properly to those people. Oh, I feel as if all my worry clouds have just lifted."

"It's a thought," Barry mused. "I already told Jim I'd take the Oregon group. But if you really want me to, and there'll be no problems with Selena, I suppose I can take the California people instead."

"I want nothing more in the world, and you leave Selena to me."

Barry grinned and turned to leave.

Pamela laughed. "You don't have to go immediately to change your plans."

"That wasn't my intention," Barry said firmly. "If I'm to be your man, I was about to solve the Nazareth Tedder problem. I don't know if I can, but it's worth a try."

"I see," Pamela said thoughtfully, not wishing to pin him down on specific details. "Well, go then!"

She watched him go, realizing how much she really had missed him. But she also realized that it was the need to possess him, not love, that filled her with desire.

"Yes," she mused aloud, "if you are going to be my man, Barry Fitzpatrick, then we'll have to start considering what cut of a man we can turn you into once we are in California. Fur business? Humm! Sounds respectable—as long as you're not a trapper."

Without mentioning his talk with Pamela, Barry took Howard Tedder to the Herberts' section of the settlement. They found the black wet-nurse and the baby. Barry was seeking in one of the warm cookhouse lean-to's. A packing box served as the baby's crib. Barry bent down and picked up the blanket-wrapped child. It instantly set up a horrible wail. Barry was so startled that he almost dropped his precious burden.

"Here," Tedder said, taking the child, "you ain't had no fatherin' to do."

As if he had uttered some magic word, the baby snuggled into the crook of his burly arm and quietly went to sleep.

"Beautiful!" Tedder breathed, tears welling his eyes. "She's like my little Maybelle. What are they callin' her?"

"Haven't yet."

"Oh, my gawd!" Tedder whispered. "That ain't proper."

Tedder put a big finger under the baby's chin and lifted her little face.

"My granchile, with no name. What's this world comin' to? Talk with her about a weddin'?"

Barry fidgeted, looking for the right words.

"None?" Tedder guessed. "Thought as much after you left an' I talked with Naz. He likes her all right, but not her high-flown ways. Says she's cream an' he's milk an' he knows he ain't gonna rise. Ain't one fer forcin' unhappiness, but what about this darlin' tyke?"

Barry shrugged. "Her mother doesn't want her."

Tedder nestled the baby even more protectively. "To hell you say. Well, her grandpap wants her. An' to hell with them fer not namin' her. Good Lord done take away my Lydia and my Maybelle, but He done replaced them. I'll care fer her, Barry, till my Nazareth's found him a proper wife. Li'l darlin'," he cooed, "your grandpap may be a sentimental ole fool, but he sure would like to call you Lydia Maybelle."

Barry couldn't help but smile. "Mighty long handle for such a small bundle."

Tedder frowned. "Don't sound too good, either." Then he grinned. "How about just Lydia May? Yah! Lydia Mae Tedder. Welcome, chile, to a great and glorious world. Oh, Gawd love ya!"

Barry's solution for the child was quietly if joyfully accepted by Pamela and Selena. It was as if the baby itself had been of no consequence to either. But the life that had gone out of Howard Tedder was magically restored. The wet-nurse now came to his cabin for the feedings, but Howard saw to all of its other needs. The greatest change, however, was in Nazareth Tedder. He would stare down into the makeshift crib unable to believe that it was a product of his seed. Two days later Lydia Mae had a crib whittled out of cedar log. Howard gently introduced her to her new bed, but instinctively it was Nazareth's finger that she reached out to grasp and she kept her sky-blue eyes on his face.

"Think she knows who I am, paw?"

Howard chuckled. "Don't you ever let her forget."

"You sure are becomin' a grandpappy fast."

Howard turned away on a frown. He was happy to see Nazareth reacting to the child the way that he was, but Theo marrying so young still troubled him. Nor could he fault his daughter-in-law. Pearl was loving and respectful and it was good to have a woman's cooking again. But marriage had turned the shy Theo even further into himself. While Nazareth was learning to accept his child, Theo seemed to go out of his way to reject Pearl's daughter by Lester Hartwicke. Howard feared that the sensitive Theo had pictured himself as a knight in shining armor riding to the rescue of a fair damsel in distress, only to find that armor rusts, the moat is hard to get back across, and marriage is a forever thing.

22

A fever spread through the settlement that is most common in the rural section of every country when winter-hard ground begins to thaw. Men born to the earth fret to set down plow, furrow deep and fill their lungs with the pungent aroma of nature's promise.

No one needed to coax or command the emigrants to move on once spring came. From dawn to dusk axles were greased, wheels set back in place, canvas sewn and recoated with waterproofing tallow, supplies checked over and cabins vacated of furniture.

The decision for California or Oregon was something for serious weighing now at the last hour, as it affected the future of every man, woman and child in the train. Some saw their fortunes lying in neither direction.

Jim Bridger stared at one woman incredulously.

"Now, really, Doc Bertie," he began, "let me hear that again."

"I thought I was quite plain the first time," Bertha said, almost angrily. "I want to remain here—presto!—for the time being. Other trains will be coming now and you will be able to offer them the services of a doctor. I will keep my adopted children with me, of course."

"Well," Jim drawled, "if that don't beat all. Best idea I've ever heard tell of, Doc Bertie. We'll set ourselves up a real horse-pital."

Now there, Bridger thought after she left his cabin, is the sort of gritty woman that would survive in the west. Not much on looks, two husbands buried, kids to raise not her own, and yet she could still chart her course like a captain plowing his ship around Cape Horn.

Then he frowned. There was another woman sort of like her for grit that had Jim mighty worried. He had held his silence during the winter months, giving Barry time to work out his own problems with Pamela Buttle-Jones. He had held his silence when Barry asked to lead the California train, mumbling he would think upon it. He was still thinking. In Bridger's world everyone was equal. He didn't cotton to airs. Barry was rather special in his eyes. He had known him since he was a pup and had attempted to instil in him every bit of his knowledge and lore. Having been an orphan since thirteen, Bridger was as wise to the ways of men and women as he was to every animal of the forest. There was something about Pamela Buttle-Jones that just didn't set right in his craw.

To catch a bear you had to set a trap. He sent a boy with a message for Pamela and settled down to wait. It would not take long, he knew. But he was unprepared for how little time it actually took. A scant five minutes later, his door was being pounded upon madly.

She went and opened the door. Pamela stood there, trembling all over.

"You!" she raged. "What right have you to meddle in my life?"

"Hush, lady," he said quietly. "Ain't no business of the whole settlement."

"I'll make it their business," Pamela threatened, storming inside. "You have no right to take Barry off the California train."

"I've every right," Bridger growled. "He's my employee, not yours."

"That can easily be changed," Pamela said. "I can snap my fingers and he'll come running."

Bridger grinned. "Then start snappin', lady."

That's exactly what Pamela didn't want to do, not yet. She was up against a wily old fox who would not easily be cornered.

She sighed. "Would it change your mind to know that Barry and I are vastly in love with each other?"

He shook his head. "That's my very reason. When I started training these pups to be trail guides I said no romantic involvement. Don't give a hankerin' damn if'n they screw around a bit, that's natural. But when they set their cap for a single skirt they forget the rest. Trouble comes and they worry only 'bout the safety of that one and not the whole damn train. Don't you think I see'd that in him this winter while you was pussy-footin' him around? Ain't gonna have that happening on the California trail."

"Then you're going to find yourself without a guide. I'm going to let him know your foolish reason for sending him to Oregon. He is too good for this business, anyway. I have plans for him that would make you head swim."

"Will he go along with your plans?"

"I know he will," Pamela said simply.

"Don't play yourself for the fool! Barry's no fringe-laced dandy you can tug about by a ring in his nose. You'd best lay all your plans out before you snap your fingers."

She had no intention of doing that. Her plans might well alter drastically once she was in California. She would have to fight Jim Bridger without telling Barry a thing. She would have to make the people see that Jim Bridger was not fit to lead them anywhere.

Bridger studied her, his brow furrowed in a frown. He could smell that she was about to change tactics, but wasn't prepared for the one she pulled.

With lightning speed, Pamela ripped the dress away from her breasts and started to scream:

"No! Keep away from me! Help! Rape!"

"What in the hell?" Jim snarled, and grabbed for her arms. She twisted her body into him, to make it look as if he were trying to kiss her.

The cabin door came flying open. Ned Conroy and Arabelle Cornithwyeth stood gaping at the scene before them.

Aware of their presence, Pamela held on to Bridger and screamed: "I'd die first before I'd get into your bed. Now let me go!"

She could feel his grip loosening slowly, until at last he stood back, looking at her. His face looked so baffled and beaten that for one moment she was sorry for him.

"Take me away," Pamela whimpered, and put out her hand to Ned Conroy.

Slowly, clumsily, Ned took it. He stood there holding it a long time, looking down at the marvelous ivory curve to her bare breasts. Then, suddenly, he let her hand drop.

"Woman's work," he spat. Turning, he went through the door with the vision of her breasts still before his eyes.

Arabelle quickly wrapped her shawl about Pamela and hauled her away with a snort of pious contempt for Bridger.

Bridger stood there a long time after they were gone. I'll be damned! he thought. I *will* be damned!

The bear had captured the trap.

Pamela cried all the way back to her cabin, pleading with Arabelle to find Barry for her. Once alone, she smiled wickedly to herself. She had recalled seeing Ned and Arabelle arguing near the cabin when she had entered. She couldn't have finer allies to bring about the ruination of Jim Bridger.

But Barry, when he arrived, was not the putty in her hands that she had anticipated. He stood still, his eyes somber and questioning, until she was finished relating her tale.

"Pamela, I—" Barry began.

"He's hateful," she said quietly. "He was going to ruin me so you would never want me again."

"I've been a fool! Forgive me."

Pamela's brows rose sharply.

"Forgive? What are you talking about?"

"He doesn't like the guides to get romantically involved. He didn't know of our love."

She stood there looking at him, her eyes widening and darkening in her fine face.

"He made a mistake," Barry went on hurriedly. "I should have married you last Christmas and it never would have happened. Don't blame Jim, blame me."

"You're insane," she screamed. "The man tries to rape me and you stand defending him! What manner of beast are you?"

"Now just calm down," he soothed. "Something isn't right."

"Of course it isn't! He's sick in the head, and you follow along as a close second."

"That's what I mean. Under all that gruffness there is not a gentler, kinder man in the world. It's not that I doubt your word, Pamela. But I think it only fair that I go have a talk with Jim."

"I don't believe you," she snapped dangerously. "If I were a man I would be going there to kill him."

"I'm sure you would," Barry said. "But I like to ask questions before I shoot a man."

Pamela's gaze was cold and austere.

"Walk out that door, Barry Fitzpatrick, and

you will never see me again. If you don't believe me, and the witnesses, then you and your Jim Bridger can rot together in hell."

The silence stretched itself between them, rearing up like an unconquerable mountain.

"I see," Barry said slowly. "You would have me find him guilty without a fair trial."

"Yes. If you really love me."

"That's not my way." Barry shook his head. "Even if I had seen it happen, I would want to find out his reasons why. It baffles me. It's just unlike him."

Just as she had with Jim Bridger, Pamela was losing her grip on the situation. She didn't dare let Barry hear Bridger's version of the meeting. She had expected Barry to be fiercely jealous and sever his ties with the mountain man without explanation. She had one last arrow in her quiver to fire.

"Then go to him," she said softly, "but as a man and not as a fool. You must know that to save his reputation he is bound to lie and make me out as the scarlet woman."

She lifted up her face and gazed full into his eyes. They were very blue and clear. But there was something else there that she could not mask from him—cold calculation. It was the look that had habitually been in her eyes before the death of Lord Lester and her confession. She was forgetting how deeply Barry had been able to delve into her soul to find the real woman hidden there. Now all Barry saw was her shallow hardness.

He turned to leave and she came to him, but he did not kiss her. Instead, he looked down somberly into her eyes.

"I'll know if he is lying to me," he said gently.

At first Jim Bridger flatly refused to discuss the matter with Barry. He was furious with himself for having been so easily stampeded. He was a rage of orders and demands. He wanted the trains ready to depart at dawn the next day. He had made his intentions known when Arabelle arrived with her delegation of women.

"Sir," she demanded piously, "we insist that you remove yourself as a guide. After what I have witnessed, neither I nor any of these ladies would feel safe in your company."

Bridger eyed her narrowly. "Lady, I ain't ever raped a thing in my life—man, woman or beast —and lookin' over yore gaggle of geese, I can't see a one I'd like to take on as my first. Fitzpatrick's the guide fer Oregon, lest he wants to quit me right here and now. I'll take the Californy train. Any don't want to follow Jim Bridger can jest wander about in the desert out yonder. We pull out at dawn!"

Barry came in after they left.

"Well?" Bridger demanded.

"I'm waiting," Barry said quietly. "I still want your side."

"Nope," Bridger said stubbornly. "I blame myself an' that's all I'll say, boy. Never should have messed into your affair. She must want you pretty bad to go to all this trouble."

"I should have known," Barry said miserably. "Of all the low, contemptible tricks. . . ."

"Damnation to hell fire," Bridger roared. "See what you done made me do? Said I weren't gonna say a damn word."

Before Barry could tell him that he had sensed the truth before he even came over, Pearl came through the doorway with her baby in her arms. Behind her slunk Theodis Tedder.

" 'Nother damn delegation?" Bridger demanded.

"Excuse me." Pearl flushed. "We can come back later if you . . ."

"Stay! Stay! What's yore problem?"

Pearl looked with confusion from Bridger to Theo. Then her pleading gaze landed on Barry.

"What is it, Pearl?" he said gently.

"We," she stammered, "Theo and me, we've been talking about leaving and all. My sister is staying here, you know, and Theo's family is going on to California." She looked to Theo for help, but he stood mute.

"Yes," Barry urged.

"We think we made a mistake."

Bridger looked at her with some astonishment.

"Now, really," he began. "I married you legal like. What's the mistake?"

"We are," Pearl said simply. "Theo was being kind to me, and I'm grateful. But there's no reason for him to be unhappy now and think that he has to care for me and the baby. Ain't his baby, you know." She gulped. "Can you unmarry us?"

Bridger sat down solidly on a stool and scratched his head.

"Depends," he drawled, searching for the right words to say. "Depends upon whether . . . ah . . ."

"Oh," Theo jumped in quickly, "we discussed that, suh. Mr. Fitz, here, can vouch that I ain't

ever really been with no girl before Pearl. An'
what with the baby and all I ain't ever had a
chance to be with her yet, either."

The utter honesty of these two young people
left Bridger floundering.

"I see," he gulped. "You ain't yet, so . . . ah
. . . well . . . Barry?"

Barry was startled at being given the decision
to make.

"You talk it over with your sister, Pearl?"

"Yes, sir. She ain't rightly happy, but says I
can stay here and help her as a nurse. Maybe
when I'm older I'll find the right man."

"Theo? What about your paw?"

Pearl giggled and answered for him. "Papa
Tedder says he'll be sorry to lose me as a cook,
but thinks we are both being right sensible."

Sensible, Bridger thought. If there were more
sensible people in the world like these two there'd
be lots less unhappiness, grief and even wars.

"I guess," he said, "if I can say that you are,
I can just as well say that you ain't. Good luck
to both of you."

Theo looked at Pearl wistfully. "Someday,
when I knows myself better, Pearl, I'll come back
fer you."

She smiled sweetly. "That's mighty fine for
you to say, Theo. I'll save up all my dances for
you."

Pamela's wagon, on the way to California,
passed the spot where Lord Lester had died in
an avalanche.

Looking at the mountain side, one last faint hope left her. New avalanches had followed the first, turning the gorge into a boulder field. There was no telling where the gold-encrusted carriage might be buried. Alone on her wagon seat, here at the fateful spot where her life had altered its course, Pamela sat with a leather pouch clasped in her hand. There were tears in her eyes. Then she roused herself. The gold she had, it was not a great amount, but it was enough to give her a show of respectability.

"I will not be poor again!" she said in her heart.

Traveling as a single train for the last time, the wagons laboriously ground a route through the South Pass and down onto the Snake River valley. The wagons closed up once more and held that position, the lessons learned during the previous spring having been quickly recalled and put back into practice.

In the great valley of the Snake a hundred-odd wagons pulled out of the caravan silently, one after another, and took a new trail that led them southwest. The Oregon-bound emigrants watched them, tears in their eyes, for friendships were being broken up.

Sorting out and directing the wagons, Barry felt the separation more than most.

Although a majority of the Tennessee farmers, including Ned Conroy, had elected for Oregon with him, Howard Tedder was taking his family to California.

As the Tedder wagons passed, Barry wordlessly offered his hand to Tedder. Just as silently it was accepted and firmly shook. The two did not need words to express their mutual respect. They would miss each other greatly.

Barry was losing another of the men he had come to rely upon for leadership. Now it was hard to recall what a worthless pup Harmon Herbert had been just a year before. But the happiness in Mary Sue's face more than made up for all of the trouble the Herbert train had caused him.

As the Herbert wagons passed, one by one, each black man took off his hat in salute. The women waved and the children called out Barry's name in friendship.

The remaining Russians were as quiet and docile as ever. They didn't know what fate lay in store for them at Fort Ross, let alone when they returned to their homeland. But at least Russia was a place they knew. The others faced new lands unknown to them.

Barry steeled himself to pull the next group of wagons out of line. He had been avoiding Pamela and was determined to do so again.

The first Buttle-Jones wagon was being driven by David Faraday, who nodded a curt farewell. Beside him sat Selena, who purposely turned her head away from Barry in disdain.

Pamela drew her horses to a halt right beside Barry's horse.

"Keep 'em moving!" Barry exploded, but Pamela did not move.

"I have things to say to you," Pamela said.

"You're holding up the whole train."

"Then I'll pull out and bring up the rear," she

said gently. "I can't leave without saying goodbye. It won't take long."

She urged her horses forward and to the left.
As the following wagons moved to close up the
gap, Pamela agilely jumped down from hers and
strode toward Barry. He was tempted to stay on
his horse, but realized there had been sincerity
in her tone. Besides, there could be no harm in
saying goodbye to another old friend. The term,
oddly, fitted Pamela.

"All right," Barry said curtly, dismounting,
"You'll have to be brief. I have to keep the
wagons separated."

Pamela put her hand on his arm.

"Goodbye," she said quietly, "doesn't seem
enough. . . . Are we ever to say hello again,
Barry?"

How easy life would be, Barry thought miserably, if only he had learned to lie.

"I don't rightly know."

"Honest, as usual. But we can let bygones be
bygones, Barry, can't we?"

"That's fine for you and me," Barry said
grimly, "but you're forgetting Jim Bridger."

"No, Barry," she said, "I am not forgetting.
I will make my apology to the gentleman on the
way to California. He has handled my womanly
foolishness with rare delicacy. But I had to speak
to you first."

"Because you love me?" he asked sarcastically.

"Why else would I have done what I did, if
not to keep you with me?"

Pamela looked him full in the face. Because
there was some truth in her statement, he detected no attempt on her part to lie.

"No, Pamela," he said, "it's not that easy. My life is too terribly simple for you. You know what you have and what you want for yourself and Selena."

She put her fingers to his lips to still his words and moved close to force him into putting his arms about her. He let her lay against his chest, but his whole body was rigid, with no surrender in it.

"No, Pamela," he said.

Slowly, quietly, she pulled away.

"I'm not going to try and press you, Barry. I did that once. I will go along with the suggestions you made about California, even though you won't be there to help me with my plans for Selena. Someday, nothing or nobody'll stand in our way any more. Please believe that, Barry."

Almost in one motion she went up on her tiptoes, kissed him quickly and raced back to her wagon. Then she cracked the whip sharply and moved the wagon into line. She got a fleeting glance at Jim Bridger's face as he came riding up; it was filled with disapproval.

Ah, well, Pamela thought, let him stew over that for eight hundred miles. She was not about to waste her time or breath in apologizing to him. She had made her points with Barry and that was all that counted.

The night before, when she was determined not to say goodbye to Barry, the one English family going to Oregon had come to say farewell to her.

"Mi'lady," Stephan Butterick had said, with due respect. "My Amy and me will be sorry to

leave you, but from what I've learned this winter I think my chances of a new life will be
better in Oregon."

"And what is it you plan on doing?"

"Fur business, mum. I've been learning the
curing and tanning of the pelts from the trappers. Fitzpatrick says I have a natural talent that
is needed."

"Does he?" Pamela mused. "But is there
money in curing?"

Butterick nodded sheepishly. "Not meaning to
blow my own horn, mum, but Fitzpatrick says a
properly cured pelt brings double the price. He
has offered to introduce me to trappers in Oregon
who will be grateful for my services."

So. Pamela mused on. Barry apparently knew
many in the fur business. This John Jacob Astor,
he had said, had a company in Oregon as well
as one in California. They had to be linked up
in some way.

"This is most interesting, Stephan," she went
on, all innocence. "But how do they get the furs
to where they are needed?"

"By clipper ship, mum. The ships come to
Oregon and California. Some go back around
the world and Africa to England. The others go
down around Cape Horn and back up to New
York. It's the sea voyage that makes the curing
of importance. Of course, I shall have to start
very small."

Pamela smiled to herself, a new scheme spawn-
ing in her brain. She pulled out her coffer chest
and took out two hundred in gold coin.

"It's not much of a pension," she said sadly,
"after all your years of faithful service."

Butterick's eyes bulged. "Oh, mi'lady, I thought to get naught. How can I ever thank you?"

Pamela smiled sweetly. "There's no need to thank me, Stephan. And perhaps we can still be of service to each other. As you know, my funds are now quite limited and I'll not be able to start a new trade as you are doing. If these ships dock both in California and Oregon, then we will be in quite close communication. If you had a bit more capital, to start out on a larger scale, would you consider taking on a silent business partner?"

"Oh, mi'lady," he enthused. "It would be a pleasure."

She turned instantly doleful. "It will be a risk, both of us being unknown in the business. If only we could persuade someone more familiar with it to assist us and guide us."

He frowned. "I've thought the same, mum. Fitzpatrick would be the perfect man, but I wouldn't dare approach him."

"Nonsense!" she insisted. "He's the one who says that you have promise. Do you think he wants to be a guide all his life? Would you want to be? He's your man, of course. But my name can't be connected with the enterprise. You understand."

Butterick blushed. Everyone was well aware of the fool Lady Pamela had made of herself over the guide. He thought himself discreet enough to refrain from gossip.

"Yes, mum," he answered.

"I have given you two hundred and shall add another two to that. It should be sufficient for you to persuade Barry Fitzpatrick to join forces with you. And a year from now, you catch one of those ships and come and make an accounting to me on my investment. Oh, one minor point—I want Barry Fitzpatrick to be on that ship with you."

With the conversation with Butterick still fresh in her mind, Pamela looked back, saw Barry mount his horse, say a few words to Bridger and ride away to get the Oregon Trail caravan formed up.

I'll have you yet, Barry Fitzpatrick, she thought. As a man, as a lover, as a business partner, as a slave. I'll make you rich enough, powerful enough, sophisticated enough, to measure up to what I want you to be. I'll make the gold lost in the avalanche seem like pocket change in a Cockney's snap purse. And you, you will be unable to say no to me ever again.

Barry closed his eyes and a grimace of pain crossed his face. For the first time in his life he had come near to hating Jim Bridger. The man's words, after he'd seen him kissing Pamela, had dripped acid. He'd cursed Barry for a fool, had then waited for an answer, his jaw stuck out, his eyes glaring.

To keep from punching Bridger out, Barry had turned his horse quickly away and joined his own train. He knew that an explanation on his part about Pamela's apology would sound false. Nor did he want it to sound as if he had backed down to Pamela to force the apology from her.

He didn't want to hate. He didn't want to

hate anyone. Pamela had hurt him deeply, but not deep enough for him to hate her forever. He couldn't discount what she had meant to him. She had been a teacher, in a way he had never been taught before. Never again would he ever be able to bed a woman without being reminded of her. Always he had to wrestle with himself when he thought about her. He knew her lustiness to be enormously gratifying, knew that his pleasure in bed with her had all but blinded him to the power she loved to hold over people. She wanted to own him, he knew that. The love that he felt for her had allowed him to overlook the possessive side of her character. But could he cope with it for a lifetime? She had all but stated that she would wait for the day when they could be together.

Under what rules, he thought soberly.

And what new rules did Jim Bridger expect to enforce?

"There's gonna be a whole new code set down," Bridger had growled, "when I get myself back from Californy. Cock-lovin' bitches like that she-liar ain't gonna stampede Jim Bridger eber again. Gonna train my guides different or cut thar balls off!"

Stupid solution, Barry thought. Threats like that, made in anger, missed the point. Wouldn't change a thing on the wagon trains. Wouldn't reduce the arrogance of the bastards who thought they knew more than the guide; wouldn't lessen the tensions that arise between different kinds of people suddenly thrust into a so-called melting pot. There was the goddam melting pot anywhere in America, Barry thought savagely—just a bunch of folks claiming their own and jawing at each other and sometimes killing each other when they couldn't get it. And there never was going to be much melting: that's something that had to be faced up to pretty damn quick.

Like, he reasoned, every wagon train west was going to have its Arabelle, its Colonel Herbert, its Bradford Cornithwyeth—its own big share of arrogance and conceit and selfishness.

But would these forthcoming wagon trains need Barry Fitzpatrick?

That question and like thoughts were still on Barry's mind after his Oregon train had forded the Snake River and the other train was far gone over the horizon.

He would soon be back in the trapping country he loved. Rushing rivers where the beaver grew enormously fat, where bears were almost as numerous as elk, where a man, alone or with a trapper friend, could lie on his back at night and look at the sky.

He had almost laughed aloud when Stephan Butterick had nervously proposed a business venture between them. A business? Up to his neck in the greed he deplored, cutting throats for money and power before they cut his? Hell, no!

But then he'd thought, did he want to go backwards or gamble going forward to some place he'd never been?

Did he want to continue playing nursemaid to wagon trains full of uncaring emigrants just to get back to the mountains for a while? And then do that again and again?

Did he want to chuck it all and climb back into Pamela's bed and let her make his decisions for him?

Barry just didn't know; no one way seemed of greater merit than the others. Maybe, when he got over being tuckered out from this trip, he'd be able to think some more and get it clear and straight. . . .

But he felt alone, and lonely. Riding through that great vast wilderness of forest, rivers and mountains he kept turning to remembered faces to counsel him—the face of his uncle, Tom "Broken Hand" Fitzpatrick, who'd brought him up, Bridger's face, Pamela's face. . . .

He even tried to recall Jessie Fremont's face, her voice, and any of her words of wisdom. All he got in return was the voice of the wind whispering through the tall pines.

No, he thought. No, Barry Fitzpatrick, you can't ask of another to feel your way. It's for you, and you alone, to know what it is.

He rode on towards Oregon.

THE WILDERNESS SEEKERS

The Indians called it Kan-Ta-Ke ("Beautiful Meadow" but to the pioneers who made their way to Kentucky over the Wilderness Road in the 1770s it was "The Dark and Bloody Ground" where American patriots still fought for their lives against redcoats and their savage allies thirteen years after the British surrender. Among these brave venturers were:

JOE FLOYD: At twenty, a giant of a man, fleeing the terrible consequences of his own strength, searching for a new life and love . . . .

TWO HEARTS: A "white Indian", captive of the Shawnee since childhood, torn between two worlds, honor-bound to war against the man she loves . . . .

MARGARET FLOYD: Gallant and beautiful, she fought side-by-side with her men against the wilderness—living in terror of the forbidden passion that raged within . . . .

CORN BURNER: Treacherous chief of the Shawnee, sworn to have Two Hearts in his tent—and Joe Floyd's scalp on his belt . . .

THE CONESTOGA PEOPLE

Filled with hope, they headed Westward into unknown danger with Barry Fitzpatrick at the fore. It was the largest wagon train ever to leave Independence, and it was in trouble before it had traveled ten miles Westward. Among the diverse people aboard the Conestoga wagons were: a cold-blooded murderer, a 14-year-old wanton, an aristocratic lady with a stolen treasure, a mulatto with a secret white lover—and one wily and powerful man who swore the wagons would never get through.

In this novel, recreating the drama of the great Westward trek, we meet historic figures such as John C. Fremont, the famed explorer, his wise and beautiful wife Jessie Benton Fremont, and Jim Bridger, the legendary frontiersman. In vivid detail, we experience the saga of a turbulent journey toward a rendezvous with destiny.

THE CONESTOGA PEOPLE continues the epic of the great Westward thrust begun in THE WILDERNESS SEEKERS and THE MOUNTAIN BREED.